Tributes to
Brandenburg:

"Compelling characters such as Ursula Bellon and Eckhardt, Christina, Meira, Herbert, and many others are beautifully developed and the relationships between these characters are finely explored. The author captures the passage from the last summer of the "Belle Epoque" and plunges the reader into the challenges of WWI, exploring themes of family, politics, business, and survival.

With a keen eye for detail which will arrest the attention of fans of WWI history and the general climate in Europe during this turbulent period, Cloud weaves a tale that reads like history…

…James Cloud's novel is a classic, a vividly and skillfully rendered story that captures the heart of a city during the war, rife with historical references, seething with compelling and interesting social and political commentaries, and featuring historical personages. Details are relevant and the scene setting is done to perfection. An expert, sensational story that unveils the face of Berlin during WWI. Brandenburg: A Story of Berlin is well researched, entertaining, and hard to put down for fans of historical novels with hints of romance and intrigue, and a setting against the backdrop of the war."

—Ruffina Oserio *for Reader's Favorite*

"James Cloud is a master teacher. Through credible characters and a thorough understanding of cultures and locale, he has given us a window into life in Germany in the period surrounding WWI. It is a compassionate view of how ordinary people struggled and made choices in order to survive the mayhem created by forces beyond their control. Brandenburg ends in suspense with the rise of Hitler to power. I can hardly wait for the sequel. Well done!!"

—Ricardo Suarez-Gartner

"One of the best historical novels I have read!

Using his background in the German language, the German culture, and interwar history, Mr. Cloud produced a novel that is historically accurate and entertaining. I wish he could have taken it through the WWII years, but fear that the Joy of the narration which characterized MOST of it would have died!"

—Amazon Customer

"…Through the eyes of a young Prussian aristocrat and his beautiful Jewish wife, along with their best friends, a working-class girl and her farming-stock husband, the author examines the class structures and the political pressures that were exerted on Germany during this period that would lead to one of the darkest times in world history…

…This book did a wonderful job, for me, in laying the groundwork for what was soon to plunge Germany and the world into further chaos, as Adolf Hitler was appointed Chancellor in 1933. That this story ended there gives me hope that there is a sequel coming…"

—Grant Leishman

"What a great book! I love historical fiction and this book was an excellent read for me. I could not put it down. The author, James Cloud writes as though he were in Berlin in the period just before WWI, setting the stage and introducing us to his characters, along with their triumphs and struggles while we get a front row seat to their lives. Very well written!!"

—Billy Mack

"…This engaging book bring together a welding of history and humanity in a time many of us have a hard time understanding. The characters from different backgrounds and classes are brought together to show how the events preceding World War II, created by World War I, effected the people of Germany. Although a work of fiction, we are able to understand in a human way the thoughts and feelings of the people of that time..."

—Deborah G.

"Superb historical novel and well written. Highly recommended. James Cloud has written a gripping historical novel as people, families, culture, prejudices, hatreds, Love, compassion. and kindness come alive on every page--superbly done."

—Patricia J. Miller

"…Historical fiction can be a tough balancing act but James Cloud writes superbly, blending the two into a stunning and vivid portrayal of roughly 30 years of life in Germany….

…Historical fact is artfully interwoven into the story as the characters witness and react to their surroundings and events that transformed not only Germany but all of Europe. Without 'taking sides', Cloud presents a straightforward account of life at the time while allowing you to feel every triumph and tragedy along with the characters. The writing is clear and impassioned and the descriptions take readers to the places mentioned. Well written and deeply moving, Brandenburg: A Story of Berlin is a wonderful story that should definitely be read and shared…"

—Melinda Hills

"What a great book!! I enjoyed learning the historical facts and the stories about the people who lived through the war. How their lives changed in order to survive the devastation and loss they had to endure. The author fully describes the characters emotions, fears, and bravery in a way that captivated me to keep reading and learn more.

I hope James Cloud writes a squeal! I am confident it will be just as captivating enjoyable to read!"

—Evelyn Upstill

"…Four families in particular are connected to the various conflicts and tensions of the time, and Cloud uses them as prime examples of life from the German perspective during this important historical time.

I am fascinated by the city of Berlin and its clash of cultures, and James Cloud's deep and detailed explanation of history and attitudes really shed some brilliant light on things that I've wondered about for many years. It's clear that Cloud has a wealth of authentic sources and information when describing Berlin, both at war and in recovery from war, but he picks and chooses his moments well so that no moment is ever overloaded with facts. At the heart of everything is the city and the impact on its culture and inhabitants as a whole, presenting a holistic view of real experience that places no blame or bias anywhere. Overall, I'd definitely recommend Brandenburg: A Story of Berlin to fans of wartime research as well as those interested in the shaping of culture."

—K.C. Finn

"I am astounded at how great it is written, how easy it is to read, and how correct all the history of Berlin is. It is very interesting and very easy to read and also follow the events that took place in Berlin in those terrible times. I would highly recommend this book to all the people that like history. I am German and I learned what those poor people in Berlin went through. I, for one, am anxious to see what the next book will have to tell me..."

—Linda Boyd

"A great book about history. Well-researched and well written. I enjoyed getting to know the history of Berlin better. Having a story of people woven into the facts made it seem more real and interesting. I am looking forward to a sequel about World War 2. History keeps repeating itself."

—Carol Reed

"...The backdrop of Brandenburg weaves seamlessly between the front lines and the daily life of everyday families in Berlin, portraying the deep struggles of all who fought and those who were left behind.

Brandenburg is exquisite in both its style and its substance, particularly as James Cloud takes a compassionate approach in the portrait painted of individual German families. Not only is the book rich with historical detail, but it also shows the emotional toll through the points of view of four main characters and chronicles their lives and those of their families. I loved how thoroughly fleshed out Cloud's protagonists and, truly, all of his characters are. It takes a skilled narrator to engage a reader to a young teenager who jumps at the opportunity to fight for the axis power, his home, the fatherland. But to go beyond simple curiosity and to draw such emotion that a reader feels a genuine kinship? That is the type of story that anyone who enjoys historical fiction wants to pick up and read. Brandenburg: A Story of Berlin has a gorgeous intensity to it that cannot be missed. Highly recommended."

—Jamie Michele

"A book to help understand Germany and its people. I read this book when it was first published and enjoyed it immensely. The author taught me world history in a very enjoyable manner as I read it from the perspective of four families living in Berlin Germany. I lived in Berlin in the early seventies and fell in love with the city and the people. Reading this novel took me back to the wonderful years I spent there. The description of the streets, buildings, eating establishments, night clubs, and people brought back found memories. I could tell Mr. Cloud loved the city and its people as I did. The author describes the city and historical events in great accuracy. This book helped me to much better understand the events leading up to World War I and the coming to power of Adolf Hitler.

…I have now completely read it twice. I enjoyed it even a little more the second time around because I gained a greater understanding of how the conflicts of politics, race, religion, and traditions impact people and families…

…I would suggest this book to anyone interested in world history and especially anyone who is acquainted with the city of Berlin. Thank you, Mr. Cloud, for your knowledge, insights, talent, and abilities."

—J. Luke

"'We are at war and it seems to me both sides are doing inhuman things to each other.'

…Often history books are very one sided and leave out the humanity of an 'enemy'. Brandenburg does an exceptional job of giving us insight to how families in Berlin viewed the war during World War I and leading up to when Adolf Hitler is appointed Chancellor of Germany in 1933. When it comes to war time novels, we often forget how many families were actually affected by the war and the enemies often lose their humanity. Cloud does a great job of integrating history and the humanity and hardships of everyday life for his characters. Cloud's research and first-hand experience make this a great historical account. A must read.

—Mark Byrd

Brandenburg

A STORY of BERLIN

www.JamesCloudBooks.com

ISBN: 978-1-987-43638-9
ISBN-10: 1-987-43638-5

Cover design by Mary Ann Cherry
www.maryanncherry.com
www.maryanncherry.net

Second Paperback Edition

DISCLAIMER

This is a work of fiction. Names, characters, businesses, places, events, locales, and incidents are either the products of the author's imagination or are actual events and historical persons used in a fictitious manner. Any resemblance to actual persons, living or dead is purely coincidental.

Man's inhumanity to man
belongs to no race
and
carries no passport.

James Cloud

DEDICATION

Dedicated to the citizens of Berlin.

IN APPRECIATION

My thanks to Steven Huffaker and Mary Ann Cherry, without whose support and encouragement this book may never have been completed.

Contents

Prologue i

Part I **Genesis**

Chapters 1 – 9

Part II **Descent**

Chapters 10 – 21

Part III **Decay**

Chapters 22 – 43

Part IV **Humiliation**

Chapters 44 – 59

Part V **Resurrection**

Chapters 60 – 82

Part VI **Gathering Darkness**

Chapters 83 – 105

Epilogue

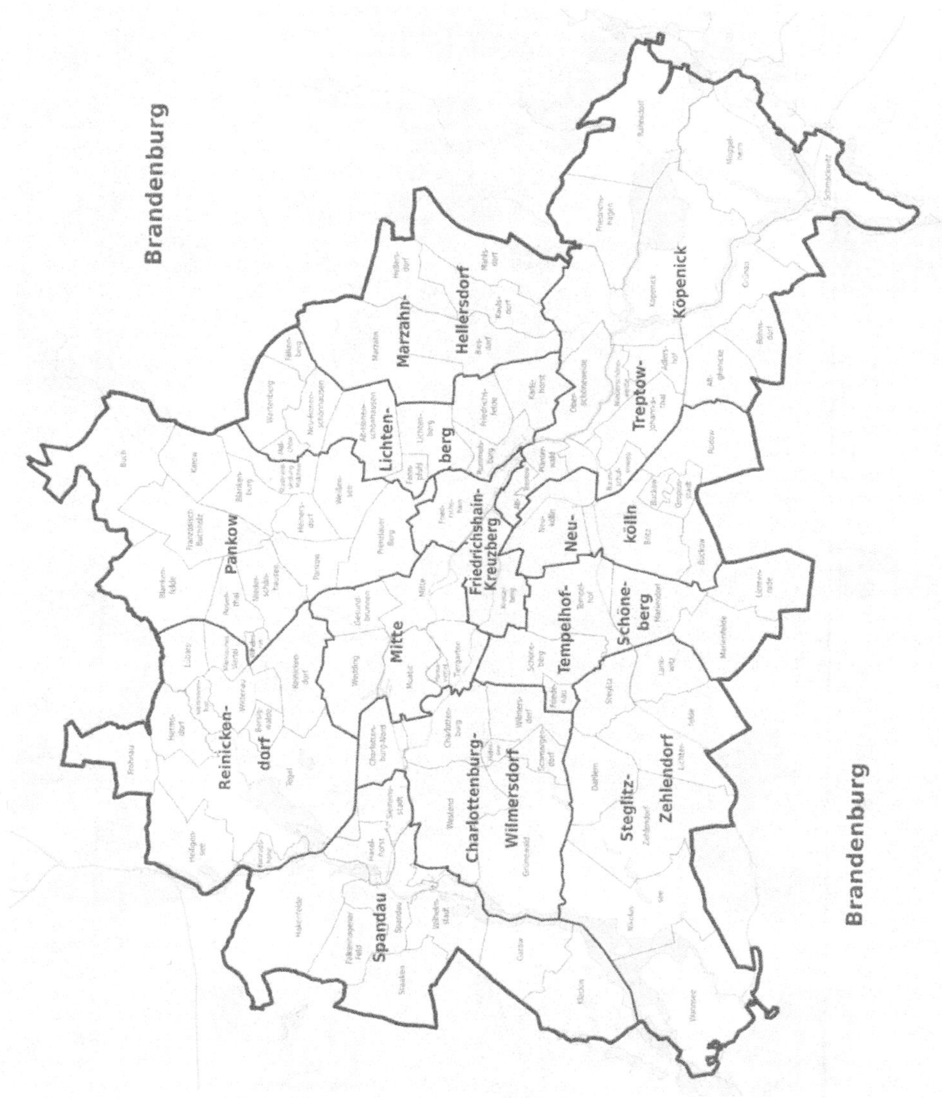

Berlin Administrative Districts

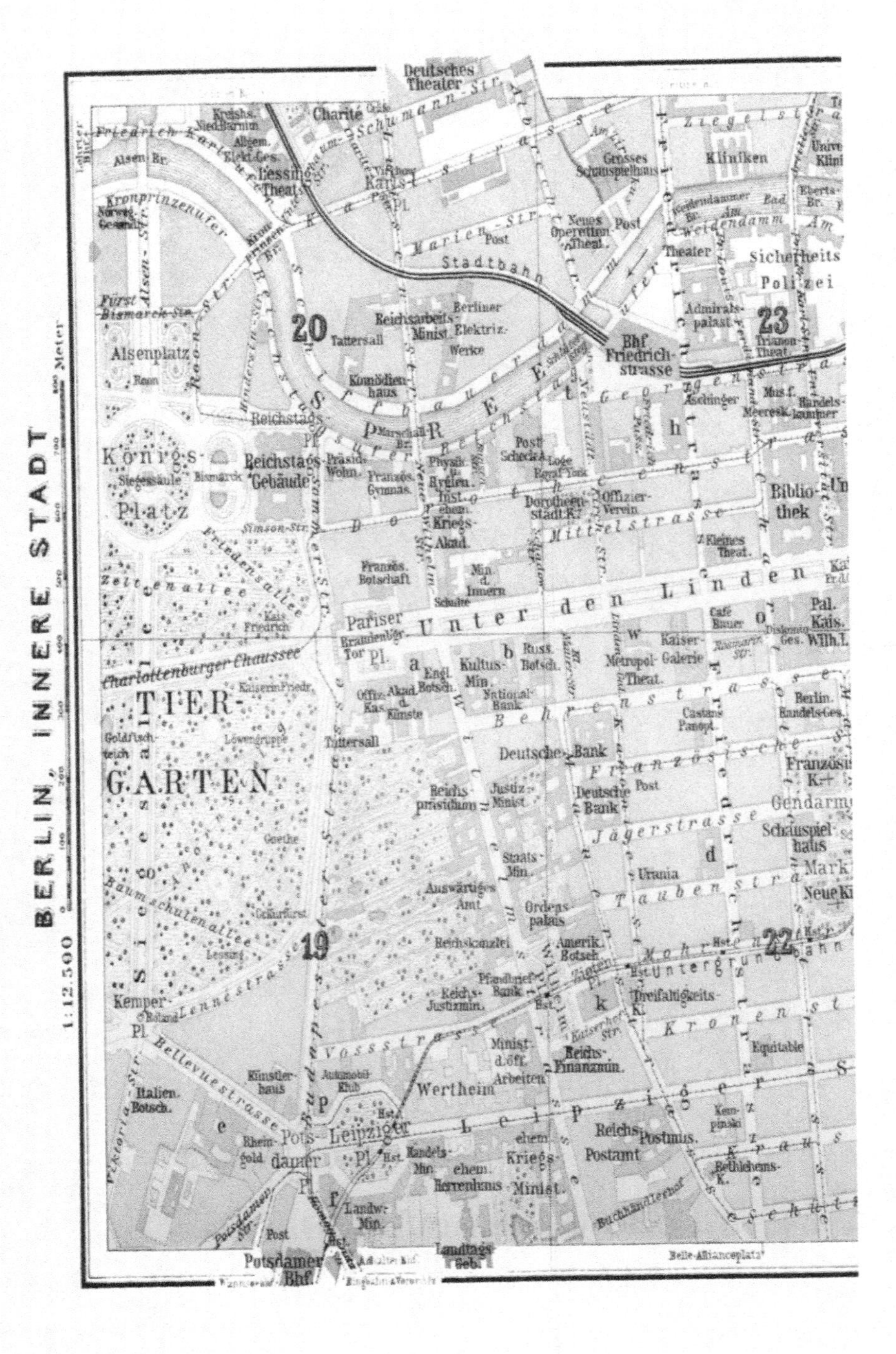
BERLIN, INNERE STADT
1:12.500
Meter
Deutsches Theater
Charité
Schumann-Str.
Ziegelstrasse
Kliniken
Alsen Br.
Lessing Theat.
Grosses Schauspielhaus
Kronprinzenufer
Marien-Str.
Neues Operetten Theat.
Post
Theater
Sicherheits Polizei
Stadtbahn
Alsen-Str.
Fürst Bismarck-Str.
20
Tattersall
Reichsarbeits-Minist.
Berliner Elektriz.-Werke
Admirals-palast
23
Trianon-Theat.
Alsenplatz
Bhf. Friedrich-strasse
Komödienhaus
Aschinger
Königs-Platz
Siegessäule
Bismarck
Reichstags-Gebäude
Präsid. Wohn.
Französ. Gymnas.
Loge Royal York
Bibliothek
Simson-Str.
Dorotheenstädt. K.
Offizier-Verein
Mittelstrasse
Kleines Theat.
Friedensallee
Zeltenallee
Französ. Botschaft
Min. d. Innern
Unter den Linden
Café Bauer
Pal. Kais. Wilh. I.
Pariser Pl.
Brandenbgr. Tor
Russ. Botsch.
Engl. Botsch.
Kultus-Min.
Metropol-Theat.
Kaiser-Galerie
Charlottenburger Chaussee
TIER-GARTEN
Tattersall
National-Bank
Behrenstrasse
Castans Panopt.
Berlin. Handels-Ges.
Goldfisch-teich
Deutsche Bank
Französische
Reichs-präsidium
Justiz-Minist.
Post
Gendarmen
Schauspiel-haus
Goethe
Jägerstrasse
Staats-Min.
Urania
Auswärtiges Amt
Taubenstrasse
Ordens-palais
Baumschulenallee
Reichskanzlei
Amerik. Botsch.
19
22
Lessing
Pfandbrief-Bank
Dreifaltigkeits-K.
Kemper-Pl.
Lennéstrasse
Reichs-Justizmin.
Kronenstrasse
Vossstrasse
Minist. d. öff. Arbeiten
Reichs-Finanzmin.
Equitable
Bellevuestrasse
Künstler-haus
Automobil-Klub
Wertheim
Italien. Botsch.
Potsdamer Pl.
Leipziger Pl.
Leipziger Strasse
Kempinski
Reichs-Postmus.
Rheingold
Handels-Min.
ehem. Herrenhaus
ehem. Kriegs-Minist.
Postamt
Krausenstrasse
Bethlehems-K.
Landw.-Min.
Buchhändlerhof
Post
Potsdamer Bhf.
Landtags Geb.
Belle-Allianceplatz

Hapsburgs' rule. When they learned of the Archduke's impending visit to Sarajevo, they decided it was time to strike, but they would need the help of the *Black Hand.*

When *Black Hand* leader Dragutin Dimitrijevic', who was instrumental in the overthrow of Serbia's last king, heard of *Young Bosnia's* plan, he was immediately ready to assist. He believed that the royal visit was in preparation for a coming Austro-Hungarian invasion of Serbia. (No record has ever been found to show that such an invasion was ever contemplated.)

Three *Young Bosnia* conspirators were escorted across the border from Serbia in early June by members of the *Black Hand.* One of the three youths was Gavrilo Princip. Once inside Bosnia, he and the other *Young Bosnian's* met with six members of the *Black Hand* and proceeded to Sarajevo a few days before the Archduke's visit.

The route of the royal motorcade had been published in newspapers in order that spectators could position themselves to view the royal couple as they passed by. The motorcade was to move down the Appel Quay along the northern side of the Miljacka River. Knowing the route from the newspapers, the plan was for Princip and the others to split up and take positions at strategic points along the route. Two of them would stand near the Cumurja Bridge, where they would be the first to see the procession. Two others waited further up the Appel Quay. Princip and Trifko Grabez stood toward the center of the route near the Lateiner Bridge.

"Are you really sure we should be doing this, Franzi?" questioned Sophie as they began their journey. "Originally, we were supposed to come to observe military exercises outside the city, and we've been warned there is unrest here and it could be dangerous."

He patted his wife's arm. "Don't fret, my dear. Governor-general Potiorek assures me security measures have been taken to assure our safety. He feels that our visit will do a great deal to show our solidarity with the Bosnian people. We must also demonstrate that we represent the Hapsburg crown and will not be intimidated." He smiled and squeezed her hand.

As the procession sped past the first of the *Young Bosnians*, leaving them no chance to enact their plan, and approaching the Lateiner

Bridge, the motorcade was forced to slow due to the size of the crowd which had gathered to see the Archduke. Cabrinovic, who had waited on the opposite side of the street, saw his opportunity. He took aim and threw an object towards the car. Just missing his target, the object bounced off the back-convertible cover of the Phaeton, down the trunk, off the bumper to the ground, and rolled underneath the following vehicle. An explosion rocked the car, lifting the front wheels off the ground and sending a fireball and shrapnel into the crowd. Three security officers and several bystanders were seriously wounded.

"Franzi!" screamed Sophie. She grasped his blood-soaked uniform sleeve. Withdrawing her hand and seeing blood on her palm, she screamed again.

"I'm alright, Sophie," Franz Ferdinand assured his wife. "It's not mine."

After missing his target, Cabrinovic began to run towards the nearby Miljacka river. Swallowing a capsule as he neared the bank, he jumped. With a tiny splash as he hit the surface of the water, Cabrinovic found himself kneeling in the river, which was 5 inches deep due to the hot summer weather. Standing up in the ankle-deep water, he began to feel sick. His suicide attempt from cyanide and drowning had failed and only induced vomiting. Police pulled the would-be assassin from the river, and the angry crowd began to beat him before he was taken away in handcuffs.

The shaken Archduke and his wife were driven to the City Hall for the scheduled reception. Franz Ferdinand interrupted the mayor's speech of welcome: "Mr. Mayor, I came here on a visit and I am greeted with bombs! It's outrageous!" Sophie whispered in his ear to calm him, and after regaining his composure, Franz Ferdinand apologized and asked the mayor to continue. Then he had his own blood-soaked speech brought to him and made a few remarks about the day's events. He thanked the people of Sarajevo for their applause and stated, "I see an expression of their joy at the failure of the attempt at assassination."

After their appearance, Baron Rumerskirch, the Archduke's chamberlain, urged the couple to remain at the City Hall until troops could be brought to provide additional security. But the Governor-

General, Oskar Potiorek, rejected the suggestion because, "the soldiers coming straight from maneuvers would not have dress uniforms appropriate for the occasion."

"Don't you think we should abandon the planned program in order to visit the wounded victims of the bombing at the hospital?" asked Franz. "After all, that bomb was intended for us."

"Absolutely we should," she responded. "It's the first thing we should do. I've just been told that some of the most severely wounded were members of our own security detail. Had it not been for us, they would likely be safe."

They returned to their car and rejoined the motorcade. The heightened security details called for an alternate route to the hospital, avoiding the crowds at the city center. The new route would travel straight along the Appel Quay, but this was never communicated to the drivers. Unaware of the new security plan, Leopold Lojka, the driver of the Archduke's car, took a right turn at the Latin Bridge, following the two cars ahead of him. Governor-general Potiorek, who was riding with the Imperial couple and seeing the driver's error, shouted for him to stop. The driver braked abruptly, and when attempting to reverse, stalled the engine. The car was stopped in front of a delicatessen, from which Gavrilo Princip had just emerged. Surprised to see the target of the plot sitting directly in the car before him, he withdrew a pistol and began to fire.

Sophie, seeing her husband covered in blood again, cried out to him, "What has happened to you?"

The Archduke muttered, "It's nothing," although he appeared to have fallen victim to this second assault.

As the driver raced towards the Hotel Konak, where the couple had a reserved suite, Sophie slumped over in her seat and lost consciousness. The Archduke too, fell silent.

At the hotel, the regimental surgeon, Eduard Bayer, removed the Archduke's coat, which revealed a bullet wound in his neck just above the collarbone. Blood gurgled from his mouth, and after a few moments, it was over. He was dead.

Sophie was laid out on a bed in the next room and when her clothing was removed, a bullet wound in her lower right abdomen was discovered, and she too, was dead.

PART I

GENESIS

Chapter One

Declaration of War

August 1, 1914

The air outside the historical city palace of the Hohenzollerns, the *Stadtschloß* in Berlin, buzzed with an electric energy that mirrored the political climate. Over 10,000 people waited restlessly anticipating the appearance of their Emperor, Wilhelm II. He was scheduled to appear on the balcony to announce the outcome of the ultimatum delivered to Russia. The excitement of the crowd matched the escalating tension of the previous weeks.

Back and forth saber-rattling between the great powers of Europe had been going on for years before the assassination of Archduke Franz Ferdinand as they jostled for power on the continent and overseas in their imperialistic efforts in Africa, Asia, India, the Pacific islands, and elsewhere.

Two days after the assassination, Austria-Hungary and Germany demanded that Serbia undertake an investigation. The Secretary General of the Serbian Ministry of Foreign Affairs, Slavo Gruic, replied that nothing had been done and the matter "did not concern the Serbian Government." This precipitated an angry exchange between the two adversaries which resulted in Austria-Hungary's declaration of war against Serbia on the 28th of July, 1914. Russia then mobilized its army along the Austrian border and ordered general deployment the next day. This set off full mobilization by Austria-Hungary, followed by the Germans. Under the Secret Treaty of 1892 between Russia and France, each was obligated to assemble its army if any member of the Triple Alliance – Austria-Hungary, Germany and Turkey were to mobilize. Then England honored its commitment of a call to arms if Russia or France were to become involved in a conflict.

Eckhardt Meinert and his fiancé, Ursula Bellon, found themselves caught up in the anticipation of the crowd, reflecting the fervor that had gripped the city. His broad shoulders and calloused hands hinted at a life spent working in the fields of his father's farm in Blaubeuren near Ulm. His clothing was simple and practical. His rugged handsomeness was a striking contrast to the typical young men of Berlin, capturing the attention of women whose glances and whispers of admiration trailed in his wake. Despite the bustling crowd, his keen eyes observed the surroundings with a hunter's instinct, noticing details others might overlook.

Ursula's complexion, with a hint of olive undertones, glowed with a natural radiance. Her overall presence exuded a balance of elegance and approachability, a testament to the fusion of her French-Huguenot roots with the dynamic spirit of Berlin. Her abundant hair, a rich shade of brunette, cascaded in loose waves around her shoulders, framing a face that defied the hardships of her inner-city upbringing. Ursula, a stunning presence in the vibrant city, was a woman of captivating beauty and undeniable charisma.

They had found each other during the previous winter at Café Kranzler, a large coffee and pastry shop on Unter den Linden. Eckhardt's Swabian roots clashed with the brash Berlin atmosphere of the café. Ursula's hazel eyes and vivacious manner, however, had drawn him like a moth to a flame.

As they got to know each other over the next few months, the young couple had many intense discussions concerning the involvement of Germany in the coming conflict and how it would impact their lives. Eckhardt, as many young men in Europe, was looking forward to enlisting in the military. He wanted to wreak revenge upon the adversaries for the insults and offenses, real or imagined, inflicted upon their nations.

“I can’t wait to see the Emperor,” said Eckhardt, his eyes gleaming with eagerness. “I’ve been waiting for this moment.”

Ursula, like many women, awaited the commencement of hostilities somewhat differently. She nodded, her hazel eyes reflecting a mixture of anxiety and pride. “It’s surreal, isn’t it? We’re about to witness history. But I’ll be worried about you if you have to leave me to go fight.”

The adoring crowd cheered as the Emperor finally appeared on the balcony of the palace. Wilhelm II flung his arms wide and declared in a booming voice, “Germany is now at war with France and Russia! I no longer recognize any parties or affiliations. Today we are all German brothers, *and only German brothers*.” The crowd roared and tossed their hats in the air.

Wilhelm’s face did not reflect the jubilation of the crowd. It is reported that upon signing the order for German mobilization due to pressure from the General Staff, he had said, “You will regret this gentleman.”

As the crowd dispersed, the young couple joined them. Ursula brought an energy that seemed to defy the hardships of her inner-city upbringing. Her quick, nimble steps navigated the crowded boulevard with ease, a testament to the resilience that had shaped her. Her confident walk whispered tales of a life of struggle, but her warm smile illuminated the gray Berlin winter.

Eckhardt’s sturdy figure moved with a quiet strength. His measured and purposeful steps contrasted to the urban chaos and hurried pace of the city dwellers around him.

As people gathered in their neighborhood pubs to celebrate, beer and schnapps heightened the already festive mood. Glasses and mugs were raised to the Emperor, to the nation, and to themselves for the good fortune of being German – and especially Berliners!

Their optimism was understandable, as their country had astonished Europe and the world with its meteoric rise under the leadership of Bismarck after their victory over the French at the end of the Franco-Prussian war in 1871. The development of technology, industry, science, the arts, and the military from 1871 to 1914, had made Germany the foremost economic and military power on the Continent. At the same time, its ascension caused the neighboring countries, particularly England, France and Russia to become ever more apprehensive and suspicious. It was the resulting tension which had greatly precipitated the crisis of August 1914.

Eckhardt and Ursula moved with the lively crowd down Unter den Linden. The bustling east-west boulevard, lined with linden trees, connected the historic Stadtschloß to Pariser Platz and the grand Brandenburg Gate. They encountered their friend, Herbert Lenz, with a striking girl on his arm.

"Hey you two, meet Meira Friedlander," Herbert exclaimed, a sly grin playing on his lips.

Herbert Lenz moved effortlessly through the crowd, an air of aristocracy clinging to him. With a confident stride and impeccable grooming, he exuded the ease of one born into privilege. His gaze, though friendly, carried the assurance of a man accustomed to a world of luxury. The subtle playfulness in his grin hinted at a rebellious streak beneath the refined exterior – and also at one used to getting his way.

Meira Friedlander exuded an elegance in her manner, and her stylish outfit, clearly showing that she came from a well-to-do family, added a touch of stylish grace to the group. Her long black hair set off piercing blue eyes that reflected a world of affluence. The delicate glint of an amethyst pendant hinted at a life of comfort. Despite the opulence, there was a determination in her gaze, a defiance against societal expectations. As Eckhardt silently observed the two, he thought them a good match since Herbert was from a prestigious family also.

Her father was a Jewish businessman who owned a large clothing store on Kurfürstendamm, the main boulevard in the Charlottenburg district. Her family were upper-middle class liberal Jews who owned a home in that upscale western suburb.

Meira, typical for children in Jewish families, worked in her father's store along with her older sister, Edna, in the ladies clothing section. Meira harbored a secret ambition to eventually enter the Friedrich-Wilhelms University to study Biology and later Medicine. She knew it was a ridiculous hope for any woman – especially for a Jewish woman.

Herbert Lenz was the son of the renowned and much respected surgeon at Charité Hospital, Dr. Hans Joachim Lenz. Herbert and his younger brother, Karlheinz, lived with their parents in a spacious modern villa on Goßlarstraße in the prestigious leafy suburb of Dahlem. Although Herbert was friendly and well-liked, he had a rebelliously curious nature that had often gotten him into trouble from early childhood and had caused conflict with his conservative, disciplined father and his mother – a descendant of an old aristocratic Prussian family. They were members of the Protestant Evangelical congregation of the Kaiser Wilhelm Memorial Church on Kurfürstendamm in the center of Auguste-Viktoria-Platz (modern day Breitscheidsplatz).

When Herbert had completed his *Abitur* (secondary diploma), it was assumed he would apply to a university. The clash between generations, particularly with his aristocratic mother, reverberated when Herbert announced he would seek employment and "get to know himself " instead of pursuing higher education, as was expected of young men of his social class. He then secured a clerical position at Siemens, where he had met Eckhardt Meinert. They agreed to meet at a pub after work where they discovered a mutual enthusiasm for German football and tried out for the Viktoria 89 Berlin team. Although they didn't make the cut, they nevertheless attended football matches together.

The two girls, walking together behind the boys down the crowded boulevard, were getting acquainted. Ursula asked Meira, "How did you two meet?"

Meira laughed, "Herbert was purchasing a new coat in my father's store, and we first met when I happened to wait on him."

Herbert, taken with Meira's striking appearance, was determined to know her better. Since it was near closing time, he loitered about the Friedlander store one evening, until he saw her leave and begin to walk toward the U-Bahn entrance. He hurried through the turnstile after her and made sure he was in the same car when the train started. Then he worked his way through the crowd until he was near enough to "accidently" push against her.

"Excuse me, Miss. Sorry to be so clumsy." He smiled broadly. "Oh, hello. Nice to see you again. Thank you for helping me select that fine cashmere coat. I wouldn't have found something so nice without your help."

Smiling back, she replied, "I'm glad you're happy with the coat. Do you often take this train? I've never seen you here before."

"Well, actually I was just walking down Ku'damm and saw you go down the subway entrance and on the spur of the moment decided to try to catch up with you."

She looked at him in surprised amusement. "Really? What did you have in mind?"

"I wonder if you would join me for coffee at a little café just off Ku'damm in Uhlandstraße. If we get off at the next stop, it's just a short walk."

Thoughtfully, she considered this. She knew her father would not look favorably upon her socializing with a Gentile man, but as she considered herself an independent woman, she decided having a coffee with Herbert should be up to her. Besides, he was very engaging. And good looking.

Eckhardt and Ursula had met during the previous winter at Café Kranzler. One Friday afternoon after finishing their shift at Siemens, Herbert, Eckhardt and some of their friends sought refuge in the smoky warmth of the renowned café from the bitter cold and gray dampness of Berlin's winter twilight.

Café Kranzler, nestled in the heart of 1914 Berlin, stood as a beacon of warmth and sophistication amidst the winter chill. The exterior, adorned with elegant architectural details, drew patrons in with the promise of respite from the cold.

As patrons entered, they were greeted by the rich warmth of the interior – polished wood, plush upholstery and the soft glow of ambient lighting. The gentle hum of lively conversations and the clink of fine china created a harmonious atmosphere, blending the nostalgic charm with the contemporary vibrancy of Berlin society.

Café Kranzler's large windows offered a view of the winter landscape outside, where the city's architecture was adorned with a dusting of snow. The luxurious drapes, drawn partially to allow the winter sunlight to filter through, created a play of shadows that danced across the tables and ornate decorations.

The staff, clad in impeccably tailored uniforms, moved with precision and grace, attending the needs of the patrons. The central focal point of the café was the impressive pastry counter, a display of artfully crafted delicacies that tempted the senses. The scent of freshly brewed coffee, mingled with the sweet fragrance of pastries, created an irresistible allure.

Each table was adorned with delicate linens and fine china, providing an intimate setting for patrons to enjoy their coffee and pastries. The air was filled with the soft murmur of conversations, punctuated by laughter and the occasional clinking of silverware against porcelain.

The winter scene outside became a picturesque backdrop to the elegant tapestry within Café Kranzler. Patrons, wrapped in their winter attire, savored the warmth of their surroundings, creating an ambiance that captured the essence of 1914 Berlin in all its refined splendor.

"Brrrrr!" cried Herbert as they burst through the entrance. "We practically sprinted here to escape the chill!"

Ursula and other patrons, startled, looked up at the commotion. A group of young women sitting at a table near the edge of the room smiled and snickered. Herbert, like many cocky young Berliners, considered himself irresistible to the ladies. Turning to his friend, he said, "Hey, watch this! Get ready for some excitement, my friend," and began to stride toward their table.

Eckhardt, pulling at his sleeve, exclaimed, "Where are you going?"

With a smirk, Herbert replied, "We have to meet those girls!"

After a slight hesitation, Eckhardt followed him. Wide-eyed, the young women, giggling, put their heads together and whispered, "They're coming over here!"

Herbert, bowing, declared, "Ladies! Allow me to introduce myself. Herbert Lenz at your service!"

More giggling.

Ursula, raising an eyebrow, coolly and unimpressed replied, "And what service would that be?"

Herbert, his head thrown back, replied, "The service of bringing a touch of sophistication and excitement to your day!"

Ursula rolled her eyes and exchanged glances with her friends.

"Well, Mr. Lenz, we're just here for coffee and pastries. Sophistication is optional."

Herbert, unaccustomed to such a saucy comeback, was momentarily speechless. Turning his attention to Ursula's friends, he continued to flirt. Ursula, meanwhile, gazed openly at Eckhardt, who was amazed that she even noticed him and began to blush.

Amused, Ursula enquired, "And who might you be?"

"I'm just here to enjoy a cup of coffee," murmured Eckhardt. Ursula's vivacious manner fascinated the shy Eckhardt.

"Why do you allow your loudmouth friend to dominate the scene? Are you too standoffish and proud to introduce yourself and be sociable?" she teasingly asked him. Berliners enjoy sarcastic humor and understand one another when they banter in their racy dialect.

Herbert could not pass up an opportunity to respond to her sauciness. "Leave Eckhardt alone. We'll put him in training, so he can shake off his rural lethargy and learn to keep up with our Berlin girls."

Eckhardt now turned a deep crimson and stammered an apology in his heavy Swabian accent that set him apart from the cocky Berliners.

"May we sit down and join you for a cup of coffee?" inquired Herbert, somewhat subdued. Some of the girls eagerly made room for them. Introductions were made all around.

Gradually, Eckhardt managed to seat himself closer to Ursula, and they became involved in conversation. "What did he mean by 'rural lethargy'? Where *are* you from?'' Ursula asked him. "And what brings you to Berlin?"

"I was born and grew up on a small farm near Blaubeuren, about 12 kilometers from Ulm, but I knew early on that farm life was not what I wanted. There is a trade school in Ulm where I enrolled in the electrician program. I served an apprenticeship under a licensed electrician and later worked for a small company there. After a year, I learned about the apprenticeship programs with Siemens in Berlin. I passed the entrance test and started last Spring."

"Where'd you meet Herbert, and what can you possibly have in common with someone like him?" she inquired. "*Mr. Lenz* is apparently quite enamored of himself."

Rushing to his friend's defense, "Herbert's a great guy once you get to know him. His father is Dr. Lenz, and they're a great family. We met at Siemens. He works in the Personnel Department scheduling new applicants for testing. We became good friends, and we now share a room in Tegel near the Siemens plant."

Ursula's eyebrows rose. "So, he's the son of *the* Dr. Lenz? His father is Dr. Hans Joachim Lenz, the surgeon at Charité Hospital? Isn't it odd that he works instead of going to university? Did he ever explain that to you?"

"If you knew Herbert well, you'd understand. He's independent and doesn't want to flaunt his privileged background. He wants to prove he can stand on his own two feet. I respect Herbert a lot. My humble background makes no difference to him. But enough about him. Tell me about yourself," he urged.

"I live in Wedding with my parents, two brothers and a sister." She paused. Seeing no reaction to the revelation of her living in the working-class district of Wedding, she continued. "My father is a motorman with the city transit authority. As a matter of fact, he drives a streetcar built by Siemens. After finishing school, I was accepted in the sales training program at KaDeWe. That's the big department store on Wittenbergplatz in Schöneberg. I've worked there for over a year now."

"Oh, I've heard about that store. It's supposed to be very fancy. Too fancy for me," Eckhardt quipped. "What does KaDeWe stand for?"

"It's short for Kaufhaus des Westens. I felt it was almost too fancy for me when I started there," she smiled. "But everyone has made me feel very welcome, and I've already gotten a raise."

Eckhardt leaned toward her in fascination as she spoke. Her lovely, delicate features radiated an elegance that belied her humble background. *Yes*, he thought to himself. *She looks like she belongs in a beautiful place like that department store – or even in a palace.*

As Ursula compared the two friends, she was somewhat put off by Herbert's cockiness, but she began to realize, on the other hand, that she was smitten with Eckhardt and his shyness.

"What are your plans for Christmas?" Ursula asked suddenly.

Surprised, he responded, "I don't have any. I don't have enough time to travel home to Blaubeuren."

"I want you to meet my family!" Ursula declared. "You must come and have Christmas dinner with us."

He stared at her, open-mouthed for a moment, then hesitantly responded, "Do you really think that would be a good idea so soon?"

Surprised at herself for blurting out without even thinking about how her parents might react, she blushed. But now committed, decided to see it through.

"Yes. I'm sure they'll want to meet you. I'll speak to them right away."

"Well, if you are sure it'd be alright. I'd sure like to."

"Let's meet here for coffee on Friday afternoon, and I'll tell you what my parents said. Shall we say at 6 o'clock?"

"That'll be fine," he replied.

Chapter Two

Patriotism and Jubilation

"What do you think of the Emperor's declaration, Eckhardt?" asked Herbert, as the four of them walked down Unter den Linden.

Eckhardt, typically for him, walked head down with a thoughtful frown on his face before answering. "I think he stated the case as well as he could have, but I also think these people – who are so overjoyed at the prospect of 'teaching the Allies a lesson' – might be surprised to get a lesson out of this situation themselves."

"What kind of talk is that?" Herbert retorted. "You're being a defeatist before the war even starts. Don't you think Germany can beat the French?" He frowned. "We've already demonstrated we can do that back in '71. And as for the British, they're too spread out in their Empire and so sure of themselves, they're ripe for a whipping!"

"We'll see," said his friend. They strolled on in silence for a few minutes.

Finally, Ursula spoke up brightly, "Let's go have some have fun! I'm already tired of hearing men argue over the war."

Meira joined in to suggest that they take the subway out to Luna Park near Hallensee to enjoy the open air and the rides. This was agreed to and they ventured forth.

Luna Park was usually crowded during the summer months. But today, with people in a holiday spirit, the games and rides were filled to overflowing. There were long lines at the ticket booths, and there was much jostling and pushing. But the overall mood was cheerful and good-natured. Such scenes were being reenacted at places of entertainment all over Europe. The citizens of the nations at war were sure it would be a short conflict, and their countries would be victorious.

Eckhardt and Ursula, walking a few paces behind the exuberant Herbert and the amused Meira, wondered what the parents, Jewish and Protestant, would think of their children's friendship. Jews in Europe had been counseled by their leaders for some time to assimilate themselves into the communities where they lived. There was, as always, an undercurrent of antisemitism in gentile society, but this had steadily diminished as Jews became more and more involved in commerce, the arts, science, and even politics. However, romantic relationships, and most particularly marriages between the two groups, were still not encouraged, even indeed discouraged by religious leaders and families on both sides. But Herbert was nonetheless entranced with Meira's beauty and charm. She was somewhat withdrawn from the conversations and interactions going on around her. She responded with shyness, but courteously when spoken to. But she brightened when she spoke to Herbert.

Luna Park was a wonderland of bright lights and color. The calliope music from the carousel, the chorus of excited voices and laughter, and the delicious odors from the food vendors all combined to surround the four young people in an atmosphere of pleasure.

"Let's eat!" shouted Herbert above the din. "I want Currywurst." The tempting aroma of the curry-seasoned pork sausage frying on the nearby open griddle prompted Ursula's, "Me too!"

"I'm having Schaschlik, announced Eckhardt. "What about you, Meira?"

Becoming more relaxed, she decided to go along with the moment. After a pause, she responded, "I think that would be a good choice for me, too. The smell of that Currywurst is very tempting, but being Jewish, I'd better do what would make my parents happy and go for the lamb Schaschlik."

This brought a chuckle from Herbert, who replied, "Yes, we'd all do well to stay on our parents' good side."

The loudspeakers suddenly burst forth with the familiar jingle for Schultheiss beer, and many in the crowd lustily joined in: *"Was trinken wir? Schultheiss Bier!"*

"Good idea!" cried Herbert. "Let's get some beer!"

They collected their food and drinks and found a table near the bandstand where a Bavarian brass band was belting out old favorites, such as, *Oh, Susanna*, *Es gibt kein Bier auf Hawaii*, and *In München steht ein Hofbräuhaus*.

They enjoyed themselves and forgot about the war. The boys were both expert marksmen – Eckhardt by hunting for food in the forest near his childhood home and Herbert by hunting for sport on his Grandfather's estate. They were happy to demonstrate their skills at the shooting gallery by winning small stuffed facsimiles of the Berlin mascot, the black bear, for each of the girls.

The long, soft summer twilight lasted almost until closing time, due to Berlin's northern latitude. They stayed to see Luna Park's famous fireworks display, which illuminated their faces as they looked upward.

Herbert glanced sideways at Meira. Her large beautiful eyes reflected the color and brightness of the bursting lights. *What will mother think of her?*

Eckhardt's thoughts were on the exploding bursts of light, color and sound. *I wonder how we'll feel when the explosions are mortars and shells.*

Berlin's nightlife of cafes, restaurants, bars and other public places of entertainment stay open until the early morning hours. When Luna Park began to empty, the quartet of friends traveled by bus to the hubbub of Kurfürstendamm. The boulevard was at its best, with theatres such as the beautiful, newly opened, Marmor Palast letting out, and outdoor cafes, restaurants and night clubs thronged with crowds of well-dressed people enjoying the heady atmosphere of the day. All the talk was about the Emperor's announcement. Confidence that it would be a short, decisive war in Germany's favor was felt all around. People were proud to be German and especially proud to be Berliners.

The wide sidewalks along the bustling thoroughfare were adorned with large glass showcases strategically positioned to capture the attention of passersby. These showcases displayed a dazzling array of luxurious items. The girls strolled along the wide sidewalk, peering into the glittering shop windows and showcases, and admiring the stylishly dressed people. They ended their tour at a small outdoor café. Eckhardt and Herbert ordered cognac, but Ursula and Meira preferred red Berliner Weiße, white sour beer flavored with raspberry syrup with a thick head of foam on top.

They savored the end of the memorable day, which they later would recall as the great turning point in their lives. The men discussed their enlistments, for like most young men of that naïve time, they were fervently patriotic. The girls were apprehensive but proud of their young heroes. This was the last of the golden days of their innocence and youth. The darkness of an incomprehensible nightmare was descending.

§§§

Later that evening, stepping off the streetcar and approaching her dingy Wedding tenement, Ursula cringed with distaste. As she entered the building where she had been born and grown up, her nostrils were assailed by the damp mustiness and the stench of boiled cabbage and lidless toilets.

How could I have been so unaware of this ugliness until now? It's only since I've been surrounded by the beauty and elegance of KaDeWe that I've even noticed it.

She went up the stairs and entered the apartment where the mouth-watering odors of her mother's cooking made her forget the ugliness of the tenement.

Christina Bellon, standing at the charcoal-heated range stirring a kettle of potato dumplings, turned to smile and greet her daughter. "How was your day?"

"Great. I've been at Kranzler's for coffee with friends," Ursula responded.

"Hmm. Kranzler's. I haven't been there for years. Too ritzy for the likes of us," came the mildly disapproving reply.

"I work hard, and that's a good place to meet new friends. Certainly, not people from around here." Christina frowned but continued her cooking without further comment.

"I met a fellow today…"

Waiting to see how her mother would react, but getting no response she continued, "You have to meet him, Mama. His name is Eckhardt Meinert, and he's a sweet guy. He's kind and thoughtful. He caught my eye the first time I saw him. He's tall and handsome, so shy and unconceited – just the opposite of his best friend, Herbert Lenz. Let me tell you about him. His father is the chief surgeon at Charité and lives in Dahlem." Christina's eyes widened.

Overhearing this conversation, her father, Detlev, who had been quietly sitting at the kitchen table, scowled and shook his head. "I hope you don't get the idea that you're equal to people like them. Dahlem is a different planet!"

Ursula turned and frowned at her father and then continued, "Everybody likes Herbert, but he's cocky and thinks he's God's gift to the women! But the minute you talk to Eckhardt, you feel *his* gentleness. He and Herbert are best friends, and they work together at Siemens. Isn't it funny how opposites attract?"

She cocked her head. "Can I invite Eckhardt for Christmas? He's all alone here in Berlin. He can't go home for the holidays because they only have Christmas day and the weekend off."

Her mother listened to all this enthusiasm with a secret smile as she worked at her stove. After a moment, she said softly, "Of course, dear. We'd be glad to have him spend the holiday with us. You'd better warn him, though. Your father will drag him off to the pub to meet his drinking friends."

Ursula laughed at this and replied, "I don't think that'll be any problem at all. Eckhardt comes from southern Germany, and they pride themselves on their beer."

When Christmas rolled around, Eckhardt felt he couldn't arrive empty handed to the Bellon's. He couldn't afford to buy all the family members a gift, so after careful consideration, he decided on a nice bottle of wine that they could all enjoy. He was glad he did because when gifts were passed out there was a present of a warm scarf for him.

Eckhardt was taken into Ursula's family. Her father was delighted to have another man in the house with whom he could discuss football. Her mother was impressed with Eckhardt's quiet manner and the appreciation he showed for the Christmas dinner, especially for his repeated compliments on the goose stuffed with raisins and plums. Ursula's younger sister, fourteen-year-old Brigitta, was immediately smitten with him. Her brothers, ten-year-old Rudolf and Emil, six, were excited when Eckhardt offered to go with them after dinner to kick football at the nearby park. All in all, it had been a good day.

Chapter Three

The Warriors Gather

August 2, 1914

War hysteria was rampant in the European capitals of all the belligerents. Enthusiastic crowds surged through the streets of London, Paris, Saint Petersburg, Vienna, and Berlin. As the young men reported to their respective army registration stations, they were accompanied by escorts of sweethearts, wives, relatives and friends.

Military bands played stirring marches which enlivened the holiday spirit. Everyone assured each other that their cause was just and that, after all, God was surely on their side.

In Berlin, Eckhardt at age 21 and Herbert 20, were already registered for military service as required by Imperial German law. All males from age 17 to 45 were required to do so. They, along with their peers reported to their respective district enlistment offices to undergo physical examinations and to receive their uniforms, which included belts with buckles embossed with the motto, *Gott mit uns*. Eckhardt and Herbert had previously taken a room together in a rooming house in Tegel near the Siemens plant, which was arranged for them through the personnel office at Siemens. This allowed them to register at the same enlistment office and to be assigned to the same regiment. It had been suggested to Eckhardt that he seek a deferment through the firm, as his work could qualify him for it. He had decided that he would rather serve in the army with his friend. After all, it was going to be a short war, and would no doubt be an adventure for the two of them.

Upon completion of their enlistment, Eckhardt and Herbert received their assignments to present themselves with their unit on Monday, August 3, in front of the Stadtschloß. There they would be reviewed by the Emperor from his balcony. They would then join the huge farewell parade to Görlitzer Bahnhof for their departure to a training area a few miles behind the front lines for six weeks training. However, this being their last free night in Berlin, they had agreed to meet Ursula and Meira at Clärchens Ballhaus on Auguststraße near the

Friedrich-Wilhelms University. They felt quite proud in their new uniforms and were pleased to see the girls in smart new frocks and hats in the latest fashion. They were seated at a table in the main ballroom, and after taking in the festive atmosphere, both couples moved onto the dance floor and began to enjoy the new dance step recently introduced from America, the foxtrot. Herbert, being the confident young man about town that he was, and Meira an energetic girl, began to demonstrate their considerable skill. Eckhardt, being not so sure of himself, had to rely upon Ursula to guide him through the new experience. As the dance proceeded, they began to move together, and Eckhardt held her more closely. When the dance ended, Eckhardt was relieved to be able to escort Ursula back to their table, while Herbert and Meira took the next dance, an exotic tango, a dance from Argentina that had been popular for some time.

Eckhardt and Ursula had by this time been considering marriage, and Ursula was ready to take this step. Eckhardt, more cautious by nature, had explained that he felt it unwise to commit until he at least knew where he would be sent after basic training. He knew that this would take place somewhere a few kilometers behind the lines on the Western Front, after which he would be sent directly into combat.

Ursula, not thoroughly convinced his resistance was due to practicality, stated, "As long as you promise you love me, I will respect your decision for now. But when you come home on your first leave, I will expect you to make a choice. Either you'll let me share whatever you endure, or we'll part and free us both to move on with our lives. In spite of all the confidence we hear everyone expressing now about the outcome of this war, we can't know for sure where we'll be in the coming weeks and months. If things go as well as we hope, we can enjoy the good times together. But if there are hard days coming, I'll need your strength and you'll need my support."

Eckhardt considered her words, held her close, and murmured, "I've never known anyone like you. I know I won't change my feelings. Please trust me. I love you and want you, but I don't want us to make this decision in a moment of passion."

The situation between Herbert and Meira had proceeded very differently. They both were Berliners of similar upper middle-class backgrounds with conservative parents who would not approve of their children's involvement with each other. Herbert's family of Prussian Lutheran faith would have considered open expressions of antisemitism to be in bad taste but nevertheless would have considered a marriage between their son and a Jewess of any stripe to be socially unacceptable. Meira's parents on the other hand, although they were members of the liberal Jewish congregation attending the new synagogue on the Fasanenstraße in Charlottenburg, and who were willing to assimilate into the general non-Jewish community, would have drawn the line at their daughter being married outside the Jewish faith. Therefore, neither Herbert nor Meira at this point would have considered marriage as an option. Herbert, with his happy-go-lucky attitude, and confidence in his ability to sway and even seduce the ladies, was strictly out for a good time with a good-looking girl. Meira, as an independent thinker who considered herself capable of taking care of herself, enjoyed Herbert's friendship. Also, he was handsome, fun, and a good dancer.

They celebrated with champagne and a sumptuous dinner and danced to interchanging orchestras until very late. Upon enlisting, the boys had to give up their room in Tegel and take a room in a small hotel near the Museum Island. The girls had taken another room in the same hotel to be near the boys when they assembled to march to the station.

After the girls bid the boys goodnight, Ursula and Meira turned off the light and settled in for a short night in their respective beds. They lay in the dark for some moments. Ursula then whispered, "How do you feel about Herbert now, Meira?"

Meira did not respond immediately, but then murmured, "I'm not quite sure. I find him very attractive, and he is an excellent dancer, but we can never be anything but good friends."

"What do you mean 'just good friends'?" responded Ursula. "I can assure you that may have been the case before tonight, but I could see how he looked at you when he thought you weren't looking. I wonder if you're being totally honest with yourself."

Meira pondered this and finally said, "I can't allow myself to think about that now. Besides, I wanted to ask you how you explained being out tonight to your parents."

"I've been working at KaDeWe for almost two years and have considered getting my own place, if I could afford it. My parents know I am capable of taking care of myself, and they know Eckhardt and know we might be out late, as it's his last night in town. I've also told them how we feel about each other, and they're delighted since they've gotten to know him."

In a soft voice, Meira stated, "I envy your independence, but with Jewish parents it's a very different matter. If my family knew I were going out with a young man who's not Jewish, it would be a catastrophe. I've even lied to them by telling them that I'd be staying overnight with a girl whose family they know. They trust me, so they never question what I tell them."

"And yet you say that in spite of all the risk you've taken, you feel that Herbert is just 'a good friend'?" The stillness in the dark room was heavy, but Meira only responded with a sigh.

The next morning the regiments assembled at various locations throughout the city. The crowd near the Zeughaus (armory) on Unter den Linden had already been able to observe the changing of the guard at the nearby Neue Wache, which took place several times every day. Large military bands nearby played many favorites, including the marches *Badenweiler Marsch*, *Preußens Gloria*, *Wach am Rhein*, and *Berliner Luft* – praising the air of the city, which is reputed to have many invigorating qualities. Women and girls carried bunches of flowers to give to the troops, and flags were seen everywhere. The excitement in the air was tangible. As the men formed up their ranks and upon command fell into step, they moved as solid units down the wide boulevard toward Pariser Platz. The crowds moved alongside them, with young women dashing up to thrust flowers into the soldiers' hands and even to kiss them. The bands set the tempo for everyone, and unit after unit they marched through the Brandenburg Gate and met up with other regiments. These had convened in the western parts of the city and had marched through the Tiergarten and along the broad Charlottenburger Chaussee. The parade then turned southeast in the direction of Treptow and their embarking point at the Görlitzer Bahnhof.

The crowd – consisting of families, wives, children and girlfriends – followed the marching throng to the station. There, they laughed, cried, and said their farewells to their dear ones, accompanied by confident shouts, "We'll be home by Christmas!" As the train pulled out of the station, the band played the old Berlin favorite, *Solang Unter den Linden*. Hands were extended out of the train windows and grasped by wives and sweethearts running alongside the train until they reached the end of the platform.

On Unter den Linden, a soft breeze rustled the Linden leaves which seemed to send forth a sigh that could have been heard across Europe, *But which Christmas?*

Chapter Four

Farewells

Ursula and Meira tearfully watched the train depart the station. They slowly walked out the front entrance into the bright sunshine. The beautiful weather mocked the broken-hearted women who had just seen their men depart – some for the last time.

"Meira, we are going to need each other's support. Let's please keep in touch," Ursula said to her new friend.

"I agree," responded Meira, as they embraced.

As they turned and went their separate ways, Ursula carried a sadness in her heart, not only of seeing Eckhardt leave, but also a feeling of apprehension. In spite of the assurances that the war would be short and ended by Christmas, she had a nagging fear that much of the confidence shown by everyone around her was not as genuine as they would like to pretend. She was confident however that Eckhardt would show himself to be steady and strong in whatever situation or crisis he might be. She had felt his unassuming strength from the very beginning of their relationship. She hurried along to catch the streetcar, eager to return to her job at KaDeWe, which she enjoyed, and which would help to keep her mind occupied.

Meira considered the feelings she had experienced at Herbert's departure. It had affected her more than she had expected. Up to that point she had regarded him as a good friend whose company she enjoyed, but she had not been prepared for the sense of overwhelming sadness she felt when the train pulled out of the station. She wondered then how she would explain her overnight absence and the late arrival at work to her father. She almost never stayed out all night, and then only to sleep at the home of a relative. She knew that if he were to learn that she had been in the company of a soldier – especially a non-Jewish soldier – and had stayed in the same hotel with him, even though in a separate room, it would precipitate a crisis of unimaginable proportions. She decided that for the time being, she would have to lie – something that was totally against her nature. As the younger of two daughters in the family, she had always been the apple of her father's eye. She anguished at the thought of hurting him and her mother. She was surprised at herself for considering the friendship with Herbert to be important enough for her to put herself in such a situation.

§§§

Eckhardt and Herbert found themselves packed in the corridor of the coach as the train pulled out of the station. Those fortunate enough to have found seats, were jammed together with five or six men in seats designed for four people. The doors of the toilets at each end of the cars were open with soldiers seated only to have a place to sit. When someone had to use the toilet, the occupant would grudgingly step out to allow the intruder to attend his bodily needs. Sometimes arguments ensued when the newcomer refused to leave afterward.

"Well, buddy, we're on our way," Herbert said to his friend, as he gave him an elbow jab in the ribs. "Those are some girls we've managed to find. I can't imagine how Meira is gonna explain me to her parents. And when my mother catches wind of her, it'll be some show. And Ursula is such a beauty. She could have any guy she wanted. I can't understand what she sees in a big ox like you," he teased Eckhardt.

Eckhardt smiled and replied, "Me neither."

There was much loud talk and laughter as the young soldiers settled in for the journey, and everyone still maintained a holiday mood as they went forth on what would be for them the greatest experience of their lives. At the time, it did not occur to most of them that many would never see Berlin again.

As time passed, the laughter and talk subsided and they began to consider what might lie before them. Many began to reflect upon those they had just left behind. Eckhardt remembered that evening in Kranzler's when he had first caught a glimpse of Ursula. He could hardly believe that she had been as attracted to him as he to her. Their relationship had steadily progressed to the point where they now found themselves. He felt badly that he had had to be firm in his insistence that they not marry at present. He knew Ursula had been prepared to give herself to him, but he was glad that he had kept a tight rein on his feelings. Especially the night before, as he kissed her goodnight in the corridor outside the door of the room she and Meira had occupied. He wondered about the future and when he might find it prudent to advance their plans to marry, as he knew Ursula wanted.

Herbert thought of Meira and how she fascinated him with her beautiful face and figure. He was used to being in charge in his relationships with girls and found it intriguing and yet annoying that with Meira, he felt that although she obviously enjoyed being with him, there was a reserve about her he could not penetrate. She had been very honest with him about her background and had also indicated that although open-minded, she was nevertheless Jewish and proud to be so.

He recalled how he had first seen her in her father's store and how he had been instantly taken with her. She had been a totally new experience for him. He wondered if her reserve might not be a large part of her desirability. He was also surprised at himself for not having been more insistent the night before when she had made it clear in the hotel the evening was over as she kissed him on the cheek before entering the room she shared with Ursula. He wondered if some of Eckhardt's controlled behavior might not be rubbing off on him.

§§§

"Meira, I want to talk to you right now!" Meira's father shouted as he slammed the front door on a Thursday evening in December. She and her older sister, Edna, stood at the kitchen sink helping their mother prepare foods for the *Shabbat*, which began the next day. It had been more than four months since the war started, and she had seen Herbert depart on the train. She rinsed her hands and wiping them on her apron walked down the hall to her father's study. Such an outburst was uncharacteristic for her father, a kindly man who was respected and liked by many.

"What's the matter Papa? Why are you shouting at me?" she asked as she entered his study, a room where she and he had had many affectionate discussions and where she had always felt safe.

"Rudolf Eisenstadt came into the store just before I was closing up this evening and asked me if you were seeing a young man who has joined the army. He and his wife were at Görlitzer Station seeing their nephew off, and they saw you with a soldier. You were standing quite close to him and apparently involved in a deep conversation. Who is he? You told us you had been with Rahel Hirschberg and her friends, and that you had stayed overnight with her. After Eisenstadt left, I telephoned Hirschbergs and spoke to Rahel. You were never with her that night! When did you start lying to us? I am astonished that you have kept this from us all these months."

The anger and hurt on her father's face cut Meira to the quick and rendered her speechless. The color drained from her face as she looked at him, dreading to tell him the truth, which she knew would hurt him more than anything she had ever done.

"You might actually know him, Papa," she began with trembling voice. "His father is one of your customers, Dr. Lenz, a head surgeon at the Charité Hospital. His son's name is Herbert Lenz, and I met him last winter on the subway after he had been to your store to buy a topcoat. We have been seeing each other along with his friend, Eckhardt Meinert, who works with him at Siemens. Eckhardt has a fiancé who works at KaDeWe. I promise you Herbert and I are just friends, and we have never been alone together."

Red-faced, her father responded, "Dr. Hans Joachim Lenz? Of course, I know him. He is a highly respected surgeon, and one of my oldest customers. He is a fine man, and one who interacts with all kinds of people. He might be open-minded about his son befriending a Jewish girl, as long as it were to remain only on a friendship basis, but I can assure you his wife would view it quite differently. She comes from an old Junker family in Pomerania and is a staunch Protestant. Her social set is made up of people who have nothing to do with Catholics and Jews. She would be outraged to know her son has been seen in your company. Furthermore, you 'promise' that the situation is just as you have described? What else can you 'promise' me? Where did you spend the night?"

Meira felt the room beginning to spin around her. How would she ever convince her father that her virginity was still intact after having spent the night in the same hotel as Herbert, albeit in separate rooms?

As she began to relate the events of that night and came to the part about the hotel, her father's face flushed deep red, and he stood up and roared, "Enough! You lie to us, stay out all night in a hotel in the company of gentiles and expect me to believe you? Get out of my sight while I decide what to do with you!"

She turned and started down the hall toward the staircase leading up to her room, convulsed in sobs. Her mother came out of the kitchen to see what the matter was. Meira could not face her mother, and sobbing, she stammered that she was going to her room.

Chapter Five

Blockade

The British blockade of Germany's ports had its beginnings ten years prior to the outbreak of war in 1914. It is now known that when British naval authorities viewed the growing development of the German navy, the planning of a blockade of Germany took place. Therefore, when war broke out, the blockade was ready to be implemented. The strategy was to literally starve the German civilian and military population into submission, thereby bringing the war to an end. However, one cannot assume that the blockade was a strategy solely developed by the Royal Navy. In fact, it was executed by the Royal Navy but was controlled by the British Foreign Office.

At the outbreak of the war, the British issued a list of goods designated as "contraband" which included foodstuffs. This effectively prohibited then neutral America from trading with the Central Powers. In November 1914, the British declared the North Sea to be a war zone warning that any ships entering that area do so at their own risk. The Germans regarded this as a brazen attempt to starve the German people into surrender and prompted Germany to retaliate in kind. Meanwhile, the French established a blockade of Austria's Adriatic ports. The ensuing shortages were thus felt by all the Central Powers.

As tragic as it was for citizens of those countries, it still has been acknowledged as one of the main weapons which eventually brought about the Allied victory. But the resulting effect it had on the civilian population was horrendous and has been described by some historians as an atrocity. The exact number of civilians who died of starvation and disease as a result of the blockade has been estimated to be between half and three quarters of a million.

Both Germany and Britain relied on imports to feed their people and supply their war industries, thus both tried to blockade one another. The big difference was that the British had the Royal Navy which was far bigger than the German navy, with the British navy being able to operate throughout the British Empire across the world, while the German navy was restricted mainly to ports in Northern Europe and the Baltic. This led to Germany developing their submarine fleet in order to raid commercial vessels carrying goods to Britain. As the war continued, the Germans were forced to resort to unrestricted submarine warfare against Allied shipping. This resulted in the subsequent sinking of the RMS Lusitania and other civilian vessels with Americans on board, which did more to inflame U.S. opinion against Germany than the blockade itself and brought America into the war two years later.

However, the British Government has since released documents which reveal that the Lusitania was carrying munitions when it was sunk by a German submarine in May 1915, with a loss of over 1,100 passengers, including Americans. Divers have found munitions in the hold, which substantiates the German claim that the ship was indeed carrying war goods and was therefore a legitimate military target. It should also be noted that the German Embassy placed warning notices in American newspapers reminding the public that vessels flying the colors of Allied nations, particularly Great Britain, represented nations at war with Germany. Thus, those boarding such vessels did so at their own risk.

Chapter Six

War and Privation

Christmas 1914 in Berlin found many homes with only women and children to celebrate the holidays. As the men in the army would be able to expect home leave after a year at the front, many women prepared for the holiday by securing as much food, clothing articles, and toiletry items as possible to send in Christmas packages to their men. Ursula was impressed by the crowds of women shopping for these things at KaDeWe. In spite of the increasing shortages of basic food and coal, there still seemed to be an abundant supply of wines, liquor, chocolate, and tobacco. She herself had spent much of her time during the months since summer knitting socks and sweaters for Eckhardt and other men in her family serving at the front.

The big change that occurred in Ursula's life was the day when Meira appeared in KaDeWe while she was serving a customer. Meira had always looked calm and composed and had always seemed to be in complete control of herself. On this day however, she looked pale and utterly distraught. She hung back until Ursula had finished with her customer, and then almost in a whisper said she needed to speak to her privately.

"My father found out I was with you at Görlitzer Railway Station to see the boys off. I had to tell him about Herbert. I tried to explain that nothing happened between us at the hotel, but he was beyond reason, and told me I had to leave. I can't ask any of my relatives to take me in, because I'm sure they've already heard from my mother that I was with a *goy*. I don't know what to do nor where to go. I hate to ask, but could I stay with you until I can figure out what to do?" She then broke down into heaving sobs.

Ursula was taken aback and was tempted to point out that there were already six people in their three-room flat in one of the multi-story tenements in Wedding, but she caught herself and responded, "Of course you must come and stay with us. I'm sure we can work it out." In her mind though, Ursula had no idea how she would approach her parents with this new development.

Meira's face brightened, and she stated she'd come back in two hours when Ursula would be off work. She would browse through the huge department store and wait for Ursula at the main entrance facing Wittenbergplatz. She then walked to her favorite section, the ladies' clothing department. Although her father's store carried a line of high quality goods in ladies' apparel, the huge selection in KaDeWe far outstripped anything to be seen anywhere else. She noted the clientele and realized that the women shoppers represented a wider range of economic classes than one would ordinarily see in her father's store.

After she had finished serving her last customer, Ursula hurried down to meet Meira wondering how she would approach her parents with the new houseguest. Uppermost in her mind was not only the question of how to accommodate someone else in the already filled apartment, but also not knowing how her family would react to a person of a higher social status – and a Jew at that. It was something she considered with apprehension. Wedding, being a working-class Protestant district, was not where one would normally encounter an upper middle class Jewish person from Charlottenburg. Ursula's parents were hardworking people who were congenial and comfortable with neighbors and friends of similar backgrounds, and they were not especially anti-Semitic, but they had almost never had any interaction with Jews. Therefore, they hardly gave them any thought. But to live under the same roof with someone so far outside of their range of experience, was something they would never have anticipated.

On the surface, one would not have suspected that the bustling crowds represented a nation at war. The streets were filled with vehicle and pedestrian traffic, and the stores, restaurants, cafes and theaters were brightly lit. Ursula and Meira made their way without delay to the apartment near Leopoldplatz in Wedding.

Seeing the nearby pub on the corner, Meira said, "Why don't I wait in there while you go ahead and tell your parents about their new houseguest?"

"That's a good idea. It'll be just my mother now, because my father works in the evening. You wait there and stay warm, and I promise not to make you wait long," replied Ursula.

When Ursula entered the warm apartment, she found her mother busy laying out the cold cuts, cheese and bread for the evening meal.

Her younger sister, Brigitta, was helping, and the two little brothers, Rudolf and Emil, were arguing about which of them would be first to wash his hands in the basin of water on the sideboard.

After kissing her mother on the cheek, and admonishing the two boys to stop their squabble, Ursula whispered to her mother, "Could I speak to you for a moment in the bedroom?" After closing the bedroom door, Ursula began, "I have a good friend who is in a very serious situation. I've told you about Eckhardt's friend Herbert, and how he has become acquainted with a very nice girl, who was with us when we all went out celebrating the night before the boys left for the front. What I didn't tell you is she is the daughter of Benjamin Friedlander, the owner of Friedlander's Clothing store on Kurfürstendamm."

Her mother shook her head in disbelief. "How did you ever become involved with her? How would a girl of your background ever have anything in common with a well-to-do person like that? And anyway, aren't they Jewish?"

Ignoring the question, Ursula continued, "She and Herbert are friends, and he is Eckhardt's best friend, so that is good enough for me. Besides, she is a very pleasant person and has become my friend as well. But there is more. Her father has thrown her out of the house, after he learned she is associating with Herbert, a non-Jew. She has asked me if she could stay with us temporarily, until she can make other arrangements, and I told her she could. She's waiting for me down in the pub on the corner."

Her mother considered this revelation, while Ursula waited for an answer. Finally, her mother responded, "Well, if you've already told her she could come here, and she is waiting for you, you'd better go and get her. I have no idea what your father will say, but I'll try to figure out how to break it to him."

"Thank you, Mama. I'm sorry to drop this on you so suddenly, but the poor girl came to me this afternoon at work and was distraught. I don't think she has eaten for a while, and she is utterly exhausted."

Meira was indeed weak and exhausted. After her confrontation with her father the evening before, she had walked the streets and had ridden streetcars until service ended at 1 a.m., and thereafter had crisscrossed the city on night buses. As daybreak came, she had eaten a scanty breakfast of a hard roll and tea at Aschingers on

Alexanderplatz, a stand-up all-night eatery, and thereafter nothing for the rest of the day. As she waited for Ursula to return and fetch her, she fidgeted on the edge of a chair near the door of the pub. Although her clothes were somewhat disheveled from her sleepless night, it was apparent to the regulars and to the barman that she was dressed in more expensive attire than was ever seen in the neighborhood. Also, as an unfamiliar and unaccompanied woman, attention was drawn to her and commented on in quiet mumbling by those seated at nearby tables partaking of their beer and schnapps. She was relieved when Ursula appeared and led her away.

When she was introduced to Ursula's mother, she took the hand offered in welcome and observed the humble yet comfortable home of the Bellon family. Brigitta greeted her cordially, and the boys stared with wide-eyed wonder at the exotic creature. Christina Bellon was polite, but reserved, as she considered the upcoming necessity of explaining the situation to her husband. As they were seated around the table in the corner of the kitchen, Meira wondered what the sausages might contain. Her mother, being somewhat more conservative than her liberal husband, had always kept a Kosher kitchen, and of course pork products would never have been seen on the table in the Friedlander house. Not wishing to offend her new hosts by enquiring about the sausages, she limited herself to slices of cheese and bread.

Brigitta, Ursula's 14-year-old sister, was entranced by the new guest, and looked at her stylish dress with uninhibited curiosity. She had, of course, often passed by the windows of the Friedlander establishment when walking along the Kurfürstendamm and had been fascinated by the beautiful fashions displayed there. However, she had never been so close to such things before and longed to reach out and touch the fine fabric.

Ursula's mother worked clearing the table after the meal and turned the matter over in her mind again and again. What strange people these must be to turn one of their children away. Although she was a person of limited education and acquaintance with those outside of her family and community, she herself couldn't imagine ever turning one of her children out of her home. She was thoroughly dedicated to her husband and family.

Detlev Bellon was a mild-mannered man who had been in love with his wife from their childhood. They had been born and raised in Wedding, surrounded by working class families like themselves. He had been employed by Straßenbahn Berlin after finishing his basic schooling at age 17.

He made his way home after completing his shift at 1 a.m. and considered how lucky he was with his wife and their children. The outbreak of the war had unsettled him, as it had some of his friends. He was thankful to have sons too young to be conscripted into the army but was concerned about young men from his extended family and from families among his friends and colleagues.

As he neared the corner pub near his home, he looked forward to his nightcap of beer and Jägermeister. As he parted the heavy leather curtain inside the door, he was cheered by the warm smoky atmosphere. Because of the late hour, only a few diehards and late shift workers like himself were to be seen. As he stood at the bar and ordered his drinks, Max the bartender, an old acquaintance, casually asked him, "Who's the high-class gal your daughter is hanging around with?" Puzzled, Detlev queried, "What are you talking about?"

"An attractive young woman came in here earlier this evening and sat in that chair by the door. She was wearing some pretty classy duds, but they looked like she had slept in 'em. Ursula came in later and took her out. I've never seen her before and she certainly didn't look like she was from around here."

Detlev turned this over in his mind as he left the pub and walked the short distance to his apartment building. He trudged up the two flights of stairs and entered the warm kitchen which was near the front entrance. He removed his heavy parka, hung it up on the coat hook, sat at the table and began to eat the bread and sausage his wife had left for him. He then opened the cast iron door of the tile stove and placed two more briquettes inside. The glowing coals grumbled as he did so. Pondering the information Max had given him, he decided he would pursue the matter in the morning, as he was tired and yearned for his bed. He removed his shoes and walked softly through the small parlor where he noticed the shape of an additional person asleep on a pallet next to Ursula and entered the bedroom he and his wife shared with the two boys asleep on trundle beds. He removed his outer garments and slipped under the thick down comforter next to his sleeping wife.

Chapter Seven

Revelation and Introduction

After 1880 and the conclusion of the Franco Prussian War, Berlin underwent a massive expansion and an unprecedented population explosion. Indeed, Berlin became a "boom town" with a huge industrial expansion. Major companies such as Siemens & Halske, AEG and Borsig moved their plants from the city center to the outskirts in order to build their enormous factories.

Former towns such as Charlottenburg, Spandau, Schöneberg and Lichtenberg became absorbed into the booming metropolis, but remained officially separate communities until 1920. People from all over Germany, and even from other European countries, fleeing rural poverty, streamed into the city seeking employment in the burgeoning new industries. Before 1880, Berlin's population had been less than 500,000, but by 1914 had increased to almost two million.

Huge tenement blocks were built which became known as *Wohnbaracken* (residential barracks). The apartments at the fronts of the buildings facing the streets were typically spacious with several rooms. The apartments or flats in the inner courtyards, however, were small with one, two, or sometimes three rooms. These were heated with free-standing tile stoves and kitchen ranges which consumed soft coal briquettes. There was no running water, except sometimes a faucet in the hall with no potable water, but only water for cleaning, which could be boiled. There were no bathrooms, but they had communal toilets that were shared by several families. Some of the earliest constructed buildings would have them outdoors in the courtyard, but later construction placed them inside the building between floors on the mezzanines. Washing could be performed in basins with boiled water from the hall faucets. For a full bath, one went to one of the nearby public bathhouses, and for a small fee, got a small cake of soap and a hand towel. Shower facilities were located in large open shower rooms with several showerheads. Life in these tenements was harsh and even unhealthy. For instance, the infant mortality rate in them was extremely high. Before WWI the infant mortality rate in the middle class Tiergarten area was 5.2 percent, while 42 percent of newborns died in working class Wedding.

Christina Bellon opened the bedroom drapes and gently awoke her husband. The apartment was quiet, as the younger children had been fed earlier and sent off to school, and Ursula and Meira had also left to go to KaDeWe, where the two of them would try to secure employment for Meira. It was midmorning and the winter sunlight penetrated the dingy ice-covered windows of the room. Although there was the typical tile stove in the corner, the rooms, except for the kitchen, were not usually heated, as the allotment of briquettes were reserved for cooking. These were purchased at the coal yard on the corner and were delivered by a man carrying them in a rack on his back like a hod-carrier and were placed in the hall near the entrance door.

Detlev made use of the chamber pot which was kept under the bed, which Christina emptied every morning in the toilet located a half-flight down on the mezzanine and shared by the two apartments on the floor above and the two apartments on the floor below. Having slept in his long underwear, Detlev then went straightaway to the warm kitchen and slipped on his trousers, which his wife had laid by the tile stove to warm. She had already laid out his breakfast of cheese and rolls with coffee. As he spread marmalade on a roll, he asked Christina, "Who was that sleeping on the floor next to Ursula last night?"

She was silent as she washed the dishes used earlier. "Ursula had a friend stay over last night," she responded. "She's a friend Ursula is going to help get a job at KaDeWe." Her husband stared at her as he digested this new information.

After a moment's consideration, Detlev replied, "Actually, I wasn't surprised to see her. Max told me about a high-class girl waiting for Ursula in the pub last night. Apparently, she caused a stir, because he said she obviously didn't come from around here. Who is she and what's her name?"

As she dried a plate and put it in the cupboard, Christina replied, "She's Meira Friedlander. Her father owns Friedlander's on Ku'damm."

Detlev being by nature a congenial, generous person, replied, "Of course if Ursula considers her to be a friend needing help, this girl must be sheltered and fed. But we are so limited as it is that we must make other arrangements as soon as possible."

Relieved that her husband had taken the new revelation so well and had not commented on the fact that Meira was Jewish, she offered, "As a matter of fact, I was talking to the custodian yesterday, and he mentioned that Mrs. Krause just upstairs is moving. Her daughter who lives in Steglitz wants her to move into her house. Since Mr. Krause passed away last summer, Mrs. Krause's health has steadily declined, and her daughter is worried that her mother can no longer manage the stairs since her last stroke. I will speak to him as soon as possible and inquire if the flat is still available. Anyway, Ursula has talked about getting her own place. Perhaps she and Meira could manage to share the expense."

"Yes, but do you suppose this girl would be willing to live in Wedding? You said her family are the Friedlanders who own the store on Ku'damm."

Christina, a practical person, replied, "Well, I think that is something she and Ursula will have to work out. Under the circumstances, we can only make the suggestion."

§§§

The Christmas shoppers descended on KaDeWe as soon as the doors were opened at 10 a.m. The luxurious department store was made more beautiful than usual by the tasteful holiday decorations. Ursula reported to her department and then got permission to accompany Meira to the personnel office. Meira had brushed and pressed her dress and had had Ursula help her rearrange her hair before leaving the apartment. In spite of the harrowing experience of the past two days, she was therefore able to restore her appearance to a considerable extent. The receptionist gave her the application forms and asked her to be seated. Because of her unusually well-groomed appearance, and because Ursula had, as a store employee with a good record, vouched for Meira, the receptionist promised to see if the personnel manager might interview her right away.

Meira entered the women's fashion center just as Ursula was assisting a dignified older woman trying on a mink coat. She then stood back and observed how the woman responded to Ursula's comments and suggestions, and how appreciative the customer was for the input. Having worked in her father's clothing store since she was a young girl and having been involved with most aspects of the clothing industry, including accompanying her father and older sister on buying trips within Germany and to other European countries, Meira could see that Ursula had a talent for selling and dealing with customers. As soon as Ursula had made the sale and packed the luxurious coat, the customer was beaming as she walked away with her new purchase.

"Ursula, I've been hired!" Meira exclaimed as she embraced her friend. The Personnel Manager had been impressed with the well-dressed Meira, her manner and elegant bearing, and with the experience she had gained working for her father. Friedlanders was an establishment well-known and respected in the city, and Benjamin Friedlander was acknowledged as a businessman with a reputation for honesty and for offering quality merchandise. The fact that Meira had been involved in the selection of such merchandise indicated to the personnel manager that she had much to offer the Ladies Apparel Department of KaDeWe. He had set up an interview with the manager of that department, who had been also impressed with her. In fact, the department manager had indicated to her that after a trial period on the sales floor over the holidays, he would invite her to the showing of the new fashions for the Spring collection. Ursula, excited to have Meira start right away, began showing her around the department. Meira was overwhelmed by the vastness of the inventory and recalled that although her father's store was a large establishment, it could not compare in size and variety of goods to KaDeWe.

Due to the crush of Christmas shoppers, Ursula was asked to work late, and Meira gladly did the same. As they boarded the streetcar that evening, they were cheered by the outcome of the day's events but were somewhat apprehensive about returning home to find out how Ursula's father had reacted to Meira's becoming a houseguest. As soon as they stepped in the door of the Bellon apartment, however, they could see by Ursula's mother's expression that all would be well. After relating all that happened during the day, they helped Christina set the table and serve the evening meal. Ursula was relieved and grateful for her father's generosity, but not really surprised, as she had always regarded him as a kind and generous man.

"I have good news," Christina declared. "I spoke to the custodian today, and Mrs. Krause is moving. Her apartment will be available right after the first of the year." As she related this information to Ursula and Meira, she was hopeful that they would be pleased. After a moment, Ursula stated that she was appreciative that her mother had made the effort to inquire about the soon-to-be-vacant apartment, but she had hoped to eventually find something closer to her job in the city. Also, although she had never said anything to her parents, she had hoped to move away from Wedding into a district where one could be closer to restaurants, cinemas, and cafes. However, under the circumstances with Meira now living with her, she realized that this new opportunity should not be quickly dismissed. She wondered how Meira would react, having lived all her life in pleasant Charlottenburg, and now perhaps having to consider living in Wedding. Meira surprised Ursula with her positive response. She expressed her appreciation to Christina, and stated that if Ursula was willing, she would be happy to share the apartment with her. What she did not mention was that being separated from her own family, she would feel comforted to be near Ursula's. Both girls once again expressed appreciation for Christina's effort. She then told them that they would have to go to the building manager's office to pay the necessary deposits and fill out the paperwork. Meira explained that she would have to telephone her sister Edna and ask her to bring some of her clothes and personal effects to the Bellon apartment as soon as possible, as she had no change of clothes.

Detlev Bellon was curious what the new houseguest would be like. Due to his work schedule, he had not yet met the young lady, but he had received enthusiastic reports from his family. Christina had described her as a congenial person who exhibited good upbringing, and who had eagerly taken part in assisting with cooking and chores. Christina had been somewhat taken aback when Meira, as tactfully as possible, had informed her that her religious beliefs prevented her from partaking of any pork products. This presented Christina with a dilemma, as pork is a mainstay of the German diet. Meira suggested that perhaps the easiest way around this would be for her to purchase non-pork meats, fowl and fish, and also to prepare these herself, which would cause the least inconvenience. Christina agreed to this but insisted that Meira would join the family when pork was not served. This seemed to be agreeable to everyone and the matter was not brought up again.

§§§

With Christmas drawing near, traditional Weihnachtsmärkte (Christmas markets) sprang up in many different locations around the city. One of the biggest was in the northeast district of Spandau, and it had been a Bellon family tradition since Detlev and Christina had married to visit it. Having been an employee of the city transit authority, Straßenbahn Berlin, for over fifteen years, Detlev by seniority had been given Saturdays and Sundays as his regular days off. Therefore, the family had always planned to visit the Weihnachtsmarkt in Spandau on the Saturday before Christmas. Many merchants from the city and farmers from the surrounding countryside displayed their wares in booths set up around the town square in the beginning days of December. Among the traditional holiday treats to be had were Glühwein, Gebrannte Mandeln (roasted brown sugar-coated almonds), and Spekulatius, spicy Christmas cookies molded in shapes of animals and holiday figures. Everyone in the Bellon household was looking forward to the special Saturday because of the much-anticipated visit to the Weihnachtsmarkt, and because it was a time when the Christmas tree would be purchased. Also, this year would be special because of the inclusion of Meira in the family festivities.

§§§

"Miss Friedlander, I am happy to meet you and welcome you into our house," Detlev assured Meira upon meeting her the following Saturday morning as his family made ready to sit down to breakfast, and then leave for their big day.

"Believe me, Mr. Bellon, the pleasure is all mine and I cannot express enough gratitude to you for your hospitality and for the kindness of your family," Meira graciously offered in response. The warmth of the occasion was felt by all present, and they made ready to enjoy the day together.

Because of the latitude of Berlin, the days of December are very short, with only an average of six hours of real daylight, with long twilight at the beginning and end of the day. Therefore, the Bellon household were up before six o'clock that Saturday and were on the way by seven in order to make the journey by a combination of subway and streetcar to Spandau. The temperature hovered around minus 2 degrees Celsius or 27 Fahrenheit and people were walking briskly to their destinations. The beauty and festive atmosphere of the Weihnachtsmarkt made everyone soon forget the weather as they wandered among the booths and decorations. The Bellon boys, Rudolf 10 and Emil 6 were mesmerized by the wonderful atmosphere, and pulled on their parents to look at the many toy displays, shouting, "Oh, look at that!" or "Oh Papa, come over here and see this!"

Ursula and Meira were amused by the boys, but 14-year-old Brigitta pretended not to be involved in such unsophisticated behavior. "Boys," she sniffed, "are such nuisances."

After stuffing themselves on goodies and hot drinks, the Bellon family and their guest finally made their way homeward as the night descended and temperatures dropped. Before returning to their apartment, they walked to the nearby Leopoldplatz where Christmas trees were for sale on a corner. After much discussion and deliberation, a pretty spruce was selected and taken home to be placed in a bucket of water in the hallway awaiting the arrival of Christmas Eve the following Thursday.

Chapter Eight

Christmas Eve in Wedding 1914

Shops and businesses closed early on Christmas Eve and people flocked to their homes in anticipation of the traditional activities and gatherings of families and friends. Dinner might include deep fried carp and potato salad with wine and schnapps. The Christmas trees would be trimmed and lit with candles and gifts would be distributed. Many would later attend special Christmas Eve services in their respective churches.

As the celebration went forth in the Bellon household, the warmth and affection they had for one another was felt by all. Meira, who had never before been part of a Christmas celebration, was touched by the laughter and good cheer, and wistfully remembered the Hanukkah celebrations in her own family. She realized how much alike people are when they celebrate together. When it was time for the family to go to the nearby Evangelical Protestant church for Christmas Eve services, Meira at first hesitated when invited to go along with them, but then decided that in order not to offend she would accept the invitation. The church was lit with many candles and the organ played traditional hymns. As the building was not heated, everyone was bundled in warm coats, hats and gloves. When the congregation and choir sang *Stille Nacht, Heilige Nacht*, everyone's breath was visible, but the atmosphere was warm and cheery. The minister delivered a short sermon, followed by a prayer for the nation and for the young men away at the front. "Let us thank God that He will bless our Emperor and lead our valiant warriors to victory. *Gott mit uns*."

At this point, Ursula was misty-eyed thinking of Eckhardt, and wondered how he was faring on this day which symbolized peace and love for all mankind.

Meira thought about Herbert and his cheerful good nature and was surprised to discover how affected she was by the thought of him. Many in the congregation were in mourning for loved ones who had been swept away in battles fought from the beginning of the war.

Ein frohes Weihnachtsfest und ein glückliches Neujahr (A merry Christmas and a happy New Year) was exchanged between neighbors and friends as they departed to their homes.

The small apartment was warm and inviting with the paper decorations which had been made by the two boys, Rudolf and Emil. The decorated tree stood in the corner of the family room, which doubled as the bedroom for the girls. Wrapped presents were arranged around the tree and the boys' anticipation and excitement was almost uncontrollable.

Everyone hurriedly removed their outer garments and made ready for the lighting of the tree candles which was done by Detlev. The candles gave off a warm glow and candles were lit on the windowsill to heighten the effect.

As their means were limited, the gifts were modest. Christina had knitted each family member a new pair of gloves, and had included Meira as well. Detlev had purchased new shoes for the boys, and a modestly priced, but well-made coat for Christina. At KaDeWe, Ursula had selected a beautiful shawl for her mother, and a fashionable muff for Meira. While at the Weihnachtsmarkt she had observed that the boys had been fascinated with a toy train made of wood and had furtively purchased it and hidden it in her large handbag. For her father, she had found a beautiful Meerschaum pipe, which he had long admired at the tobacconists in the next block. She had selected a beautiful amethyst ring in the Jewelry department of KaDeWe for her sister Brigitta. Meira had purchased a large box of luxurious Josty chocolates in the confectionary department at KaDeWe for the whole family.

When Christina, to whom the present had been given, removed the Christmas wrap, the boys, were dazzled by the green and gold foil-covered box and the beautifully arranged delicacies within. As they in wide-eyed wonder moved toward the open box, Christina warned, "We have never had something like this in our home and I will be in charge of the chocolates! They will be rationed and appreciated and not gobbled up."

Detlev grinned at this. His wife was a giving woman who was not inclined to voice a quick opinion, but when she had made up her mind about something, and especially an instance where running the household and disciplining the children was involved, she could be immovable.

"How about some Christmas music? I expect you all to sing," Detlev said after the gift-giving was done. He had a small accordion, which he had inherited from his father, and which he played in family gatherings, and on special occasions. This was always welcomed by the family. He brought it out and began to softly play *O, Tannenbaum* as everyone gazed at the small tree with its glowing candles. Soon Brigitta, who had a clear sweet voice began to sing the old familiar words, *"O, Tannenbaum, O, Tannenbaum, wie treu sind deine Blätter."*

The family, one by one, began to join in until the small room rang with the joyous music. This was followed by other familiar favorites: *O, Du fröliche* (Oh, ye joyous one), *Still – still – still, Ihr Kinderlein kommet* (You little children come), and finally, *Stille Nacht, heilige Nacht* (Silent Night, Holy Night).

Chapter Nine

The Christmas Truce

"*Stille Nacht, heilige Nacht, alles schläft, einsam wacht...*" Eckhardt heard men's voices singing from somewhere down the trench line. He had been dozing as he rested in his bunker in a German trench on the Western Front near Verdun, Belgium. Upon completion of their training in early September, he and Herbert had taken part in the First Battle of the Marne, where Germany's drive through Belgium had been halted. The armies had then been bogged down, which resulted in the beginning of trench warfare. This led to the development of a meandering line of trenches extending for several hundred miles from the northern coast of Belgium near the Dutch border to the Swiss border near Basel.

Within hours of the beginning of the battle, rain began to fall and continued throughout the first five months of the war. The battlefield soon turned into a quagmire and the soldiers found themselves standing in cold water sometimes over their boot tops. However, shortly before Christmas Eve, the rain stopped, and the temperature dropped below freezing. In the higher places the water had drained out of the trenches and the ground became solid. After being able to rotate to the rear and dry out their clothing and receive hot food and coffee, the men were grateful for the cessation of the rain in spite of the colder temperature.

As he came out of the bunker, Eckhardt realized that in addition to the beloved hymn being sung in German, he was hearing a response of "Silent Night, Holy Night" being sung in English by the British troops in their trench less than 100 yards away. As he walked along the trench, he saw some of his comrades placing small Christmas trees with lit candles on the parapet. Some were even standing up in full view of their adversaries, some of whom were doing the same. "What's going on here?" he inquired of a soldier standing nearby.

"Someone further down the line began shouting 'Merry Christmas' in English to the Tommies over there," the man responded. "Then the singing started, and now I hear that both sides are discussing a cease fire."

At this, Eckhardt saw several soldiers raising signs with the message, 'You no shoot – we no shoot.' "Incredible!" Eckhardt exclaimed. "I wish Herbert were here to see this." Herbert having contracted a serious case of dysentery two weeks previously, had been sent to a field hospital several miles from the front.

The other soldier did not respond as he climbed the small ladder leading to the top of the trench, and with many others began to walk across No Man's Land toward the British lines. British Tommies were doing the same, and the two groups met and began to shake hands and talk. Some of the Germans had worked in England before the war and could converse surprisingly well in English. Occasionally, one could hear a conversation which revealed that a German was familiar with the hometown of his British conversation partner.

After some hesitation, Eckhardt decided to join the group between the two trench lines. He climbed up the ladder and walked across the rough terrain of No Man's Land, which was strewn with barbed wire. Shortly thereafter, he encountered a young man in a muddy olive drab uniform, who appeared to be about the same age as himself. The two young soldiers stood arm's length apart, each appraising his adversary, unsure of what to do next. Smiles began to break through their countenances. The young Englishman man extended his hand to Eckhardt, and they shook hands warmly, falling into a conversation of broken English and German. Soon it became clear that an interpreter would be needed. Standing near a group where much English was being spoken, Eckhardt asked an older German, who appeared to be fluent in the language, if he could help out.

"Certainly, son. Glad to." The man introduced himself as a member of one of the Saxon regiments from further down the line.

"Where did you learn to speak such good English?" Eckhardt inquired of the man.

"I was a barber in Liverpool for almost ten years. I really enjoyed England, and the Brits are alright fellows. It's a real tragedy that we're fighting each other now. I would have stayed there, except for this damned war. But when it started, I couldn't turn my back on the fatherland, and so I came back to serve, and here I am," the man concluded with a look of sadness.

Eckhardt found this very perplexing. He wondered what he would have done in the same situation.

"You and your new Limey friend need shearing. Let me give you a haircut – on the house. I carry my clippers and scissors with me everywhere. A Christmas present to you both." He then repeated the same offer to the Englishman in his language. After being seated on a nearby crate, both young men were soon handsomely groomed, for which they both responded with gratitude.

With the help of their older friend, they were introduced to each other and learned that they were both from small country towns: William from Calne in Wiltshire, and Eckhardt from Blaubeuren in Wuerttemberg. They showed one another photographs of their families, and also pictures of their respective sweethearts. Eckhardt proudly showed him Ursula's photo which she had sent in a letter soon after he and Herbert had left Berlin. The young Englishman displayed the picture of a pretty delicately featured girl named Elizabeth.

Soon the suggestion began to make the rounds that they should use this special opportunity to collect their dead comrades, some of whom had been lying on the ground and entangled in barbed wire for days, weeks, and even in many cases months. Due to natural decomposition of the corpses, and also having been eaten by the rats which infested the trenches and battlefields, this was a gruesome task. Both sides agreed it should be undertaken. They collected the remains, and where possible grouped them in their respective nationalities, but when identification could no longer be determined, they were placed in common graves, thereby consigning them to resting places with Germans and Englishmen resting together. Prayers were offered in both languages, and the feeling of common humanity was felt by all present.

After the burials were completed, the men began to exchange souvenirs, uniform buttons and helmets being the most popular items. Then as the night continued, holiday foods began to make their appearance, the commodities having been provided by the armies of both sides. Roast goose, Westphalian ham, Corned Beef, plum puddings, cakes and breads of various kinds were brought forth and accompanied by beer and liquors of many varieties. After having eaten their fill, and sampling each other's traditional holiday specialties, they became thoughtful and a wistfulness settled over the gathering as they considered the tragedy of their situation, and the necessity of returning to battle and to the slaughtering of one another. The night was cold and clear, and they gazed at the stars, which they knew were shining on their homes and loved ones. Then they began to return to their trenches and prepare to resume the business of taking one another's lives.

PART II

Descent

Chapter Ten

The Schlieffen Plan and Disillusionment

The Schlieffen Plan was the name applied to the strategy behind the German invasion of France and Belgium after the outbreak of World War I. Field Marshal Alfred von Schlieffen, Chief of the Imperial German General Staff from 1891 to 1906, had developed a victorious strategy for one-front war during the Franco-Prussian War in 1870.

After that war, official German historians and other historians, labeled the plan "a blueprint for victory," a claim which has since been invalidated.

Upon von Schlieffen's retirement in 1906, Colonel General Helmuth von Moltke the Younger was appointed Commander-in-Chief of the German Army and has since been blamed by some German historians for ruining the Schlieffen Plan.

The strategy had been for the German Army to drive through neutral Belgium and continue on straight to Paris. This resulted in many Belgian civilian casualties. Allied propagandists used this as an opportunity to intensify anti-German sentiment.

The Germans managed to advance to within 30 miles of Paris, before being stopped by the French Army, but with a loss of 250,000 French casualties in the Battle of the Marne in September 5-12, 1914.

The First Battle of the Marne was a counter-attack by the Allies, the French and the British Expeditionary Forces. This forced the German Army to retreat to the northwest along the Marne River, resulting in an Allied victory. The war then became bogged down in a four-year long stretch of trench warfare. Von Moltke was subsequently dismissed.

§§§

War fever continued unabated during the first months following the outbreak of the war. Soldiers marching to the railway stations continued to be showered with flowers and the air was filled with a festive atmosphere. People gathered at newsstands and kiosks, anxious to receive news of the war, as if they were following the progress of a sporting event. They gathered in their pubs, cafes and restaurants to exchange views and to toast and congratulate themselves for living in the greatest city in the greatest country on earth.

Volunteers, including some of the prettiest girls, dispensed food, good coffee and chocolate at the railway stations. There was plenty of everything and plenty of patriotic enthusiasm.

Bands played continually, and everyone was celebrating what they were sure would be a short war. But the reassurances of, "Germany will win, and the boys will be home by Christmas!" rang false when the war had not ended by Christmas of 1914. Then disillusionment set in and the mood became darker.

Chapter Eleven

Reflections

Herbert was dozing when an orderly awakened him with the news that his Christmas mail had arrived. In the two days since Christmas he had been in a despondent mood. He had been severely ill during the first week after his admission to the hospital. He had had a high fever with spells of vomiting and diarrhea and had suffered hallucinations during the first days after his admission. Although he had been diagnosed with Bacillary Dysentery, the less serious form of Dysentery, as opposed to Amoebic Dysentery, he had nevertheless been seriously dehydrated and could not keep anything in his stomach, even vital liquids. In the days just before Christmas, his appetite had begun to return, but not enough for him to be able to partake of the holiday delicacies served to other patients in his ward. And now, even though his stomach had settled enough for him to take solid foods, his mood had been so depressed, that he had no interest in eating. His usual confidence and optimistic outlook, for the moment, had deserted him. Herbert, used to being admired and attractive to others, was mortified to have the bedpan brought to him in full view of his fellow patients, more than twenty of whom shared the ward with him.

"Letters from home!" shouted the orderly. "Your mail has been rerouted, Herr Lenz, but I see you have a couple of packages as well as some letters." Herbert sat up with a start and reached out for his mail. He eagerly opened Meira's letter first.

My dearest Herbert,

Ursula tells me that Eckhardt has written her, you are in a hospital with a serious case of dysentery. I am so sorry that you are ill, but I am also relieved that you are safe behind the front lines. Please let me know, as soon as you are able, how you are coming along. I have sent you a package, which I hope you have received. I have included some extra socks. I wish I could claim to have knitted them, but I must confess they were bought at KaDeWe, where I am now working. You will no doubt be surprised to learn this.

A few days before Christmas, my father learned from one of his customers that you and I were seen at Görlitzer Railway Station on the day you and Eckhardt left for the front. He pressured me into telling him about staying with Ursula in the hotel where you and Eckhardt were also staying. He was furious and threw me out of the house. Not having anyplace else to go, I appealed to Ursula to stay with her until I can decide what to do next. She and her family have been gracious enough to allow me to stay in their small flat in Wedding.

Ursula has also helped me get a job at KaDeWe where she works. Fortunately, another apartment will be available in the same building after the beginning of the New Year which Ursula and I are going to share. I cannot express my gratitude enough to Ursula and her family for their kindness in helping me at this most difficult time.

I hope and pray that you will recover soon, and that you will be uplifted at this time of the year and enjoy the holidays. I also hope you will not be too downhearted being away from home and your family. This being your first Christmas alone, ill and in a foreign country, must be very difficult for you. I am very happy to have met you, and hope to know you better. Please be assured I am thinking of you, and I pray you will get well quickly.

Affectionately,

Your friend, Meira.

Herbert held the letter in his hand for a few moments, feeling as though it were an unbroken link with home and with Meira. He had missed Meira, Eckhardt and the other comrades in his unit, but had neglected to give a great deal of thought to his own family. When he read about the dilemma Meira had had to deal with before the holidays, he regretted that he had inadvertently contributed to the confrontation she had with her father. In his heart, he was extremely grateful to Ursula and her family for the generosity and open-heartedness they had shown Meira. He wondered how his family would have reacted when faced with a similar situation. He could imagine that for his mother, taking in a Jew would have been out of the question, but his father? Dr. Lenz was a conservative, intelligent man, but not a man without empathy. He had interactions with Jewish colleagues on a daily basis, and had no qualms about patronizing Jewish businesses such as Friedlander's, but having a Jew live under his roof? Herbert wasn't sure. As for his younger brother, Karlheinz, he was a sullen, moody youth and hard to read, as teenagers often are.

He then opened the package which Meira had sent. In it were the socks, as well as some delicacies including a tin of smoked salmon, a small box of chocolates and some Turkish cigarettes. These items, as well as major food commodities would soon be curtailed as the war ground forward. The shortages of vital goods would soon begin to be felt by the German population as the British more fully implemented their naval blockade which had begun on November 11, 1914.

He then opened the letter from his father.

My dear son,

I speak for your mother and brother when I state that we miss you being away from us at Christmas for the first time since you were born. We try to keep informed about the events of the war, and of course our thoughts are of you.

We are sorry not have been at the station to see you off when your train left last summer, but I had a serious surgery scheduled that day, which the patient's family did not want undertaken by anyone other than myself. As you know, your mother doesn't feel comfortable dealing with large crowds on her own, and she wouldn't allow your brother to go off by himself.

You know how disappointed I was when you decided not to go to the university after you completed Abitur, but I admire you for going out on your own and taking employment at Siemens. In normal times, I am sure you would have eventually decided how you wanted to plan your future and perhaps have returned to take up a profession. Of course, now the matter is taken out of your hands with the outbreak of this war. It is unfortunate your choices have ruled out the possibility of being in officer training now, and you are thereby limited to serving as an enlisted man in the trenches with common soldiers. As for me, although I regret your decisions, I support you and am only concerned for your safety.

You know your mother, and for her it is not so simple. All of her friends' sons are officers, and two are in the flying corps. She feels humiliated when asked about you and having to explain your situation. You mustn't think she is not concerned for you, but you know how important it is to her to save face.

We will be going to her father's estate in Pomerania for Christmas, and wish you would be coming with us. In the meantime, take care of yourself, and I hope you are with Eckhardt for the holidays. Even though he is not of your class and background, he seems to be a good friend as you have described him, and for that I am grateful. Please write more often and keep us informed as much as the censor will allow.

With best wishes,

Your Father

Herbert folded the letter and turned over in his mind what his father had said about his mother. Yes indeed, he knew how important keeping up appearances was to her. Perhaps that had a lot to do with his decision to break away from the protocols of living in the upper-class manner. From the time he was a small boy he had been an independent thinker and was friendly to anyone who showed him the same consideration.

He opened his father's package and was pleased to receive more chocolate and cigarettes. He preferred the ordinary Juno cigarettes, but his mother had purchased the English Sobranie gold-tipped variety, which now because of the war were no longer available. Nevertheless, a pack of the exotic brand, which had probably been obtained through the black market, was included in his package. He was amused that no doubt this effort had been made by his mother. Was this her way of being considerate and presenting him with a special gift, or was it another effort on her part to maintain status? He knew that he would have to use them up before returning to the trenches, as smoking such an item in the presence of his comrades would have been seen as pretentious, which he would avoid at all costs.

Chapter Twelve

Slaughter Resumed

Eckhardt leaned against the soggy side of the trench and pondered the events of the past few days. He thought about Herbert and how he missed him. He reread Ursula's letter, which had arrived three days after Christmas along with the package she had sent. The soldiers were grateful for mail which was given priority by the German postal service and delivered quickly to the front. He had done a double take when he learned about Meira living with the Bellon family in their humble flat in Wedding. He was saddened, but not surprised that her father had thrown her out of their home. He had heard that many Jews did not look kindly on their children becoming intimately involved with non-Jews. He also knew that many Christians held the same kind of bias against Jews, and even against other Christians of different faiths. Ursula assured Eckhardt, however, that Meira had won over Ursula's family, and even accompanied them to Christmas Eve service. He was gladdened to learn that Ursula and Meira now worked together at KaDeWe. It would be good for both of them.

After the joy of the temporary Christmas Eve truce, he and the soldiers on both sides of the lines settled back into the dreary day-to-day business of mutual slaughter. The battles resumed with artillery firing into the enemy's lines to precede the charges made across No-Man's land, leaving the dead and dying entangled in the deadly embrace of the barbed wire strung out between the trenches. The cries of the wounded could be heard up and down the line of trenches throughout the day and into the night, punctuated by curses and screams as rats attacked the helpless wounded and the dead lying in the rain and mud. The survivors of the attacks would themselves become victims of the brazen rodents which ran across their faces as they slept, and as they became fatter and bolder, would even snatch food from the soldiers' hands as they ate. As there were no waste facilities at the front, food scraps were heaped in garbage cans, which in turn were emptied over the parapets on the ground in front of the trenches on a daily basis, which of course drew the rats in hordes. Shooting the animals was not allowed, in order to conserve valuable ammunition. As a result, attacking the rats with bayonets and clubs became an important pastime. Faced with these terrors, among many others, the weary men stood in their rain-soaked muddy uniforms and awaited the whistle signaling the next charge.

§§§

Ursula absentmindedly set the table for the evening meal, as she recalled the last evening she and Eckhardt had spent together, and the farewell next day at the train station. She thought about his shy manner, and how he had become the focus of most of her thoughts. The news of the war was very disturbing, and she thought about how confident people had been the previous summer. She recalled the exuberance the young soldiers had displayed as they shouted, "We'll be home by Christmas" as the train rolled out of the station.

She recalled the anti-war demonstration that had taken place on July 28, before the outbreak of hostilities, and how Eckhardt had confided to her that he wondered if perhaps the demonstrators were not right. But he advised Ursula not to repeat his concerns, especially to Herbert, who was a confident believer in the supposed superiority of Germany's military power. Herbert had even mocked the pacifist remarks he had overheard his own father make one evening at the dinner table after the demonstration had been reported in all the newspapers. It soon became evident that many Berliners did not entertain a deep enthusiasm for the war, and those who did were typified by young men like Herbert – generally of middle and upper middle-class bourgeois background, including many secondary school pupils and university students.

Then, after Germany's humiliating setback at the hands of the French in the first battle of the Marne, their optimistic mood turned to despair and anger, and tension in Berlin increased noticeably. Resentment against foreigners also increased dramatically, and the "Germanisation campaign" that had begun was stepped up. She recalled an ugly incident she and Meira had witnessed one evening as they were waiting for their bus. An older couple standing near the bus stop were overheard speaking English. Two middle-aged women immediately set upon the dumbfounded couple and berated them, assuming they were British. A young man who was a student, and spoke English, intervened and interpreted for the frightened couple explaining that they were American. The United States at the time was still neutral, so other bystanders turned on the two accusers and scolded them for setting such a bad example for Berlin. The two chastised women ducked their heads and silence prevailed among the crowd as they continued to wait for their bus.

The gloom of the post-holiday winter days deepened the melancholy she felt. As people learned about the British blockade, they began to buy up food and other goods in large quantities. Ursula and Meira had already seen this happening in KaDeWe and in the markets throughout the city. Consequently, food prices were driven up, and the authorities tried to intervene in the production and distribution of food. Maximum prices were imposed followed by rationing.

§§§

"I'm sorry, Meira, but Papa found out from Mama that I've been bringing your things from home. He's ordered me to stop and I'm not to see you," Edna Friedlander told her sister over the phone.

Meira replied she understood and apologized for putting the older girl in a difficult position. She had learned through the confrontation with her father, how unrelenting he could be, and knew that any appeal to him would be useless.

Hanging up the phone with a sigh, her shoulders slumped. She walked away from the phone booth and pulled her coat collar tighter around her neck for protection from the biting cold. She thought about how much her life had changed during the past year. Last winter she had been sure of herself, and certain how much control she had over own life.

Now exiled from her comfortable home, and living in Wedding with Ursula's family, for whose kindness and generosity she would be ever grateful, she wondered where her life was going. She thought about Herbert and how attracted to him she was, and how he was a totally different man than the kind she would have ever considered before. But she thought of the young men she had grown up with and had known all her life and admitted to herself that they all paled by comparison. Not only because he was a handsome Gentile, but also because he had shown an independent, almost rebellious determination to be his own man. It then occurred to her that in this regard, they had more in common than she had realized before now. Both of them came from upper middle-class backgrounds, and their parents were in both cases conservative, and even snobbish each in their own way. Although Meira did not yet know Herbert's mother, she would discover from future discussions with him how much Mrs. Lenz and Mr. Friedlander were alike, in that they both would react similarly when they learned of their children's relationship. For Herbert to be intimate with a Jewish girl would have outraged his mother, and for Meira to even consider taking up with a Gentile had already infuriated her father.

Although she enjoyed her time with the Bellons, and had found the Christmas traditions she had shared with them to be beautiful and comforting, she nevertheless missed her own family and the familiarity of her own faith. Fridays were especially difficult for her when she thought of the evening meal and foods served for the beginning of the Jewish Sabbath. She, like everyone else, was depressed by the effects of the war and the adjustments and difficulties it brought about. She thought about Herbert being alone in the hospital and yearned to be able to talk to him and comfort him.

The wind picked up and caused the bitter cold of the Berlin winter to penetrate her clothing and remind her of how she looked forward to meeting Ursula at their bus stop. She was cheered by the realization that she and her friend would be able to move into their own flat the following Monday. Tomorrow being Saturday, they planned their shopping excursion to purchase some of the basic household necessities. Christina had already offered to accompany them to several of the flea markets to be found in Wedding and Kreuzberg. She saw Ursula ahead waiting at the bus stop. Ursula saw her coming and smiled.

Chapter Thirteen

Shortage and Rationing

The patriotic enthusiasm of Berliners shown in August 1914, at the outbreak of the war, had largely evaporated by the end of the year, due to increasing shortages of food and growing distrust of the government. The citizens who had been swept up in the surge of pride in Germany's meteoric rise after 1871, were not aware of the precarious situation the country was in before the start of hostilities in 1914.

Those inside the military and political establishments realized that Germany was in no position to sustain a long war but had not made this information public. Berlin, which had seen its population more than double in the previous thirty years, had to rely on a third of its foodstuffs being imported. As early as Autumn 1914, shortages had begun to appear in the markets and shops in the city. Nevertheless, on January 28, 1915, when bread rationing was announced, the population was caught by surprise. Rationing was also accompanied by rapid price increases of basic food commodities.

Working class families, such as the Bellon family, were directly affected by these occurrences, but the suffering was not shared equally by the entire population. The upper middle-classes, such as the families of Dr. Lenz and Benjamin Friedlander, were unaffected by the shortages, as they could afford to purchase items on the black market. This soon became apparent to the lower classes, and the seeds of resentment and class division which had been planted in previous years, now began to germinate and grow.

Christina Bellon, along with most other Berliners, would remember February 23, 1915, as the day the blockade began to be a personal hardship, and not just a news item. Bread rationing was begun on that date, and ration cards were initially distributed by the bakeries and bread shops. She had awakened at 4:00 a.m. in order to secure a place in line at the door of Schröder's bakery across the street from her tenement building when it opened at 7:00 o'clock. She dressed in the icy room and hurried downstairs and across the street, only to discover that a line of housewives had already formed in front of the shop. As the war progressed such queues would wind along the front of the building and around the corner, with many people lying on straw mattresses on the sidewalk throughout the night.

As Christina waited, a woman standing in front of her turned and asked if any members of her household were at the front.

"My husband is 41 and works for the transit authority, and my two sons are little boys," Christina responded.

"Consider yourself lucky," stated the woman. "I have a son who enlisted at the very beginning and was in the march through Belgium. He is somewhere in France, and has not been hurt so far, God be praised. My sister lost a son just before Christmas on the Western Front, and also has another son who had enlisted a month before his brother was killed."

Christina expressed her condolences and wondered how many similar tragedies she would hear about in the coming months. She reflected that Ursula was also deeply concerned about Eckhardt. He had written in his last letter about the Christmas truce, and having made the acquaintance of the young British soldier. She turned to her conversation partner and related this to her, whereupon the woman retorted that she considered such fraternizing with the enemy to be a disgrace. "Anyone who takes part in that should be shot!"

Stunned, Christina realized that she would have to be careful about discussing the incident with strangers. This would be the first of many experiences she would have where people would put forth such strong opinions.

As the stress of the war and deteriorating conditions at home caused reactions like the one she had just witnessed, Christina realized she would more and more have to question her own opinions and beliefs. Was it wrong and unpatriotic to remind oneself that the war was a human tragedy, and that people on both sides shared the same emotions and concerns? She would discover that pacifist views had best be kept to herself, unless she were willing to endure this kind of anger and hostility.

When the door of the bakery was finally opened, the applicants were presented with elaborately embellished ration cards alluding to the Lord's Prayer with the phrase, *Unser täglich Brot gib uns heute,* give us today our daily bread.

The municipal authorities had designated the weekly ration of bread per person to be about 2 kilos. This represented about half the normal prewar consumption. Mr. Schröder declared that bread day would be every Thursday. At this early stage of the war there was little grumbling, as people were still willing to make sacrifices for the war effort.

Ursula and Meira had moved into their apartment a little over a month before and had therefore established a separate household from the Bellon's. Being a longtime customer of Mr. and Mrs. Schröder's bakery, Christina was allowed to receive ration cards and bread ration for the girls, but Mr. Schröder admonished that they would have to come in and sign for them later in the day. In the future, they would have to bring in their cards personally, in order to get their bread ration. Christina had hoped to be able to take care of this for them, as they would henceforth have to get up early enough on bread day to procure their own bread allotment before going to work.

Upon receiving her ration cards and bread, Christina hurried home in order to prepare breakfast for Rudolf and Emil before they left for school. Detlev, working the evening shift for the transit authority, would require his breakfast later in the day. Christina thought about the conversation she had had with the woman in the bread line and did indeed consider herself to be fortunate that her menfolk were safely at home – at least for the present. Many other families across the width and breadth of the city, and across the country, were in mourning for lost fathers, husbands, sons and brothers, as well as having to adjust to the increasingly difficult life of a country at war.

§§§

Detlev Bellon made his way home after his evening shift in the bitter cold of the February night, and was cheered by the light from the windows of his pub. As he entered and parted the leather curtain inside the door, he was greeted by a nod from Max, who as bartender scrutinized all who entered his establishment. The smoky atmosphere was only broken by murmured conversations of the few late-evening regulars lounging at the bar or huddled at the tables along the wall. Those at the bar were for the most part loners, who from time to time would exchange a word with Max, or someone sitting next to them. The conversations revolved around the war and the increasing hardships caused by it. Others were seeking solace for the loss of someone at the front. Some would turn their heads in the direction of the door when a person entered to see whether or not it might be a familiar face as usual, or whether by chance a stranger might enter and provide some new distraction. A pair of Skat (a popular card game) players at the corner table were absorbed in their game and took no notice of people coming or going. Max, anticipating that Detlev would take his usual place at the bar, set out the Schultheiss beer and Jägermeister which had been the preference of most regular customers, including Detlev, for as long as Max had been bartender the better part of twenty years.

"Na, Maxie, how's it going?" Detlev began.

"With me it's always the same. Changes in the neighborhood I hear though. But with this damned war we can expect a lot more changes, I guess," countered Max.

"Oh yeah? What've you heard lately?" inquired Detlev.

"Well, I'm surprised you haven't brought me up to date about that classy girl who was waiting here before Christmas for your daughter. You seemed surprised when I told you about her, but you haven't said a word about her since. My wife heard from Frau Schröder that your wife registered your daughter Ursula and a girl named Meira Friedlander to receive ration cards. The two of them now share a flat in your building, I hear. That Friedlander girl wouldn't be the same girl who was waiting here that evening, would it?"

Detlev was startled by this revelation. How quickly one's business makes the rounds in a close neighborhood! Although he didn't feel that there was any malice behind Max's questioning, Detlev nevertheless was annoyed by the unexpected probing.

"Yes, she's the person you saw here. She and my daughter are friends and work together downtown," Detlev responded.

"Friedlander. Isn't that the name of that high-class clothing store on Ku'damm? Is she from that family?" Max continued.

"Yes. She and her father have differences is why she came to stay with us." Detlev was aware that conversations near him had ceased, as people began to tune in on his exchange with Max.

The man sitting nearest blurted, "They're rich Jews, aren't they?" It was a statement more than a question.

"Okay. That's enough!" Max declared firmly. "Sorry, Detlev. Didn't mean to put you on the spot and drag all your laundry out in public."

"That's alright, Max. I know you didn't mean anything by it. We've found Meira to be a wonderful girl and she's welcome in our house. And she's a good friend to my daughter!" he stated, with a challenging look around the room. The erstwhile intruder ducked his head and focused on his beer.

"Sorry I brought it up. If she's a friend of yours, she's as welcome here as any woman, if she ever wants to come by with you," Max stated, throwing a warning look at the curious faces nearby.

Suddenly, Detlev felt an urgency to drink up and leave. As he departed, he could feel the questioning glances on his back. He could imagine that his blue-collar neighbors had never expected to see such an exotic person living in their midst. And a Jew! He could also sense that there was a mixture of innocent curiosity and mild hostility in their interest.

Chapter Fourteen

The War Intensifies

On February 4, 1915, Germany declared the waters around the British Isles to be a total war zone, and publicly warned that ships could be sunk without warning. The British reacted by imposing a total sea blockade on Germany and prohibiting importation of all goods, including food. The French launched an offensive against the German lines in Champagne. They were bogged down in muddy winter weather and hampered by a lack of heavy artillery. In March, after suffering 240,000 casualties, the exhausted French broke off the offensive.

After six weeks in the hospital, a dispirited Herbert returned to the front and took his place with his unit. Due to his illness, he had lost almost twenty pounds, and was a shadow of his former robust self. Eckhardt, delighted to greet his friend, was taken aback by the lackluster response given to his extended hand.

"What's gotten into you, buddy? You have always been the life of the party – the voice of optimism. Remember how that drill sergeant rode your ass at training camp because your father is a renowned surgeon at Charité? You amazed us all how you took it."

Typically, sons of upper middle-class families were trained as officers in European armies, and enlisted men were from the working class. Herbert, by not entering the university upon completion of his secondary education, and by taking employment as a worker at Siemens, had relegated himself to the same socio-economic class as Eckhardt, the son of a farmer.

Herbert, however, had endured the bullying better than the sergeant in question had expected, and even had begun to gain the man's respect, as well as that of his comrades – especially Eckhardt. His Berliner's cockiness had served him well. He had, as well as most young men of his class in Europe at the time, been buoyed up by patriotism and a self-assurance that his country's cause was just.

But now, Eckhardt had never seen Herbert like this. When he tried to question his friend as to what had changed him, his efforts were brushed off with a murmured noncommittal response.

Then during a conversation among the men in the bunker when the Christmas truce was referred to, Herbert became very agitated and shouted that he had heard about the "disgraceful fraternization with the enemy" and declared, "all involved should have been shot!"

Hearing this, the men began to move away, leaving Eckhardt alone with Herbert, who turned to him, challenging, "I hope you weren't involved in that!" Finally, Eckhardt responded, "Yes, Herbert. I was." Herbert only glared at him before turning and stalking out of the bunker.

Eckhardt sat staring at the carbide lamp in the corner and turned all that had transpired over in his mind. He knew that now would not be the time to try and explain his experience with the young British soldier and the events of that amazing night to Herbert. He also knew his friend well enough to know that such an outburst was not typical of him. Herbert was emotional and passionate, but unfair judgment of others was not part of his nature. In fact, he had always shown forth a cheerful acceptance of others, uninvolved with any consideration of class or background. He had been well-liked by the workers at Siemens and by his comrades in the army. What had brought about the withdrawal and barely civil behavior he had shown since his return from the hospital? Eckhardt suspected it had little to do with illness or with the Christmas truce.

As he walked away from his friend, Herbert was surprised at himself for his outburst. He had an urge to turn around and apologize, but he kept walking.

What's wrong with me? he asked himself. He knew Eckhardt well enough to know that his being willing to meet the enemy on neutral ground had nothing to do with a lack of patriotism. Eckhardt was an open-hearted soul ready to acknowledge the humanity of any man, but nevertheless a good soldier who would never waiver in performing his duty, no matter how disagreeable it might be. He could differentiate however between the necessity to shoot an enemy soldier and outright cruelty.

The reports of the killing of civilians by German soldiers during the invasion of Belgium in the previous summer had deeply affected both Eckhardt and Herbert. The official German version was that the civilians had been sniping at the troops, but that explanation was not satisfactory to many, as women and children had been found among the dead.

Herbert reflected on his experience in the hospital. Just as Eckhardt had surmised, the main reason for the change in Herbert's personality was rooted in experiences he had undergone during his hospital stay. Soon after his admission to the hospital, Herbert received mail including letters from Meira. The young corporal delivering the mail would often good naturedly tease recipients of letters from their girlfriends and call out the names of the senders. On one such occasion, he called out, "Lenz! Another love letter from Miss Friedlander." Immediately a voice was heard, "Friedlander! That's the name of that fancy Jew store on Ku'damm!"

A young man, Jakob Beck, from the blue-collar district of Berlin-Kreuzberg, had soon realized that Herbert was the son of the renowned surgeon, and therefore from a prestigious family in Dahlem. The fact that Herbert was in an enlisted men's ward, instead of in with officers, raised questions among the other patients. Animosity between Herbert and Beck began to develop. The heckler and two of his friends were soon seizing every opportunity to harass Herbert and embarrass him in front of the other ward occupants. The situation became increasingly tense, until one evening after lights out, Beck blurted, "That girlfriend of yours, Lenz, is a Jew, ain't that right?"

Herbert, taken for a moment, then retorted, "What's that got to do with anything?"

"The Jews are getting rich from this war, you know," added another of the annoying trio. "They're in cahoots with their brothers in England, who are behind the blockade driving prices up here.

"They all stick together no matter which country they live in," piped in the third.

"Where did you hear that propaganda?" came from the back of the room.

"Leave Lenz alone!" offered another soldier.

"Yeah, we're tired of listening to your crap. You three are feeling good enough to lay around here and make trouble," somebody else shouted.

The argument developed into an uproar that brought the night nurse into the ward. She switched on the lights and demanded, "What's going on here?"

"Sorry, sister. Beck and his two cronies won't leave Lenz alone, and we're all tired of listening to 'em. They ought to get kicked out of here and sent back to the front. They want to fight, so let 'em do it out there."

"Alright Corporal Drescher. That's enough! You don't have the authority to decide who comes and goes here. If I have any more trouble with anyone in this ward, I'll put that person on report which will be passed on to his commanding officer. Now, I want it quiet in here! Do I make myself clear?"

The men were subdued and murmured, "Yes, sister. Sorry sister."

Women who served as nurses in field hospitals in any army were a hardy bunch, who were not easily intimidated. They were often nurses of long experience, who knew how to maintain control, and at the same time were capable of doing their job under extremely difficult circumstances. They were certainly not overwhelmed by rowdy young soldiers.

After the lights were out and the men began to settle down again for the night, Herbert told himself that he would single out Drescher and extend him his gratitude for speaking up for him. He still felt the sting of Beck's remarks about Jews and was disappointed with himself for not speaking up more in their defense and in defense of Meira. He felt that Beck and his kind were insulting her personally.

Herbert turned all of these events over in his mind as he continued to walk away from Eckhardt and determined that he really must make things right again with his friend.

Chapter Fifteen

Lost hopes

The original German strategy at the outbreak of the war had been to implement the Schlieffen Plan in order to bring about a swift defeat of France and then to transfer the bulk of the German fighting force to the Eastern Front to combat the Russians. However, the successful counter-offensive by the French caused the German retreat in the First Battle of the Marne in September 1914. The war then bogged down and both sides settled into trench warfare that would continue on the Western Front until the end of the war.

The German setback in the West left only one German army to defend East Prussia against the Russians. The Russian advance was nevertheless stopped by the Germans at the Battle of Tannenberg in August 1914. However, a second Russian invasion in Galicia succeeded in throwing back four Austrian armies and leaving Russia in almost complete control of the region at the end of 1914. After the beginning of 1915, large German forces were transferred to the East to hold off further Russian advances in East Prussia.

§§§

Frederika Lenz had been born and had grown up on her father's large estate near Danzig in Pomerania. She and her older brother, Michael-Friedrich von Hohenberg, had been raised in the tradition of ancient Junker families. Their privileged upbringing had included schooling for her at a prestigious boarding school in Danzig, and for him at a boys' military academy in the province of Brandenburg near Berlin.

The Russian advance at the outbreak of the war had caused great anxiety among the Junker families, the von Hohenberg family being no exception. The German victory at Tannenberg had brought great relief to Frederika Lenz, and she, like others of her class, felt confident that the established order of things as she had always known it would continue far into the future.

Her eldest son, Herbert, had caused her considerable dismay from the time he was a small boy. He had shown a cheerful disregard for the order and values that she held dear. He was always interested in making friends with those around him. He had a small child's curiosity about the doings of the servants and treated the male members of the staff as pals, even as he grew into young manhood.

His father was amused that his adolescent son would rather be in the garage working under their Mercedes limousine with the chauffeur, than playing tennis with his classmates from the private school he attended. When Herbert announced that upon completion of his *Abitur*, he intended to postpone entering the university, and get a job, in order to "get to know himself better." His father was a bit taken aback by this announcement, but his mother was beside herself.

She, herself, growing up had never doubted that the pattern laid out for her and children of families like hers, was right and her responsibility was to not disturb the social order. She accepted the inequality of the classes as a God-given institution. In nature, the species remain in their assigned places, and human beings should do the same.

Herbert's insistence on doing things his own way, had caused concern for other members of his mother's aristocratic family as he grew up, but his most recent act of joining the army as an enlisted man had brought strong criticism from her father and brother. When she and her husband and younger son traveled to the family estate for the Christmas holidays, after the outbreak of the war, Herbert's status as a common soldier was the topic of conversation for the whole two weeks. Friedrich-Wilhelm von Hohenberg was a graduate of the Prussian Military Academy and had served as a major on the staff of General Field Marshal von Moltke during the Franco-Prussian War. He had retired to his Pomeranian estate in 1905 with a substantial pension. His son, Michael-Friedrich, had followed in his footsteps, and had likewise graduated from the Prussian Military Academy. He had received an appointment to the General Staff in 1908.

With this long line of military leaders on his mother's side, it was obvious to everyone, except to Herbert, that he should have kept tradition and followed suit. His grandfather and uncle argued that even now, with their influence, arrangements could be made to get him out of the trenches and into the academy.

Frederika now felt she had a convincing argument to persuade her son to remove himself from a situation that had been a source of great agitation and embarrassment to her since the beginning of the war.

§§§

Aerial photography was implemented by the British for the first time during the Battle of Neuve Chapelle in March 1915. The 1:5,000 scale maps, were distributed to each corps of the army. These were used during the British offensive, which determined the manner which trench warfare took for the remainder of the war on the Western Front.

Giving great attention to detail, the British First Army achieved tactical surprise and the subsequent break-through. But infantry-artillery co-operation broke down due to communication failures, giving the Germans time to receive reinforcements and establish a new line.

Herbert and Eckhardt were part of the big German counter-attack, which involved twenty infantry battalions, or about 16,000 men. It was a horrendous failure. The resulting carnage left all who witnessed it in a state of shock.

Herbert thought about the letter he had received from his mother during the previous month, putting forth her father’s and brother’s idea, that he should consider taking them up on their offer to use their influence to get him out of the trenches. They suggested he accept a field promotion and an appointment to a clerical job behind the front lines, and ultimately seek entrance to the Prussian Military Academy. His first reaction had been to ignore this plea, but his latest experience had made him give it further thought. He had witnessed bloodshed before, but nothing on the scale of what he had recently seen. His strongest objection to the idea was because of his loyalty to his comrades in his unit – especially to Eckhardt.

He approached his friend soon after he had berated him for his part in the Christmas truce and the contact he had made with the enemy. After deep consideration, he realized Eckhardt was not a grudge-bearing person. He could see that reaching out in friendship to anyone who did the same, even an enemy, was in line with Eckhardt's character.

When Herbert apologized to him, Eckhardt smiled and replied, "Don't give it another thought. I knew you weren't yourself, and that was probably because you were still recovering from your bout with the green apple quick step."

Herbert blushed, and muttered, "Yeah. No more green apples for me."

Eckhardt chuckled, put his arm around his friend's shoulder, and gave him a squeeze.

Herbert wished he, himself, could claim such a forgiving and generous nature.

He was therefore hesitant to bring up the proposal put forth by his mother and her family. He knew Eckhardt put great stock in loyalty to one's friends and comrades and wondered how he would react. It caused Herbert to question himself, just how capable was he of returning such loyalty.

He had turned the matter over in his mind night after night before the recent battle, but after the setback his army had just suffered, he began to wonder just how much sacrifice one should be willing to endure. He and many others began to realize, that not only was Germany not going to enjoy a quick victory, as had been supposed on that bright morning in August after war had been declared. On the contrary, it became more and more apparent, it was going to be a long conflict, and the tide seemed to be turning against his country. Just how valid was the boast embossed on their belt buckles: *Gott mit uns*?

Chapter Sixteen

Women's Challenges

As the blockade continued, the difficulty of securing food became more critical. The curtailment of food imports represented only one aspect of the problem. The importation of fertilizer was also cut back so that Germany's agricultural production was vastly reduced. Also, the lack of manpower due to the induction of men into the military threw the burden of farm work and food processing onto women, many of whom had never worked outside the home before. Even though about 900,000 war prisoners were made available to assist with planting and harvesting, the lack of experienced farmers, together with these other issues caused Germany's agricultural output to decrease dramatically. The lack of fodder also meant that much of the country's livestock, especially hogs, had to be slaughtered. The meat resulting from this was quickly consumed with no reserve following behind.

In the meantime, the implementation of rationing sparked a rapid increase in hoarding, which resulted in rapid price increases of still obtainable commodities. As a result, shortages of food available to working class families became even more critical. Consequently, food riots soon broke out in the cities, with Berlin being one of those most severely affected.

In February 1915, the report of women and children storming a Berlin municipal market desperate for a kilo of potatoes, spread across the city. This caused unrest in the population, especially among the so-called "women of little means" who queued for food and began to protest food shortages, not only in Berlin, but in cities across Germany. These women began to bring about the establishment of a new alliance, which over time laid the groundwork for women's acquisition of previously unknown social and political power. Members of the bourgeoisie, or middle class, showed surprising support for the poor women. Soon resentment developed against the agricultural producers and merchants who were seen as profiteers.

The issue of growing food shortages, which brought about malnutrition and even starvation, along with news of Germany's reversals suffered at the front and the mounting casualties, motivated approximately 2000 women to protest the war in front of the Reichstag on May 28, 1915. Such an action would have gotten attention anywhere, but in an authoritarian society, such as Germany, it was an unprecedented event.

By the autumn of 1915, Christina Bellon and tens of thousands of other Berlin women were engaged almost full time in the struggle to obtain food for their families. This involved travel to and fro across the width and breadth of the vast metropolis, and eventually even forays into the surrounding countryside in the quest of food.

The Bellon household was indeed fortunate to still have a full-time employed male providing steady income. But even though this was available, it was neither sufficient to meet the demand of rising prices, nor was it useful in obtaining what was simply not available.

One early Thursday morning in October, Christina hurried across the street to Schröder's bread store to take her usual place in line for her weekly ration of bread. After waiting for more than two hours, she heard from others standing in line ahead of her, that the store had unexpectedly been closed, as there was no more bread available. A collective wail of panic arose from the crowd of women who had been waiting in the morning chill. This soon turned to anger, and some began to pound on the closed door shouting accusations. "What have you done with the rest of the bread allotment, Schröder? Are you selling on the black market like the rest of the swine across this city?"

The Schröders cowered behind the closed door and debated how they could defuse this dangerous situation. Finally, after a few minutes, Mr. Schröder opened the door to explain that he had not received his full allotment of flour. He had decided that he must continue to meet the specified ration of two kilos of bread per person, until he received a directive to change the ration quantity.

"I considered reducing the amount for each of you, but I decided that would have made the ones who came before you angry, and I might be reported to the central rationing office for cheating."

In despair, Christina returned home in a daze, not knowing how she was going to provide for her family. In the entrance of the apartment building, she met Ursula and Meira leaving for work. Almost in tears she recounted her experience at the bread store.

"Never mind, Mama. We picked up our ration earlier, before the bread ran out, and we'll divide it up with you and Papa."

Christina, who was trembling with relief and gratitude, replied, "Thank you, girls. We'll have to use it sparingly, but I don't know how I could have faced the kids, if I told them there was nothing. But I'll discuss this with Detlev, and we must get together this evening when you two get home and decide what we can do from now on."

Meira listened to this conversation and told herself she must do something to assist this family in their desperate circumstances.

Chapter Seventeen

Verdun

February 21 – December 18, 1916

Erich Georg Anton von Falkenhayn, born September 11, 1861 in Burg Belchau, West Prussia, was a many faceted man. In many ways, he typified the Prussian Junker. He was descended from an ancient line of the Prussian aristocracy with connections to titled nobility and even to the Royal Family.

He became a cadet at age 11 and joined the Army in 1880. He was then appointed an infantry staff officer thereby launching a career as a professional soldier. As a young man, he served in China during the Boxer Rebellion between 1896 and 1901.

After his service in Asia, Falkenhayn experienced a meteoric rise in his career. He was posted in *Braunschweig* (Brunswick), and promoted to the rank of major-general in 1912. In 1913, he became Prussian Minister of War, which was his position at the outbreak of World War I, and after the First Battle of the Marne on September 14, 1914, he succeeded Helmuth von Moltke the Younger as Chief of the German General Staff.

He was credited with preventing inhumane excess against the Jews in Palestine in 1917, which at that time was under control of the Ottoman Turks, who were part of the Central Powers. Winston Churchill praised him as by far the most competent of the German generals in World War I.

Falkenhayn was the typical Prussian general, in the sense that he was a militarist of undeniable competence, but had contempt for representative democracy, as was evidenced by his address to the Reichstag in 1914, when he stated that the Army is removed from the influence of the constitution and political struggles in order that it could become what it was, namely "the secure defense of peace at home and abroad."

In late 1915, Falkenhayn wrote a memorandum to the Kaiser in which he put forth the conviction that the war could only be won by inflicting massive casualties on the French army, thereby eliminating its will to continue to fight, and forcing them and the British to sue for peace. His was not the intent to outmaneuver the French, but rather to lure them into a trap that would lead to a battle of attrition. His intent was to cause them to "bleed to death." He called his plan *Operation Gericht*, or "place of execution."

On the morning of February 21, 1916, German artillery opened fire on the French army defending the fortified city of Verdun. The nine-hour long barrage was intended to break the morale of the French, but instead dragged both sides into a ten-month-long bloody cycle of attacks, counterattacks and almost uninterrupted bombardments, that turned Verdun into a hell on earth. The French eventually turned the tide of the German advance, and regained lost territory, but not before the two armies had suffered more than 800,000 casualties between them. The Battle of Verdun came to be known as the longest and one of the most vicious battles of World War One.

§§§

On February 1, 1916, German reinforcements were moved to the 20-kilometer front in anticipation of attacking the French defending the city of Verdun, but the offensive was delayed by inclement weather until February 21. Herbert, Eckhardt, and their comrades, expecting the bombardment to begin on a daily basis, grew restless and depressed. The combination of waiting and the miserable weather, caused their anxiety and despondency to increase. Their uniforms were constantly damp and their feet were never warm. Many suffered from coughs and constant nasal congestion brought on by repeated colds and sore throats. When they were awakened by the roar of the artillery on the morning of February 21, many expressed relief that it had at last begun. They had been assured by their leaders that the artillery which had been amassed, would surely bring the French swiftly to their knees.

Herbert had always been impressed with Eckhardt's steadfastness and self-control, and now awaiting orders to advance when the barrage ceased, he found himself, as well as others in his unit, looking to Eckhardt for leadership and assurance. In spite of himself, he found his mind returning to the proposals put forth by his mother's father and brother offering to release him from the trenches. He had not yet revealed his dilemma to his friend but felt that he could not carry the matter alone much longer. Herbert and Eckhardt were among the first troops to attack the French trenches, which had been bombed out by the barrage. The surviving French were not in a condition to offer much resistance, and the Germans were able to make rapid advances along the east bank of the Meuse River. Eckhardt commented on the courage shown by the French troops in the face of such overwhelming force. Herbert and those in his group, were affected by Eckhardt's attitude, and were influenced to treat prisoners in a humane manner.

One day after having overrun the devastated enemy positions, they came upon a wounded Frenchman mired waist-deep in the mud of a bombed-out trench. Some Germans having found him earlier, had encircled the unfortunate fellow, and were debating what to do about him. Some had even begun to harass him and threatened to shoot him. Eckhardt upon seeing this, took charge and ordered the agitators to desist from their cruel behavior. He then organized an effort to extricate the terrified Frenchman from his predicament.

Some long pieces of wood salvaged from the shattered French dugout, were placed lengthwise across the boggy surface in front of the wounded man, and Eckhardt lying on his belly on the boards, threw a length of rope to him, which the Frenchman was able to tie around his chest. This was not done without difficulty, as the man was wounded by a shell splinter in one shoulder. After the rope was secured, Herbert and the others began to pull the man out of the sucking mass of mud. Due to his wound, the Frenchman cried out in agony and then passed out. Herbert and his comrades continued to pull on the rope, and gradually the quagmire released its victim. The German medics were summoned, and the wounded man was removed to a field hospital behind the lines.

Herbert, recalling the Christmas truce in which Eckhardt had participated, and coupled with this recent experience, was convinced that his friend was a truly extraordinary man. In the face of battle, Herbert had witnessed how Eckhardt carried out his responsibilities as a soldier, not shrinking from firing upon the enemy, as was expected of him, and encouraging his comrades to do the same. It soon became clear, however, that he did so with determination, but without relish. As soon as the fighting was over, Eckhardt reverted to a compassionate fair-dealing human being.

Not knowing a great deal about Eckhardt's family and upbringing in Blaubeuren, Herbert became curious about this, and resolved to learn more about him. Eckhardt being a private type of person would not prove easy to engage in such a conversation.

§§§

Four days after the initial bombardment, the Germans were able to make rapid advances and capture lightly defended Fort Douaumont, with virtually no resistance offered by the French. The mood among the German troops was upbeat, and confidence that the campaign at Verdun would soon come to an end, was widespread.

This was not to last however, as the French resistance was fierce, and the battle degenerated into a continued succession of back and forth struggles, with several towns and forts in and around Verdun changing hands many times. Neither side managed a permanent territorial gain of as much as one mile during the entire battle. Some historians have described the Battle of Verdun as one of the darkest moments in Western civilization, because the objective of most battles is to defeat the enemy, and then take and hold territory. But here, the goal was to produce as many dead as possible.

At Verdun, the relative safety of the trenches was eliminated by the constant artillery bombardments, so that only isolated pockets remained where the trenches had been. The flare of the bombardments was visible for miles around, and Verdun came to be known as "the Furnace."

Chapter Eighteen

Disoriented and Lost

During one bombardment in April, while their unit was moving from one sector to another, Herbert and Eckhardt became separated from one another, and Herbert found himself crouched in the remains of a bunker. The heavy spring rains had been increased by the bombardments, which often cause rainfall. Herbert, hip deep in cold water, observed that he was not alone, as the decomposed remains of three soldiers were half buried in the mud nearby. Two of the corpses could be identified by the tattered remnants of their uniforms as French, while the third, which had been reduced to a skeleton, had a German helmet perched grotesquely on the skull.

As he shivered in the gray twilight, he thought of his friend, and pushed aside the thought that he might be dead. The pounding of the artillery from both sides continued until nightfall, and then eventually subsided. After what seemed like several hours, the rain ceased, and scattered clouds parted, allowing the moon to cast light on the tortured landscape. He cautiously raised his head over the edge of the bunker and tried to see the trunks of several trees that had been near the location of his unit before the commencement of the last bombardment. The trees were not to be seen, and the terrain had been entirely transformed by the pounding of artillery. An ominous quiet had descended on the battlefield, as exhausted men on both sides hunkered down in their hiding places, their ears ringing from the roar of artillery they had had to endure for many hours.

Herbert crept out of his shelter and crawled slowly across the ground in the direction of murmured voices. As he came nearer the shell hole from where he could hear men in hushed conversation, he paused and listened intently to the muttering, but to his dismay he identified the voices as French. A wave of panic swept over him and his head reeled in confusion. How had he become separated from his comrades so far from the German lines. He lay in the darkness and tried to decide what to do next. He had no watch, and therefore did not know how much time remained before daylight.

During the artillery barrage Eckhardt and others of his unit had taken shelter in the command bunker, muttering and cursing the misery of their situation. As soon as he sat down against the wall of the bunker, he began to look around for Herbert. Realizing that he was nowhere to be found among the men clustered around him, Eckhardt made his way outside and peered over the parapet of the hole that had been a trench. Not seeing his friend anywhere, he returned to the bunker and began to inquire whether anyone had seen him. Due to the roar of the artillery, most of the men, involved with their own concerns for survival, merely shrugged or shook their heads. Some just stared at him blankly, not hearing or registering his questions.

Eckhardt, having grown up as the eldest of seven children in a poor farm family, had learned self-sufficiency at an early age. Hard work and having to make his own way in life as a young teenager, had made him strong, both physically and mentally.

Herbert, on the other hand, although of an independent nature and willing to make his own way, by virtue of his upper middle-class background, was not able to adapt to the harsh circumstances of a frontline soldier as well as Eckhardt and others of the working class. Therefore, Eckhardt was alarmed and deeply worried, hoping for a good outcome, but also prepared for the worst.

Herbert cautiously moved away from the group of Frenchmen and turned back in the direction from whence he had come. He bypassed his former hiding place and continued to crawl, keeping the moon on his right, hoping to avoid crawling in circles.

Eventually he drew near the remains of a trench and paused again to listen for voices. Then he heard a German voice:

"Halt! Hände hoch! Identifizieren Sie Sich!"

"Ich bin es, Herbert Lenz."

"Vorwärts treten!"

With great relief, he hurried in the direction of the voice, keeping his head down and his hands in the air. He reached out to extended hands and was immediately surrounded by comrades.

As soon as he had shared breakfast with his new comrades, Herbert was directed to his own unit, which was a few hundred yards from the hole where he had taken shelter the day before. Everyone on both sides were recovering from the previous day's barrage and were enjoying the temporary lull in battle. Almost as if by agreement, the two armies were sunk in lethargy and indifference, and momentarily held off firing on one another, taking the opportunity to refresh themselves before the start of the next bombardment.

Herbert was able to make his way back to his unit without mishap and was heartily greeted by his friends. When he and Eckhardt caught sight of one another, they were hardly able to contain their relief and joy. When he related his near confrontation with the Frenchmen the night before, he was congratulated on his escape. After the initial excitement of his return, Herbert settled into contentment at being back with his comrades, and especially with Eckhardt.

Eckhardt, after hearing how his friend had managed to keep his wits about him and extricate himself from a very dangerous situation, regarded him with increased admiration and respect. He wondered if he were to be caught in a similar predicament, would he be able to remove himself from it any better.

Chapter Nineteen

The Somme

The bombardments resumed, and the rains returned. The two armies continued to endure and suffer or die.

The back and forth struggle continued throughout the months prior to July 1, 1916, when the French and British forces combined to initiate a large offensive against the Germans south of the River Somme in France. The first day of the battle brought about a devastating defeat for the German Second Army, which was forced to retreat from its former position by the French Sixth Army. But this day was also the worst day in the history of the British Army, which suffered 57,470 casualties by the end of that day.

This offensive necessitated the division of the German forces at Verdun, which affected Eckhardt and Herbert, as their unit was reassigned to the Somme. As terrible as the conflict at Verdun was, many historians regard the Battle of the Somme as one of the bloodiest conflicts in military history, with a total of over a million casualties from all armies engaged. For many people, the Battle of the Somme became a symbol of the horrors of war and has been designated "141 days of sheer horror." Indeed, many soldiers on both sides became traumatized from seeing their comrades blown apart and cut down by gunfire before their very eyes, and large-scale mutinies began to take place among the French forces.

Eckhardt, through his recently elevated respect for Herbert, was amazed at the steadfastness of his friend in the face of the massive bombardments and attacks.

On September 15, 1916, the British introduced the first armored vehicles on treads in military history. Originally, they were disguised as water tanks. However, the first reaction of the German troops was shock and terror, after witnessing the destruction of this new vehicle. The machines were deployed to run parallel to the German trenches, and fire into the helpless troops huddled there. It was during one such encounter in the third week of September that Herbert and Eckhardt gazed transfixed in horror at the growling, clanking monsters as they crawled across the devastated landscape, crushing barbed wire and human remains into the mud. As one came toward them, the men began to scramble into their trenches and cower helplessly together. Herbert and Eckhardt squatted against the wall, as the machine made its way along the parapet of their trench firing into the mass of men below as it went. The deafening roar of the motor with its machine gun fire was blended with the screams of the wounded victims. The vehicle came directly above the place where Eckhardt and Herbert were hunched together. As they were showered with mud splattered by rapid-fire bullets, Herbert screamed when a bullet shattered his left knee. Eckhardt, lying next to him, was unscathed, while men were being shot to pieces all around them. This military vehicle was known forever after as "The Tank."

After the fury of the attack subsided, medics were able to transport the many wounded to field hospitals behind their lines. Herbert was helped out of the trench by Eckhardt and a medic, and placed in a horse-drawn ambulance, along with three other wounded men. As the ambulance pulled away, Eckhardt fought back tears wondering if he would ever see his friend alive again.

But the success of the new weapon was short-lived, because the tanks were subject to mechanical breakdown, and in addition, by October, the heavy rains turned the battlefield into a huge sea of mud. The tanks were then unable to navigate in the morass, and on November 18, the Allied commander, General Douglas Haig, called off the Somme offensive, after more than four months of slaughter.

Chapter Twenty

Missing in Action

Frederika von Hohenberg-Lenz replaced the telephone receiver on its hook in a shocked daze. After not hearing from her son, Herbert, for more than a month, and having a letter from herself to him returned on November 12, 1916, marked, "Whereabouts of addressee unknown," she had asked her father, retired Major Friedrich-Johann von Hohenberg and her husband, Doctor Hans-Joachim Lenz to make urgent inquiries to Hebert's company commander about his disappearance.

Her husband's telephone call informed her that her son had been wounded at the Somme on September 21, and had been sent by ambulance to the rear, but the ambulance had never arrived at the field hospital. Her father, upon hearing this news, was outraged and threatened to take the matter up with the highest authority. The considerable influence of both her father and her husband was brought to bear on the military leaders, who promised to exert the utmost effort in their behalf in locating her son. After several months of exhaustive inquiry, however, their effort was to no avail.

Her father ranted that she and her husband should have exerted more effort in influencing their son to accept his offer of a posting away from the front. In addition to their understandable worry and grief, they were hurt by this criticism, and tried unsuccessfully to convince the old man that they had done everything to persuade Herbert to take advantage of the offer.

Herbert's independent streak had been demonstrated many times during his growing-up years, and was well-known by all who knew him, including his grandfather. Therefore, the distraught parents felt that they were being unjustly persecuted.

§§§

Ursula passed Eckhardt's letter of September 22, to Meira, which read:

My Dearest Sweetheart,

I want to assure you that all is well with me and I've been lucky so far to emerge from the most recent encounters out here unharmed. I wish I could say the same for our dear friend, Herbert. We came under attack by the British yesterday. They are using a new weapon, the Panzer. They're using it to fire into our trenches, and Herbert was wounded in the left knee.

The good news is that he was otherwise unhurt. We sent him to the rear, where he will receive good care in the hospital. It also means that for him the war is probably over. He should be able to mend quickly from his operation and come home. I am sure Meira will be happy to hear that and tell her not to worry.

I should also be eligible for a home leave, as I haven't had one since the war started. I'll let you know as soon as I can when to expect me.

All my love to you, and please give my best wishes to Meira and your parents.

Yours devotedly,

Your Eckhardt.

Meira frowned and laid the letter on the table as she took in the news. Turning to her friend, she declared, "Although I'm shocked to hear that he's been injured, at the same time, I'm relieved he's alive, and he'll probably be coming home soon."

As she turned all this over in her mind, she was able for the very first time to say the words to herself, *I really truly love him.*

If only she could be with him to help him through his ordeal. She realized that now the time was right for her to confront her family and tell them unashamedly, that she was sure Herbert was the right man for her, religion and tradition notwithstanding.

Then, in her excitement, she exclaimed, "Oh Ursula, I am so grateful he is alive and I must write him right away. My poor darling!" Tears coursed down her cheeks.

Ursula, in all the time she had known her friend, had never seen Meira, who had always maintained a dignified composure, show such great emotion. If she ever had had any doubts as to Meira's feelings for Herbert, they were now forever banished.

Meira sat down and began to pour out her heart to Herbert:

My darling Herbert,

I have just read about your terrible ordeal in Eckhardt's letter to Ursula. How I wish I were with you now. I am so grateful you are alive and will be able to return to me soon. I have never told you before, but I want you to know that I love you.

I am sorry I couldn't bring myself to tell before you left Berlin, but I was afraid that loving you would bring on much trouble with our families for both of us. But now I don't care. If we can build a world for the two of us, our own Kingdom for Two, then I can face whatever might come our way, as long as I have you.

Please do whatever the doctors tell you and get well. Please let me know as soon as you can how you are doing, and count the days with me until I can hold you close.

God be with you, love of my life,

Meira

Meira folded the letter, put it in the envelope and placed the stamp on it with trembling hands.

"I must post this right away," she said to Ursula.

"Let me write an answer to Eckhardt and I'll go with you," responded her friend.

"Oh, forgive me, Ursula, but I must go now."

Realizing that Meira was not thinking clearly at the moment, Ursula did not contradict her, but good naturedly watched her as she threw on her coat and dashed out the door. Realizing that Meira needed some time alone to sort out her emotions, Ursula thought perhaps it would also be better for her to be alone to respond to Eckhardt.

Eckhardt, always eager to receive letters from home, but especially from Ursula, tore open the envelope.

My darling Eckhardt,

I allowed Meira to read your last letter with the news about Herbert, I hope you don't mind.

She was of course shocked to learn that he was injured but at the same time greatly relieved he is alive. I am also thankful that you are safe and well, although I worry about you constantly. Please do all you can to keep yourself out of harm's way.

Meira has told me that she feels she must inform her family about her relationship with Herbert, realizing that they might disown her. But as how they have already "suspended" her membership in their family, she feels the need to get the issue clarified once and for all.

As for us here at home, the situation in the city continues to deteriorate, and keeping ourselves fed is a daily challenge. One must be careful when traveling across town, as food riots have broken out at times, and the danger of violence increases.

We have now realized that what we read in the papers is just news of the various political factions blaming each other for this disastrous war. I'm sorry to trouble you with this. Forgive me. You have enough to do just to take care of yourself.

Please give Herbert our best regards from all of us here when you see him.

As always, all my love,

Your Ursula

Eckhardt was dismayed to have Ursula's letter blacked out by the censor and wished he knew more about what was happening at home. However, he immediately wrote her back:

My dearest darling Ursula,

I have bad news I wish I didn't have to pass on to you. I was able to get a 24-hour pass to visit Herbert in the hospital, but when I got there I was informed that his ambulance never showed up. I know this will devastate Meira, and I am grateful she has you. She will need all the support you can give her. It is such a shame that she can't be comforted by her own family.

I'm sorry I can't be there to help you and your family with the difficulties you have to undergo. Don't worry about passing on bad news from home. We are better informed about what is going on there than the authorities think. When someone comes back from leave, we hear all about it through the grapevine. As long as the censors don't cut it out, feel free!

There is nothing really new going on out here. We are in a stalemate, and when we take prisoners we learn they are just as sick of it all as we are. I shouldn't say such things, but I think the censors know we aren't fools. I think they spot check the mail and a lot gets through in both directions.

Enough complaining! The important thing to keep in mind is that we love each other and we will get through this.

Please give my warmest regards to your family, and please assure Meira that I will pass on any information that I get about Herbert.

With all my love,

Your Eckhardt

He received his letter back with an admonition that his attitude was unacceptable and needed to be corrected.

§§§

A few days after Ursula received the last letter from Eckhardt, Meira's letter was returned with the notation that Herbert could not be found. As she had already learned from Ursula that he was missing, she was prepared for the news. Recovering her composure, she resolved to take matters in her own hands and find him.

"I am going to volunteer as an army nurse and request that I be posted in or near the sector where he was supposed to have been sent," she informed Ursula after receiving her returned letter. Although initially astonished to hear this, upon further consideration Ursula realized that such an undertaking would be in line with Meira's personality. She had always demonstrated to those around her, that she was her own woman, and was not easily swayed from a course of action after she had put her mind to it.

The next day she requested the afternoon off from her supervisor at KaDeWe and presented herself at the army recruiting station near the Zoo Station. She was registered and assigned to the nurses training program at the Beelitz-Heilstätten hospital southwest of Berlin. After six weeks of intensive training, she was sent to a military hospital that had been converted from a sheep barn near the town of Roye in the Department of the Somme.

Chapter Twenty-one

Foraging

By the end of November 1916, food supplies were increasingly earmarked for diversion to the military, and the food shortage in the working-class districts of Wedding, Kreuzberg and Prenzlauer Berg had become so severe, that due to the body's lowered resistance brought on by malnutrition, typhus began to appear, especially among the young and the elderly. The search for food had become a full-time job for Christina Bellon and other working-class women. Arising before dawn had become routine, and she spent the main part of her day crisscrossing the city by tram, bus and subway. She was more fortunate than most, and because of her husband's employment with the city transit authority she had a pass providing her with transportation for half-fare.

With competition for the meager food supplies, she had learned to develop warning signals which helped her avoid situations where conflict was imminent. Once at a stall in an open market in Kreuzberg, she was standing in line when a squabble broke out between two women over a few withered potatoes, both insisting they had been at the head of the line. The argument involved others in the line, and a young crippled war veteran tried to intervene. One of the women struck him a blow which landed him on his back. The crowd became enraged that someone would strike a crippled soldier. The other woman in the dispute punched the offender in the face and it became a hair-pulling, punching brawl. Christina withdrew from the melee, just as two policemen blew their whistles as they ran toward the fight.

Resentment grew across Germany, but especially in the capital where corruption of the black market, and the upper classes' blatant use of bribery, became general knowledge among the poor and underprivileged. Soon thoughts began to turn against the Emperor and his court as the comings and goings of gleaming limousines at the City Palace were observed by those in ragged clothing shivering or sweltering at nearby tram and bus stops. Also, the points of discussion in the working-class pubs across the city began to revolve around the blame for the war. As in any war, the working class was the most represented in the growing lists of casualties appearing in the newspapers. What of course was often not considered, was that officers in World War I were also at great risk, as they literally led their men in the suicidal charges between the trenches directly into enemy machine gun fire.

After a time, Christina and others began to spend more time during the warmer months foraging in the countryside, where farm produce could be purchased. But as the British blockade intensified, even the farmers suffered shortages of fertilizer and fodder for their animals and were forced to slaughter livestock. The chain effect was severely felt by the autumn of 1916.

§§§

After the combined efforts of Frederika's father and her husband to find her son Herbert produced no results, she withdrew from society because of grief and humiliation. She became lethargic and unresponsive to attempts to reach her. The hardships of war having made it difficult for her to maintain the standard of living which she had always taken for granted and having to admit to herself that there were indeed limitations which she and her family had to accept, Frederika Lenz became practically reclusive. She no longer had interest or ambition to involve herself in the struggle for necessities of life, especially food and fuel.

As her despondency deepened, she spent more and more time gazing at photographs of her children, her firstborn, Herbert, her deceased daughter, Gerlinda, born two years after Herbert and who had succumbed to whooping cough at the age of three, and her youngest, Karlheinz.

For those who had the means such as Frederika Lenz, the shortages of food could be overcome by bribery and through the black market. But the lack of coal forced the railroads to reduce traffic, and the resulting loss of fuel for domestic use was felt by almost all citizens. It was no longer possible to heat large villas in Dahlem, and the tenements in the poorer sections had to rely upon sporadic deliveries of coal which allowed nothing for heating and only sparse allotments for cooking.

In light of these grim realities, Dr. Hans Joachim Lenz persuaded his wife to take their youngest son, Karlheinz, out of school and retreat to her father's estate in Pomerania. There the availability of food was significantly better than in the city because of proximity to the farms on the estate. But this was in no way equal to the abundance which had been available during peacetime. Consequently, in early November the two of them boarded a First-Class carriage of the Prussian Northern Railway at Stettiner Bahnhof for the long trip eastward. It was with sadness and relief that Hans Joachim Lenz watched the train depart.

He dismissed the remaining members of his household staff, his chauffeur and younger male members having already been inducted into the army and closed up the Dahlem villa for the duration. He then took lodgings in the nearly vacant student housing facilities connected to the Friedrich-Wilhelms University adjacent to the Charité Hospital. Most of the male students had departed to the Front, making the dormitories available for use by the hospital staff. This change in his living status allowed him to devote more time to his surgical practice, which had seen a surge in demand by wounded from the Front.

PART III

Decay

Chapter Twenty-two

Frederika Augusta von Hohenberg

Hans Joachim Lenz had grown up in Königs Wusterhausen, a small town 18 miles southwest of Berlin where his father had been a family doctor, as had his father before him. Hans Joachim followed the family tradition, and upon completion of *Abitur* had been accepted into the pre-medical program at the Friedrich Wilhelms University.

As a medical student, he had shown considerable promise and gained the respect of his professors and fellow students. But being a young man in the golden years of late nineteenth century Berlin, he soon became familiar with the attractions of the booming capital and its many pleasures and amenities.

Many landed aristocrats in nineteenth century Europe maintained town houses in the major cities in order to partake of the pleasures of the winter season – the opera, concerts, balls, parties and fine restaurants, thereby escaping the winter solitude of their country estates; so it was with Frederika von Hohenberg and her family. Graf von Hohenberg kept a large villa in the district of Zehlendorf – like Dahlem – another of the most prestigious suburbs of the capital. Frederika had looked forward to the winter season as far back as she could remember.

During performances at the Berlin Philharmonic, there is an intermission where one can enjoy champagne and light refreshments. It was at one such event in December, 1883, that young Hans Joachim was introduced to a dazzling beauty by her escort and cousin, Dr. Dietermann von Buchholtz, a widower and renowned physician, one of his father's former classmates and good friend who had established a very successful private clinic and practice in the capital among members of the aristocracy, and even some of the royal family. It had originally been planned that her brother, Michael-Friedrich would escort her to the gala concert, the Bach Mass in B Minor, but he had taken ill with a bad cold and had asked their cousin to escort his sister. As the renowned performance was the highlight of the concert season, Frederika, a devoted music lover, would not want to miss it. The dazzling young blond blue-eyed Frederika Augusta von Hohenberg had been accustomed to young men flocking at her feet since she was a girl, but there was something about the shy young Lenz with his boyish good looks that attracted her immediately.

Being the son of a small-town doctor, Hans Joachim was intimidated when he heard the name *von Hohenberg*. This signified a member of the aristocracy, which in Wilhelminian Berlin carried great prestige. He knew he was in over his depth, and after bowing and mumbling the expected acknowledgements, was ready to retreat to the nearest corner, but Frederika intervened by asking him if he would be so kind as to get her a glass of champagne, at which her cousin grinned knowingly. Hans Joachim's face, crimson with embarrassment amused her as he was totally at a loss how to behave in such a situation. The cousin, enjoying the little drama immensely, excused himself, as Frederika was in good hands, was she not?

She held out her arm to be escorted to the refreshment stand. Being slow to comprehend what was expected, Hans Joachim stared at the outstretched arm, before realizing she meant for him to escort her. After a pause, he took her arm and they proceeded through the crowd.

As she sipped her refreshment, she surveyed the bashful young man, and after some moments, referring to the renowned Bach Mass, inquired, "How do you feel about Baroque music, Herr Lenz?"

Not being at all knowledgeable about Baroque music, he hesitated and then replied, "Well, I find it very complicated."

With an amused smile playing about her lips, she pressed him, "What do you mean 'complicated'?"

Being at a loss for an answer, he searched frantically in his mind just as the gong sounded announcing the resumption of the performance, warning all present that the doors to the concert hall would be closing in five minutes, as no one is allowed to enter during a performance.

Her cousin then appeared to escort her to their seats, which were in a private box. Hans Joachim, being a student and only having purchased one of the least expensive seats in the gallery, bent to kiss her hand in farewell, and then mumbled that he was pleased to have met her. As they separated, his brow furrowed in bewilderment, wondering why she had found him worth her notice, because it had been clear by her eyes and smile that she was indeed attracted to him.

As they made themselves comfortable in their red velvet upholstered seats, Frederika turning to her cousin and asking how he came to know young Lenz, learned that he and Hans Joachim's father had attended medical school together at the university some twenty-five years earlier and they had maintained contact over the years. As she considered this information, she resolved in her mind she would somehow contrive to see the young student in the not-too-distant future.

Chapter Twenty-three

Dissolution of Security and Feminine Assertiveness

On June 21, 1916, as Benjamin Friedlander stepped into a taxi to be driven to his store on Ku'damm, the driver asked him whether or not he had heard about the French plane which had flown over the city during the night dropping leaflets. When Friedlander replied that he had not, the driver handed him one which proclaimed, "We could drop bombs on the open city of Berlin and kill women and children, but we merely drop this proclamation."

As he read, he had an increased feeling of foreboding, which had intensified since he banished his youngest daughter from the house. His wife had berated him for his determination not to contact her, and he had felt the disapproval in the frowning glances of his daughter, Edna, but he would not permit mention of Meira's name.

When he entered his store, he noted there were few customers, which had been the case since conditions in the city had deteriorated. He had been forced to terminate several of his employees as business declined. He had attempted to provide help with food for his remaining staff, but as his own resources dwindled, he had to cut back on that as well.

As he walked through the store to his office at the back, he overheard customers and employees discussing the audaciousness of the French flyer who had dropped the leaflets. By the next day the papers revealed the whole story.

Sub-Lieutenant A. Marchal had left Nancy, France on the evening of June 20 in a special type of Nieuport monoplane. His intent was to fly across Germany at low altitude dropping copies of his proclamation on Berlin and to land in Russia. However, he was forced to land near Cholm in Poland where he was taken prisoner.

Benjamin Friedlander's reaction was the same one felt by the citizens of Berlin. How was it possible for an enemy flier to have penetrated into Germany as far as the capital unhindered? The implications were discussed in the pubs and in gatherings across the city. It was evident that Germany was far more vulnerable than the authorities had led the populace to believe. Throughout the summer months of 1916, the news from the Front became ever more dismal, and the casualty lists in the newspapers grew.

§§§

On a bleak and rainy day in November, Edna Friedlander went to KaDeWe where she had from time to time surreptitiously made short visits to her sister. Her father had forbidden her mother and her to contact Meira. When she learned from another employee that Meira no longer worked there, she sought out Ursula, who related the account of Herbert Lenz having gone missing and Meira's subsequent decision to join the army nursing corps in order to look for him at the Front. When Edna related this earth-shaking news to her parents, her mother broke down and was inconsolable. Her father was visibly shaken and speechless.

Since he had banished his daughter from the house, Benjamin Friedlander had vacillated in his thinking. On the one hand being tempted to weaken and contact her, but then reminding himself of her rebelliousness and deceit which led her into a relationship with an unknown Gentile.

When he had recovered himself, his indignation overtook him, and he reviled Edna: "How dare you disobey me when I had specifically forbidden you to make contact with her? She has continuously made bad decisions, since she got involved with that Goy! Now look what she has gotten herself into! She's proud, disobedient and stubborn. She is not a good Jewish woman, and you are on the same path!"

"Who's proud and stubborn? Were you so hard on her because you were concerned about her?" Or were you just offended because you lose face as the 'Jewish father'?" his wife intervened.

"Don't you dare speak to me like that, woman!" he roared.

"I'm going to say what's on my mind from now on!" his wife flung back. "If you don't like it, that's just too bad!"

"You were determined not to believe her when she insisted that nothing had happened between her and Herbert," interjected Edna. "If he had been Jewish, would that have made a difference?"

"I'm not discussing this any further and you will both do as I say! There is to be no attempt to contact that girl, is that understood?" he shouted.

"She's my daughter, and I will try to find out what's happened to her!" Golda Friedlander shouted back. "Why can't you even say her name?"

Benjamin Friedlander stalked out of the room.

Chapter Twenty-four

Christmas Leave 1916

Ursula shivered in the gray dampness of the Görlitzer Railroad Station. She and a multitude of wives, children and family members waited with anticipation, and in many cases with dread, for loved ones returning home for holiday leave or for treatment and hospitalization. As the train crawled into the cavernous terminal, the locomotive's steam intensified by the bitter cold momentarily enveloped those waiting on the platform. Nurses and Red Cross workers surged forward with stretchers and wheelchairs to receive the wounded. Canteens staffed by volunteers with coffee, refreshments and cigarettes waited with their offerings arranged on tables covered with clean white cloths.

The wounded, having first priority, were unloaded with their bloody bandages, missing limbs, and disfigured faces visible to the waiting civilians. Ursula was, as were many others, shaken by the display of war's carnage. She felt hot tears on her cheeks as she surveyed the shattered forms of young men. She was moved by anger at the stupidity of war and thought of those who were responsible for the tragedy and waste with a sudden rush of hatred.

After the wounded had been removed and were being attended by their caregivers, the soldiers who were still whole, or only slightly wounded and ambulatory, began to emerge from the passenger cars. Those waiting surged forward and enveloped their men in embraces. Emotions were expressed by all those arriving and those waiting with tears, laughter and fervid expressions of joy. Seeing Eckhardt making his way forward as he searched the sea of faces for a glimpse of Ursula, she pushed her way through the crowd and shouted repeatedly above the din "Eckhardt, Eckhardt. Over here, darling!"

Hearing her voice, he searched in that direction. Seeing her working her way toward him, he broke through the throng to her. As they met, they embraced and kissed and cried.

"Oh, sweetheart. I was so afraid I might not see you again," she blurted.

He, usually being very under control and steady, found himself shaking from emotion and tearful as he had never been.

"Ursula, Ursula. Darling are you really here?"

They were locked in an embrace and oblivious to the crowd surging around them.

Finally, they regained their composure and made their way toward the entrance. As they emerged from the station, snow was falling, but neither was aware of the cold as they made their way to the tram stop.

§§§

Christina Bellon had exhausted every effort to collect food items for the upcoming holidays and for Eckhardt's visit. Ingredients for traditional Christmas delicacies had virtually disappeared from the stores and markets. Chocolate, coffee, sugar, spices and seasonings were almost unobtainable. But Christina had managed to scrape together some of the precious items by responding to every rumor and tip she heard. She crisscrossed the city for weeks, wheedling, coaxing and bartering, getting a little here and a little there. She bartered portions of her own bread ration and articles of clothing in exchange for a measure of sugar or a few squares of baking chocolate. Eventually, she had a supply of ingredients for some Christmas treats.

Built into the brick wall of her kitchen was a ventilation shaft with a small larder shelf fronted by a cast iron door. In this she kept a large tin breadbox wherein she placed her precious commodities in order to protect them from the ever-present rats, which could climb up the shaft and enter the larder shelf from behind.

The rats were a constant menace in the tenements and were especially a threat to families with small children, as the bold creatures had been known to attack babies in their cribs. From time to time notices were placed in the hallways by the building custodians advising that rat poison was laid out. Parents were advised to not allow small children and pets to play in the corridors or stairwells and warned that care should be taken when using the unlit toilets.

Christina enlisted the help of her daughters, Ursula and Brigitta, as she began her holiday baking a few days before Eckhardt's arrival. She had had to set aside some briquettes over the past weeks for this. Soon the kitchen was filled with tantalizing aromas and heat from the baking. The boys, Rudolf and Emil, huddled around the small table to watch the women perform their magic, and begged to be allowed to lick the residue of batter from the spoons and bowls used for the baking. In the excitement of the activities, the joy of better times returned to the humble home.

§§§

Eckhardt had arrived in Berlin on a Saturday evening and was therefore greeted by the entire Bellon family, including Detlev. As he and Ursula entered the small home, they were welcomed by the open arms of both Christina and Brigitta. The boys ran to Eckhardt with boisterous shouts and embraced him around his legs, while Detlev, smiling broadly, extended him a cordial clasp of both hands.

Not coming from a close family, himself, Eckhardt's usual reserve melted in the warmth of the Bellon home. Soon he was inundated with questions led by the boys excited queries, "Did you kill a lot of froggies and Limeys, Eckhardt?"

Laughing, he assured them that he had not killed any more than necessary. Disappointed at this unexpected answer, their faces fell as they thought this over. After everyone had regained a measure of composure, Christina commented that he was thinner than she remembered, whereupon her husband humorously remarked that everyone was on a weight-loss campaign, or hadn't she noticed? Everyone laughed at this and Eckhardt was happy to be back in the presence of Berliners and their sarcastic wit.

"Have you seen Meira since she arrived out there," inquired Ursula.

"No, I haven't been able to get in touch with her," Eckhardt responded.

"Do you think she has much chance of finding Herbert?" continued Detlev.

Eckhardt considered how to answer this question, which of course had been on everyone's mind, including his.

"Well, you have to understand that tens of thousands of men of both sides are moving to and fro every day, and men are lost and come up missing all the time. Do I think it's likely she'll find him? I wish I could with confidence say yes, but when you see the chaos we live in out there, I just don't know. Of course, like everyone else, I am hopeful. Please believe me when I say that the authorities have done what they can under the circumstances. But, as I said, they are dealing with tens of thousands, and there is just so much time and resources that can be expended for one individual. I know that isn't what you want to hear, but people back here can't fathom what it's like out there, and I couldn't either until I saw it myself."

A pall fell over the room as everyone took this in. Finally, Christina muttered, "I wonder what her parents think."

Ursula responded to this by relating the appearance of Edna Friedlander at KaDeWe during the previous month. After she had informed the girl that Meira had gone to the front to look for Herbert, she'd asked Edna whether she thought this news might soften Mr. Friedlander's heart. Edna had then explained that, as a Christian, Ursula could probably not understand the offense that a disobedient child—especially a girl—would cause to a traditional Jewish father in such a situation. At this, Detlev and Christina stared in disbelief.

"What kind of man would throw out his own child in times like these," grumbled Detlev.

"The poor girl," added Christina.

"I miss Meira," volunteered Brigitta.

The boys, not totally understanding the adults' conversation looked from one person to another.

§§§

As the evening drew to a close, the question of sleeping arrangements came up. "Since Meira left, I have been sleeping back here with my family as before," stated Ursula. "As a matter of fact, I'm probably going to give up the flat after the first of the year, but you can sleep there tonight, sweetheart," she said to Eckhardt. "I saved a few briquettes and I went up earlier and started a fire in the stove."

"You shouldn't have wasted your fuel on me. I'm used to sleeping outdoors in the rain. But thanks," he responded.

After saying goodnight to Ursula's family, he and Ursula withdrew to the hall where they embraced and kissed.

"I'm looking forward to spending the day with you tomorrow," she murmured. "I've taken off from work for the time you are here, so we can do whatever you like."

"It really doesn't matter what we do. Let's just let each day take care of itself, as long as we're together. You have to get back inside out of this cold hallway. You're not dressed for being out here," he responded.

She kissed him again.

Chapter Twenty-five

Weihnachtsmarkt 1916 and Eckhardt's Revelation

The next morning dawned bright and sunny and cold. When Eckhardt entered the Bellon kitchen, everyone was already up, dressed and hurrying about. The family had already eaten their meager breakfast, and a plate with a slice of bread and cheese awaited him on the table. Christina had brewed a pot of tea and she poured him a cup as he sat down.

"Well, are you ready to help us keep these boys under control at the Christmas market today, soldier?" Detlev asked.

"Christmas market! Do such things still exist?" asked Eckhardt with a grin.

"We couldn't deal with these kids if it didn't," responded Christina.

Brigitta chimed in, "I think the whole thing is childish and boring."

"Oh, Brigitta! Don't give yourself airs. Besides, I hear Axel Herzog will be there helping his mother manage her stall selling Christmas ornaments she makes. I've seen you watching him out of the corner of your eye at church," teased Ursula.

"Oh, Ursula! I hate you!" cried Brigitta red-faced as she flounced out of the kitchen.

"Now Ursula, you behave yourself," Christina reprimanded her daughter. "Do I have to remind you that you looked at the boys when you were her age?"

"Mother! I never *did* act as silly as that!" Ursula retorted.

"Nobody's as stupid as Brigitta," blurted 10-year-old Rudolf.

"Yeah. Girls are really dumb," added little Emil.

Detlev winked at Eckhardt as the two of them grinned at the female drama being played out before them.

"Okay everybody," Detlev directed. "That's enough. Let's get dressed and go before we waste any more time here."

§§§

Compared to pre-war years, the Christmas market in Spandau offered meager pickings for Christmas 1916. Most people had to make do with the shortages of materials and goods, but the cheery atmosphere was being maintained as people were determined not to let the war rob them of their much-deserved holiday. Many men in uniform like Eckhardt, were everywhere to be seen, and most of them escorted young women on their arms.

Eckhardt and Ursula walked ahead with their heads inclined toward one another in murmured conversation. Walking a few paces behind, Christina observed the pair and whispered to Detlev, "Do you think he'll propose to her?"

"Now Christina, you leave that alone" muttered Detlev. "Let them decide what's right for them. I can understand Eckhardt's hesitancy. He has a lot to face and it's understandable that he doesn't want to leave Ursula a young widow if anything should happen to him."

"Don't you see how Ursula feels?" countered his wife. "She'll be devastated if anything happens to him, whether they're married or not. And besides, she would have her widow's pension if they were married."

"Well, I hope that's not the main reason you'd push them to get married," retorted Detlev.

Hearing Detlev raise his voice, Ursula turned and asked, "What are you two bickering about back there?"

"Oh nothing, sweetie. I'm just trying to get through to your bull-headed father."

"And your mom is being pushy again."

Eckhardt chuckled. "Your parents are funny. Anyone can see your dad adores your mother, and she feels the same way about him. I wish my parents had been like that," said Eckhardt wistfully.

"Tell me about your parents, Eckhardt. You've never talked about them."

Eckhardt continued to walk without answering. After a few moments, he began, "My father is so different from your dad. I can't remember him smiling or laughing, except at a dirty joke, or when he hears about someone he doesn't like getting beaten up.

He would leave and stay away for days at a time, and when he came back, he was always angry at my mother for something. He would even accuse her of flirting with other men. If you knew my mom, you would soon see that the last thing on her mind would be flirting with anybody. He didn't drink a lot, but when he did, he was worse than usual.

I think the main reason he would come back was to get mom pregnant again. I have two brothers and one sister older than me, and they left home years ago and haven't been back since. Then there are two little kids, a boy and a girl, and mom is pretty much raising them alone. Last I heard about my father, he was living with some woman in Munich," Eckhardt said with tears in his eyes.

After a pause, Ursula turned to him. "I'm seeing a side of you I've never seen before. You've always been so calm and steady."

Taking his hand in both of hers, she continued, "My poor darling. You've been carrying this inside all these years, and now I'm glad you feel you can let it out to me. I hope you will always feel you can share anything with me." She smiled and patted his hand. They continued to walk for several minutes, oblivious to the boisterous shouts and laughter of those around them.

Then, Ursula said, "It's amazing how different you are from the man you just described."

"I hope you're right. I've always sworn to myself that if I would ever be anything like my father, I would kill myself!"

Ursula was taken aback at such a passionate outburst. She could see that still water really runs deep, and there were things buried deep in Eckhardt's psyche that she would never have suspected.

After a few moments, he brightened and said with a smile, "Let's not talk about any more dark things today. Let's go see what those boys are up to."

Rudolf and Emil had been darting about inspecting the toy displays. As expected, the offerings were scanty, but nevertheless they had spotted some carved soldiers and a fort which had been made at home by the vendor and his wife, she having been the artist who had painted them in bright colors.

As Eckhardt and Ursula walked up and looked over the boys' shoulders, Ursula motioned to her parents to come over and look. When Christina saw the price on the poster beside the fort, she stated flatly, "You can forget that, boys. That's way more than we can spend in times like these."

The boys were crushed, and their faces registered deep disappointment. Eckhardt, taking all this in, pulled Detlev aside and murmured, "Let me help out with this, Detlev. This war is being thrown up too much as a reason to not enjoy life when we can. Look around. What else do you see that's gonna cheer up those little guys?"

Detlev responded, "Thanks for your offer, Eckhardt, but I can't allow you to use your money for foolishness. They need to understand that everybody's making sacrifices now, and they can't expect to have something just because they want it."

Ursula, seeing her father and Eckhardt with their heads together, moved closer and asked, "What are you two up to now?"

Eckhardt explained what they had been discussing, and Ursula interjected, "Eckhardt is right, Papa. Just because the adults get into a war, is no reason kids should have to pay for it. Let us both help you and Mama do this for the boys."

Detlev pondered for a moment and then motioned to his wife to come over and related the conversation to her.

"What do you think?" he asked her.

"Oh, I don't think we should do that. If we go overboard for the boys, what're we gonna do for Brigitta?"

Everyone was silent for a moment.

"Where's Brigitta anyway?" said Detlev.

"I saw her going in the direction of Mrs. Herzog's booth a few minutes ago," answered Christina.

Eckhardt laughed. "Well, I guess you had that right this morning, Ursula."

"Well, at least we know she's interested in a nice boy. We've known Axel since he was little. He and Brigitta went to school together. He's a year older than she is," explained Christina.

"Let's just pray that this war will be over before he's old enough to be drafted," added Detlev.

After much persuading by Ursula and Eckhardt, Detlev and Christina relented and agreed to let them help with the purchase of the soldiers and fort. It was then decided that Ursula and Eckhardt would take Rudolf and Emil to get Spekulatius and Gebrannte Mandeln, while Detlev purchased the coveted toys for the boys.

As the darkness descended, and the chill increased, it was decided that Brigitta should be collected from her deep conversation with Axel Herzog, and the family then made their way to Leopoldplatz in Wedding to select the Christmas tree as in years past. Everyone was in a holiday mood, except for Brigitta, who sulked because she had been interrupted in the midst of her discourse with Axel. Even the boys had recovered from their disappointment of being told they should not plan on the soldiers and fort for Christmas.

After carrying the Christmas tree upstairs and placing it in a bucket of water in the hall, Detlev proposed that he and Eckhardt stop in at the corner pub for a short one. What he really wanted was to show Eckhardt off to his friend Max, the bartender, and to any of his drinking buddies who might be there. This was agreed to by Christina and Ursula, with the admonition that they not to stay too long, because Ursula wanted Eckhardt to herself as much as possible.

Upon entering the smoky pub, Max greeted them and gave Eckhardt an appraising look.

"Is this Ursula's soldier you've been talking about, Detlev?" he pointedly asked. "He's a big one, ain't he? Where're you from, fella?"

Blushing and still taken by surprise by Berliners' directness, Eckhardt replied he came from a little town near Ulm. Hearing his strong Swabian accent, Max grinned and chided him, "What do you think of our Berlin girls?"

"I'm not an expert on Berlin girls in general, but if Ursula's any example, a man would be a fool not to grab one the first chance he gets!"

This brought laughter from Detlev, Max and a few nearby listeners, one of whom quipped, "Yeah, but you'd better be careful what you grab." More laughter.

"What'll you have, young fella?" Max asked Eckhardt with a grin.

"Same as Detlev," he replied.

"Schultheiss and Jägermeister, Detlev?" Max inquired.

"Not today. Why don't you recommend something special for our war hero, here?" Detlev responded.

Leaning forward, Max said in a low voice, "I've got some *Bols* Dutch gin I managed to get from my contact in Holland. For you two, it's on the house."

Detlev looked at his old friend in surprise. "How do you manage such things? I need to ask you more often about your 'contacts' and what you have hidden in your cellar."

Max grinned again. "I have to be careful who knows about these things. Let's just say I have foreign visitors 'bearing gifts' who come from time to time."

"Well, serve it up, *'Hausmeister'!"*

Max poured out three small glasses of the precious stuff, one for each of his 'guests' and one for himself. They touched their glasses together and repeated together, *'Zum Wohl'*. Here's mud in your eye! Cheers! Bottoms up!

After discussing the war, current problems, and politics for a short while, Detlev declared, "We'd better be getting back. I promised Ursula I wouldn't keep you away too long. With four women in the house, we're outnumbered, son. Underage boys don't count" he grinned and said to Eckhardt.

"Good to meet you, young fella'. Come back anytime" Max said, shaking Eckhardt's hand.

Chapter Twenty-six

Glories of Antiquity

The next morning after everyone had had breakfast, Christina pulled Ursula aside and whispered, "I think I have an idea about Brigitta's Christmas present. Last week I was in Kreuzberg in a flea market, and I saw a beautiful pair of tortoise shell combs inlaid with mother of pearl in a display case with old jewelry. They were expensive for a flea market – 50 marks, if they're still there. Perhaps I could barter for them with some cash included. I wish I could go there today, but they'll be closed on Sunday. I'll go there first thing after I pick up my bread ration and wait for them to open. What do you think, Ursula?"

"That's a wonderful idea. Brigitta's very proud of her beautiful black hair, and the combs would be the perfect gift. I wish I could go with you, but I have to work, and I can't jeopardize my job. The store has already let more than half of the staff go because business is so slow. The shelves are half empty and most people are more concerned about necessities than luxury items."

Eckhardt had planned to make the most of his time on Ursula's days off and was looking forward to taking her to the Museum Island to visit the Pergamon Museum. It houses monumental buildings, including the Pergamon Altar from about 166 BC. It was taken in 1897 from one of the terraces of the acropolis at the ancient Greek city of Pergamon in Asia Minor (now in modern Turkey). Other exhibits from antiquity are the Ishtar Gate of Babylon and the Market Gate of Miletus. When Eckhardt asked Ursula if she had ever seen it, he was surprised to hear that she had not, she being a native Berliner.

When they set forth, Ursula was flushed with excitement. It was a clear day, cold but with the pale winter sun shining on the city. They rode a bus to Brandenburg Gate and then decided to walk up Unter den Linden under the bare Linden trees. In spite of the cold, there were a fair number of people taking advantage of the clear weather walking on the famous boulevard.

When they reached the corner of the Linden and Friedrichstraße, they were drawn to Café Kranzler, the landmark coffeehouse where they had first met before the war. As they entered the warm steamy interior, they smiled at one another as the memories rushed back. When they walked past the glass display case, they quickly ascertained that the selection of pastries was meager, compared to what one would have seen there in former times.

Fortunately, the table where they had sat on that long-ago evening was available. They felt somewhat guilty asking whether or not coffee was obtainable. But when they did, they were offered a substitute made from grain. They requested that two crème-filled pastry horns be brought with their "coffee." As they sipped the suspicious brew, they agreed it was not comparable to real coffee, but wasn't too bad. A small creamer was brought with a small portion of cream and two small sugar cubes. They knew the price for the rare treats would be exorbitant, but they didn't care. This moment was about more than refreshments or the cost. They savored their intimacy and smiled into each other's eyes. For a long period, no words were spoken, but their clasped hands and their glowing countenances said everything.

They reluctantly left the congenial atmosphere and continued their stroll up the famous boulevard. As they neared the Lustgarten across from the City Palace, they noticed several gleaming chauffeur-driven limousines driving past. They wondered who the passengers might be. They couldn't see into the interiors of the vehicles, but perhaps one contained the Emperor himself?

They then turned left and made their way to the Museum Island located in the middle of the Spree river and crossed over the connecting bridge. As they entered the great building, they were relieved to escape the bitter cold outside, even though the cavernous rooms were not heated. They then realized how thoroughly chilled they were from their long walk. They paid the admission price and entered the huge room housing the famous altar.

Ursula looked wide eyed and open mouthed at the magnificent structure. It was as large as the face of a big temple, the huge staircase measuring twenty meters wide. The intricacy of the marble sculptures along the frieze over the huge steps was overwhelming. They both were awe struck by the beauty and grace of the ancient work, which had been created more than two thousand years ago. They stood taking it in, and then walked slowly forward to study the carved figures in greater detail. The atmosphere of reverence in the great room, which contained a large number of visitors, was impressive. Everyone seemed to be overwhelmed by what was before them. There was only a soft murmur among the people as they commented to one another on the great work. After walking around the huge structure several times, Eckhardt suggested they move along in order to see more of the impressive museum before closing time.

Next, they entered the vast room containing the Ishtar Gate. This was the main entrance into the city of Babylon (in modern Iraq) and was constructed about 575 BC under the direction of Nebuchadnezzar II. The front of the gate is covered with blue-glazed bricks adorned with alternating rows of dragons and bulls made of yellow and brown glazed tiles. The gate measured more than 11.5 meters high. The blue enamel on the tiles is thought to be of lapis lazuli, though this has been questioned by some historians. As with the Pergamon Altar, Eckhardt and Ursula were rendered speechless by the magnificence of the structure. They walked back and forth through the gate and marveled at the precision and artistry.

Finally, they heard the gong reminding everyone that the museum would be closing in fifteen minutes. The visitors made their way to the outside entrance and into the gloomy darkness of a Berlin winter evening.

Chapter Twenty-seven

Die Hochzeit
(The Wedding)

Lying alone in the dark in Ursula's bedroom, Eckhardt thought of the remaining days of his leave and resolved to spend every available moment with Ursula, making memories which might have to last for the rest of her life in case something should happen to him. It occurred to him that perhaps he should grant her most fervent wish – a proposal. In addition, it was now time to consider that if the worst should happen, she would also be eligible to receive a widow's pension. He stretched out his arm in the narrow bed as if to reach out and draw her next to him, but he felt only the coldness of the empty side of the bed. He ached to hold her close to him in the dark intimacy of the bedroom. *Yes! It was time.* He would arrange a special situation and give her his most wonderful Christmas gift that she wanted more than anything else – a life together in marriage.

§§§

Ursula gazed at the dim light coming through the ice-covered window of her parents' apartment. All was still in the room, and she wondered how Eckhardt was doing upstairs in her bed. She wished she didn't have to be apart from him, because the remaining days of his leave were precious. She wanted to draw him into herself and merge their spirits. Creeping into her mind like a malicious gremlin, came the question of what she would do if she were to lose him. In a sudden panic, she pushed the frightening thought out of her head. *No! That can't happen! That mustn't happen! I will him to be safe!*

The next morning as soon as they had had breakfast, Eckhardt suggested to Ursula they take a stroll. It was a clear sunny day and they did not mind the cold. They proceeded to the tram stop on Müllerstraße and there decided to take a ride going northwest toward Tegel. When they came to the cross street of Barfußtraße they got off and walked to

Schillerpark. At this point Ursula asked where Eckhardt was taking her. He responded with a smile and declared that he had a request which he hoped she would accept.

They continued through the park until they came to the St. Aloisyus Church. They entered the church where some people were kneeling at pews in various parts of the main chapel. Being Protestant, Ursula had never been in a large Catholic church before. Religion had never been an issue between them before, and she was somewhat puzzled why he had brought her here now.

"Dearest Ursula, I love you. I have given this much thought, and I know I have disappointed you in the past by insisting we should put off considering marriage until this war is over, but I've come to see things differently. Dear darling girl, will you have me now? Will you marry me?"

Although she had played out this scene in her imagination innumerable times, she was nevertheless startled at the question.

"Oh, sweetheart! I have dreamed of this moment over and over. Will I have you! I have wanted you from the beginning. Yes, yes, yes!"

They embraced, and he held her for several minutes.

"I know you're not Catholic, but I won't push you on that. We can first be married by the registrar, and then you will have time to think about the religious issue, is that alright?"

"Yes, of course. I love you no matter what. But if we're going to do this, I want to go to the registrar now. Today!" she responded.

They hurried to the registrar's office where they posted the banns as required. Normally, the entire procedure from registering marriage intent until the couple can be married before the registrar, takes a minimum of two weeks. However, because of the war, they were advised that if they were willing to hand carry the paperwork back and forth between the various offices, they could expedite the process and be married before the end of the week. Of course, they heartily agreed to this arrangement. They spent the day traveling to-and-fro across town, waiting in drafty corridors, along with other young soldiers and their brides-to-be who had the same intentions.

When they returned home that evening and related their news to Christina and the children, Christina embraced Eckhardt and gave him a kiss on both cheeks. The boys whooped and embraced him about the legs, and even "dignified" Brigitta smiled and gave him a peck on the cheek.

They waited up for Detlev to return from his shift and told him all that had transpired during the day. He clasped both of Eckhardt's hands and gave him a hearty handshake, and stated, "Well done, my dear fellow. Welcome into our family. You know you already have a place here, and Christina and I couldn't be happier."

Christina then broke out a bottle of claret she had been hoarding for Christmas, and a toast was given all around. Except Brigitta and the boys had to make do with a small glass of raspberry flavored drink that Christina had also put by. Brigitta, of course, was put out not to be included with the adults

Eckhardt and Ursula passed their time together and enjoyed the venues that were still available in the capital. They went dancing at Clärchen's Ballhaus, where they had passed the memorable evening with their friends, Herbert and Meira on the last night before the men left. On this, and on several other occasions, they were prompted to wonder about their absent friends. There were many discussions about Herbert and what might have happened to him. As for Meira, it was hard to imagine the chic, sophisticated, urbane young woman dealing with the filth and horror of a field hospital in the middle of a bloody war. However, Ursula and Eckhardt both agreed, though reserved and dignified, Meira did not lack determination and resilience.

The following Friday, on December 22, having made all the necessary arrangements and having had all the paperwork approved and recorded, they and Ursula's family, including Detlev, who had taken time off from his work, all appeared before the registrar at ten o'clock in the morning. The brief ceremony was concluded, and they were congratulated by the registrar and his secretary.

Due to the food shortages in the capital, many good restaurants had been closed. Those remaining, such as in the Hotel Adlon-Kempinski, had increased prices to exorbitant levels. Detlev had therefore made arrangements with his friend Max at the corner pub to provide a lunch consisting of sausages and potatoes from the pooled resources of Max, Detlev and Christina. Although the environment was humble, the atmosphere was jovial as the family and some friends repeated their toasts and congratulated Eckhardt and Ursula.

Memories were built in such scenes played out across the city, and across Europe, throughout those difficult days, which would be wistfully remembered by many in the hard years yet to come.

The days flew by much too quickly, and then it was Sunday, December 24, Christmas Eve. Once again, the Bellon family made ready to celebrate the beloved holiday. Two years before, the holiday guest had been Meira, who was now sorely missed. But this time Eckhardt was to be part of the celebration. As in the past, church services were attended in the evening, and there were many young men missing from the congregation. They were either at the front, missing or dead. The mood in the church was more somber than in years past, but old friends were nevertheless gladdened to greet each other with holiday wishes. As if to put the war aside for the moment, people did not spend much time discussing it.

Detlev and his family, including Eckhardt, whose presence was cherished, returned to the humble home and began their celebration. The resplendent candle-lit tree radiated an embracing glow upon the homemade paper ornaments, which had been placed around the room. Christina's baked goods and treats were savored and commented on, especially by Detlev, who praised his wife's diligence and ingenuity in procuring the precious ingredients under the extremely severe conditions. Finally, the gifts were distributed, and there were a few pleasant surprises. The two boys, Rudolf and Emil, whooped with joy when they ripped open the bright red tissue paper to find a box filled with the coveted soldiers and fort, which they had given up hope of ever receiving. This brought grins to all of the adults. Brigitta, striving to show her usual teen's aloofness and detachment, was open-mouthed when she found the beautiful tortoise shell combs in the box in her lap.

"I hope you like them, Brigitta" said her mother.

"Like them! They're magnificent! How did you ever manage to find them, Mama?"

With a cunning smile, Christina responded, "Oh, I have my little resources."

Detlev beamed with renewed admiration for his wife's amazing capacity to surprise.

As in years past, the adults received knitted goods from Christina. Detlev had somehow managed to find a source through his colleagues for salted herring, which was his gift to the whole family. When queried by his wife as to how he had come by such a rare commodity, he smugly refused to name his benefactor.

Before Montauban in France was retaken by the British and French during the previous July, Eckhardt had found a small shop in the village which had some small bottles of perfume. He was able to barter with the shopkeeper for some with rations, which he hoarded for just such contingencies. These were his gifts to Usrula and Christina. For Detlev he had saved some boots that were in very good condition. These had been given him by a comrade who had to have both legs amputated after being wounded in an artillery barrage. As they were too small for himself, he had saved them for Detlev who declared that they fit him very well. From Ursula he received some soft woolen long underwear which she had managed to put aside before they were sold out at KaDeWe.

The next day, Christmas, found the three Bellon women in the kitchen preparing the holiday dinner. A retired forester in the Spreewald, which is about 100 km southeast of Berlin, was a lifelong friend of Christina's father and had promised to procure three rabbits for her. She had made the trip by train three days before Christmas, bringing a bottle of Schnapps for the old man, which Max had saved for him. The rabbits had already been cleaned by her forester friend, allowing her upon returning home to wrap them in a pillowcase and hang them outside a window in the winter cold.

The dinner was a great success, and the spirit of the day, increased by the joy of Eckhardt and Ursula's marriage made Christmas 1916, one of the best for the Bellon family. The war was pushed aside in their thoughts, which were taken up by the love they had for each other.

Chapter Twenty-eight

The Turnip Winter

The day after Christmas, Ursula and Eckhardt returned to the Görlitzer Station where he would board the train to the Front. They were saddened that their honeymoon had been limited to the night they had spent together in Ursula's flat, but they nevertheless were happy that they were at last one and had consummated their "Kingdom of Two." Like many other young couples on the platform, they clung to each other and promised to write daily, or as often as they possibly could. Ursula kissed him and held his hand as long as she could as he got on board. When he had fought his way through the packed corridor to a window seat, he leaned out and extended his hand, which she grasped as the train began to pull out of the station. She finally had to let go as the train picked up speed. She stood watching until it was completely out of sight. She then turned and walked tearfully back toward the entrance of the station. *Oh, God, please bring him back to me, even injured, if it must be, but bring him back.*

Early on the Thursday after Christmas, as Christina took her place in line at Schröder's Bakery, she saw a group of women at the head of the line in an angry confrontation with Mr. Schröder. She inquired from the woman ahead of her what was the matter.

"I'm not sure, but I heard something about turnips" replied the woman.

"Oh, no," moaned Christina. "I have heard that at other bread stores there was no more flour and there would be shortages indefinitely. I had hoped that would not be the case here."

As they were speaking, some women passed by carrying shopping bags filled with ugly yellow turnips instead of baked loaves of bread.

"My God," exclaimed another woman standing in line behind Christina, "What are we supposed to do with those?"

As the line moved forward, Christina thought about what resources she might find among her many contacts both in and outside of the city. Then the dismal realization came to her as she looked at the desperate women around her, that these were her competition, even more so than before, and they were undoubtedly thinking the same thing. Finally, she reached the open window where she accepted her portion of turnips from the downcast Mr. Schröder. His stricken face reflected his regret at having to deal with his longtime customers in such a manner.

"I'm sorry, Mrs. Bellon. We must get through this and believe better times will return." He continued, "Please believe me, it's no better for Mrs. Schröder and me. We can't even get enough flour for ourselves."

"I understand, Mr. Schröder. Please give my regards to your wife," Christina answered.

"Why are you consoling him?" the woman behind her shouted. "He's lying! You know he's kept back some flour for himself."

"For heaven's sake woman. Get control of yourself!" Christina admonished. "I've known Mr. and Mrs. Schröder all my life. I grew up around here, and Mr. Schröder always passed out cookies to the children at Christmas and Easter, until this damned war came along. Don't you think we're all desperate? How dare you take out your frustration on this good man!"

The woman, with head hung in shame, muttered an apology as she was given her portion of turnips.

Chapter Twenty-nine

Sister Friedlander

"Sister Friedlander!" shouted the head nurse through the doorway of the nurses' station as Meira sat with her head laid back and eyes closed while holding a cup of tea. She had been on duty for the past ten hours without stopping as the wounded were brought into her assigned ward.

"See to the man in bed 27. His amputation needs dressing again. And when you have done that, help Sister Reichelt with the new arrivals. Two must be stripped and prepared for surgery right away."

Her five-minute respite was over. So it had gone, day in and day out, in the months since she had arrived at this field hospital several miles behind the front lines at the Somme. In what little time off she had, she made enquiries about Herbert at the various hospitals and dressing stations ranging up and down the front line. Soon she began to realize that as more and more time passed, he was regarded as lost and became merely a statistic among the thousands of cases of missing men.

She had hardly noticed the passing of the holidays of Hanukkah and Christmas. Most of the time she was on her feet helping to deal with the deluge of broken bodies. Her short nights were spent in exhausted sleep when she often dreamed of Herbert.

She had a recurring nightmare in which she heard him crying out to her. She would awaken sweat drenched and shaking with tears streaming down her face. She had written several times to Ursula pouring out her frustration, anguish and disappointment.

She fought constantly against the dark shadow that crossed her mind, when she would receive yet another negative response to an enquiry; perhaps she should accept as fact that he was lost and dead. As soon as such thoughts crept into her mind, she reminded herself, that no, she had a feeling deep inside, almost like a whisper from some spiritual source, that he was alive out there somewhere, and was depending on her to find him. When this happened, she would whisper to herself, “Wait, darling! I will find you and take you home.”

Chapter Thirty

Frederika and Hans Joachim

As she gazed out over the marsh-like expanse of the fields on her father's estate, Schloß Hohenberg, Frederika Lenz pulled her fur-collared coat closer as protection against the biting wind. She had taken long walks around the perimeter of the estate in order to escape the enveloping depression and grief over the loss of her son. Her father had exhausted his resources and connections with the military in the search of his grandson. Herbert had vanished with the departure of the ambulance that was to take him to the field hospital the previous September, and it seemed as if he had never existed.

The usual Christmas celebrations of the von Hohenberg family had been extremely muted, and the prevailing air of grief and gloom had infected the whole household. It had even been felt among the remaining members of household staff.

In addition, due to the combined effects of lack of fertilizers and experienced farm laborers, many having been drafted into the military, and also unusually poor autumn weather, the potato harvest of 1916 had been dismal and much of the harvest shipped to the cities had rotted. The one crop which had been plentiful was turnips, which traditionally had been raised as animal food. But the root vegetable became virtually the only food available during the winter of 1916-1917.

Like most agricultural establishments in Germany that year, the von Hohenberg estate was forced to rely upon stored food items kept in its cellars and storerooms. Having foreseen the coming crisis more clearly than many others, the old Graf had wisely been putting aside storable food items, including smoked meat products, dried fruits and vegetables, bottled fruits, vegetables and meats. This had served the members of his household well, and he had initially tried to share food with starving families in the small village nearby, but as the food crisis deepened, he had had to restrict his humanitarian efforts drastically.

However, he now continued to make turnips available to those in desperate need.

Frederika considered all these issues and was grateful that at least she and her youngest son, Karlheinz, had the refuge of the estate. But she worried about her husband in Berlin. She had written to him several times a week exchanging news about their mutual efforts in the search for Herbert and also about their challenges dealing with the current situation. Her husband only had time to write short notes, being almost overwhelmed with his work at the Charité Hospital. Occasionally, they were able to exchange short telephone calls, but the phone lines were not readily available to the general public due to the pressing demands of the military. At one point, she had considered returning to the city but was strongly dissuaded from this by both her father and her husband.

As she continued walking on that dismal January day, she thought about her husband and how she missed him. Spoiled and self-centered as she had always been, she nevertheless had been captivated by the shy young medical student on their first meeting at the philharmonic those many years ago. She couldn't put her finger on why she had been so taken by him that night, but over the years it became more and more clear to her that it had had a great deal to do with his simple goodness and consideration for others that she had sensed immediately.

She recalled how she had contrived to see him again after the concert on that long-ago evening. Her parents had always hosted a large dinner party during the Christmas season of 1883, to which many prominent members of Berlin society were invited.

Seated next to her at the table, was a young officer and friend of her brother from his regiment, Lutz von Hauenstein. Throughout the course of the dinner, Frederika's cousin, Dr. Dietermann von Buchholtz, watched with detached amusement as the young man put forth great effort to hold Frederika's attention. She answered his questions courteously, but with disinterest. She contributed to the conversation with polite but brief comments, and seemed to be preoccupied with other thoughts, as he put forth eager observations about the other guests, the current political situation and whatever else occurred to him.

After dinner was finished, and the gentlemen prepared to withdraw to the library for brandy and cigars, and the ladies were gathering in the small drawing room, Dr. Buchholtz caught Frederika's attention in the hallway outside the dining room. He whispered to her that he had some news from the young Hans Joachim Lenz whom she had met at the concert two weeks before. Did she recall meeting him, and would she like to hear about it now or later in the evening?

"Oh yes, I recall him perfectly well! Please tell me what he has said about me!" she blurted.

"Did I say he had said anything about you, Frederika?" her cousin asked with a smirk.

She blushed crimson at being caught off guard and cursed inwardly at appearing so eager to hear about the young medical student.

"He asked me to inquire whether or not it might be possible you would consider seeing him again."

Giving up all pretense at appearing cool and dignified, she responded, "Oh yes. When can I see him?"

"I thought it might be advisable that I be present for the sake of respectability. Therefore, might I suggest that we meet for lunch at the small Hiller Restaurant sometime after the holidays?"

Wanting to make it sooner than that but deciding that she had already embarrassed herself enough by appearing too eager, she replied that perhaps her cousin should arrange it as he saw fit. As a result, he related to her the next day that the date was set on a Friday in the middle of January.

Friday, January 19, 1884, was a day which Frederika would later recall as a major turning point in her life. The lunch was served in the elegant restaurant but Dr. von Buchholtz realized that, as soon as the two young people saw each other, he and the surroundings faded into the background.

After that, they met often in small restaurants, theaters, Kranzlers, and as the weather improved, in the Tiergarten, and at the newly opened zoo, the first in Germany.

Eventually, as their relationship became more intense and it became clear that they loved each other, Hans Joachim cautiously raised the question whether she would consider marriage. She, realizing she would have to face her family, and that their class difference would become an issue, determined she would put the matter to her mother first, her father and brother both being extremely proud of their aristocratic place in society.

Her mother listened as Frederika explained how she had met Hans Joachim, and how she had felt drawn to him from the beginning. Her mother, being a dignified but empathetic person, sat without responding for a few moments, and finally replied, "Well, you know your father is a good-hearted man, but also a great believer that people are generally better off staying within their social level. He is a product of his background and a descendant of one of the oldest Junker families in Pomerania and has always hoped and assumed that his children would carry on that tradition. But you have seen over your lifetime that he's very compassionate and has always treated his farm workers and their families well. I'll try to catch him when he's in a good mood. Leave it to me. I know him, and he will protest at first, but ultimately, he'll want you to be happy.

As for your, brother, leave him to me also. His objections will come from a different source. He's young and full of himself, and I hate to say it, but my son is a snob. Hopefully, he will grow out of it. He'll rant, but I know how to handle him. After all, if we can bring your father around, then Michael Friedrich will have to get over it, and I'll see to it that he won't take out his disappointment on you. If your father is by then won over and supports you in this, Michael Friedrich will have to get over himself."

Frederika, with tears coursing down her cheeks, embraced her mother. "Thank you, thank you, thank you, Mother! Wait 'til you meet him. He's a sweet, kind man. He is dedicated to helping others, and he's well-liked by those who know him. I'm convinced he will make an outstanding doctor, and I'll be proud to bear his children."

§§§

As she continued her stroll around the estate, she recalled that long-ago conversation and tears welled up in her eyes, as she thought of her mother and how she had indeed finally convinced her father to agree to meet Hans Joachim.

As her mother had predicted, her brother responded with, "Who is he? The son of a country doctor! I've introduced you to some of my friends, any one of whom could be a better match for you. As for Lutz, you practically ignored him when I introduced you to him at Christmas dinner."

At this point, her father, as her mother had said he would, spoke up. "That will do Michael Friedrich! Your sister has convinced your mother and me, that at least we should meet this young man, and when we do, you will show him the courtesy I would expect from my son. If you feel afterward, that he's not what Frederika has led us to believe, I will hear you out, and we'll go from there. In the meantime, you will behave like a gentleman, and show yourself to be a man of good breeding. A true gentleman never shows contempt for those he considers beneath his station. Are we clear about this?"

"Yes, Father. I will do as you ask."

§§§

Soon afterward, Hans Joachim was invited to dinner at the von Hohenberg villa, and as Frederika expected, he was shy and reticent when introduced to her family. Throughout the course of the dinner, her father inquired why he had chosen the field of medicine. Hans Joachim explained that his father had been his inspiration.

As a small boy, he had often accompanied him when he made his rounds in and around Königs Wusterhausen. Many of his patients were laboring class people of limited means who sometimes had to pay his father in kind, with knitted socks, gloves, scarves, etc. The farmers in the surrounding countryside had sometimes paid with meat, poultry, and other farm products. His middle- class patients, who could afford to pay with cash, had in addition presented his father with small gifts on his birthday, and at Christmas. In any case, his father had never turned anyone away, and his name was spoken with respect, and even affection throughout the community.

After he had spoken of his father, Frederika's family listened without comment, until her mother spoke up. "I can see you come from good stock. A father would be proud to have a son speak of him as you have just done."

Her father nodded. "Yes, indeed. Such men are rare, and apparently the apple has not fallen far from the tree."

Her brother was subdued. Later, after Hans Joachim had left, he apologized to her. "I hope you will forgive me, sister. I can see now what the son of a country doctor can be. I am glad you allowed us to meet him."

§§§

Frederika completed her walk around the estate as the night closed in, and she returned to the schloß. As she turned all the memories over in her mind, she confronted herself.

She had a sudden realization that in the intervening years she had not thought of her husband's meeting with her family for a long time. She was ashamed to admit to herself that she had allowed herself to become caught up in the society of the capital, and in many ways, had not lived up to the values she knew were so important to her husband.

She thought about the conflict that had arisen when Herbert announced he did not wish to attend university and instead wanted to become a worker at Siemens.

I see now that I have been motivated by petty ambition to maintain face with my society friends. I have even been ashamed of my son. My darling son! How like his father he is.

Dear Herbert, how I miss you! If only I could hold you close now! Oh, my boy! Where are you?

Tears rushed to her eyes.

Chapter Thirty-one

Gershom and Rahel

Benjamin Friedlander looked around his store as he prepared to lock up on a bleak February day in 1917. As he looked at his depleted merchandise, a few women's dresses and men's suits displayed on mannequins, and half-empty shelves of shirts and blouses, he wondered if he would have to close his doors before this wretched war ended. Wholesalers were unable to purchase goods from factories that were desperate for fabrics and materials made unavailable by the blockade. Feeling that he would like to close the door and walk away, he then thought of his father.

Gershom Friedlander, who had been forced to leave the home where his family had lived for more than seven generations in the village of Furmanivka near Odessa, Russia, had been the tailor in the small community. During the pogrom of 1859, he and his wife Rahel had had to leave in the middle of the night with only the clothes on their backs and make their way through Poland to Berlin. Fortunately, they had left Furmanivka in the late Spring, so that during the following weeks the weather became increasingly more pleasant. From time to time they had to seek shelter in barns, caves or even under trees when rain fell.

Rahel was pregnant with their first child at the time, and they had to rest when the walking became too much for her. One day she went into labor and suffered a miscarriage by the side of the road somewhere near Krakow in Poland. The five-month old stillborn baby, a boy, had to be buried in a field near the road. Gershom carried his wife on his back as they continued on their way to Germany. They had to beg and steal food wherever they could find it, and prevail upon the kindness of strangers, and when possible, Gershom would do menial labor on farms in exchange for food. Occasionally, they were able to ride in a farmer's wagon, which gave Rahel a welcome respite from the arduous journey.

Finally, after nearly three months on the road, they arrived in the German capital malnourished and at the point of collapse. They were taken in by a Jewish family in Kreuzberg who dealt in used clothing, which was obtained from other indigent people who went begging from door to door in more prosperous districts. As soon as Gershom and Rahel were able, they helped with sorting, mending and washing clothing items to be resold in the small shop, and also in a stall in the open-air market, as weather would allow. For their effort, they were provided room and board and were able to occupy a corner of the cellar of the small shop. In addition, they were paid five marks per week. Little by little, Gershom and Rahel were able to save enough to begin to purchase some used clothing items for refurbishing and resale. Over a period of several years, they built up their trade, and eventually were able to buy out the inventory from their benefactor, who was by this time an aged widower and no longer able to keep up with the demands of the business.

In the meantime, Rahel suffered another miscarriage in 1863, another stillborn baby, this time a girl. Then in 1865, she brought forth a healthy son, Chaim, and another, Benjamin, in 1869. As a child, Benjamin helped in the family business and watched as his father was able to gradually deal in new merchandise and was also able to buy a used sewing machine with which he was able to put his tailoring skills to work.

At first, they sold simple inexpensive items of everyday clothing and men's work clothing, which sold well in the working-class district of Kreuzberg. Word got out that Gershom produced quality work, and he was able to branch out making men's suits and ladies dresses, which attracted a higher-class clientele. Benjamin enjoyed watching his father work, and soon he was able to produce simple items himself. Between the two of them, they were able to sew tailored suits, dresses and coats, which in addition to their ready-made clothing, began to substantially increase the family income.

The oldest boy, Chaim, hated the clothing business, and at the age of sixteen left Berlin to take up work in the Krupp steel works in Essen, where he displayed business skill, and in later years moved into middle management. Benjamin, however, became interested in both men's and women's fashions, and as Berlin grew more and more prosperous during the boom years of the late nineteenth century, it became a fashion center of central Europe.

On summer evenings after the shop closed, Benjamin could be found strolling on Unter den Linden observing the smartly dressed men and women as they moved about entering and leaving the restaurants, hotels and theaters. Then in the western district of Charlottenburg, elegant shops opened on the newly developed boulevard, Kufürstendamm. Benjamin looked in the windows of the shops and in the glass display cases along the sidewalks where beautiful merchandise of all varieties was to be seen. He told himself that one day he would have a store on this beautiful thoroughfare.

When Benjamin turned seventeen, Gershom and Rahel began to encourage him to consider looking for a wife. He knew several girls among the circle of family friends, and his father had several men hint to him that they would gladly negotiate for a dowry if Benjamin would agree to a marriage arrangement. Benjamin respected his parents greatly and agreed to consider a match that they would select, on the condition that he would not be forced to accept a bride against his wishes.

A short time later, Gershom came home one evening and announced he had some exciting news, which he would reveal at the dinner table. After Gershom said the prayer and they began to eat, he declared that he had found a vacant store with living quarters upstairs closer to the city center on Leipzigerstraße near Spittelmarkt. This would allow them to leave Kreuzberg and put them in a better position to attract more prosperous customers. In the weeks following, every spare moment was used to clean, decorate and furnish the new quarters. A new sign was proudly hung over the doorway with the name *Friedlander und Sohn* emblazoned in gold lettering.

Chapter Thirty-two

Benjamin and Golda

One day soon after the opening, Benjamin was unpacking new shirts and putting them on the shelves when a middle-aged woman entered the store and began to look over the women's coats on display. She was accompanied by a pretty young girl, whom Benjamin noticed immediately. His mother, who also worked in the new store inquired whether she might be of assistance. The lady stated that she was looking for a new winter coat for her daughter. Finally, with Rahel's assistance, she selected a fine dark green fur-collared coat which would go well with the young girl's auburn hair and hazel eyes. She turned to the girl and asked, "What do you think, Golda?"

The girl murmured, "It's beautiful, Mama." The woman then requested that the coat be delivered to the nearby bank on Friedrichstraße where her husband Josef Eisenstadt was the director, and who would take care of payment. The bank was the prestigious *Mendelssohn & Co.*, one of the oldest banks in the capital. After Frieda Eisenstadt and her daughter left, Benjamin, having overheard the conversation, told his mother that he thought the girl, Golda, was very lovely. That evening, Rahel told her husband that Benjamin had commented on the Eisenstadt girl, and perhaps he should make enquiries to see if he could find out more about her family.

Upon hearing this, Gershom's eyebrows went up and he pointed out to his wife that perhaps a bank director's daughter might be a little out of reach for their son. His wife responded, "Nevertheless, I think we should find out more about them. After all, it can't hurt to find out which synagogue they attend and where they live."

Soon thereafter, Rahel persuaded Gershom to open an account at Mendelssohn's bank. As his store prospered, he was able to deposit increasingly large sums into the account, which gained him new respect among the bank employees. His store began to make a name for itself as his growing line of merchandise was augmented by his tailor-made offerings, which were produced by himself, Benjamin, and another skilled Jewish tailor newly arrived from Poland. All in all, *Friedlander und Sohn* became known as a store which carried quality goods and provided excellent service, and Gershom became a respected member of the business community in central Berlin.

Several weeks after opening his account at Mendelssohn's, Gershom and Benjamin were in the bank one afternoon when Mrs. Eisenstadt and Golda entered the main lobby returning from a shopping excursion. As they walked toward the staircase leading to the upstairs executive office of Mr. Eisenstadt, Benjamin nudged his father and whispered, "Look Papa. There she is. Isn't she pretty?" He then stared so openly at the girl that he caught her eye. She looked his way and frowned slightly before dropping her gaze. Realizing that his stare had made her uncomfortable, he ducked his head, red-faced with embarrassment.

As they walked out of the bank, Gershom chided his son, "So that's the girl your mother has been making so much fuss about."

"Well, what do you think, Papa?"

"Yes, I guess she's a passable looking girl" his father said with a smirk.

"Only passable?" responded the offended Benjamin. "I think she's lovely!"

Gershom regarded his son thoughtfully and after several moments said, "Well, if you're determined to meet her, we'll have to see what we can do."

§§§

Mrs. Eisenstadt, sometimes accompanied by her daughter, continued to shop at Friedlander's and always was waited upon by Benjamin when Golda was present. He made a point of cordially greeting them – and looking directly at Golda when he did so – causing her to lower her eyes when she responded, often blushing at the same time. Her mother became aware of the interest the young man was showing her daughter, and one day leaving the store she questioned Golda, "What do you think of young Friedlander? He likes you, you know."

"Do you really think so, Mama? He seems very nice."

She looked at her daughter as she considered the situation in her mind. The Friedlanders seemed to be good hardworking people, and she knew that they had arrived in Berlin years ago in poverty. One had to admire how they had built themselves up. Young Benjamin was not a bad looking boy, was obviously very supportive of his parents and deeply involved in the family business. She had heard something about an older son who had left some time ago to make his way in the Ruhr region around Essen or Dortmund, but Benjamin had remained to help his father develop the store. One could not help but admire such loyalty. They were still not very sophisticated people, but they nevertheless seemed to be a family that had all the makings of success. Yes, young Benjamin would bear watching. She would advise her husband to keep an eye on their financial development. Who knows what possibilities might develop in the future, and perhaps in the not too distant future at that.

§§§

Thereafter both young people would contrive to see each other. Golda would insist on accompanying her mother to Friedlander's when she went shopping there, and Benjamin would always make a point of waiting on Mrs. Eisenstadt and her daughter. After a few months, and with his mother's support, Benjamin prevailed upon his father to make contact with Mr. Eisenstadt to explore the possibility of a betrothal arrangement and to negotiate a dowry.

Meanwhile, in the intervening months, Josef Eisenstadt had watched the business and personal savings accounts of Gershom Friedlander increase substantially. His wife had predicted accurately when she declared that the Friedlanders would soon become a family of substance. Therefore, when his secretary informed him one afternoon that a Mr. Gershom Friedlander had requested an appointment with him, he was not unprepared.

As Gershom entered the elegantly appointed office, he stepped forward and clasped Josef's outstretched hand in a firm handshake. They introduced one another and agreed that they had looked forward to finally meeting in person. Gershom took the seat offered to him by his host and they exchanged pleasantries, enquiring after the welfare of one another's families. After a brief comment on the fine weather they were having, they moved on to the subject of the mutual interest their respective children had expressed in each other. The fact that the wives in both cases had also been influential in bringing about this meeting was not mentioned but understood by both men.

Josef Eisenstadt congratulated Gershom Friedlander on the growth and success of his store, which was rapidly gaining respect among the members of the business community and commented that his wife enjoyed making purchases there. Gershom thanked him for this, and stated that he, as well as his wife and son, enjoyed having made the acquaintance of Mrs. Eisenstadt and Golda, which incidentally brought them to the purpose of this meeting.

Benjamin launched forth. "Would you permit my son, Benjamin to call upon your daughter, with the intention of proposing marriage to her?"

After a thoughtful moment, Josef Eisenstadt responded, "I'm sure I can speak for my wife and myself, when I say that would be agreeable. And if all goes well between our two children, when we mutually determine the time is right, would you be prepared to discuss a dowry?" Gershom replied that he would then indeed be prepared to enter into such negotiations.

They cordially concluded their meeting and were inwardly both eager to relate the outcome of the discussion to their families.

Smiling to himself, Benjamin thought about the excitement he had felt when his father had brought home the news that he could begin a courtship of Golda Eisenstadt, which after a few weeks led to the fathers reaching an agreement as to the dowry and the subsequent plans for the wedding.

The wedding took place in May, 1890, in the "New Synagogue" on Oranienburger Straße. As they stood under the canopy, Benjamin lovingly regarded his bride, as she lifted her veil to drink the ceremonial wine before the glass was wrapped in a napkin and placed on the floor. Benjamin smashed it with his right foot and the guests shouted, "Mazel tov!"

Chapter Thirty-three

Family Feud

Benjamin's thoughts returned to the present with all its travails as he bade his store manager goodnight. As he stepped outside, he saw an amputee seated on the sidewalk against the wall of the building next door. As he drew closer, he realized the man was wearing the soiled and tattered remnants of an army uniform. He was playing a folk tune on a harmonica and looking hopefully at Benjamin as he walked nearer. Benjamin placed a ten Mark banknote in the man's hat and regretted that he could not do more for him. Wounded and blind veterans reduced to begging on the streets of the city had become more and more common as the war dragged on. He pulled the collar of his topcoat tighter around his neck as he hurried to the tram, his automobile having been parked in the garage for more than a year. He felt that being seen in an expensive vehicle, when so many were suffering the lack of necessities, would have made him feel ashamed.

As he entered the front hallway of his house, Benjamin noted the chill in the room and quickly took the cardigan off the hall tree near the door and replaced it with his topcoat. Due to the coal shortage, all the steam radiators in the house had been turned off in all rooms except the bathroom and kitchen, where the heat had been turned down low to keep the pipes from freezing. Upon entering the kitchen, where everyone spent most of their awake time in the winter months, he received only murmured replies when he greeted his wife and eldest daughter. He noted that his wife was red-eyed, as if from weeping, and inquired what was the matter.

"Meira has joined the nursing corps and is on the Western Front" blurted his daughter, Edna.

"What are you talking about?" he asked.

"I met Meira's friend, Ursula Bellon, on the subway today, except now she is Ursula Meinert. She and Eckhardt are married."

"Why would your sister do that?" Benjamin asked in an agitated voice.

Mother and daughter exchanged furtive glances. Golda frowned at her daughter with a slight shake of her head, as if to warn her not to say anything more.

"Why would she do that?" Benjamin prodded.

"I don't know. She probably wanted to do something for the war effort," lied Edna.

Turning to his wife, Benjamin said, "Why are you so quiet? I know there's something you aren't telling me." Whereupon his wife broke down in sobs.

"What the hell is going on here?" he shouted.

Edna rushed over and put her arm around her mother's shoulder. "Don't you shout at us!" she flung at her father. "You might remember you wouldn't listen to Meira when she tried to explain about staying out that night. If you want to know anything, try listening, instead of bullying people!" she continued.

Taken aback by this new show of defiance from his eldest daughter, who had always been submissive and obedient, Benjamin was momentarily speechless.

There was a heavy silence in the room as Golda continued to weep on her daughter's shoulder.

Finally, Edna said, "If I tell you, will you promise not to shout and really listen?"

With a sigh of resignation, he answered, "Yes, I promise. Only please tell me why your sister did this."

"You remember she told you that she was with Herbert Lenz that night?"

"Yes, I remember. What's this got to do with him?"

"They've been writing to each other and are in love."

"In love!" Benjamin interrupted sharply. "With a Goy!"

"There you go again!" Edna retorted. "You promised to listen. Never mind. You'll never learn!" she said as she started to turn away.

"I'm sorry. I'll shut up." Benjamin replied. "Please go on. I really will listen to what you have to say."

Pausing and turning around, Edna said, "Alright. But if you raise your voice again, I won't try to talk to you."

"I promise." Benjamin mumbled contritely.

"Well, last September Meira was informed by Eckhardt Meinert that Herbert had been wounded and was sent to a field hospital by ambulance, but the ambulance never showed up, and he went missing."

Wincing at hearing his daughter's name, Benjamin red-faced, struggled to contain himself, as Edna shot him a warning glance.

After a moment's hesitation, Edna continued, "Because she couldn't get any answers, Ursula said Meira decided to join the nursing corps and requested to be sent to a hospital near where Herbert went missing."

"What? Is she out of her mind? And after I told her she could have no future with a gentile? See what happens when a Jewish girl becomes involved with a Goy!" Benjamin shouted.

"Stop calling him that!" Edna flung back. "And you wonder why we can't talk to you!"

Suddenly Golda interceded. "Stop! Stop! Stop! Our daughter is out there somewhere in the face of danger and all you can think of is your injured manly pride!"

Benjamin looked at his wife in astonishment. Never in all the years of their marriage had she ever spoken to him in such a manner.

Unblinking, Golda stood her ground and stared him in the eye. Then she said, "I'm going to bed. I've had all I can take for now!"

"What about dinner?" he asked.

"Fix it yourself! I'm going upstairs!" She left the kitchen and closed the door behind her.

Father and daughter looked at each other, lost for words. Afterward, a meager supper was eaten with no further conversation.

Chapter Thirty-four

A New Opponent

May 12, 1917

My darling Ursula,

It seems like years since we were together. How I miss you and hope this wretched war will end soon. We are all sick of it – the British and French, as well as the Germans. When we take prisoners, it's surprising how many smile. When we ask why, they tell us they're glad the war is over for them. I think of how different it was when we left Berlin on that long-ago summer day. We were proud to be going to defend the honor of the Fatherland, as the Emperor told us that morning on the balcony of the City Palace. We were so confident that we were doing the right thing, and we were so sure it would all be over before the end of that year. How foolish we all were!

Enough of that. I must end this as the mail collection is coming. But I have to tell you about the most amazing experience I had yesterday. There was a lull in the shooting and we were watching airplanes overhead engaged in a dogfight. There were so many circling around each other, and occasionally smoke would be seen coming from one of them. A couple seemed to explode, while others were flying and smoking all the way down to the ground. Then we saw one had been hit and was smoking as it flew in our direction. It flew so low as it passed over our trenches and it came down behind our lines. Some of us jumped out of the trench and ran in the direction where the plane had gone down. When we got there, the plane was pitched forward on its nose and burning, and we could see that it was American by the markings. The pilot was lying on the ground quite a distance from the plane. Three of us reached him first and we could see he was still alive and I turned him over. He was conscious and looked up at me. Using my limited English, I told him to stand up. He startled me when he answered in German. He thought his ankle was broken, but he had managed to drag himself away from the plane.

After I recovered from my surprise, I helped him sit up. I asked him where he had learned German. He said at home with his parents, who had left Germany before he was born. They came from Dessau.

He then told me his father worked for Ford Motor Company in Detroit as a die maker. He said he himself was studying engineering at the University of Michigan when the war broke out and he had joined the Army Flying Corps two years ago. The medics arrived and loaded him on a stretcher, but I walked alongside as they carried him to a dressing station.

When some of the others heard him speaking German, they were angry and thought he was a traitor, but I explained he was a German-American. Soon a small crowd gathered around him as he waited for a truck to arrive and take him to a prison camp to await transport to Germany.

As we waited, one soldier asked why America was fighting against Germany and how could he fight against the Fatherland. The American was silent for a few moments and then proceeded to tell us that Americans were angry at Germany because our submarines sank so many ships, including American, after President Wilson had asked our government not to. He said they were outraged at us for being the first to use gas. We are also blamed for our airships bombing civilians in London, and besides, we were the ones to start the war in the first place. I tried to tell him that was not really true, but he ignored it. As for himself, he was sorry to fight against Germany, but his parents were patriotic Americans and they felt America had provided great opportunities for them and their family. I was flabbergasted! I couldn't believe that a son of German parents would say such things.

We are at war and it seems to me both sides are doing inhuman things to each other. By the time the truck arrived to take him away, all of us were upset. I'm sure there is some truth to some of the things he said, but I also believe their propaganda has exaggerated the truth. I am sorry to tell you these sad things, but I would like you to discuss them with your father and find out what people at home think.

With deepest love,
Your Eckhardt

P.S. I was able to get a 12- hour pass and I went to see Meira at the field hospital. She is so thin and exhausted. She still hasn't heard any more about Herbert. She cries when she talks about him.

§§§

American public opinion, at the beginning of hostilities, were in favor of neutrality. This was especially true among Irish Americans who were opposed to aiding Britain in light of the Irish independence movement. German Americans had family ties to Germany, and Scandinavian Americans had a feeling of kinship with Germanic culture and ethnicity. Then, Jewish Americans were opposed to aiding Czarist Russia, from whence many had been driven out.

However, tales of German atrocities in Belgium emerged, the veracity of which historians still debate. The public was outraged because of the sinking of the passenger liner *Lusitania* in May 1915, (which has since been proven to have carried munitions in accordance with German claims). Submarine attacks were increased on all vessels bound for British ports. Emperor Wilhelm II declared this was done to stop the supply of goods bound for Britain, thereby forcing them and the Allies to sue for peace, which would shorten the war. All these issues caused American public opinion to turn strongly against Germany.

President Wilson tried for two years to dissuade the German government from allowing submarine attacks against ships of neutral nations, specifically those from the United States. Initially, Germany had respected these pleas, but as the tide of war began to turn against the German forces, especially on the Western Front, the decision was made to resume attacks on all ships which could be suspected of aiding Britain, realizing that this action would increase the likelihood of bringing America into the war.

Finally, the German Foreign Secretary, Arthur Zimmermann, sent a telegram to the Mexican government offering to help Mexico regain its territories, which had been lost to the United States in the Mexican War, in return for Mexico joining the German cause if the United States joined the Allies. This information was made public just as German submarines resumed attacking American ships. President Wilson then asked Congress to declare war on Germany. This declaration was made on April 6, 1917, and the U.S. declared war on Austria-Hungary on December 7, 1917.

Chapter Thirty-five

Declaration of Independence

Meira had been on duty for nine hours with only a short break for a light lunch. She had become accustomed to the routine in the field hospital, located several miles behind the front lines. Whenever there had been an artillery barrage followed by a charge across no-man's land, there was always a surge of wounded which followed. Today the good weather had seen an increase in action on the front. The battle lines had hardly moved in the past two years of war. Most of the trenches had been steadily occupied during all that time.

As she assisted the younger nurses in preparing the broken bodies for surgery, she wrote the names taken from their identification booklets on the ward roster. She checked the boxes next to the religious denominations accordingly: *E* for *Evangelisch* (Protestant), *K* for *Katolisch* (Catholic), and *J for Jüdisch* (Jewish). As she moved along the rows of beds, she noticed a young man watching her. As she drew near, he smiled broadly at her and stated, "You must be Meira Friedlander."

Startled at this, she replied, "Yes, and how do you know that?"

"Your uncle, Chaim Friedlander, goes to my synagogue in Essen Werder. He told my father he had a niece serving as an army nurse on the Western Front in Roye near the Somme. When I was sent to this sector, my father sent me your name and I wondered if I might find you. Then when I was hit by shrapnel in my left leg and sent here, I knew I had to find you."

While listening, she noted his name *Aaron Levine* on the roster and checked the box marked with *J*.

"Well, it is indeed a small world, *Herr Feldwebel* (sergeant) Levine" she responded.

"I'm very happy to make your acquaintance, Sister Friedlander and I hope to see you again soon."

She smiled as she moved on down the row of beds. Soon she was caught up in the urgency of moving patients into surgical units and thought no more about young Levine.

Two days later, the head nurse in her unit met Meira in the hall and told her a young soldier named Aaron Levine had asked to see her. As she was on her way to the canteen for her lunch break, she thanked the head nurse and said she would look in on him when she could. Later that afternoon, after going off duty, she went to his ward and found him sitting up in bed looking at her with a broad smile.

"Well, *Herr Feldwebel*, how are you feeling today?" she began.

"Much better, now that you're here."

Taken somewhat aback at his forwardness, but not really offended, she retorted with a smile, "I'm flattered that I have such a healthy influence on you. Some of my patients think I'm a witch, because I'm not very patient with uncooperative men and their false modesty. I've seen everything since I've been here, and when I need to bathe someone, or redress a wound, or put a bedpan under a man, I expect cooperation without drama."

He grinned and replied, "Well, I guess that puts me in my place, but I'm still happy to see you, and when it comes time for me be taken outside, I want you to do it."

"Well, that depends on what I have going on at the time, but I'm happy to help you when I can, just as I am for any other soldier. Can I get you anything now? Perhaps I can bring you a book from our small library, or a newspaper" she offered.

"No newspapers! They're only full of gloomy stuff and I have seen enough of that already."

"Well, I'll see what I can find for you, but I have to go now."

"Will you look in on me tomorrow?" he urged.

"I will if I can, but in the meantime, you'll have a ward nurse to look after you. Goodbye."

"Goodbye, Sister. Thank you for coming in."

As she walked away, she smiled to herself and thought, *If Papa could see this little drama, he'd be delighted that a 'nice Jewish boy' is flirting with* me.

Little did she realize that something had previously been set in motion that was going to cause widespread shock waves for herself and others in two families.

Spring gave way to summer, and Aaron Levine became more and more intense in communicating his admiration for Meira. She, on the other hand, remained courteous, but professionally detached in her interactions with him. As per his requests, she took him for tours about the grounds, at first in his wheelchair, and then as he mended, she accompanied him on his crutches as they took slow walks. Finally, on a lazy afternoon when the action on the distant front had subsided, and there was relative peace and quiet, they sat under a fine linden tree and he began to press her for her remaining so detached.

"Do you find me unattractive, Meira?" he asked.

Startled, she stared at him.

"Why would you ask me that?" she responded after a few stunned moments.

"I've made every attempt to let you know that I'm very attracted to you. Although you're always courteous and pleasant, and you've helped me through this ordeal, for which I am grateful, it seems like you're pushing me away."

After a hesitation, she replied, "You need to understand that I'm in a very strenuous position, and I have to remain strong in order to deal with the misery, tragedy and ugliness I see every day. I have to remain emotionally detached, or I won't be able to function.

This is neither the time nor the place for romance. No, I don't find you unattractive, but I can't even allow myself to even think about that. You're my patient and you are entitled to the best care I can give you, but you're not entitled to get involved in my emotions or my personal life. I think we should go in now."

He was subdued and embarrassed and wished he had not pushed her to this point. They walked back to the building with nothing more said, and the beautiful day became depressing for both of them.

§§§

Ephraim Levine read his son's letter with great interest and knew his wife would be delighted. After the anxiety they had experienced upon receiving notice of Aaron's battle injury, this letter would brighten their lives. He had met a girl from Berlin who had captured his attention, Meira Friedlander. She was the daughter of Benjamin Friedlander, the well-to-do owner of the renowned clothing store on Kurfürstendamm. He wrote she had not responded well to his overtures, but he was convinced that it had nothing to do with him personally and was due to her wanting to maintain a professional distance as his nurse. He, however, was convinced she was the right woman for him. She was beautiful, very intelligent, and caring for others. He, Ephraim Levine, being a doctor and a professor at the medical school at the University of Duisburg-Essen, would appreciate her as a professional, if he could see how she conducted herself as a nurse. Aaron asked his father to approach his friend, Chaim Friedlander, to request a meeting between the fathers to see if Meira's father would urge his daughter to look at young Levine in another light.

Ephraim smiled to himself as he admired his son's determination to win over this remarkable girl. He was already in agreement with Aaron's strategy. Jewish fathers usually have great influence when they agree with their children's choices of potential spouses. He had no doubt that a girl from such a respectable Jewish family, who showed such initiative, would make a good wife for his son, and a good mother for his grandchildren.

§§§

Meira stared at the letter from her father with outrage and disbelief. Benjamin had broken his promise to himself not to communicate with his daughter. But after learning from his brother, Chaim Friedlander, of young Aaron Levine's feelings for Meira, and his wish to have the fathers meet and discuss a betrothal announcement and negotiations of a dowry, he felt he must seize this opportunity.

She was furious with her father for not recognizing her for who she was, and with Aaron Levine for thinking that such machinations going on behind her back would influence her to think of him more favorably. It was true that sometimes in the still of the night when she was lying in her bed, she wondered if she was being unfair in not considering what young Levine had to offer. What if Herbert was dead? Would she regret not moving on with her life? But then the feeling came over her again that she knew Herbert was out there somewhere, and if she persevered and endured, she would find him.

No! She would put an end to this once and for all, and tell Aaron Levine that any chance he might ever have had of winning her was now and forever nonexistent. He should get on with his life and leave her in peace. She decided that it was also time to reveal her relationship with Herbert to her parents and her reason for having joined the nursing corps. She knew that by doing so, she would most certainly destroy any chance, as slight as it was, of ever being able to bring about a reconciliation with her father.

However, this experience would serve to increase her determination to stay the course as a nurse and double her efforts to find Herbert. Her anger only caused her to feel refreshed and rejuvenated in her quest.

§§§

Benjamin Friedlander announced to his store manager he would be leaving early as he had some family business to attend to at home. Red-faced with rage, he stormed out of the store and stalked to the tram stop, oblivious to the beautiful late summer day being enjoyed by those around him.

He stormed into his house and shouted he needed to speak to his wife and eldest daughter immediately. When they had gathered in the front parlor, he began his tirade.

"We will consider that other daughter no longer part of this family. She's dead to us and I do not want to hear her name spoken ever again!"

Golda and Edna sat white-faced with shock before Golda finally posed the question, "What has she done now?"

Her husband retorted, "She has turned her back on her family and her faith. She had the opportunity to be courted by the son of a fine

Jewish family in the Ruhr Valley and she has completely flung it back in his face! I had written her a letter relating that the boy's father had contacted me through my brother suggesting we meet to discuss possible dowry arrangements, and she had the gall to tell me to mind my own business in a letter I received from her today at the store! Mind my own business! Since when is the marriage of a daughter not the business of a father?

But worse than all of that, the reason she's serving as a nurse at the front is because she's chasing after a gentile who has been listed as missing. She is nothing but a camp follower. A whore!

She tries to sugar coat the news by telling me this Goy is Herbert Lenz, the son of Dr. Joachim Lenz, and that his mother is Frederika von Hohenberg, the daughter of a retired colonel of the General Staff, one of those militaristic war-mongers that dragged us into this war in the first place. Does she think that's supposed to make any difference? She should have been strangled in her cradle!"

Golda, after a moment's hesitation, racked in sobs, pulled her apron up over her face and rushed from the room. Edna stared at her father with shock and dismay and then followed her mother. Benjamin, left alone, turned over in his mind what he had just said and slumped down in a chair, bowed his head, let the tears begin to course down his cheeks, and gave himself over to more grief and despair than he had ever felt in his life.

Chapter Thirty-six

Women take up the Slack

As the warm summer months of 1917 began to fade in Berlin, the already beleaguered population began to brace themselves for the oncoming winter months with dwindling food supplies and resources. More and more food commodities were directed towards the armed forces, and with the tightening of the British blockade, civilians were reduced to even more meager conditions. As hundreds of thousands succumbed to typhus and other diseases due to malnutrition which lowered the body's resistance, already low morale turned to bitterness and anger.

In addition to the hardships brought on by the blockade, the shortage of human resources also caused conditions to deteriorate on the home front. The shortages included the transfer of many farmers and food workers, miners, factory workers and workers in many industries into the military. The draft age of 17 to 45, had initially targeted men in their early twenties. But as the war continued to consume men by the millions, younger and older men were called up.

Detlev sat at the bar in his pub and thoughtfully gazed at the middle-aged woman tending bar who had replaced Max, who had been drafted some months earlier. He thought about women like Christina who were left behind and already worn thin with the endless struggle of finding food for their families. Finally, he finished his beer and trudged homeward.

Upon entering the apartment, he was surprised to find Christina sitting at the kitchen table and looking at him with tear-filled eyes. With a sinking heart he knew why, when he saw the official brown envelope lying on the table.

"Well, it's come, hasn't it?" he murmured.

"Yes, sweetheart."

He took the envelope from her outstretched hand and withdrew the notice. He was to report for registration at the Tempelhof induction office in three days' time.

Christina stood up and they embraced for long moments as her tears soaked his neck and collar.

§§§

Ursula awoke the next morning to find her brothers and Brigitta in the kitchen eating their meager breakfast of skim milk and two small portions of turnip porridge.

"Mama is still in bed with Papa, because she is not well" volunteered Brigitta.

"Mama not well?" Ursula responded. "I have never known Mama not to be up before any of us. I wonder what can be the matter? I hope she isn't coming down with something. She's constantly exhausted searching for food."

She tiptoed to her parents' bedroom and softly knocked. Upon hearing her father calling her in, she opened the door to find them both sitting up in bed in a deep discussion.

"Your father has been drafted," stated Christina before Ursula could say anything.

"Oh, Papa," blurted Ursula.

"Please help Brigitta get the boys off to school and we'll talk when you get home this evening."

At a loss for words and realizing that her parents wanted to be alone, she closed the door and returned to the kitchen. After she had seen the boys off to school, Ursula sat at the table and weighed the news in her mind. She slowly ate her own breakfast, and then got ready for work. As she traveled across the city, she looked at people on the sidewalks and realized again how shabby everyone looked. The thought crossed her mind that it was amazing how she and everyone else continued to try to maintain the effort of living. What was it all for?

Throughout the day, her thoughts turned to her parents, and she wondered how the family would adjust to this new trial. She thought about her mother trying to carry the responsibility for all of them after her father was gone and resolved to try in every way to lessen her burden.

When she returned home that evening, she found her mother had just returned from a foraging trip outside the city and had managed to find a chicken which was roasting in the oven.

"Your father is giving notice to his boss and we'll have a good meal when he returns this evening" declared Christina. "I have decided I will offer to take his place as a tram driver" she stated further. "We'll need the money, as his army pay won't be enough."

"You will do no such thing, Mama. Those boys need you here, and who will continue to supply food for them? I'll give my notice at KaDeWe and take his place. The store will probably be relieved, because business has fallen off so sharply, they've had to let some of the younger ones go already."

Brigitta sitting nearby and taking this in, spoke up, "Oh, do you suppose I might be able to work at KaDeWe? I would love to work in the clothing department. I'm seventeen and I'll finish school this year."

"Well, as I just said, Brigitta, the business has drastically fallen off and they are cutting back, not hiring."

At this, Brigitta's face fell.

"Never mind, dear. I'll need you to help me with my foraging when you're done. But for now, you concentrate on your schooling" counseled her mother.

"Oh, Ursula, now we'll have two men to worry about—you with Eckhardt—and me with Detlev" Christina murmured as she embraced her daughter.

There was no other sound in the humble kitchen, except the coals grumbling in the stove.

Across the great metropolis, and across the countries on both sides, this scene was repeated as the great monolithic war machine continued to devour the flower of that generation and their loved ones.

Chapter Thirty-seven

Rising and Falling Hopes

Eckhardt leaned against the side of the trench and gazed out over the sodden landscape of No-Man's Land. As the autumn rains began to fall, a quiet settled over the battlefields of the Western Front, interrupted off and on from July to November, 1917, by the Third Battle of *Ypres* in western Belgium, also known as the Battle of *Passchendaele*. He and others had had their hopes momentarily lifted in the Spring of that year, by news of the outbreak of a revolution in Russia, which led to a cessation of Russian participation in the war, and the withdrawal of Russian troops from the Eastern Front. Then, shortly thereafter, these hopes were again dashed with the entrance of the United States in the war in April.

The morale among the troops was declining rapidly, as they felt ill-used and ill-informed by their leaders. The patriotic fervor of preceding years had subsided, and bitterness and discouragement took its place in the hearts and minds of the troops and their loved ones at home. The inclusion of ever younger, as well as older draftees in the army, was seen as a true indicator of how bad the situation had become.

The news that Ursula's father had been drafted came as no real surprise to Eckhardt. But he nevertheless was very depressed, when he thought of the additional hardship placed on Ursula and her family. He answered her letter with the reminder that she was to use his army pay to supplement the household income, and to tell Christina not to hesitate to use it in any way she saw fit. He felt guilty, as did many of his comrades, that they were better fed than the civilians at home, although the troops were not adequately fed, either.

His musings were interrupted by the alarm bell announcing a gas attack. The Germans had been the first to use poison gas on the Western Front on April 22, 1915, at the Second Battle of Ypres in Belgium. In the years following, both sides continued to develop and use it. Soon, however, all combatants developed sophisticated gas masks and clothing, which essentially negated the strategic importance of these weapons, but the psychological impact remained powerful.

Eckhardt frantically reached into his pack for his mask, but in his excitement dropped it into the mud at his feet. He scrambled on his knees looking for it, and was assisted by the soldier next to him, whose mask was already in place. The two of them were struggling to get it on Eckhardt's face just as the first whiff of the deadly chemical poured over the parapet of the trench. The instant burning of his eyes and throat alerted him that he had come in contact with it, although in a very small amount. Nevertheless, his gasping and choking alarmed his comrade, who immediately called for the medics. Some others had been affected to greater and lesser degrees, which occupied the medics for a few minutes before they could attend to Eckhardt. He was then placed on a stretcher and removed to the rear, where he was placed in a motorized ambulance. Everyone by this time was wearing gas masks, except for those who had been caught unawares and had already succumbed to the effects of the gas.

As the ambulance bounced over the shell-pocked road to the hospital, Eckhardt began to violently vomit, which brought relief. The attending medic tried to administer warm salt water to the patients, one of whom died on the way. The resulting retching produced a yellowish frothy fluid, and this action seemed to make breathing easier. Before reaching the hospital, one more patient died, and Eckhardt and the remaining survivor were rushed to the clearing station where gas victims were treated. By this time, their faces were violet red, and their ears and fingernails were blue. Their skin was cold, and their temperature was subnormal. They were quickly wrapped in blankets, and warm saltwater continued to be administered to induce the vomiting. Although conscious, both men complained of severe headaches which were followed by extreme weakness in the legs. The doctors agreed that if they could survive the next twenty-four hours, they had a good chance of recovery.

§§§

Ursula read in the letter written by the nurse attending Eckhardt, that he had been hospitalized following a gas attack. She felt panic overtake her, until she read in the next line that although his recovery had been slow, he was now almost recovered from the pneumonia that almost always results from such a trauma. She was heartened to learn that as soon as he recovered more strength, he would be sent home.

Chapter Thirty-eight

A Trip to Zossen

Since Ursula had begun her job as a tram driver, after her father had departed to the front in the summer of 1917, she and her mother had used every spare moment in search of food. Late in October, Ursula encountered an old schoolmate, Gudrun Stegmeier, traveling on her tram. The woman sat in a seat directly behind Ursula, and after exchanging greetings and a back-and-forth questioning about their families, the woman leaned forward and whispered to Ursula, "My uncle, who is a farmer near Zossen, has some cabbages and onions, if you are prepared to pay his prices. He also can offer a few eggs, and occasionally some ham. But these are very expensive, and you must not tell anyone, or he will be arrested for black marketing." She then handed Ursula a note with directions to the farm outside Zossen, and whispered instructions that he was to be told Gudrun had sent her.

Ursula nodded her head that she understood, and as the woman left the tram, they exchanged smiles and promised to keep in contact.

As soon as she had completed her shift later that evening, she hurried home to inform her mother of this great news. They decided they would take the electric railway first thing in the morning to Zossen, about 25 miles south of Berlin in the district of Brandenburg. Ursula stated she would call in sick on the telephone at the nearby post office, and they would take the boys, Rudi and Emil with them. Brigitta was also enlisted as the extra pair of hands would help tremendously. She and her brothers were delighted to be allowed to take a day off from school and take part in what appeared to be a great adventure.

Before dawn the next day, they woke the groggy boys, who protested at being awakened. As soon as everyone had had a skimpy breakfast, they collected four large suitcases and two smaller ones, and ventured forth, walking to the Leopoldplatz subway station to catch the first subway to Lehrter Railway Station, the starting point for the electric railway to Zossen.

As soon as they were seated in the electric railway coach, the boys' excitement spread to their mother and their sisters. The early morning sun shone through the windows as the train left the station. Soon they were travelling through the southern Berlin suburbs of Tempelhof, Mariendorf, Marienfelde, Lichtenrade, Schoenefeld, and on to Zossen. As the density of the city was left behind, the boys were astonished to see the open fields, lakes and trees of the countryside. They had not been outside the city since they were small boys before the war. After about one hour of travel, they arrived in the small rural community of Zossen.

It was a cool but bright sunny morning, and they were in a holiday mood. After asking the directions to Wünsdorf, south of Zossen, they began walking along the road which was bordered by fields and woods. After walking for a little more than half an hour, they came to the private road which led to their destination. Twenty minutes later they came to a clearing in which was a stone barn. They saw an elderly man sitting at an ancient grindstone sharpening tools. As they approached him, he stopped working and looked at them with suspicion. Ursula then stepped forward and explained that she was an old school friend of his niece, and that she had been told he might have some food items for sale. She quickly added that they were prepared to pay well. He then smiled, and rising from his seat, motioned them to follow. They entered the barn, and the odor of hay and livestock permeated the air. Entering an empty horse stall, he took a wooden pitchfork and began to remove a layer of hay from the floor. He then bent over and grasped an iron ring and lifted a trapdoor, revealing steps leading down to a cellar. Taking an oil lamp from a hook beside the stairway and lighting it, he descended into the darkness, directing them to follow. In the large cool cellar, there were open wooden barrels filled with produce packed in sawdust. On a wire strung across the rafters were a few hams. On a shelf in baskets, beautiful white and brown eggs could be seen.

The boys' eyes were wide with astonishment, as the farmer began to retrieve cabbages and onions from the barrels. He surprised the women when he brought forth some potatoes, which had not been expected. The women made their selections and began to pack them in the suitcases. Two hams were purchased and wrapped in old newspapers in order to mask the smell as much as possible. When the suitcases were filled to capacity, and the agreed upon prices were paid, Ursula and her mother gratefully thanked the man, even though compared to normal peacetime prices, they had paid an exorbitant price for what they had received. The filled luggage pieces were taken up the stairs, and after enquiring if they might return when the need arose, and receiving the answer that they would be welcome, as long as they understood that there could be no guarantee as to what would be available in the future.

They began their trek back to Zossen and the electric railway to take them back to the city. When they finally made their way back to the small railway station, they determined that the next train to Berlin would be along in about an hour. The boys, by this time, were beginning to complain that they were thirsty and hungry.

A small kiosk across the street from the station offered water, some diluted fruit juice, and small slices of bread spread thinly with butter. Ursula crossed the street with the boys while Christina and Brigitta waited with the precious suitcases. As Ursula was paying for the snacks, she heard Christina's and Brigitta's screams intermingled with a man's cursing. Turning, she saw her mother and sister struggling with a man and two boys attempting to wrest suitcases from their hands. Ursula and the boys ran across the street and she attacked the man from behind. Brigitta was punching the bigger boy, while Rudi and Emil began to pound on the other. As the man turned to defend himself from Ursula's blows, her mother kicked him in the ankles.

Two soldiers on leave seated nearby moved to assist the women, but seeing them coming, the man and the boys fled down the street cursing as they ran, threatening to return. The soldiers, after seeing the hasty retreat of the thieves, assured the women that they would be standing by if they were bothered again. Thanking the young men, Christina offered them money, which they graciously declined. They then returned to their seats.

Exhausted and shaken, the women turned to the boys to determine if they had been hurt. They were unscathed but in tears, as in the confusion they had dropped the snacks which had been purchased.

Assuring them that the snacks could be replaced and praising them for their courage in helping defend the women, Ursula took them by the hand to the kiosk for more snacks, which were quickly purchased, in order that Christina and Brigitta would not be left alone too long. They kept a sharp lookout for the thieves, but the rest of the time passed without incident. No one spoke on the ride back to Berlin, and the boys soon nodded off as the women gazed out the window.

Chapter Thirty-nine

Salvation and Renewal

The serpentine length of the train slowly made its way into the cavernous interior of the Anhalter Station to excrete its load of broken and damaged human flesh before engorging a fresh cargo of young humanity waiting on the platform. Ursula anxiously searched among the wounded emerging from the train for a glimpse of Eckhardt. Then, she realized that the tall emaciated figure approaching her was indeed her beloved. She had expected the ordeal that he had endured would have left its mark on him, but she was not prepared for what she now saw. In place of the well-built, heroic Eckhardt, who had always carried himself with a confident athletic stride, a gaunt, ghastly pale and unsteady shadow of a man appeared before her.

"Ursula!" issued a raspy voice.

She ran to him and embraced him, feeling how his clothing hung loosely around his shoulders, where previously there had been muscle. Her tears intermingled with his as they stood clinging to one another. He shook as they clung to one another, oblivious to the crowd surging around them

"Oh, my darling. How glad I am to see you" she breathed into his ear.

She became aware of his faltering steps as they began to make their way out of the building and into the chill damp of the overcast November day. She still had not recovered from the shock of seeing how changed he was from his former self, but now realized that she must adjust her pace for him to keep up with her. They took their places in the crowded tram where middle-aged women surrendered their seats for them. Ursula sat close to him holding his gloved hand in hers, while he gazed without comment through the frost glazed window.

When they reached Leopoldplatz, they laboriously made their way to the apartment building and up the stairs. Stopping before the door of Christina's flat, he asked, "Why aren't we going up to our place?"

"Since Papa left for the army, Mama and I decided to heat only one flat. I'm still paying rent for the upstairs flat, but it makes no sense to heat both. "While you rest, I'll go up and heat ours and get it ready for you."

They entered the small kitchen, which was still warm from the range used to make breakfast. With Christina long since departed on her daily food-finding rounds, and Brigitta and the boys at school, the flat was still. Eckhardt sighed with relief for finally having peace and quiet after the hectic train journey. He gazed lovingly at Ursula as she moved about preparing his meal, the first after almost a day and a half traveling with only army issue biscuits and water. As she worked, she related the experience she and Christina had on the foraging trip to Zossen, and their narrow escape from the food thieves.

He listened and realized that he and others at the front were for the most part not really aware of what their families had to endure on the home front. But then he recalled how he had seen that what Belgian and French civilians had to go through, was very much the same thing. Once again, a reminder that the senselessness and tragedy of war knew no borders.

§§§

As the days moved into December, the outlook for Germany became ever bleaker, both at the front and at home. The government's lack of preparation for a long war in 1914, and the General Staff's underestimation of their opponents came home to haunt them with a vengeance by the end of 1917. All of the combatants, with the exception of the Americans, had by this time used up their supply of young manpower and were forced to send young boys of sixteen and men in their fifties in poor condition into battle. The new replacements were not inspired with the nationalistic enthusiasm of 1914, nor excited with battle. Indeed, they hated it, and resentment soon turned to talk of revolution. The ever-tightening British blockade eventually caused the death of 474,000 German civilians due to malnutrition and disease. The German military also seriously underestimated the Americans, and assumed that they were softened by good living, undisciplined and unaccustomed to hardship. This showed a serious lack of understanding of American history. These young men descended from pioneers and immigrants who had survived the hardships of the American frontier. This foolish attitude was soon replaced by an awakening. German commanders then reported that the Americans who were soon pouring into France at the rate of 10,000 per day, were remarkably fit, in fine spirits with good attitude, and displayed an enthusiasm reflected in the popular American hit, "Over There."

By December, 1917, 150,000 Berliners were totally dependent on government food assistance, and soup kitchens appeared all over the city. The growing discontent led to the outbreak of massive worker strikes. There was, however, a boost in morale after Russia withdrew from the war and 44 German divisions on the Eastern Front were transferred to the Western Front. The German population placed hopes on what General Erich Ludendorff (the victor at the Battle of Tannenberg against Russia in August, 1916) said would be the "Peace Offensive" on the Western Front.

§§§

As winter deepened, Eckhardt did not seem to recover as Ursula had hoped. When she had to leave him in order to go to work, he seemed only to want to stay in bed, and his lethargy worried both her and Christina. As much as she could, Christina tried to arrange her foraging during the early hours of the day in order to be with him when Ursula had to leave in the evening for her shift on the tram. But this meant that Ursula also had to be available when Brigitta and the boys returned from school after 3 p.m. On some days, Brigitta would be with her friends and occasionally slept over at one of their homes. The boys, Rudi and Emil, would often go upstairs and persuade Eckhardt to play board games. Rudi was especially fond of chess, but the mental concentration would often tire Eckhardt, and he usually gave up early in the game.

The commodities acquired in Zossen were largely depleted by Christmastime, except for one of the hams, which Christina held back with determination for the holidays. As Christmas approached, it was hoped that Eckhardt would be able to go to the *Weihnachtsmarkt* (Christmas Market) as in the previous year, but it was not to be. He simply could not face the ordeal of travel across the city in the bitter cold. Therefore, it was decided that Christina and Brigitta would take the boys and Ursula would remain behind with her husband.

When he learned of this decision he protested and stated that he would be fine by himself, and Ursula must go with the others. Ursula, however, adamantly refused, and he relented, inwardly relieved that she would not leave him. Experiences like this began to undermine his self-esteem, and he began to feel that he was becoming a millstone around her neck. At night after she was breathing in sleep beside him, he would go over and over these thoughts, and resolved that after the beginning of the new year he would put forth a plan he knew would not please her, but that he nevertheless felt he must insist upon.

Christmas Eve arrived, and the little family managed to acquire a tree and put up holiday decorations in the flat. Christina found time throughout the year to knit gloves and scarves for all, especially for Detlev away at the front, and had bought some small puzzles for the boys. Eckhardt insisted that he would accompany them to the traditional Christmas Eve service in their church. Ursula and Christina both argued against this, as they were concerned he might become ill sitting in the unheated church in his weakened condition. But he prevailed and making sure that he was dressed as warmly as possible, they set forth. In spite of the cold, Eckhardt seemed to brighten being out of the house and out on the street with the holiday crowds.

He was greeted by neighbors and acquaintances at church, and the pastor extended him a warm handshake. Due to war losses, there were many vacant seats, and many familiar faces were missing. A few wounded veterans and soldiers on leave made up the majority of the male congregation, except for some old men.

After the service, while walking home past Leopoldplatz, Eckhardt requested that they pause a moment while he sat on a park bench to catch his breath. His damaged throat tightened in the bitter cold and his breathing was labored. Ursula urged her mother to get the boys home out of the cold and declared she would sit with Eckhardt for a few minutes. But the boys insisted that they would sit with Uncle Eckhardt, Ursula on one side and they on the other. Christina and Brigitta waited patiently while this was going on. This cheered Eckhardt, and he fondly placed one arm around Ursula and the other around his nephews. He marveled at how much Brigitta had matured during the past year. Previously, she would have complained about having to wait in the cold, but now she placed her arm around her mother's shoulders and smiled at her brothers as they snuggled up to their uncle, whom they obviously adored. After a few minutes, he stated he was ready to continue on their homeward journey.

When they reached Christina's flat, the boys displayed their usual excitement and boisterously asked when the presents would be opened. As in former years, the paper decorations were in place and the tree was beautifully lit with candles. But the holiday mood was still diminished by the absence of Detlev and Meira.

They had received a parcel from Detlev with small quantities of treats long absent from the shops in Berlin. Two chocolate bars for the boys were especially admired, and the boys generously passed them around so that everyone might have a small nibble. After the presents had been opened, the mood became somber, and Detlev's accordion was sorely missed, but they nevertheless sang the stanzas of the old favorite, *Stille Nacht, Heilige Nacht*.

Chapter Forty

Imperial Twilight and Pandemic

Eckhardt had not been in close communication with his mother since before the war, but he had sent her intermittent accounts of himself throughout the years. He now decided to fully apprise her of his condition and inquire if he might come to Blaubeuren for an extended visit. Within two weeks he received an enthusiastic letter, assuring him that he would be most welcome at any time for as long as he wished. In the meantime, he had a medical examination at the military hospital in Tempelhof, had been declared unfit for return to duty and was placed on indefinite medical leave. He was to report again in three months.

After having made these preparations, he revealed his plan to Ursula. At first, she protested, but after explaining that he had first gotten the idea because he saw how much hardship caring for him had been placed on her shoulders.

"I certainly don't think the cold dampness of a Berlin winter is as beneficial for my lungs as the fresh country air of Blaubeuren. My mother's house is on the edge of town close to the forest and open fields where I can walk and get more exercise. Mama knows all the farmers around there and has access to fresh food and dairy products. Besides, I haven't seen her for several years, and if I return to the front, who knows when I'll have another chance like this again. Also, not having to look after me will make things easier for all of you here, and I think a temporary change will do us all some good."

Ursula gradually came around to his way of thinking and became supportive of the plan when it came time to inform the rest of the family. Christina was quick to see the wisdom of Eckhardt's thinking and assured him that although he would be missed, she could see that such a change would no doubt be beneficial to his recovery and overall well-being. When Rudi and Emil heard of it, they protested loudly, as they had come to see in their uncle a surrogate father, which helped ease their longing for Detlev. Brigitta was saddened, and it became evident she had developed a girl's crush on him. But everyone finally agreed that for the moment, Eckhardt's welfare was of primary concern.

On a snowy day in February, Ursula accompanied her husband to Lehrter Railway Station for the journey to Ulm, which lies 12 miles from Blaubeuren. They tearfully embraced on the platform and Eckhardt assured her that as soon as his strength was sufficiently restored, he would return to her. As expected, the train was loaded to capacity with military personnel, but seeing how unsteady and unwell Eckhardt appeared, a seat was surrendered to him by a young recruit. He joined others at a window to wave at Ursula as the train slowly departed. He watched her run alongside the train as she had always done when he left before. He gazed at her with a heavy heart until she was out of sight.

§§§

In the weeks following Eckhardt's departure, Ursula, Brigitta and Christina were, as always, engaged constantly in the struggle to keep food on the table. But in spite of their efforts, all the members of the household seemed to wither and weaken. The bitterness of the northern German winter, the lack of fuel and poor diet gnawed at their health and well-being. The passengers on Ursula's tram had the same gaunt and sallow complexions as everyone else, and the usual rash of winter colds and coughs seemed to intensify during the winter of 1918.

One morning in March, a young woman who was sitting two seats behind Ursula looked especially bad. She was perspiring heavily and coughing continually. Suddenly she fell out of her seat, and some alarmed passengers seated nearby rushed to her aid. Ursula stopped the tram at the next stop, and as quickly as possible she and two passengers helped remove the woman and laid her on a bench. A policeman standing nearby was summoned and called an ambulance. He then saw to it that the unconscious woman was taken to a hospital. Ursula and the assisting passengers returned to the tram and continued on their way.

When she returned home that evening she related the incident to her mother. Brigitta upon hearing this, spoke up to say that the same thing had happened to a girl in her class that morning. Two days later, while eating her lunch in the company canteen, Ursula felt light-headed, and shortly thereafter had to rush to the nearest restroom to vomit. The light-headedness turned to dizziness accompanied by a severe headache. Chills overtook her and she began to perspire copiously and began to cough. Knowing she could not begin her shift in such a condition, she informed her supervisor, who stated that he would call in another operator as a substitute and advised Ursula to go home.

She was barely able to sit up on the tram which took her to Leopoldplatz, where she began to walk to her building. She fought her way to the entrance door and again had to vomit, embarrassing herself. She managed to get inside the building and sit on the bottom step of the stairway leading upstairs. Vertigo so completely overtook her that she had to lean helplessly against the wall. Shaking with chills in her now perspiration-soaked clothing in the frigid unheated hallway, and fighting to cling to consciousness, she began to feel real panic that she might pass out at any moment.

Just then, the outside door opened and the porter, who lived in the flat nearest the entrance on the ground floor, entered and saw her. With alarm, he rushed over to her.

"Mrs. Meinert! What are you doing out here . . .," he began.

"I am so sick. Please help me."

"Of course," he responded, and began to lift her to her feet. Laboriously, the two of them made their way up to her mother's flat. Fortunately, Christina was home as Emil had also come home earlier from school with a cough and complaining of a headache. Seeing Ursula with her cadaverous appearance, she quickly took over from the porter, thanking him profusely for coming to her daughter's aid.

Christina helped Ursula to her own bedroom, helped her lie on the bed, removed her sodden clothing, then covered her with a sheet. She then fetched a basin of cool water and began to wipe the perspiration from her daughter's skin in order to bring down the fever. As soon as this task was completed, she clothed Ursula in one of her own cotton nightgowns and covered her with a light down-filled comforter. As the room was unheated, Christina laid a small fire of briquettes in the seldom-used tile stove in the corner. Realizing that the fever would bring on dehydration, Christina brought a half-filled bowl of potato broth, which she had earlier prepared for Emil, and helped Ursula sip spoonsful. After this, Ursula seemed to be less restless, and she slipped into a slumber.

Later in the afternoon, Brigitta and Rudi returned from school reporting that several classmates had taken ill throughout the day. As they later sat at their skimpy evening meal, Brigitta complained that she was not hungry and had a headache. She retired to her trundle bed in the next room.

"I'm scared, Mama," declared Rudi. "They're getting sick just like those kids at school. What's happening?"

Christina frowned for a moment and then responded, "We have to trust in God. Let's say a prayer for our family and those other kids."

Little did they realize that they were seeing the beginning of a pandemic that would eventually cover the earth and ultimately result in deaths later estimated to be as many 50 million worldwide.

In the following hours, Christina saw her stricken loved ones suffer with the insidious evil that had invaded their home. Ursula, by nightfall, had turned blue in the face, as the circulating blood could not get oxygenated. She began to cough up a pinkish froth, which also exuded from her nose and mouth.

Emil, meanwhile, began to exhibit the same symptoms, and his condition deteriorated faster than that of his older sister. As he labored to breathe, brown spots appeared on his cheeks, and soon he was coughing up pure blood. In anguish, his mother helplessly watched him slip away, gasping for breath. As the dawn broke, he was gone.

Not being able to leave to fetch an undertaker and not having access to a telephone, she wrapped her son in a sheet and placed his body on the floor in the cold hallway by her door.

When Christina later sent Rudi to fetch a doctor at the nearby clinic, he returned after an hour to report no doctor was available, as the clinic was already overrun with patients, with many lying in the hallways, available beds having long since been taken.

"I'll stay home and help you, Mama," Rudi told his distraught mother.

She agreed that would be best.

Brigitta also spent a feverish night, but she seemed to rally in the early morning hours. But by midmorning she also began to cough up blood and was soon racked with fever. By midday she was beginning to fail. Christina watched another child die in agony.

Rudi watched wide-eyed as his mother – in her grief and frustration – looked heavenward and cursed, "God, where are you?"

Chapter Forty-one

The Lord Giveth and the Lord Taketh Away

Meanwhile, Ursula's fever broke in the late afternoon and she lapsed into a deep sleep.

Christina laid a comforter over her eldest son as he lay on his pallet on the floor of the main room, and through her tears issued a sigh of relief, that at least he so far had been spared. Not being able to lift the corpse of her youngest daughter, she left her covered with a sheet on her trundle bed in the same room. Soon thereafter, a knock came at the door, and she opened it to face two unshaven older men who announced they had been summoned by the porter. He had been told by the neighbor across the hall about the dead boy lying on the floor. They were from the nearest morgue and had the task of going through the area to collect remains of the deceased. They then produced folding stretchers and removed first the body of Emil, and then returned to collect that of Brigitta. Relieved and at the same time distraught with grief, Christina watched them carry her children away.

Although Christina had no way of knowing it at the time, the disease had already filled the morgues in the city beyond capacity, with the dead having to be stacked one on top of the other, until they had to be carted away to mass graves outside the city. Relatives wishing to retrieve the remains of their loved ones, were advised that it had to be done within twenty-four hours, which was later shortened to eight hours.

As the pandemic continued, people began to collapse and die on the streets, and were left unattended by passersby, who were terrified to come near them. They would lie where they fell and often died, being later collected in wagons manned by the staff from the morgues and mortuaries.

For unknown reasons, some, such as Christina and Rudi, were able to survive the ordeal unscathed. Others would sicken, but not be taken, and then have to suffer a recovery that could take months. Some were damaged for the rest of their lives.

In the days that followed that terrible night, Ursula was gradually able to regain her strength and after six weeks returned to her job on a part-time basis. By late Spring, she was, for the most part, recovered, except for a lingering cough that persisted throughout the following summer. She decided not to inform her husband about the ordeal until much later, as he was involved with his own recovery. She prayed that the awful disease would not overtake him in his already frail condition and was extremely grateful that he was far away from the city in the countryside of southern Germany.

Her mother became withdrawn and uncommunicative following the loss of her children. She had managed to retrieve their remains and have them placed in coffins for a double service funeral at her church, the Old Nazereth Protestant church on Leopoldplatz. She was advised by her pastor that the service would out of necessity have to be short, as many other parishioners had to be served, and he was occupied for days at a time helping his flock bury their dead. Brigitta and Emil were buried side by side in the Dorotheenstädischer Friedhof on Chausseestraße in the Mitte district of Berlin.

Chapter Forty-two

The Destroyer Not Sated

Detlev read Christina's letter relating the deaths of his children through a blur of tears. He knew of what she was reporting, as the deadly virus had begun to attack young soldiers in the trenches. He had already witnessed how healthy young men seemed to be taken, instead of older men. It was later determined that the age group between 20 and 45 were the most vulnerable.

He shared her relief however, that Ursula had managed to recover from her ordeal, and that so far Rudi had remained untouched. Christina herself had also managed to stay healthy, in spite of the extra burden of dealing with the deaths of Brigitta and Emil. He was proud of his wife and regretted deeply that she had had to go through the terrible time without his support.

After his induction during the summer of the previous year, he had six weeks of training at the training center behind the lines of the Western Front, and then was posted near Ypres, where he had taken part in the Battle of Passchendaele. He had watched comrades being mown down and blasted to bits by mortars. He had survived two gas attacks, and wondered why he been spared so far, when so many around him were killed. Then in the early Spring, the pandemic began to spread among the troops on all sides. The combination of the war, and now the added scourge of the flu pandemic, made him and many others wonder if the long-predicted end of the world had come. Was Judgement Day at hand?

Then on a beautiful day in May during a lull at the front, he was sitting with a group of comrades, which included a number of older men like himself. They were eating the stew which contained hearty pork from a pig they had found eating truffles in the woods near an abandoned farmstead behind the front. They had also managed to harvest some mushrooms, and together with the slaughtered pig, had persuaded the cook to use some of his hoarded potatoes to cook the rare repast they were now enjoying.

Afterward they lay about under a large chestnut tree, that had so far been spared from the devastation of the war. Detlev dozed off listening to the sounds of Spring, and as he closed his eyes he watched the lazy movement of clouds in the blue sky thinking, "This is how men should live."

After some time passed, he awoke to find himself bathed in perspiration, and with a sharp headache. As he sat up, he felt dizzy and nauseous. He wondered if the food had been contaminated, but then thought that that couldn't be, because it had been prepared fresh that morning. He tried to stand up and broke into a cold sweat. As he made his way back to the bivouac behind the lines where their tents and huts had been put up, he had to vomit and his breath began to come in gasps and he began to cough. Then he knew! The scourge had overtaken him. His terror was overshadowed by the immediate thought, "If anything happens to me, what will Christina do?"

He collapsed before reaching the camp, was picked up by medical orderlies and carried by stretcher to the dressing station. A harried doctor took a look at him and had him laid on the ground outside the tent, as all available cots were occupied. The coughs of the flu victims were like a steady chorus competing with groans of the wounded in the next tent, as the flu cases were kept separate from the wounded.

The constant to and fro of incoming flu patients and the outflow of those who had succumbed being removed, was a steady stream of traffic day and night.

Within several hours, Detlev, like many others, steadily worsened, and late in the evening, he breathed a last gasping bloody breath.

Before Christina opened the official brown envelope with trembling hands, she knew what news it contained.

Chapter Forty-three

Defeat and Armistice

Germany embarked on an all-out campaign for total victory with the launching of the first of five major offensives on March 21, 1918, along a 60-mile long front in the Somme. During the so-called "Michael Offensive" German troops recaptured in five days all the ground they had lost during the Battle of the Somme in 1916, but were stopped by the British 3rd Army which prevented them from taking the key objectives of Arras and Amiens.

In the second offensive, the "Georgette Offensive" of April 9-29, 46 divisions from the German 6th Army pushed the British 2nd Army back to the outskirts of Ypres and retook the Passchendaele Ridge, but their momentum was stopped by British, French and Australian reinforcements. The German loss of 330,000 casualties in the two offensives, coupled with a huge lack of reserve troops, caused these offensives to break down and collapse. Also, the death of Germany's popular hero, Manfred von Richthofen, the "Red Baron," shot down on April 21, was a serious blow to the already flagging German morale.

The third offensive, the "Bluecher-Yorck Offensive" of May 27-June 3, 1918, involved 41 divisions of the German 1st and 7th Armies which caused the Allied Armies in central France to bog down, thereby blocking reinforcements from reaching the British positions. The Germans were able to overwhelm the weak defenses of the French 6th Army east of the Aisne River. This brilliant success encouraged General Ludendorff to revise his entire strategy. He saw this as an opportunity to make a dash for Paris, and draw the Allied armies into a final showdown, which would decide the outcome of the war. The Germans made a westward dash and came within 50 miles of Paris. But the German troops, having been pushed to the limit throughout the Spring of 1918, were totally exhausted and unable to maintain the pace. The great push sputtered to a halt, and Allied reinforcements, including Americans, flooded the region.

The Germans launched their hastily-organized fourth offensive, the "Gneisenau Offensive," on June 9, and tried to revive the momentum of the dash for Paris but were stopped by the successful counter-attack of French and American troops, resulting in a collapse of the new offensive within four days.

The fifth and final German offensive of the war, the "Marne-Reims Offensive," began with 52 divisions in a two-pronged attack near Reims, France on July 15. The Allies had been expecting this and were lying in ambush. The German attack east of Reims was demolished on the same day by the French, while the advance west of the city was stopped by the U.S. 3rd Infantry Division. A joint French and American counter-attack was successful, and the offensive was finished in two days.

§§§

On July 17, 1918, the former Czar of Russia, Nicholas Romanov, and his entire family were murdered in Ekaterinburg, Russia. Civil war swept across the country and ended with a death toll of an estimated 15 million people. The assassination of the Romanovs shocked the world, but especially got the attention of the European royalty.

This tragic event foreshadowed the demise of ruling houses that had been in power for centuries. For example, the Hapsburg dynasty of Austria-Hungary had existed for 700 years.

From July onwards, the fortunes of war turned against the Central Powers, Germany, Austro-Hungary, Bulgaria and the Turkish Ottoman Empire. On August 8, 1918, six German divisions east of Amiens were crushed by the British 4th Army using 456 tanks. 13,000 German prisoners were taken. The British advance was only slowed when the Germans rushed in six divisions, their last reserves on the Western Front.

The Germans continued to fall back in the face of overwhelming odds, strengthened by the influx of Americans arriving at the rate of 10,000 a day. On September 28, in the face of unstoppable strength of the Allies and the looming possibility of an outright military defeat on the Western Front, General Ludendorff collapsed at his headquarters and informed his superior, Paul von Hindenburg, that the war was lost and must be ended.

The next day, on September 29, Bulgaria, the first of the Central Powers to quit the war, signed an armistice with the Allies. Ludendorff and Hindenburg met with the Emperor, Wilhelm II, and convinced him to likewise seek an armistice. The German army was falling apart by the day, with enormous troop losses, declining discipline, exhaustion, illness, food shortages, increasing desertions and disorderly conduct and drunkenness. The Emperor finally heeded their advice and agreed that the time had come for an armistice.

On October 2, 1918, Ludendorff sent a representative to the Reichstag in Berlin to inform the legislature that the war was lost, and discussions for an armistice should begin immediately. The politicians, from whom the truth had been kept by the General Staff and the Emperor, were shocked.

Two days later, President Wilson was informed via the Swiss, that the German government was requesting an armistice. They had contacted Wilson directly, bypassing the French and British, hoping that the American president would be more lenient. They were disappointed, however, when he responded with a list of demands to be met before any discussions could take place. These included German withdrawal from all occupied territories, and a total cessation of U-Boat attacks.

By the middle of October, the Germans had undertaken a general retreat along the Western Front, and a withdrawal from France and Belgium. During the month, various portions of the European empires began to declare independence, including Poland – formerly part of the Russian empire – proclaiming itself as an independent state. The Czechs declared independence from Austria, and Slovakia declared its independence from Hungary. Czechoslovakia was subsequently formed from these two entities.

On October 30, Turkey signed an armistice with the Allies, thereby being the second member of the Central Powers to withdraw from the war.

Mutiny struck the German Navy in Kiel and Wilhelmshaven, on November 3rd, when sailors refused orders to put to sea to engage in a final showdown with the British Navy. At the same time, Bolshevist-style uprisings took place in German cities, including Munich, Stuttgart and Berlin. These uprisings alarmed German and Allied leaders alike, who feared that a violent Bolshevist revolution, such as had taken place in Russia might overtake Germany, and an increased sense of urgency was raised in the armistice negotiations. Also, on this day, November 3, Germany's only remaining ally, Austria-Hungary, signed an armistice with Italy, leaving Germany alone in the war.

On November 9, 1918, the Imperial government of Emperor Wilhelm II collapsed, and a German republic was proclaimed. Friedrich Ebert was named the head of the new provisional government, and the Emperor abdicated and fled to Doorn, Holland, where he remained for the rest of his life.

At 5:10 a.m. on November 11, 1918, in a railway car at Compiegne, France, the Germans signed the armistice which went into effect at 11 a.m. Along the Western Front, fighting continued until precisely 11 o'clock, with 2000 casualties suffered that day by all sides. The Armistice began on the eleventh hour of the eleventh day of the eleventh month of the year 1918.

PART IV

Humiliation

Chapter Forty-four

Rebirth

"Monsieur Herbert, wake up." Madame Fournier, his "employer" and benefactress shook him awake from a deep sleep in his bed in the storage building behind her farmhouse.

"There has been an armistice and the war is over. The Germans are leaving France, and you must go with them," she continued.

The armistice! It had finally come!

"Come into the house and get your breakfast," said the kindly middle-aged woman.

"*Mercí, Madame Fournier,*" Herbert replied in his rudimentary French.

She departed. He roused himself and began to pull on his trousers, being careful to protect his left knee. Although useable, it was nevertheless still not completely healed from the wound inflicted almost two years previously in the first British tank attack. It had been necessary for Madame Fournier to cut off his blood-stained, tattered uniform. She had then provided him with some of her husband's clothing, for which he was grateful. As he continued to dress, he reflected on the day it had happened.

He remembered the excruciating pain he suffered as the bullet penetrated his knee. He was placed in a horse-drawn ambulance with two other wounded men, and he recalled the agony of the jostling they endured as the horse-drawn vehicle was pulled over the ruts in the road. He remembered hearing a mortar coming closer and the deafening explosion as it hit the earth near the road. Suddenly the terrified horses bolted and began to dash down the road, as the driver shouted and tried desperately to bring the panic-stricken animals under control. He remembered hearing an ear-splitting crack, after which they capsized as they hit a shell hole.

After that, he couldn't remember anything until he was aroused by a woman and a young girl speaking French, as they pulled him from the wreckage. He was later told by the women that they had come upon the scene some time after it had happened. He was the only survivor, having been thrown clear, and they had found him lying unconscious a few feet away from the wreck. The driver and the other two wounded men had been crushed by the vehicle as it rolled over into the ditch alongside the road. The horses had broken loose and were grazing nearby.

Madame Fournier and her 13-year-old daughter, Celestine, as he had later learned the names of his two rescuers, managed to capture the two horses and with great difficulty were able to get him onto the back of one and bring him to their farm a few kilometers away.

Upon arriving at their home, they took him down from the horse's back and laid him on the ground near the house. Madame Fournier fetched a basin of water and began to wash him, which partially roused him to consciousness.

"*Parlez-vous Francais?*" questioned the woman as she continued to cleanse him.

Herbert, having learned some basic French in his school days, responded with great effort, "*Je parle seulement un peu le Français.*" (I only speak very little French).

By this time, Celestine having returned from putting away and feeding the horses, asked her mother in rapid French, "What are we going to do with him, Mama?"

"First, we get him out of these filthy clothes, see to his wound, perhaps help him to take a little nourishment, and then put him into bed."

"Yes, but then what after that?"

"Some of the neighboring farms have been using German prisoners for farm work, and when he is well enough, we shall do the same. We shall tell anyone who asks we acquired him through the system. Anyone can see that two women need help to manage this place."

"Is that why we rescued him? Don't we hate the Germans?" pressed her daughter.

"It's war, and even though he is the enemy for now, he is a human being. He is lucky we found him and not the Resistance or a French soldier. He would have been shot or bayoneted where he lay by any of them. Also, with his injury, he probably wouldn't survive the care he would receive if we had turned him over to the military. But, Celestine, you must tell no one about this. We could be arrested and perhaps shot as traitors," cautioned her mother.

Later, when this conversation was related to him by Celestine, Herbert marveled at their compassion and felt boundless gratitude for his good luck in having been found by these two Christian women. This experience would affect him for the rest of his life.

§§§

Madame Fournier was a farmer's widow, her husband having died of consumption when Celestine was seven. Having grown up on a farm, she was practiced in caring for sick and injured animals. She cleansed and inspected Herbert's injured knee and determined that the bullet was still lodged under the kneecap in the joint. She informed Herbert of this and explained that if he wished her to take care of it, she would do the best she could, or she could turn him over to the authorities and he must then take the chance on receiving adequate professional care. Enlisting the help of the local doctor from the nearby village would be out of the question, as he likely would turn him over to the military or to the Resistance.

After a few moments of considering his options, he responded that his father was a doctor, and as a boy he had learned something about anatomy from him. He asked her to help him sit up in order that he might look at the wound himself. After the two of them had examined the wound, Herbert decided the two of them could take care of it themselves, as he could see he was in the hands of a very capable woman.

Madame Fournier, pleased he had decided to place himself in her hands, set about preparing for the surgery. She told Celestine to fetch a sheet and put a kettle of water on the stove. Then they began to rip the sheet in strips to be boiled. She went to the storage shed and gathered some knives used in butchering hogs and sheep. She heated these in the fire of the kitchen stove and fetched two bottles of cognac from the cellar.

She had Herbert undress and put on one of her nightgowns, and with her help, he hobbled to the long kitchen table, where he took a seat. She then poured a tall glass of cognac and instructed him to drink as much as he could, as she had no anesthesia. She and her daughter watched him as he began to show the effects of the alcohol, and when he seemed almost at the point of falling forward, they helped him lie down on the table.

"Are you ready, Monsieur? I am sorry I have no proper medication or ether for you."

"Yes, Madame."

"Celestine, bring him more cognac," she instructed her daughter.

After he had drunk the glass of cognac, he felt the warmth of the alcohol overtake him and his eyelids were almost closed. She then had him lie down on the table. When he dropped off to sleep, Madame Fournier set her mouth in a grim line of determination and began her grisly work.

The Hotchkiss machine gun on the tank that wounded Herbert fired an 8mm bullet which was lodged in his knee between the kneecap and the joint. After cleaning the wound and using cognac as a disinfectant, Madame Fournier could see that in order to remove the bullet, she would have to separate the kneecap from the knee. She then realized that this task would be beyond her ability. As she probed in the damaged flesh, her patient suddenly began to scream and writhe on the table. She called to her daughter to fetch a rope from the workshop. In the meantime, she managed to get him to swallow more cognac. When Celestine returned with the clothesline she had found, they tied Herbert to the table in order that the wound could be thoroughly cleaned and bandaged. She gently cut away fragments of putrid tissue and then packed the wound with strips of the sterilized sheet which had been dried in her oven and bound the knee.

Bathed in perspiration and exhausted from the surgery, Madame Fournier collapsed into a chair and observed that Herbert was still in a deep sleep. She allowed herself a glass of cognac as she observed her work. Rather than move him, she decided, with Celestine's help, to roll him slightly halfway in one direction, and then the other, and remove the bloody materials. She placed a clean sheet under him and covered him with a light blanket, leaving him loosely tied to the table. Later when he awakened they would put him in the bed in the next room. Celestine urged her mother to get some rest and she would stay with the patient

During the following days, Madame Fournier and her daughter helped their guest recover himself to the point where he was able to sit up, take nourishment, and in broken French tell them how he came to be lying by the wrecked ambulance where they found him. At first, the pain could only be curtailed by the use of cognac, both drunk as a painkiller and as an antiseptic when his bandages were changed. Finally, however, the wound healed to the point that this was no longer needed.

Chapter Forty-five

Convalescence and Friendship

Eckhardt read and reread Ursula's letter reporting Detlev's death. In the months after returning to his mother's home near Blaubeuren, he had heard with great anxiety about the scourge of Spanish Influenza that continued to sweep through the country, and to descend upon the hapless poor in the cities. Their living conditions, already taxed to the limit because of the shortages and deprivation of war, were now almost unbearable in the face of this added tragedy. When he learned from Ursula of her brother's and sister's deaths soon after he left Berlin, he was anguished because he was not there to help lighten the burden on his beloved wife and her mother.

Now, as if a hideous joke were being played by some demon on their family, it was the husband and father who was taken.

His reaction, as he took in the awful news was one of grief and rage, similar to what Ursula said her mother was feeling. They, and many others across Europe, were outraged at what their government had imposed upon them, offering very little assistance to cope with this added ghastliness. Many began to question their faith and blame their sorrows on God and even to question His very existence.

Thus far, the pandemic had spared many in the countryside and in the small villages, due to less crowded conditions and cleaner air. Consequently, Eckhardt, was on the one hand grateful to be recovering from the damage caused by the gas, and grateful that his mother and siblings were not affected, but on the other he felt guilty that his wife and her family remained in grave danger.

As spring arrived, the countryside around Blaubeuren brought forth its display of wildflowers that turned the fields and farmsteads into a medley of color. Red poppies covered the landscape as far as the eye could see. Fruit trees were bedecked with pink and white blossoms and the air was fragrant with their perfume. As he and his mother walked by the spring pond, the *Blautopf* (blue pot), and watched the ducks and swans on the sapphire blue surface, while hearing the muffled thud of the hammer mill in the background, it was easy to imagine that they were returned to a more peaceful and idyllic time. He recalled how he as a small boy, along with his siblings, would take this same stroll on summer evenings with his mother when his father was away. She would tell them stories about her girlhood in this same community, and how she would attend dances in the cultural hall upstairs in *Gasthaus Krone* where she was much sought after by the young men for dances.

She would even relate how she fell in love with their father. He had been the best dancer and was very charming and handsome. She never spoke negatively of him before her children. Only as they grew older and began to see for themselves how alcoholism had gradually overtaken him, and how abusive he had become, did they lose respect and affection for him.

She would also tell about the history of Blaubeuren. Sometimes they would hike up to the ruins of the castle *Hohengerhausen* overlooking the valley and the town of Blaubeuren-Gerhausen. As he recalled those times from his childhood and his growing up years, the horrors of war and disease seemed for a moment suspended and pushed far away.

But his time in this lovely place was drawing to a close, and he knew that soon he must return to Berlin and help take some of the burden off his wife's and mother-in-law's shoulders. His condition although much improved, was still overshadowed by a threatening cough and shortness of breath. Mornings, soon after awakening, were especially bad, and he had lost a great deal of weight, which he could not seem to regain, even though he was being reasonably well fed. Most of all, the peace and lifestyle of his surroundings had given him a much-needed psychological boost, and he was convinced he had made the right decision to come here when he did.

§§§

Herbert continued to mend slowly, but soon he was able to assist with light chores on the little farm. His hostess, although an unsophisticated country woman, showed herself to be a warm and compassionate person and had obviously passed these characteristics on to her daughter. Over time, the doctor's son and the farmer's widow found that although separated by nationality, language and social background, they nevertheless had many qualities in common. Herbert had never taken social standing seriously, much to his mother's chagrin, and Madame Fournier from childhood on had been interested in other people and was always ready to help them with their concerns.

Little by little, they had learned to appreciate one another, and Herbert was also able to enjoy a surrogate "little sister" in Celestine, who soon came to idolize him. Madame Fournier explained that she had a brother, who was in the French army, who would hopefully be returning after the war. Herbert then went on to reveal his relationship with Meira, which greatly interested the woman. Herbert was grateful for her interest, which never in any way indicated a romantic attraction, as she being a devout Catholic was still in love with her deceased husband, which was revealed when she spoke of him.

He, on the other hand, was loyal in his heart to Meira, whom he loved and missed deeply. He was very grieved not to be able to communicate with her, his friends in Berlin, nor his family, as such a revelation would bring immediate retribution and disaster upon himself and his benefactress – him for not reporting in and for desertion, and her for harboring an enemy alien.

§§§

When it came time to cultivate, plant and harvest, Herbert was kept out of sight, and on occasion when neighbors dropped by, he was rushed into the root cellar beneath the kitchen floor. He did, however, prove himself to be helpful mending and maintaining tools and harnesses. He assisted Celestine caring for the horses, pigs, chickens and sheep, and he soon learned about grooming and shearing. He also was helpful in the kitchen when the women were occupied with farm work.

One day, during the second summer while he was kneading bread, he happened to glance out the kitchen window and saw a French officer coming up the path on a motorcycle. Herbert immediately dropped to the floor and reached for the nearby root cellar trap door and lowered himself down the stairs just as the officer dismounted from his machine and stepped up to the door. The man knocked several times, peered through the window, and then slid an envelope under the door, not seeing a flour handprint that Herbert had left. As soon as it was clear, Herbert cautiously emerged from the cellar and picked up the envelope. He could see that it was an official correspondence from the French military.

When Madame Fournier and her daughter returned later that afternoon from selling produce in the nearby village marketplace, Herbert informed them of what had transpired earlier. When she opened the envelope, she read that her brother had been slightly wounded at the front, and after being treated in a military hospital would be granted a two-week convalescent leave. This posed a new dilemma. How were they to deal with Herbert when her brother returned home?

A week after receiving the letter, Madame Fournier decided to trust her parish priest with her secret. She appealed to his Christian sense of charity and pointed out that she only needed a sanctuary for two weeks. At first, he rejected the idea of having anything to do with hiding a German soldier. Then it occurred to her to remind him of the parable of the Good Samaritan by pointing out that Herbert was indeed like the man found beaten and wounded by the side of the road, and she was the Samaritan who bound up his wounds. The old priest was thoughtful for a few moments, and then relented.

"Alright. I will take him in for two weeks, but you must never reveal this to anyone under pain of death."

"I swear to you in God's name that this will go with me to my grave" she assured him.

Relieved and overjoyed, she knelt before the old man and kissed his hand.

The day before her brother's arrival, she waited until well past ten o'clock in the evening. Taking a supply of food, she slowly guided Herbert down a lane through the dark woods to the priest's small quarters—the manse—at the back of the church. He also had a backpack with a change of clothing and two blankets. Tapping lightly on the door of the manse, the old priest opened and whispered that they should quickly enter. Herbert was shown into a small storeroom where he would sleep behind the tiny kitchen.

"It's very important when services are being conducted in the chapel, you must not make a sound and stay in your hiding place" he was warned by the priest.

"You have my word," Herbert replied. "I'm very grateful for your kindness, and I'll make every effort not to be a burden or bring danger to you or Madame Fournier."

After once again kneeling and giving gratitude and promising to bring more food as needed, Madame Fournier departed. The two men regarded each other without a word, and then retired to their respective beds.

In the days that followed, Herbert and the old priest came to know something of one another's feelings about faith and religion. Herbert soon observed that his not being Catholic seemed to make no difference to his host. A good deal of the time, the priest was away making calls and seeing to pastoral duties among the members of his flock. In the evening they shared simple meals, often comprised of no more than bread and cheese, taken with a glass of simple red wine. After supper, they sometimes played chess, at which the priest proved himself to be superior. Sometimes they would discuss the war, the priest showing great patience with Herbert's rudimentary French. They shared the view that their respective countries were wasting their greatest human resources. At the end of his two-week stay, Herbert was very impressed to have made the acquaintance of a man who lived what he professed to believe.

Madame Fournier's brother's leave was passed without incident. Only once did the conversation veer off in a dangerous direction, and that was on the evening before he was to return to his unit.

While venting bitterness and hatred of the enemy, he was interrupted by Celestine who spoke up defiantly, "They are only young men like you doing what they are told, and they have mothers and families, too!" She was stopped when she saw her mother frown and subtly shake her head.

Her uncle, startled by the outburst, said, “Where did she get such ideas?”

“Celestine is very tenderhearted, and she has seen more than a child her age should ever see. She gets very upset when anyone mentions the war.” Turning to her daughter, she chided, “That’s enough, Celestine. I think it’s time we all went to bed.”

When Madame Fournier later related this conversation to Herbert, he smiled, and his gratitude to this good woman and her daughter for their loyalty to him was greatly increased.

Chapter Forty-six

Joyous Reunion

Herbert was roused from his memories by Madame Fournier bustling about helping him get ready to leave. She explained she would take him in her horse-drawn cart to the villa several kilometers away where the German headquarters had been housed. As they prepared to leave, he noticed Celestine standing by with tears in her eyes. As he followed her mother out the door, the girl ran to him and embraced him, exclaiming, "Oh, Monsieur Herbert, please don't forget us."

Herbert choked up and was moved with the realization that he and this little family had grown very close to each other, and the bond of common humanity had transcended the barrier of war. He recalled Eckhardt telling of the Christmas truce of 1914, and could now relate to the emotions the men on both sides must have felt.

He assured Celestine that he would come back someday, when peace had healed the present animosity between their two nations. As he followed Madame Fournier to the cart, he noted that she too was misty-eyed, and he reached forward and patted her on the shoulder.

As they proceeded along the road leading to the front, he was glad that he was able to wear some of Madame Fournier's deceased husband's clothing, which drew no unwanted attention from French soldiers, who made room for their cart to pass as they returned from the front.

"What will you do now, Monsieur?"

"First, I must report in to my regiment and be mustered out. I will then notify my family and friends that I will be returning home. They surely must have all given me up for dead. But there's a certain girl I need to find."

Madame Fournier smiled at hearing this, and quipped, "You will be like Lazarus to them."

They both had a chuckle at this observation and continued on.

After another hour, they came in sight of the villa set back from the road where smoke could be seen issuing from one of the chimneys, and soldiers dressed in the German field gray uniforms scurrying about loading boxes and supplies on waiting trucks parked in the yard. As they drew up to the open entrance gate to the estate, Herbert could see that his friend and benefactress was uneasy being near so many erstwhile enemy troops.

"It's alright, Madame. You can let me off here and I can manage to get to the house. I cannot thank you enough for what you have done for me, and I promise to keep in contact with you. I hope someday to bring my Meira to meet you. You'll like Meira. She's a very warm-hearted person and she'll want to thank you herself for saving me for her."

He extended his hand, and she took it in both of hers and replied, "I am very glad I met you, Monsieur. You are a fine young man, and you tell your girl she is very lucky to have you. I am glad Celestine could meet you and know there are good people everywhere. It will be good when we can forget the propaganda we are told and understand this as well. She has a bit of a crush on you, you know," Madame Fournier added as an afterthought.

At this Herbert smiled again and took her hand in both of his. As he turned and hobbled up the drive, he was filled with many thoughts about the incredible experience he had had, and the French people he had come to know and love. He turned once more and saw Madame Fournier sitting in the cart watching him walk away. Seeing him, she waved, and he waved in return. She then turned the cart around and headed back the way they had come.

When two young soldiers caught sight of the crippled soldier making his way up the drive, they stopped what they were doing and rushed to help him. As they entered the building, it was apparent that everyone was moving about vacating the premises in their eagerness to be done with the war and return to their homes and families. Herbert was taken to what had until recently been the clerk's office, where men were burning documents in the fireplace. One of his helpers called to a middle-aged man who was emptying file cabinets along the wall,

"Are you in charge here? This man needs to report into his unit, which he says is connected to this office."

The man stopped and walked over to desk near the window. "Sit down and let's get this over with," he directed. "At this stage of the game, it's just a formality anyway."

Herbert thanked his two helpers and sat in the chair before the desk. "I need your *Soldat Buch* (soldier identification),"

"I'm sorry, but I don't have it."

Herbert then identified himself and told his incredible story.

When he finished, the clerk eyed him with suspicion and except for his obvious injury, would have suggested that he might be a deserter. When this was hinted at, Herbert explained that he had just been let off by Madame Fournier and if necessary, she could vouch for him.

"You expect me to believe the word of a Frenchie? Were you sleeping with her?" he suggested. "In addition to your other problems, that would be considered fraternization with the enemy."

At this Herbert bristled. "She's a fine woman and I owe my life to her. You just said this is merely a formality."

The harried clerk considered this for a moment, then said, "Oh, to hell with it. The war's over. Let's just get your discharge papers drawn up and send you on your way.

Then he said, "Wait a minute. You say your name is Lenz, Herbert Lenz?

There was nurse who came in here about a year ago looking for a guy by that name. I remember because she said she was serving over in some town on the Somme as a nurse and she came back a few times. She was a pretty thing, Jewish I think. What was her name?" he muttered to himself.

Then turning to one of the other men putting papers into the fireplace, he asked, "*Du, Hor*st, what was the name of that nurse who came in here several times looking for a Herbert Lenz. Said he had gone missing and she had come out here to serve at the field hospital in order to look for him. Craziest thing we ever heard of! What was her name?"

After thinking about it for a moment, the man turned and said, "Friedlander, Meira Friedlander. I remember because I'm from Hellersdorf near Berlin and there's a fancy store on Ku'damm named 'Friedlanders'."

When Herbert heard this, he felt he had been struck by lightning. He turned to the man and asked, "Are you sure about that? What did she look like?"

"Very lovely. Beautiful black hair and stunning blue eyes."

Excited by this information, Herbert asked, "Where is this hospital you mentioned?"

The clerk spoke up, "Not far. About 15 kilometers west of here. Let's finish up your discharge papers and we can get someone to drive you over there."

Herbert was on the edge of his chair and could hardly contain himself as his papers were typed, signed and stamped. After what seemed an eternity, he thanked the clerk and his assistant for the wonderful news and made his way to the entrance, where a staff car had been drawn up. The drive to the field hospital seemed to take hours, when in reality it was only about half an hour.

As they drew up before the entrance of the hospital, Herbert had his door half open and nearly fell out in his rush to go inside. He thanked the driver and hobbled into the building. He went to the front desk and inquired after Meira Friedlander and was told she was in the garden at the back of the building assisting a convalescent to take a stroll.

He made his way to the rear door of the hospital as quickly as he could manage on his crutch. The weather had warmed unseasonably for November, and he could see several patients in wheelchairs and on crutches being assisted by nurses in the garden. He stood on the landing and looked carefully at the nurses. Then he caught sight of her. She was helping support a young man slowly walking toward the building.

"Meira!" he shouted.

She looked up and paused while she studied the face of the gaunt, shabbily dressed civilian on the back landing. Finally, the dawn of recognition came to her and she turned ashen white.

"Herbert!" she cried.

He started to descend the steps when she shouted, "Wait. We'll be right there!"

Ignoring her command, he continued to hobble down the steps and continue as quickly as he could in her direction. She was unable to run to him because of the patient leaning on her for support. When they were within arms-length of each other, Herbert reached out to her and grasping her by one shoulder, leaned forward and kissed her.

The young patient stared wide-eyed at this drama and then murmured, "Excuse me. Would you like me to go on by myself? I'm sure I'll be alright."

"You'll do no such thing, comrade. I'll help you on the other side."

Herbert moved to the other side of the man and put his right arm around his waist. The odd trio then proceeded to the entrance of the building with Meira, now dissolved in tears, on the right side of the patient and Herbert on the left. When they reached the doorway, Meira called for assistance, and when another nurse took over, she released the patient, who by this time was smiling ear to ear. As he moved down the hall, he called over his shoulder to Herbert, "Good job, comrade."

Herbert and Meira then fell into each other's arms and tearfully embraced.

"I can't believe this. Where have you been?" she stammered

"It's a long story, and I have the rest of my life to tell you about it. Will you marry me?" he answered.

"Yes, yes, yes, my darling. I want to spend the rest of my life hearing you tell about this miracle. Over and over and over."

Chapter Forty-seven

Heimkehr
(Return Home)

Eckhardt watched his mother wave until she was out of sight as the train pulled out of the little station in Blaubeuren. He would change trains in Ulm for the long journey back to Berlin. He regretted leaving his mother just before Christmas, but he felt the need to see Ursula and be there with her and Christina and Rudi for the first peacetime Christmas in five years. As the train moved through the Swabian countryside, he knew he would miss his tranquil homeland, but at the same time, he knew his destiny was now bound up with the great capital. He could sense relief among his countrymen that the horror of war was finally at an end, but also an apprehension of what the future might hold for this exhausted land.

When he boarded the train in Ulm, it was crowded with troops of a beaten army anxious to put the battlefield behind them, and a wistfulness caused by the memories of fallen comrades who would not be returning with them. He could imagine that the victors were just as eager to return to their homes, but with the exuberance of victory instead the despair of defeat. However, the knowledge that this was a one-way trip homeward, without the dread of returning to the front lifted their spirits. Also, the cessation of war, together with the abatement of the horrible flu pandemic helped bring a general sense of gratitude for life and the prospects for the future.

Late in the evening of the third day of travel, the train arrived in the Lehrter Station, and after the off-loading of the injured, the other passengers were able to disembark. Eckhardt expected to have to wait before he could see Ursula, but to his surprise, she was standing in the crowd closest to the train. Wordlessly, they pushed toward one another and with muffled gasps of "Oh, my darling" and "Sweetheart" enfolded each other in a long, impassioned embrace.

"Oh, Ursula, how I've missed you. You look more beautiful than I remember you."

She smiled at this, knowing that poor nourishment, exhaustion, the ordeal of illness and grief for the loss of loved ones were surely to be seen in her face, but she was grateful for hearing him say it.

"You also look much better than when you left" she replied. "Apparently the good country air and your mother's cooking has brought back the handsome hero I remember."

Arm in arm they walked out into the winter sunshine and proceeded to the tram stop. When they reached Leopoldplatz, they walked toward the apartment building. However, in spite of their elation and excitement, it soon became clear to Ursula that Eckhardt did not have the spring in his step she remembered. Indeed, as they passed a park bench, he apologized and requested that they sit for a moment while he caught his breath.

"That's the thing I just can't seem to shake off. I'm so short of breath, and I have coughing attacks that take all my energy, usually in the morning" he explained.

Ursula registered this information with deep concern, but sat beside him without comment. After a few minutes, they continued on their way, and his enthusiasm seemed to return as they entered the building and made their way upstairs. They entered Christina's kitchen and were greeted by a rush of warm air.

"Mama has been hoarding some briquettes she managed to find on one of her recent foraging trips, in order to have the place comfortable for your return, and she has even found some real coffee – heaven knows where."

His spirits were greatly lifted by the warm kitchen and the cup of coffee Ursula set before him. Eckhardt was overcome by a rush of gratitude for her and having been spared to see her and for the end of a seemingly endless war. He had been sure many times he would not survive it.

As he watched his wife sitting across from him and gazing adoringly at him, he reached across the table and took both her hands in his and murmured, "God was generous giving you to me. I will live the rest of my life doing everything I can to be worthy of you."

Chapter Forty-eight

Home at Last Together

Meira urged Herbert to allow one of her colleagues, an experienced orthopedic surgeon with whom she had with worked many times at the front, to examine his injury. It might be possible to remove the bullet. At first, he was reluctant to go through another surgery, and the following period of healing and rehabilitation, but finally he could see the wisdom of not trying to go through life with the offending thing inside him.

His surgery was scheduled for two days after his arrival, and he had the procedure explained to him by the surgeon, a kindly middle-aged man, who thought very highly of Meira. The man even went so far as to state that she was the nurse he held in highest regard, and under pressure of dealing with overwhelming numbers of wounded, she had been the stalwart of the surgical team.

Herbert was in complete agreement with the doctor's opinion of her, and inwardly congratulated himself again for having been able to win her love. He recalled how she had conducted herself after the confrontation with her father. She had been so determined to find him, that she left everything behind, and unflinchingly took on the hardships at the front.

The surgery went very well, and when he came out from under the anesthesia, after being violently nauseous and vomiting, he was relieved to see Meira bending over him wiping his brow with a cold damp cloth.

"Congratulations, darling. You did very well on the table and you are now free of that obscene thing."

She smiled and assured him that the doctor would be along to see him when he was finished with another more serious surgery. Herbert was surprised that after being able to swallow some warm broth, he felt immediately better – much better than after Madame Fournier had operated on him. Soon, as promised, the surgeon appeared and shook his hand.

"Well, young man, you should be up and around after a couple of weeks – on crutches at first of course. I was amazed when I heard that a French farmwife had operated on you before. She did a surprisingly good job, considering the circumstances she was working under. She should be congratulated for helping you avoid a serious infection, which could have finished you off. I can't promise that the knee will ever be one hundred percent, but you should be able to get around without a cane if you exercise the leg regularly."

"Will I be able to dance again?"

"Whoa! One thing at a time! It's too soon to predict that. But amazing things can happen if you're determined to help your body heal. And who knows? With this wonderful girl to help you, you're very lucky indeed."

He smiled, shook Herbert's hand and left.

Herbert looked at his sweetheart, now his betrothed, with pride and joy.

As Herbert convalesced, Meira assisted with the last patients to be treated before the staff began to vacate the hospital and prepare to return it to the French medical authorities. Then the day arrived, when he and some others were transported to the nearest railway station to board the train, which would take them over the border into Germany, where their coaches would be switched to trains of the *Reichsbahn*, (German railways).

Meira accompanied him all the way, and they gazed out the window as the German countryside swept past. As they passed through towns and cities, they noticed that everyone boarding and leaving the train seemed to be shabbily dressed and had an air of despair and resignation about them. Even though the peace was a relief to everyone, the defeat of the war had undermined their spirits.

Finally, though, they arrived in Berlin in the Görlitzer Railway Station. Meira and Herbert gazed at the cavernous interior of the terminal, and as if they had read one another's thoughts, they both began to speak in one voice.

"I'm sorry, darling. You go ahead," he said to Meira.

"I was just thinking about that beautiful August day five years ago when Ursula and I were here at this same station to see you and

Eckhardt off to the front. Everyone was excited, and the bands were playing as if you were going off on a holiday excursion. What fools we were!"

"I know. It's hard to believe we were ever that young and naïve. If we had had any idea what we were getting into, I wonder if we wouldn't have run like hell!"

They smiled at one another, grateful to be together and home at last.

Chapter Forty-nine

Shame

By the time hostilities had come to an end, Germany was a nation in upheaval. After the Emperor abdicated in November 1918, and the Imperial government had collapsed, the Social Democrat, Philipp Scheidemann, proclaimed a Republic on November 9. The new government concluded an armistice with the Allies two days later on November 11, 1918, which in reality was a surrender, as the Allies kept up the food blockade to exercise their control. The German Empire was finished, and was succeeded by a deeply flawed democracy, the Weimar Republic, so-called because its first constitutional assembly took place in the city of Weimar.

The unrest that had preceded the armistice began in October, 1918, in northern Germany in Kiel, where civilian dock workers led a revolt and persuaded many sailors to join them. This rebellion then spread to other cities, laying the groundwork for the leftist movement in Germany, which from the outset was not supportive of the newly formed Weimar Republic. The mainstay of the new government was to be found among members of the General Staff, and the business and middle classes, not among the working class. The conflict between these groups remained a source of discontent and hostility for many years.

The Treaty of Versailles was signed in the Hall of Mirrors in the palace of Versailles outside Paris on June 28, 1919, almost exactly five years after the assassination of Archduke Franz Ferdinand in Sarajevo. Among the 70 delegates from 26 nations who participated in the negotiations, representatives from Germany were not included. Historians still debate over the fairness or harshness of the treaty. Although the word *guilt* was not used, it did serve as a legal basis to force Germany to pay reparations for the war.

One of the most controversial points of the treaty, Article 231, specified:

"The Allied and Associated Governments affirm that Germany accepts the responsibility of Germany and her allies for causing all the loss and damage to which the Allied and Associated Governments and their nationals have been subjected as a consequence of the war imposed upon them by the aggression of Germany and her allies."

This understandably aroused great opposition among Germans, who viewed this as a national humiliation by forcing them to accept full responsibility for causing the war. The American diplomat John Foster Dulles – one of the two authors of the article – later stated that the wording used was unfortunate, in that it aggravated and offended the German people. Other commentators have suggested that the treaty was flawed to the extent, that instead of preventing future wars, it in fact made a future war unavoidable, and that it became the basic cause for the Second World War.

§§§

"Frederika, did you hear me? Herbert is alive and on the way home."

Frederika Lenz stared at the phone in the library at Schloß Hohenberg. She was speechless to hear from her husband, that after all this time, her son was coming home. She had prayed and hoped for such news as she had just received, and now that it had finally come, she was caught off balance and couldn't think of how to reply. Then all the pent-up feelings that she had pushed down inside burst forth.

"Oh, darling, of course I hear you, but for a moment I couldn't trust my ears. Where is he? When did you hear from him? When is he coming home?"

"Hold on! Slow down! I got a call from him this morning and tried to reach you, but with all the confusion going on with the end of the war, the phone lines are overloaded. He was just leaving a hospital in France and is heading back to Berlin on a train as we speak. He is coming back with a young lady from Berlin. Her name is Meira

Friedlander, a daughter of Benjamin Friedlander, the owner of Friedlander's on Kurfürstendamm.

This was met with a long silence. Her husband prompted her again. "Did you hear me?

"Friedlander? Aren't they Jewish?"

Her husband sighed as he heard indignation rising in her voice. He had anticipated such a response, and now considered how best to reply to it.

"Now, darling, wait until you have heard about all the circumstances. I can't really explain it well over the phone. It's quite a story, and I think you should come back to Berlin and hear it from Herbert himself."

"Yes, Karlheinz and I will be coming on the next available train. I've been meaning to bring him home soon in any case. When my father died in the influenza epidemic last month, Karlheinz took it very hard and needs to get away from here for a while."

"Yes, I think that would be wise. As I told you at the time, I'm sorry I couldn't be with you when you buried your father. We were so overwhelmed here with the epidemic and war wounded being sent back from the front."

"I know, Sweetheart. I told you then I understood, and I do. Don't give it another thought. Let's open up the house again. I think I need to get things back in order there. I'm glad we have been able to be here during the terrible times there in the city, but you, poor darling, have had to cope with that alone. But the war is over now, and with Herbert coming home, I want to be there. I'll call you or send a telegram when I know our definite arrival time. Don't worry about meeting us, if it's not possible. We can get a taxi. We can let ourselves into the house. I'm eager to see you again, and with Herbert coming home, we should have a celebration. I love you, darling."

He hung up the phone, excited to have his family together again, but apprehensive about how to help his wife accept the relationship between their son and his fiancé. He had purposely withheld that part of the news.

§§§

Edna Friedlander read and reread the letter from her sister, which she had taken from her post office box, which she had acquired after her father had forbade her and her mother to have any contact with Meira. Edna's reaction to the news that Herbert Lenz had proposed to Meira was mixed. On the one hand, she was happy for her sister having found the man she loved, the reason for which she had joined the nursing corps at the front. But on the other hand, she dreaded what her father would do if he learned what had she had done. She could not accept his command to consider Meira no longer part of the family. She then resolved to never reveal that she had remained in contact with her sister with her mother's full knowledge and support.

She hurried home in order to speak to her mother, before her father came home. As she entered the house, she went straight to the kitchen where her mother was sitting at the window gazing out at the garden. She bent and kissed Golda on the cheek, and then, taking her hand in both of her own, declared, "Meira is coming home. She's coming with Herbert Lenz!"

Her mother looked at her wide-eyed with wonder and joy. "Praise God! Finally! I have prayed for this moment."

But then a frown crossed her brow, as she lowered her voice to inquire, "What do you mean coming with that boy? I thought he'd been missing for two years and was presumed dead."

"Yes, Mama, but Meira never gave up on him and refused to accept that. Let me read what she wrote:

> *'He showed up at my field hospital injured and on crutches. My heart leapt for joy and I knew in that moment my effort in coming out here hadn't been in vain. After we embraced, he proposed to me on the spot, and we are to be married as soon as we can return to Berlin. His knee is almost healed from his most recent operation. When I see you, I will tell you the most incredible story of how he was saved and hidden by a French widow and her daughter on their farm. But for now, I am just grateful he is alive and I have him back.'*

Golda Friedlander studied her fingernails as her daughter concluded reading the letter, and asked "Do you want to read it for yourself, or shall I burn it, as I have all the others we've received from her?"

"Yes, I want to read it and we shall not burn it. I'll give it to your father to read as well. I will no longer ignore my child. Your father can do as he sees fit, but I will write Meira tonight and tell her I'm sorry I haven't contacted her in all this time.

As for her young man, he will be my son-in-law, and I will embrace him as such."

Edna looked with astonishment at her mother. She had known, that the shunning of her sister had caused her mother great anguish and grief, as well as to herself. She had learned to see her mother in a new light. She was not the obedient Jewish wife, after all.

"I agree with you, Mama. I'm proud of you, and I'll stand by you. And I will tell Papa so."

Chapter Fifty

Karlheinz

Karlheinz Lenz walked around the perimeter of the garden at Schloß Hohenberg and thought about the events of the past several months. He felt an overwhelming sense of loss with the death of his uncle, Michael Friedrich von Hohenberg, during the battle of Amiens in northern France in the previous August, and more recently the loss of his grandfather, Graf von Hohenberg. His grandmother's condition had deteriorated alarmingly as a result, and now with the announcement of the Armistice, which in reality had been a German surrender, Karlheinz felt the secure world he had known since childhood falling apart.

But the remarkable news that his mother had received from his father this morning redirected his thoughts. His brother Herbert was alive and coming home! Karlheinz was ashamed to admit to himself that he had mixed feelings about this, as he had always felt that he was the overlooked child in the family.

Herbert's optimism and open-mindedness had long been a cause of simmering envy and resentment for the younger son. He could not bring forth the easy confidence and self-assuredness that seemed to come so easily to Herbert. Indeed, he already felt he was being pushed into the background with the homecoming of his older brother.

As he walked around the grounds of the estate, he thought of the sadness that had overcome him when his mother announced they would be returning to the capital as soon as possible. He recalled the summer days of his childhood when his grandfather had taken him to the fields and workshops of the estate. He had always looked forward to the sense of escape and freedom he experienced when he left the city with his parents. Unlike his brother, Karlheinz was not a social person, and preferred the solitude and peace he enjoyed as he walked through the woods and fields.

He had completed his Abitur the previous spring and turned eighteen just before his grandfather's death and had expected to be placed in the upcoming enrollment at the Prussian War College. But with the ending of the war, that would now no longer be a possibility. So, all in all, he felt more adrift than ever before in his life.

Chapter Fifty-one

Added Despair

Ursula watched her mother descend the stairs from her flat to go forth on her excursion in the search of food. Since the deaths of her youngest daughter and son, and thereafter the death of her husband, Christina Bellon had become withdrawn, and no longer exhibited the determination and resilience that had been an example for the rest of the family. Indeed, she no longer seemed interested in what was going on around her, except for the circumstances surrounding Rudi, her eldest and only surviving son.

She still managed to acquire the bare necessities for the table, but there was no longer the excitement that she had always shown, when she heard of an opportunity to obtain some rare commodity.

Upon his return from Blaubeuren, Eckhardt, too, had commented on the big change in his mother-in-law. But he and Ursula agreed that the general despondency which affected Christina, was also to be seen in the eyes of nearly everyone around them. The wrenching changes that had taken place in the country was taking its toll. In addition to horrendous losses suffered by the army, the even greater devastation caused by deaths among both soldiers and civilians during the influenza pandemic, the collapse of the Imperial government, and most recently the defeat suffered at the hands of the Allies, all were so overwhelming that many among the population felt perhaps all was lost never to be restored. The German people had hoped that with the ending of hostilities, the food blockade would be ended. But when it was learned this was not to be for the foreseeable future, many simply gave up hope.

Like everyone else, Ursula's family suffered through the beginning months of 1919 with hope for a return of better times, but after the Treaty of Versailles was signed in Paris on June 28, the shock of the terms, which laid most if not all the blame for the start of the war at the feet of Germany, caused widespread disbelief and outrage. Radical movements began to gain traction throughout the country, among them the Communist Party, which had been founded during the January Revolt of 1918.

Chapter Fifty-two

The Way Back

As Herbert and Meira made their way through the crowded corridors of the train, they realized that finding a seat for the both of them would be virtually impossible. However, as soldiers standing outside the overfilled compartments and in the vestibules caught sight of Herbert on his crutches, they grudgingly moved aside to allow him to pass. He and Meira finally found a corner near one of the lavatories, where he was able to lean against the wall. Meira stood close to him and braced herself against him to take some pressure off his injured knee.

After a period of time, as the train moved through southern Germany, soldiers began to disembark as they reached their destinations. Meira periodically walked through the train in search of an empty seat. Then, in one of the open coaches she saw two women rising and beginning to collect their bags and bundles. She approached them and explained her situation, and on hearing of Herbert's injured leg, they agreed to stay in place to allow Meira to hurry back and bring Herbert to the seat. They both thanked the women profusely, and Herbert was at long last able to take the load off his distressed knee. He stretched out his leg and, in spite of the pain, fell almost immediately into an exhausted sleep. Meira sat next to him and rested her head on his shoulder. She too, was soon fast asleep.

After a few hours of fitful sleep, Meira awoke and took stock of their situation. She had brought bread, cheese and some sausages, along with a bottle of French wine to sustain them. When Herbert roused himself, he admitted being very hungry. Meira was greatly encouraged by this and regarded his appetite as a sign he was healing well. They allowed themselves small portions of their precious food, as it had to last until they reached Berlin the following midday. As she sliced off small portions of bread and cheese, Meira caught a glimpse of a small boy and girl seated across the aisle. She observed the little boy licking his lips.

"They're hungry" she whispered to Herbert.

He turned to look at the children and replied, "Well, we have to share."

Like most children in Europe at the time, they were gaunt from hunger, but she didn't know how to make the food last to the end of their journey. Nevertheless, she gave a small slice of cheese and bread with a sausage cut in half to each child. The grateful mother smiled and murmured a thanks to Meira. When offered an equal portion, the young mother thanked her, but refused and stated she and her children would be arriving at their destination later that evening.

As the train rocked along on its journey, Herbert gazed out the window, and in a low voice, murmured, "Look at our poor country. Why did we ever get into this tragic mess?"

An elderly man seated behind them, leaned over the seat back and growled, "I am surprised to hear such pacifist talk from a soldier. You, of all people should know that Germany was forced to fight for herself, as we are surrounded by enemies and our honor was at stake."

Herbert, red in the face, turned around and, facing the old gentleman, declared, "As in all wars, old men like you are free and easy talking about the glory and honor of war, when the young men have to do all the fighting and dying."

Open-mouthed at the outburst, the old fellow did not reply, but dropped his head and looked at the newspaper on his lap.

Meira, with a slight smile, nudged Herbert to be quiet. She had heard other young men like Herbert express the same sentiments. She, having witnessed their agony and death on a daily basis, was in complete agreement with them.

Chapter Fifty-three

Showdown

"She's doing what?" roared Benjamin Friedlander. "Marrying that gentile? Absolutely not! I won't have it! And you two conspiring behind my back! You tell me what's happening after everything has been decided. No one consults me or does me the courtesy of telling me of what she's doing until it's all over. I told you we were no longer to have any contact with her."

"Oh, stop! Just stop! You decide to cut her off, but still think you have authority over her – and everybody else in this family!" retorted his wife. "Get over yourself, Benjamin Friedlander!

You know Meira has always been able to organize her life, and she's always been successful at whatever she puts her mind to. If she has seen fit to sacrifice so much for this young man, he must be a special soul, and I for one want to get to know him and understand what she sees in him."

"I'm in full agreement with Mama," inserted, Edna. "Meira has always been the one to inspire me. It's as if she were the oldest daughter, not the youngest."

"And another thing, Benji," continued Golda, "what's the real reason for your outrage? Is it because you fear your daughter is entering a relationship that will do her damage, or are you more concerned about losing face in front of your relatives, friends and Jewish customers?"

Startled by the backlash and assertiveness of his wife and eldest daughter, he stared at them open-mouthed.

Chapter Fifty-four

Return to Dahlem

Karlheinz and his mother stepped from the train in the Stettiner Railway Station and made their way to the taxi stand in front of the building and secured a taxi. As they made their way through the city, he thought of the departure from the station in Danzig and his grandmother waving goodbye on the platform.

Frederika had been misty-eyed as the train began to move, wondering if she would ever see her mother again, as the older woman seemed more and more frail every day.

As he gazed through the window of the taxi, it struck him that there were more people begging on the streets than he ever recalled seeing before. Many of these were crippled veterans in tattered remnants of their uniforms. The upcoming Christmas holidays were almost a non-event in Berlin in December 1918. Some shops had made a meager effort to decorate their store fronts, but the ashen-faced passersby seemed to take no notice. The air of defeat and despair was pervasive, and the usual hustle and bustle of holiday shoppers was not to be seen.

The darkened villa did nothing to raise their spirits, as Frederika and her son walked up to the door. Her husband had made arrangements with their old butler to open the house and heat their bedrooms before their arrival, and he greeted them at the door with a lit candelabra in his hand, the electricity having not yet been restored. As they stepped into the unheated vestibule, they did not hand the man their wraps, which he offered to take, as was customary. He indicated that he had taken the liberty of having the cook come in earlier and prepare a simple supper for them, which would be served in their rooms. They thanked him and made their way upstairs. Upon reaching the upstairs hallway, they kissed one another goodnight and retired to their candlelit bedrooms.

The next morning, they awoke to a cold, but sunlit morning. As soon as they were dressed, they went downstairs where they were greeted by the old butler, who informed them that breakfast was awaiting them in the kitchen, which by now was cheerfully warmed. The cook was bustling about and was apologetic for the meager breakfast she was obliged to serve them. Frederika put her at ease and assured her as soon as breakfast was over, she would have trunks brought in from the front hallway, which contained some provisions she had brought from the estate. At this, the cook's face brightened, and she promised the luncheon and dinner would be the best she could manage.

Later in the morning, the electricity was turned on, and a service man came from the post which controlled the telephone service. He activated the apparatus, and Frederika promptly called the hospital to speak to her husband. She was advised that he was in surgery, but he would be notified she had called.

As she replaced the receiver on its hook, she tried to quell her impatience. She was anxious to hear when her son and his new bride-to-be would arrive. She had told herself over and over she would put her best foot forward when she met Meira Friedlander, but inwardly felt dark misgivings. As for Karlheinz, he had not reacted one way or another upon hearing of his brother's choice of bride, as was typical for his noncommittal nature.

§§§

Herbert lay on the bed looking at the ceiling and was grateful for the familiar faint odor and stillness of his old room. After two days sitting up in the coach seat on the train, surrounded by crowds of people, he was finally able to lie flat and stretch out on a real bed.

Meira was staying in Christina's flat in Wedding. They had been met at Anhalter Station two days before by his parents and his brother, Karlheinz. His father had rushed forward and embraced his son with great emotion, and then turned to Meira and took both her hands in his and declared, "I am so happy to meet you Miss Friedlander, and I can't tell you how grateful I am to you for looking after my boy."

Meira, somewhat surprised but grateful for his warmth and cordiality, replied she likewise was happy to meet him.

Frederika Lenz then stepped forward and embraced Herbert, and after kissing him on the cheek, in a low voice said, "Welcome home, my darling."

She then offered her hand to Meira, and with a cool, reserved smile greeted her, "Good evening, Miss Friedlander." Meira responded politely in the same vein.

Meanwhile, Herbert held out his arms to his brother, who hesitantly stepped forward and they embraced briefly. Meira then offered her hand to Karlheinz, and with a smile declared that she was happy to make his acquaintance. Karlheinz only shook her hand and unsmiling, nodded his head.

As the group left the station, Frederika Lenz told Herbert that his room was prepared, whereupon he replied that he would be staying with Eckhardt and Ursula in Wedding. This drew a startled and annoyed response from his mother, "We have been looking forward to your homecoming for so long. Surely you won't disappoint us by not coming now."

This caused an awkward pause in conversation, until Meira suggested she speak privately to Herbert for a moment. Stepping aside, she said in a low voice, "I would love to have you come with me, darling, but things are starting off better than we expected with you parents. Let's not spoil it now. Go with them and I'll call you tomorrow. "

He objected, saying, "I don't want to leave you and have you go off alone."

"Never mind. I know how to get to Wedding. Let them get used to me a little at a time."

Grudgingly, he admitted she was right, and returning to his parents, informed them he would go home with them.

Relieved, his father then suggested they take Meira to Wedding in their Mercedes, which he had recently taken out of storage. She protested that would not be necessary, but Dr. Lenz insisted. Finally, Meira gratefully accepted.

As they traveled across the city, they drove north on Friedrichstraße and came to the intersection with Unter den Linden and past Kranzler's on the corner. Herbert took Meira's hand and whispered, "Remember the last time we were there with Eckhardt and Ursula?"

This brought tears to her eyes, and she responded, "Oh, it's so good to be back."

Chapter fifty-five

Wedding Plans

Several days later, Frederika came up to Herbert's room and initiated a conversation concerning wedding plans, and wondered if the ceremony might not take place in the Kaiser Wilhelm Memorial Church on Breitscheidplatz. Herbert explained that although Meira was very open-minded, and not a strict follower of Judaism, she nevertheless had already stated she felt their wedding should take place in a non-religious environment. But certainly not in a Christian church where her parents would feel excluded. He went on to say with all things considered, the ceremony at the Standesamt (justice of the peace office) should suffice, with a reception afterwards in a restaurant.

With a slight frown, Frederika considered this for a moment, and then suggested in that case, she would be happy to have a reception in their home. If they were to wait until Spring, it could take place in their garden. Herbert thanked her for her generous offer and responded he would have to see how Meira felt, sure that Meira shared his desire not to wait until Spring.

Meira, meanwhile, had tried to talk to her father by telephone at his store, but was told by the manager that Benjamin Friedlander was out of town on a buying trip. She hung up disappointed, but not surprised, thinking to herself that the excuse given was surely a ruse. The blockade was still in effect, and fashion shows were still rare, if they took place at all.

She then contacted her mother again and arranged for them to meet at Kranzler's. When the conversation turned to discussing the forthcoming wedding, her mother suggested that if it were to take place in the Fassanenstraße Synagogue in Charlottenburg, her father might relent and see this as an opportunity to regain respect in their Jewish community. Sadly, Meira had to put forth the same explanation that Herbert had given to his mother, that the wedding would have to be in a neutral location.

Golda Friedlander then reacted the same as Frederika Lenz and responded with an offer to have a reception afterwards in her home.

Meira went to visit Herbert at his home a day later, he being unwilling to venture downtown with his cast and crutches. They debated the problem, and finally decided to combine the festivities of the two families and have the reception in one of the ballrooms of the Eden Hotel on Potsdamer Platz.

When this plan was presented to the respective mothers, neither was especially pleased, but then they both agreed to assist. Meira and Herbert recommended that the four of them meet for lunch at the Eden and help to choose the ballroom— and meet one another. The lunch was set for three weeks later when Herbert's cast could come off when he would be able to walk with a cane and with Meira at his side.

The lunch went reasonably well, with Golda Friedlander being the unpretentious person she was, greeting Frederika Lenz cordially. Frederika, being somewhat constrained by her class and background, at first was cool and reserved. But then as she observed Meira's mother making the effort to bridge the gap between them, she slowly began to respond to other the woman in a more relaxed manner.

The wedding took place on a day in April, and the reception was a welcome respite for everyone from the after effects of war and the flu pandemic. The two families seemed to have reached a common ground of understanding and civility, except for the absence of Meira's father. He claimed to have pressing business out of town but didn't specify what or where.

Herbert's younger brother, Karlheinz, observed the proceedings from the sidelines, and responded to friendly overtures from Mrs. Friedlander and Edna with marginal courtesy.

The happy couple permitted themselves a brief two-day honeymoon in nearby Potsdam, where they visited the palace of Frederick the Great, Sanssouci.

Chapter Fifty-six

Getting Reestablished

Upon returning to Berlin, they set about the business of finding employment and a place to live. Herbert applied for his old job at Siemens but was only able to find part-time work there. The firm was in partial operation, due to the postwar recession and the limitations imposed by the Versailles Treaty. Meira, however, was able to find a full-time nursing position at the Charité Hospital with the influence of her father-in-law. Thus, they were able to look for an apartment.

They found a comfortable flat in Berlin Mitte on the tram line along Invaliden Straße, which led directly to the hospital on Charité Platz, thus making the commute easy for Meira. Herbert, on the other hand, had to travel to Siemensstadt by tram and subway, making three transfers on the way.

Eckhardt had also applied at Siemens, but he was more fortunate as a fully licensed electrician. Because of the war, there was a shortage of skilled craftsmen and tradesmen. Thus, he was able to obtain full-time work immediately. Ursula continued to work for the transit authority, but she planned to return to KaDeWe, as soon as the store was able to recover from the shortages and would commence hiring.

Christina was showing signs of failing health, and as food returned to the markets, Ursula and Eckhardt urged her to curtail her efforts to be the sole source of food. The British Blockade ended in June 1919, and the food situation normalized quickly after that.

Rudi, by then 15, was encouraged by his brother-in-law to complete his secondary education and then enter a trade school program. But being a fatherless teenager, he fell in with some streetwise youngsters like himself, and got caught up in some risky situations involving petty theft and found himself before a judge in juvenile court.

Due to his age, he was remanded to his mother, but advised that any future interactions with the law would subject him to harsher sentencing.

When Ursula heard about all of this, she counseled with her husband, and when they visited Herbert and Meira in their new apartment the following weekend, they discussed the matter. Herbert put forth the suggestion that perhaps that the boy be sent to his family's estate and put under the supervision of their estate manager, a hardworking middle-aged Polish farmer. He might gain from being removed from the rough inner-city environment of Wedding.

Ursula picked up on the idea immediately and Eckhardt agreed. Upon returning to the flat in Wedding, they ran the idea before Christina. After a moment of consideration, she too, felt that the change might do both Rudolf and herself a great deal of good. In her weakened condition, having to raise a teenage boy alone in the small flat, sometimes overwhelmed her. She asked Ursula and Eckhardt to give support in relating the decision to young Rudi when he came home from school. They replied, of course they were willing to help her in any way she needed.

Eckhardt added that the final decision would depend on the answer Herbert would give him tomorrow at work, after he talked to Frederika. Herbert had pointed out, that he would of course have to run the idea by his mother but was sure that there would be no problem.

The next day, Herbert rang up his mother from an office phone at Siemens, and after she had heard the whole plan, she had assented to the proposal. She cautioned, however, that it must be understood, this in no way was to cause any upset or disturbance for her mother, who was by this time in a very frail condition. She even proposed that Karlheinz accompany Rudi on the journey and get him settled with the estate manager. Herbert then informed Eckhardt of the conversation with his mother.

Pleased that everything seemed to be going well, Eckhardt returned home after work just as young Rudi was entering the front stairwell. Together they climbed the stairs to Christina's flat where Ursula had just arrived from the butcher's shop with delicious cold-cuts. Rudi requested that Eckhardt join him in a game of chess, while his mother and sister prepared the evening meal. By the time the meal was ready, things were not looking well for Eckhardt in the chess match, much to his chagrin.

After enjoying a good meal of cold cuts, quark (cream cheese or junket) and fresh cut chives, which Christina had discovered at a nearby vegetable market, the plan for Rudi's future was brought up. At first, he protested that he didn't want to leave his friends and go to an unknown place so far from home. But then it was pointed out to him he could learn to ride horses, hunt and fish in the woods on the estate, and with the advent of warm weather, go to the beach near Danzig and swim in the Baltic. He could spend the whole summer away from the heat of the city and would learn some new skills from the people on the estate. Finally, he agreed it sounded like an exciting adventure after all. It would also give him something to brag about to the other apartment-dwelling brats.

After enjoying a happy evening, Eckhardt and Ursula climbed the stairs to their own flat, satisfied that they had helped her mother resolve a thorny problem.

Chapter Fifty-seven

Summer at Schloß Hohenberg

When the proposal to take Rudi Bellon to the estate on the train was put to Karlheinz, his was a mixed reaction. On one hand, he was eager as always to return to the estate and the Baltic coast and escape from the city, but having to chaperone a teenager from Wedding, who had already had difficulties with the law, appealed to him not a little bit.

"Why does it fall on me to look after a little street urchin from the ghetto. I hear he's already been before a judge. He probably smells bad and spits on the sidewalk. I've seen those little thugs on the tram and on the subway. Why did Herbert have to get mixed up with such trash, anyway."

"That will do," thundered his father, whereupon Karlheinz stood up and stormed out of the dining room. Dr. Lenz then turned to his wife sitting across from him at the dinner table, "See what your elitist attitudes have produced!"

Frederika sat ashen-faced. She was deeply hurt by the outburst and felt that the accusation was unfair. Hadn't she welcomed Meira Friedlander into the family and made every effort to make her feel accepted? She had also assisted extensively with her and her son's wedding. And finally, hadn't she agreed to Herbert's plan to send young Rudi to the estate, and suggested sending her youngest son to accompany him?

Her husband immediately apologized, "Forgive me, Frederika. That was totally uncalled for. But please help Karlheinz see this will not only help Herbert and his wife, but also help you and your mother, because there is now no male family member to oversee the affairs of Schloß Hohenberg."

§§§

Rudi sat in the corner of the first-class compartment and regarded his chaperone who sat opposite engrossed in his newspaper, or so it seemed. The train rolled through the countryside of Pomerania, which was showing forth its springtime splendor. Orchards of fruit trees were covered with blossoms and the yet-to-be cultivated fields and meadows exhibited a display of wildflowers. The woodlands were filled with trees putting forth the soft green of Spring. The train traveled northeast from Berlin toward Deutschkrone and on to Bromberg, where Karlheinz and his charge would be met by the estate manager and driven northward to Schloß Hohenberg, which lay midway between Bromberg and Danzig.

Rudi was puzzled and hurt because Karlheinz had hardly spoken to him after they said their goodbyes to their family members at the Stettin Railway Station. Rudi was a friendly outgoing young man who was used to being liked by practically everyone he met, and he had made considerable effort to engage Herbert's younger brother in conversation, until he finally gave up and withdrew into his corner.

Herbert and Karlheinz couldn't have been more different. Herbert, who made friends wherever he went and was looked up to by Rudi and his family was in sharp contrast to his younger, reticent, and even aloof brother. Rudi was beginning to fear that he might not like his traveling companion.

Karlheinz, as always, was glad to leave the city and return to the quiet atmosphere of the countryside and to the estate he loved. He was eager to assume the leadership of the running of the place, and for the chance to show his family that he was as capable in his own element, as his much-admired brother was in his.

He was vexed, however, to be made responsible for the juvenile delinquent now seated across from him. He resented his father forcing him to take this on in order to be allowed to return to his rural sanctuary. As far as the kid having run into trouble with the law, why would anyone be surprised? A tenement brat from Wedding! What would you expect?

§§§

Mr. Janek Lewandowski, the estate manager, met them at the station in Bromberg in an ancient barouche driven by a young groom and pulled by a matched pair of beautiful Trakehner horses. He greeted the travelers with a tip of his cap, to which Karlheinz responded with a nod and a terse "Good day, Lewandowski," ignoring the young groom entirely.

Rudi followed with, "Hello, sir." On the drive to the estate no one spoke until they approached the wrought iron gates at the entrance. They followed a long, graveled drive to the manor house. Rudi was transfixed as he took in surroundings such as he had never seen before. The great house dated back to the 15th century, when it had originally been built by a von Hohenberg ancestor as a small castle, but over the centuries had evolved into a beautiful baroque villa with part of the original castle retained on one wing.

Karlheinz's grandmother, the Gräfin von Hohenberg was standing on the verandah waiting for the carriage, which drew up in front of the door. Karlheinz was shaken to see how frail his grandmother had become in the months since he and his mother had left.

"Oma," he muttered as he ascended the steps and embraced her. She felt like a tiny doll in his arms.

"My boy," she responded. Then stepping back, she commented, "So this must be the young man your mother told me about on the telephone. How are you, young fellow? What is your name?"

Before Rudi could answer, Karlheinz interjected, "This is Rudolf Bellon. He is the brother of my sister-in-law's friend, Ursula Bellon Meinert. He has become a problem for their family, and we're going to see if some good hard work and discipline will straighten him out."

Turning to the estate manager standing behind the young groom, who was preparing to lead away the horses and carriage, Karlheinz directed, "Take him with you, Lewandowski, and get him settled in the quarters with some of the other young single men."

Startled to learn that he was not welcome in the house, Rudi was white-faced as he turned and followed the older man to the workers' quarters.

"Well, that's not how Frederika led me to believe the boy would be taken care of here. I've already asked the upstairs maid to prepare a room for him next to yours," remarked the Gräfin.

"No, it's better this way, Oma. He's a rebellious pup, and he mustn't be allowed to get above himself. He needs to be kept in his place, and that's not with us."

In the days that followed, Karlheinz took on his role as head of the estate with gusto. He questioned and rejected many of the decisions made by Mr. Lewandowski and took over the financial matters from him completely, including the operating allowance to which the manager had always been entrusted. The Gräfin, even in her considerably diminished state, could see that her grandson's overbearing attitude was causing friction between himself and the staff, both indoors and outdoors. Once, at dinner, he even reprimanded the old butler, many years in the employ of the Von Hohenberg family, Josef Wojewoda, for responding too slowly to a request for another serving of meat. Gräfin von Hohenberg spoke to her grandson later in the drawing room when they were alone.

"You know, Karlheinz, the manager has complained to me that you have countermanded his instructions to some of the workers in their presence, and the humiliation you caused Wojewoda this evening will be brought to my attention by him for sure. These two men, as well as some others on this estate, have been in service here since I was a young woman. My husband, and his father before him, were very selective in the people they hired, and in the case of the household staff, they have always been under my supervision. I'm not suggesting that you directly apologize to them, but if you want your servants to respect and support you, you must learn to treat them as competent and trustworthy, which they are."

Smarting from the rebuke, Karlheinz excused himself and went out on the back verandah and lit his cigar, a habit he had only taken up since his recent arrival. He looked out over the formal garden and the pond which reflected the moonlight. As he brooded, he heard voices coming from among some trees which grew along the border of the rose garden. He hurried down the steps and, as he drew nearer, he recognized the voice of Rudi Bellon.

"You, Bellon, what are you doing there? Come out right now!"

Rudi and another young man, the son of one of the estate workers stepped out on the lawn from behind the trees, where they had been sitting on a bench.

"Sorry, Karlheinz. We'd been just strolling in the woods and were sitting on that bench talking about the football match coming up on Saturday" explained Rudi.

"Here, I am *Herr Graf* to you, and you and the other workers are not to linger near the house," barked Karlheinz. "And you, Wojcek, know better. You've been told to stay away from the manor unless you are summoned, is that clear?"

Bowing, the young Pole, apologized and promised not to disturb in the future.

"Now get out of here," commanded Karlheinz.

Enraged, Rudi was about to fire back at his tormentor, when his companion tugged at his sleeve and murmured, "Let it go. We need to leave."

Karlheinz turned and began to ascend to steps, when he looked up and saw his grandmother observing the drama from the verandah. With a disapproving frown, she turned and re-entered the house.

§§§

"Madame, your mother is on the telephone" Magda, the new maid informed Frederika.

"Thank you. I'll take it in the library."

"Hello, Mother. How are you?"

"Some days good, some days not so good.

Frederika, I'm sorry to have to complain, but Karlheinz has been a big surprise. We've all worried about him for years because he has always been so moody and withdrawn, but he's found some new self-confidence, and I'm afraid I have to say it's come out in ways that are not positive."

The old Gräfin then told her daughter what had transpired between Karlheinz and Rudi. That Rudi had been banished from the house, and that he ate and slept with the farm workers.

When Frederika heard this, she was beside herself. Not only because of the treatment Rudi had received from her son, but most importantly because of the stress and disturbance it was causing her ailing mother.

"Oh, Mama, I'm so sorry. We had no intention of causing you this much trouble. Don't worry. My husband and I will deal with this. Please don't distress yourself any further. Thank you for calling and bringing this to my attention. I'll talk this over with Hans Joachim this evening. Don't say anything to Karlheinz or Rudi. We'll deal with them directly. Please take care of yourself. I love you. As I said, don't concern yourself with this any further. Goodbye, Mama."

When her husband arrived home, late that evening as he had been detained in surgery, Frederika saw to it that he was fed and had time to relax. As they went into to the library for after-dinner drinks, a cordial for her, and a cognac for him, and sat down, she proceeded to relate to him the content of her mother's phone call.

Dumbfounded, Hans Joachim stared at her. White with anger, he retorted, "What is the matter with that boy? What's gotten into him? Who does he think he is?" Rising from his chair, he stated, "I'm calling him right now. I'll straighten him out!"

"No, dear. Not now. It's late, and my mother will have retired, and this would just upset her more. I promised her she needn't be bothered by this any further."

Pausing, her husband replied, "You're right. It'll keep until morning. But I'm calling him right after breakfast, and if I don't get the feeling I'm getting through to him, I'll go up there and deal with him face to face."

With a sigh, Frederika said, "Hopefully it won't come to that. He may be proud and arrogant, but he's not stupid. You might threaten him with having to come home. I think that would get his attention more than anything. You know how he feels about the estate, and he would certainly not like to have to come back here now under these circumstances. He would lose face in front of everyone, and especially in front of that boy. He's obviously enjoying himself, playing Lord of the Manor, which must stop and which needs to be made clear to him right now."

“Very good, dear. You’re very wise. Let’s go to bed. I’m sure we’ll both be more clearheaded in the morning and better able to handle this more effectively.”

§§§

Red-faced with indignation, Karlheinz replaced the telephone receiver on its hook. He had been summoned to the phone by the butler, when he was standing on the back verandah discussing the spring planting with the estate manager, who had already divided tasks among the workers, including Rudolf Bellon.

His father had informed him that his behavior was causing distress to his grandmother and must cease immediately. He was severely reprimanded for giving himself airs by ordering Rudi and others to address him as “Herr Graf.”

“How dare you! You have no claim to that title in any way. As it now stands, your grandmother is the heiress of the estate and the titles that go with it. If she were not there, you’re not even next in the line of succession. Your mother is, and after her, your brother, as the eldest grandson, inherits the title of Graf. So, you can see where that puts you.

Come down off your high horse right now or come home! You are to apologize to Rudolf Bellon, and on behalf of your grandmother, invite him into the house to sleep and take his meals with her and you. He is our guest, not a conscripted farm laborer! He’s the brother of your brother’s best friend’s wife, therefore practically a member of this family! You will treat him as such from now on! Is that clear?”

Shaking with rage and humiliation, Karlheinz knew he had better not talk back. He softly answered, “Yes, sir.”

§§§

Even though he could tell that Karlheinz’s apology was not sincere, Rudi was nevertheless happy to be included with members of the family again. Karlheinz told him that he had misunderstood why Rudi was being sent to Schloß Hohenberg. That he had thought Rudi was a taking a summer job on the estate.

Taking this all in with a straight face, Rudi simply replied he was glad the misunderstanding had been cleared up and that there were no hard feelings, which he inwardly knew was not the case.

Chapter Fifty-eight

Dispossessed

The terms of the Versailles Treaty were made known throughout Germany and the world as soon as it was signed on June 28, 1919. In connection with this event was the establishment of the Polish Corridor from Danzig on the Baltic through eastern Pomerania and which provided the Second Republic of Poland, with access to the Baltic Sea, thereby separating Germany from its province of East Prussia. It also immediately dispossessed German landowners in the new corridor. They had the choice of either abandoning their properties or taking out Polish citizenship.

Josef Wojewoda lifted the receiver of the shrilly ringing telephone in the front hall of Schloß Hohenberg. Frederika asked the old butler to please transfer the call to her mother's bedroom.

"Mama, I'm sorry to disturb you, but I have some news that I wanted you to hear from me before anyone else breaks it to you.

We have lost the estate. The Allies have taken eastern Pomerania and given it to the Poles."

The old Gräfin could not internalize what she had just heard.

"What do you mean 'given it to the Poles'?"

"Just that! The Treaty of Versailles, which was just signed today, has designated a corridor running south from Danzig through eastern Pomerania to be handed over to Poland. Danzig is also lost. If you wish to remain on the estate, you must take out Polish citizenship."

The old woman began to stammer incoherently, causing Frederika to ask, "Do you understand what I have just told you? You must get ready to leave. Mama, are you there? Answer me."

As if in response, Frederika heard the phone drop to the floor.

Turning to her husband seated nearby, Frederika cried, "Something has happened to Mama. I heard a clatter, and now there is nothing. I must go to her."

Hans Joachim quickly moved to embrace his wife as she almost collapsed. He took the receiver from her trembling hand and spoke into it, "Hello, hello. Is anyone there?" But getting no response, he replaced it on its hook.

Marta Nawiska, the Gräfin's personal maid had been brushing the old lady's hair when the phone call came from her daughter. Marta tactfully withdrew to the large walk-in closet to select a morning frock for her employer's consideration. Hearing the phone drop followed by the sound of the Gräfin falling to the floor, Marta rushed into the bedroom and was shocked to see her lying face up, eyes staring vacantly upward, gasping for breath and drooling from her mouth. Marta raised her to a sitting position and frantically said, "Madame, Madame! Speak to me."

Getting no response except a groan and rasping breath, she pulled the bell cord by the bed. The butler appeared in the doorway and rushed over to assist. Together they carried the old woman to her bed. He immediately called the butler's pantry and was relieved when the young footman answered. He was ordered to call the doctor from the outside line. After what seemed like an eternity, the footman called back to say the doctor was in the village assisting the local midwife with a difficult delivery but would come as soon as possible.

In the meantime, Karlheinz was told by the groom what had happened as he returned from his morning ride.

Rushing into the house and up the stairs, he burst into his grandmother's room and fell to his knees beside her bed. Taking her hand in both of his, he blurted, "Oma, Oma, can you hear me. It's Karlheinz. Don't worry Oma, you'll be fine. The doctor will be here soon. Oma, answer me." Then, realizing that she was oblivious to what was being said, he burst forth in tears, and sobbing laid his head on the pillow beside her head. Just at that moment, the bedside phone rang and was answered by Marta Nawsika, who informed Frederika what had transpired.

"Let me speak to my son."

"Oh, Mama, can you come up right away? The doctor is coming, and we hope he can help Oma, but I wish you were here now," Karlheinz pleaded.

"Yes, dear. Your father and I will take the next available train. Don't lose hope."

§§§

Shaking his head, the old doctor, who had long served the von Hohenbergs, turned to Karlheinz and the butler waiting anxiously for his verdict. "I'm sorry, but your grandmother has suffered a massive stroke. Her pulse is very weak, and her breathing is labored. Her condition has been deteriorating for some time since your grandfather's death, and I must warn you not to expect her to recover. I can well imagine the news about the loss of this estate was a terrible shock. If she were able to speak, she would very likely say that she has no wish to live."

Upon hearing this, Karlheinz covered his face with his hands and bowed his head in sobs that shook his whole body. Placing his hand on the young man's arm to console him, the doctor softly said, "Let me know right away if there is a change in her condition."

Two days after the arrival of Frederika Lenz and her husband, the Gräfin von Hohenberg passed quietly in her sleep. Frederika notified Herbert, who requested leave from his job at Siemens, which was granted. He and Meira prepared to make the journey to the estate. Eckhardt and Ursula accompanied them to Stettiner Railway Station and helped them get settled in their first-class compartment.

Herbert, by this time, had recovered well from his injury and was able to get about with the help of a cane. As the train pulled out, Eckhardt and Ursula waved their friends farewell. As they walked out of the station, Ursula turned to her husband and said, "We must give them all the support we can from now on. They are not only facing a funeral, but also the task of preparing themselves for the loss of the estate. I have written Rudi to stay as long as necessary to help Herbert and his family during this terrible time."

"That's very thoughtful of you," replied Eckhardt. "I can imagine that Rudi will remember this experience for the rest of his life. Hopefully, he'll take a lesson out of this…that a person can lose worldly goods overnight.

What's really important in this life are the relationships we form, and those of us who are fortunate enough to form good relationships in our families and among our friends, are truly blessed."

Ursula clung more tightly to her husband's arm, and murmured, "Very true, and my greatest blessing is having you."

§§§

With head bowed, Karlheinz walked slowly down the alley of beech trees leading from the back garden to the fields planted in rye and Russian red wheat. As he moved further away from the house, the din of conversation from the guests gathered on the back terrace faded. The funeral which had taken place that afternoon in the private chapel on the estate had been attended by family members, lifelong friends from neighboring estates, and the household staff. The procession from the chapel to the nearby Von Hohenberg mausoleum had taken place under an overcast sky, which gave way to light rain. The coffin was taken inside and placed in the crypt next to that of the Graf. After the brief eulogy spoken by the Lutheran minister from the village, the mourners, led by Frederika and her sons, made their way to the house as the rain ceased, and the sun shone through the clouds. As soon as he could, Karlheinz excused himself as the need to be alone overcame him.

He looked across the fields and smelled the fragrance of the damp earth and air. How he loved that smell! As he walked beneath the trees, he looked at the rain-washed leaves shining in the late afternoon light and entered the woods beyond the fields.

He made his way to the pond where his grandfather had taught him to swim. He could see rings on the surface where the fish were beginning to feed and thought of the fishing excursions he and his grandfather had made during those long-ago summers. He felt the tightness in his throat as he realized this would be the last time he would walk these grounds as the last in the long line of von Hohenbergs.

The thought that someone else would soon walk here as an owner, tore at his heart. His beloved refuge was about to be taken.

As he turned back to the house, the feeling of sorrow and nostalgia gave way to anger. He thought about the moment on the day his grandmother was stricken, when he first heard of the outrageous demands of the Allies – the dispossession of his family from their beloved lands!

He had felt like an outsider all his life, except when he was here with his grandparents. Here he was truly at home, and it had always been his dream to eventually live here until the end of his days. Now it was not to be. It had been taken from him by foreigners, who were now in control of his homeland, exacting retribution for the terrible war for which none of them assumed any blame or responsibility. How he hated them!

Chapter Fifty-nine

The Uprooting

The eviction notice had arrived from the Polish government in the middle of July 1919, but Frederika had begun the process of breaking up the household immediately after her mother's death. The Polish authorities allowed the estate owners to keep or dispose of household contents, but not the land and buildings.

Frederika decided to organize an auction of the furnishings but was not optimistic this would bring in much revenue, as all German estate owners in the newly formed Danzig Corridor were doing the same. The furnishings in the large manor houses such as Schloß Hohenberg, were much too massive to fit in most modern houses and apartments, to which the majority of dispossessed Germans would be moving.

For example, the main dining table in Schloss von Hohenberg was forty feet long and would seat thirty guests. The old Beckstein grand piano was nine feet long. The clock which stood in the entry hall was over eight feet tall. Frederika selected a few pieces which she felt she could fit into her Berlin villa, but the rest were put up for sale for a fraction of what they were worth.

She disposed of her mother's, father's and brother's clothing – mostly from the prewar period and therefore out of style – by allowing the servants to take what they wanted. These items would be made over to fit by the skilled country wives and worn proudly to church and social gatherings for many years to come. She packed away the best china and family silver. As she had her own in Berlin, she could put them in the bank vault, in case she ever needed to barter or sell them in hard times.

As Herbert had to return to his job at Siemens, and Hans Joachim to his practice at Charité Hospital, Karlheinz was charged with disposing of the livestock and farm equipment. Rudi, as directed by his mother and sister, offered to help in any way he could. But Karlheinz brusquely told him his help was not needed, and he was free to return to Berlin any time he wanted. When he informed Frederika of this, she immediately took her son to task, and reminded him of what his father had told him about treating Rudi as almost part of the family. Karlheinz sulked, but agreed to obey. He then informed Rudi his help might be useful after all, and he could help by grooming the horses for sale and cleaning out their stalls.

Since the night they had been banished from the back garden, Rudi had formed a bond with the young Polish farm worker, Wojcek. When he told his friend about the assignment he had been given by Karlheinz, Wojcek assured him they could accomplish the tasks together. He showed Rudi how to brush and curry the horses until their coats shone, trim and comb their manes and tails, and file and trim their hooves until the horses looked splendid enough for show.

Then they set about shoveling out the stalls and washing them down with disinfectant. As the barns and outbuildings at Schloß Hohenberg had always been well maintained, it was not a huge task to have the stalls and stone floors of the building soon smelling fresh and clean. When Rudi told Karlheinz the job had been completed, Karlheinz was astonished, and even complimented him, "If we were staying, I can see we could make a good worker out of you."

When the day arrived for final departure, the representative from the newly formed Polish housing authority presented himself and his assistants to take possession of the keys to all the buildings on the property. Karlheinz was coldly receptive to these men, but proper in his conduct. Inwardly he was motivated by controlled hatred, but determined not to cause any more difficulties for his mother.

As the two of them seated themselves in the old barouche for transport to the railroad station, the household staff and farm laborers were standing in line before the front entrance of the house to see them off. It was hard to read the emotions of some of the people, but others, such as Janek Lewandoski, the estate manager, and Josef Wojewoda, the butler, were plainly grieved by the turn of events, which would affect their lives and break the bonds they had formed with the family in their youth.

The barouche driven by Lewandoski, and followed by three baggage wagons, on the first of which Rudi was seated next to the driver, crept down the long driveway. Young Wojcek and Rudi waved to one another, each with misty eyes. In the days they had worked together, they had formed the basis of real friendship. As they rolled away from the house, Frederika, with tears streaming down her cheeks, turned for one last look. Karlheinz sat rigidly facing forward with no show of emotion, but hatred boiled in his brain. He promised himself that one day he would return and have his revenge.

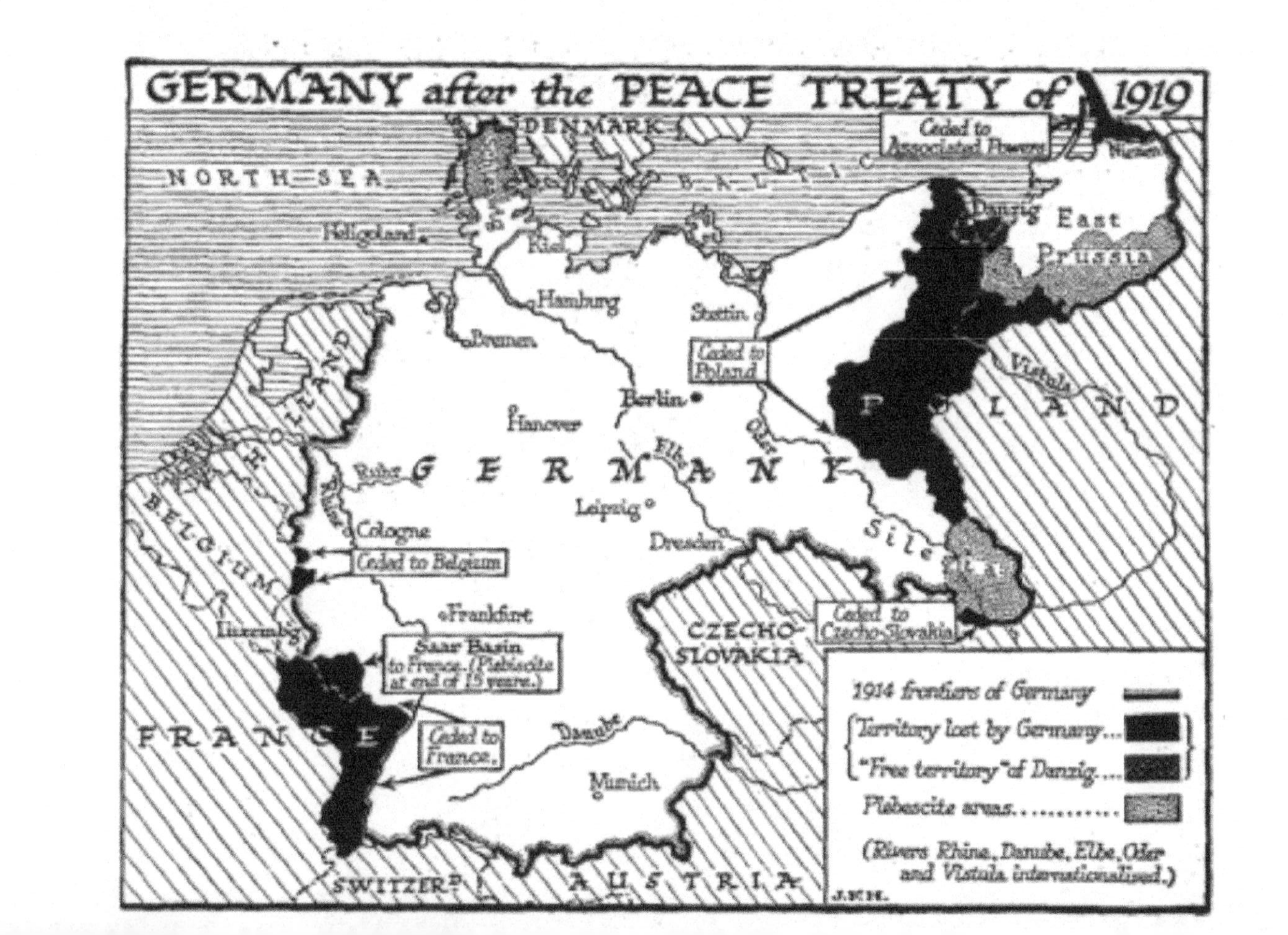
GERMANY after the PEACE TREATY of 1919
DENMARK
NORTH SEA
BALTIC
Heligoland
Kiel
Hamburg
Bremen
Stettin
Ceded to Associated Powers
Niemen
Danzig
East Prussia
Ceded to Poland
Vistula
POLAND
Berlin
Hanover
Oder
Elbe
GERMANY
Ruhr
Rhine
Leipzig
Cologne
Dresden
Silesia
Ceded to Belgium
BELGIUM
HOLLAND
Frankfurt
Luxemburg
Ceded to Czecho-Slovakia
CZECHO-SLOVAKIA
Saar Basin to France. (Plebiscite at end of 15 years.)
Ceded to France.
FRANCE
Danube
Munich
SWITZER^D
AUSTRIA
1914 frontiers of Germany
Territory lost by Germany...
"Free territory" of Danzig...
Plebescite areas...........
(Rivers Rhine, Danube, Elbe, Oder and Vistula internationalised.)
J.F.H.

Part V

Resurrection

Chapter Sixty

Weimar Republic Born in Turmoil

Berlin had been in a state of upheaval and political unrest since the last days of the war. Workers had gone on strike and participated in armed fighting in the streets. Groups of different political movements had sprung up and faced one another in confrontations throughout the year 1919.

In January of that year, the founder of the Communist Party of Germany, Karl Liebknecht and his Marxist colleague, Rosa Luxembourg, joined the uprising of the Spartacist League. This revolt was brutally put down by the new German government under Friedrich Ebert, assisted by remnants of the Imperial German Army, and militias known as the "Freikorps" (Free Corps). On January 15, Liebknecht and Luxembourg were captured by the Freikorps and brought to the Eden Hotel, where they were tortured and interrogated by Captain Waldemar Pabst, the chief of staff of the elite Garde-Kavallerie-Schützen-Division (Guard Cavalry Rifle Division), which was quartered in the hotel.

After their interrogation, they were told they would be transferred to Moabit Prison. However, Pabst had already decided to have them killed. The official statement made later, was that Liebknecht had been shot "while trying to escape," and that Luxembourg had been "shot by members of an excited mob."

This led to fighting between the Left-Wing and Right-Wing "socialists." The split has been in effect up to recent times. The KPD, or *Kommunistische Partei Deutschlands* (Communist Party of Germany) became the SED, or *Sozialistische Einheitspartie Deutschlands* (Socialist Unified Party of Germany) in former East

Germany. The SPD, or *Sozaildemokratische Partei Deutschlands* (Socialist Party of Germany) was a social-democratic party in West Germany and is now represented in all of unified Germany.

The sad irony is that neither Liebknecht nor Luxembourg were Bolsheviks. Liebknecht, as an intellectual, had a horror of bloodshed, and tiny "Red Rosa" Luxembourg had urged an end to violence. Political justice in the Weimar Republic was shameful. The end result was that all the perpetrators in the Liebknecht-Luxembourg murders were eventually acquitted. The ensuing chaos resulted in the first postwar national assembly being convened in Weimar, where the new constitution for the new Germany was written and adopted on August 11, 1919, which led to the new government being known as the "Weimar Republic."

Chapter Sixty-one

Hyperinflation

By the middle of 1920, Eckhardt and Herbert had resumed full-time work at Siemens. Despite the continuing political unrest, life began to stabilize for them and their families. Meira, having established rapport with her mother, met with her and her sister, Edna, at least weekly, and sometimes more often. Her father, however, maintained his distance from her and Herbert. Meira, with the help of Herbert's father, obtained a nursing position at the Charité Hospital and began a course in surgical nursing at the nearby Berlin University.

Ursula had returned to KaDeWe and was soon promoted to the position of a buyer in ladies' fashions. In connection with this, she was able to travel to other cities in Central Europe, including Paris, which had quickly reestablished itself as the fashion center of Europe.

As she met with other Europeans, it soon became clear to her that the resentment against Germany ran deep. Oddly, it seemed to be turned more against Germany than against Austria, which had been the first country to declare war. When she communicated this to her husband, and others at home, she was met with astonishment and anger.

"Why do people blame Germany as the country totally responsible for the war?"

This led to many lengthy debates and arguments around the kitchen tables and in the pubs of Berlin, and across the country. However, in the election of January 1919, the majority of Germans still voted for parties that favored the new democratic republic, which were the aforementioned SPD *Sozialdemokratische Partei Deutschlands* (Social Democrats), the liberal DDP *Deutsche Demokratische Partei* (German Democratic Party), and the DZ *Deutsche Zentrumspartei* (German Center Party), a Catholic political party, commonly referred to in English as the Catholic Center Party.

§§§

Working class families, such as Eckhardt's and Herbert's, found it increasingly difficult to make their money reach to cover living costs. Germany was beginning to feel the effects of creeping inflation.

In 1914, 4.25 German marks was the exchange rate to one U.S. dollar. By the end of 1920, it was 70 marks to one dollar. In order to make payments on the reparations demanded by the Treaty of Versailles, Germany began to print money without the economic resources to back it up. On the plus side, the battles of the war were fought mostly in France and Belgium, allowing Germany to come out of the conflict with most of its industrial complex intact. In May 1921, however, the London Ultimatum demanded reparations in gold or foreign currency to be paid in annual installments of 2 billion gold marks, plus 26% of the value of Germany's exports.

In June 1921, the first payment was made on time, but this led to the rapid devaluation of the mark, which rapidly fell to about 330 marks to the dollar. As a result, Germany stepped up the mass printing of bank notes to buy foreign currency to pay reparations. The German mark began to plummet to unforeseen levels by the end of the year.

§§§

As during the war years, Christina resumed her efforts to procure food for her family. As inflation drove up food costs, she found herself returning to some of her foraging practices involving travel in and out of the city. Soon, she also joined housewives on paydays at the entrance gates of the factories to collect the pay envelopes of their men, where she collected Eckhardt's pay at Siemens, Ursula not being able to because of her job. This became necessary as prices of commodities began to change hourly to keep up with the devaluation of the mark. These women then hurried to the markets to spend the cash as quickly as possible, because by the end of 1921, the price of bread could double in 24 hours.

Chapter Sixty-two

Adapting to the Times

After Rudi returned from the estate, and passed a rigorous aptitude test, he enrolled in a trade school to study auto mechanics. Automobiles became more common on the streets of Berlin after the war, and the need for trained mechanics grew apace. His uncle Eckhardt had at first urged him to follow in his footsteps and become an electrician, but like most boys of his age, Rudi was totally fascinated by the new models of cars. Many of the expensive cars were owned by people who had moved their savings out of the country, particularly into Swiss banks, and who were in a position to buy with foreign currency.

Others, seeing the specter of ever-increasing inflation on the horizon, chose to invest their money in items such as automobiles and real estate before it became too late. But Eckhardt, and other astute individuals could see that automobiles were definitely the wave of the future. Therefore, he supported Rudi in his decision to follow that path.

Ursula, too, could see the effects of the worsening economic situation in her career with KaDeWe. As the mark became more and more devalued, it became increasingly difficult to purchase foreign made goods, resulting in the return of small workshops producing domestically made clothing.

Many of these establishments were, as in former times, operated and owned by Jewish tailors. This motivated Ursula and other commercial buyers to patronize Benjamin Friedlander, who had continued his family's tradition of clothing manufacture. Although the inflation had seriously undermined Friedlander's profit margin, he nevertheless managed to provide quality merchandise to his customers. This would stand him in good stead when more prosperous times returned.

Herbert, grateful for his employment at Siemens, was chagrined that he was not the main source of income for Meira and himself. As she developed her skills as a specialized surgical nurse, she became a key member of her father-in-law's surgical team. Soon she became a supervisor of surgical nurses and was able to command one of the highest salaries in her profession at Charité Hospital. But like almost everyone else at that time, she found it more and more difficult to keep financially afloat.

Karlheinz Lenz became almost reclusive after his return to Berlin. His bitterness, due to the loss of his family's estate, ate at him like a cancer. He began to resent foreigners of every stripe, and especially Jews, who seemed to cope better in the financial crisis. What he and many who resented Jews failed to take into account, was that Jews having suffered centuries of persecution, had developed investment and saving habits that had carried them through other crises in the past. Also, they had strong family ties and understood cooperative sharing better than many of their gentile neighbors.

Frederika Lenz dealt better than her son with the loss of Schloß Hohenberg. At first, she was almost inconsolable, but with the support of her husband, for whose counsel she had always been grateful, and with the input from her eldest son, Herbert, she began to move forward.

Herbert told of the tragedies he had experienced during the war and pointed out that they as a family had managed to survive it, and the flu pandemic which followed, intact. Also, they had good homes, and except for the lingering effects he still endured due to his war wound, were healthy. All of this was very uplifting to Frederika. But it seemed to be totally lost on Karlheinz, who seemed to take perverse pleasure in nursing his bitterness and hatred.

In the background was the boiling pot of political instability and uncertainty about what the future would bring. The Berliners, who had long established a reputation for resilience and independent thinking, were getting through the bleak times they were experiencing with sarcastic wit and audacity. *Berliner Schnauze* (Berlin sassiness) would serve them well in the bleak days ahead.

Chapter Sixty-three

Anti-Semitic Assassination

Walther Rathenau left his home at 10:45 a.m. on June 24, 1922, in his open convertible and headed to his office in the Wilhelmstraße. He was serving as Germany's Foreign Minister during the early years of the Weimar Republic. His father, Emil Rathenau, was the founder of the electrical engineering company, *Allgemeine Elektrizitäts-Gesellschaft*, or AEG, which continues as a major German industrial firm today.

As a strong German nationalist, Walther Rathenau, who was Jewish, was a leading spokesman for the assimilation of German Jews, and who opposed Zionism and socialism. As a prominent Jewish politician who believed integration of Jews into mainstream German society would lead to the disappearance of anti-Semitism, he was hated by the extreme right, in spite of his fervid patriotism. He aroused the rage of the Right by negotiating the Treaty of Rapallo with the Soviet Union in 1922, and also insisting that Germany had to fulfill the provisions of the hated Treaty of Versailles. The Right only saw a Jew making devious deals with fellow Jews, the Bolsheviks. They marched through the streets shouting,

> *"Knallt ab den Walther Rathenau!*
> *Der gottverfluchte Judensau!*
> (Knock down Walther Rathenau!
> The God-Forsaken Jewish sow!)"

As he turned at the corner of Wallotstraße into Königsallee in the prestigious Grünewald district, his car was cut off by a dark gray automobile in which were seated three men. One of these pointed a submachine gun at Rathenau and fired five times. Another man threw a hand grenade into Rathenau's car, and the large gray car sped away. After a few minutes, Walther Rathenau died. Today a memorial stone in the Königsallee marks the scene of the crime on the now-named Rathenauplatz.

The assassins were members of an extreme rightist organization group, the so-called Organization Consul, which preached anti-Semitism, but whose main mission was to restore dignity to Germany within a broader nationalistic framework in the aftermath of the First World War and the humiliation of the Versailles Treaty. Therefore, some historians state that Rathenau's murder should be seen as the result of deep dissatisfaction with the Weimar government, and not merely as a result of Anti-Semitism.

The main assassins were two former officers, Erwin Kern and Hermann Fischer, who committed suicide after being surrounded by police in Saaleck castle, near Kösen. The driver of the car, Erik Werner Techow, was captured and sentenced to 15 years in prison. He was released from prison for good behavior in 1927 and volunteered for the French Foreign Legion. He later repented for his part in the assassination, and during the Second World War helped save over 700 Jews in Marseilles.

After the Nazis came to power in 1933, they declared Rathenau's assassins to be national heroes, and designated June 24, as a national holiday.

Chapter Sixty-four

Family Explosion in Dahlem

The villa owned by Dr. Hans Joachim Lenz sat on the Goßlerstraße in the prestigious district of Dahlem. The house had been built in 1910 and reflected the understated dignity of the owner. On a summer evening a few days after the Rathenau assassination, the doctor and his family sat down to dinner in the small dining room at the rear of the house facing the well-manicured garden. The double French doors were open, allowing the soft summer air carrying the fragrance of trees and flowers to waft across the green velvet of the lawn and into the interior of the room. Soft light from candles in silver candelabra in the center of the parquet-topped dining table illuminated the room. The light summer meal served on silver serving platters, had been laid out by the butler and maid on the large oak sideboard, also illuminated by candles in silver candelabra. Some of the most valuable silver pieces had been brought from Schloß Hohenberg after the breakup of that household.

As Hans Joachim seated himself at the opposite end of the table from his wife, he took in the serenity of the room, and looked affectionately at his family, finally together again after years of separation. Frederika, wearing a light summer frock and immaculately groomed as usual, returned his calm gaze, as their sons and Meira settled themselves into their seats. Both women were dressed in the current style of the early 1920s, and Meira's hair had been recently bobbed accordingly, while Frederika continued to have her golden hair arranged in the style she had always worn. Herbert and Karlheinz were dressed in slacks with open-collared shirts, and Hans Joachim continued to wear his suit and necktie.

As the first course of cold cherry soup was served, and lightly chilled Chardonnay was poured, the conversation began with Frederika commenting, "What a dreadful tragedy that was with the killing of Minister Rathenau."

Hans Joachim responded, "Terrible. I heard Walther Rathenau speak once at a dinner hosted by the German Democratic Party, and a more devout patriot you couldn't imagine. Those maniacs who killed him were some of those radicals who didn't learn anything from the war."

Herbert added, "You're right. I shudder to think what would happen to this country if people like that were in control."

A sullen Karlheinz, who had been listening to the exchange, suddenly blurted, "No, they were right! Rathenau and his Jew cronies made fortunes from the war and would sell this country out. The sooner we get rid of the *Dreckjuden* (Jew scum) the better."

Meira, sitting across from Karlheinz, blanched at the outburst and looked at her brother-in-law in shock.

He, feeling her stare, glared back at her belligerently. Frozen in disbelief, a sudden silence that descended on the family was palpable.

Herbert roared with fury, "How dare you! Where in the hell do you get such ideas?"

Hans Joachim joined in, "Yes. What kind of people have you been with?"

Karlheinz defiantly retorted, "People who have caught wise to what these Jew parasites have been up to, that's who!"

Frederika, who had planned and looked forward to this reunion, was visibly shaken by the animosity which now surrounded her table.

"Please!" she pleaded. "What has happened to all of you? We haven't been able to enjoy an evening together like this for years, and now you're at each other's throats. Whatever goes on outside should never be allowed to divide us from each other.

Turning to her daughter-in-law, she said in a quavering voice, "Meira, I'm so sorry, dear. I apologize for the bad behavior of my family, which I hope you will regard as your family, too."

Meira, tears in her eyes, responded, "Thank you, Mrs. Lenz. I appreciate that. We are hearing more and more of this kind of talk lately, which, according to my mother, my father hears in the city."

Karlheinz suddenly stood up and stormed out of the room, followed by his brother. Herbert caught up with him as he reached the front door, and catching Karlheinz by the shoulder, spun him around.

"You go back in there and apologize to my wife, right now!"

"Go to hell," retorted Karlheinz. "Why did you ever get mixed up with a Jew in the first place?"

Herbert then slammed his brother up against the wall and threatened, "You will go in and apologize to Meira, or so help me God, I'll knock you on your ass."

Karlheinz continued to struggle, just as Hans Joachim entered the hallway and began to separate his sons.

"Stop! Stop! Stop! Stop this right now, both of you. You're breaking your mother's heart, and she and Meira are both in tears. Stop!"

Finally, Herbert released his brother, who stubbornly refused to do as he had been told.

"I'm not apologizing. I've wanted to tell you for a long time, Herbert, how I feel about you marrying a Jew. I've had to suffer enough embarrassment when my friends asked me about it."

"You will apologize, or you can get out and stay out of this house until you do," shouted his father.

"Fine. I don't want to live under the same roof with Jew lovers anyway," Karlheinz shouted as he made his way to the door.

"You go out that door and you can forget about any support from me," threatened Hans Joachim.

The slam of the large oak door reverberated through the house like a gunshot. Herbert and his father looked at each other shaking and shocked.

When they returned to the dining room, the butler was standing like a statue next to the sideboard, ashen-faced. The two women whose heads were bowed, their shoulders trembling with muted sobbing, looked up as their husbands came back to the table. The mood, which had been so serene, was shattered, as were now the ties of the stricken family.

Chapter Sixty-five

Collapse of the Mark

In 1914, one U.S. dollar would be exchanged for 4.25 German marks. By June 1922, one dollar would buy 320 marks. By December of that year, the mark fell to 7,400 marks per U.S. dollar. In order to enforce the reparation payments, French and Belgian troops occupied the Ruhr valley, the industrial region of Germany, in January 1923. Further inflation was caused when workers in the Ruhr region went on a general strike, and the German government printed more currency to support their passive resistance. By the end of the year, November of 1923, the dollar was worth 4,210,500,000,000 German marks! The cost of living index in June 1922, was 41, and in December 685 – a 15-fold increase.

This breakdown was brought on by many factors, but approximately one third of the German deficit from 1920 to 1923, was blamed on the reparations Germany was expected to pay. Bankers and speculators, especially foreign, were also cited as another cause of the hyperinflation. After August 1921, Germany had begun to buy foreign currency with marks at any price, which only hastened the breakdown of the mark. The government increased the printing of paper currency, the mark thereby becoming virtually worthless.

Christina and the other women standing in line on a gray and rainy morning in late November 1923, were not surprised, when they saw Mr. Schroeder put a notice in his window that the price of a loaf of bread had gone up to 200,000,000,000 marks. After all, what was two hundred billion marks, when a wage earner like Eckhardt, as a licensed electrician at Siemens, was paid over 20 trillion? This scene was repeated in the working-class neighborhoods across Germany like Wedding and Kreuzberg.

§§§

Christina joined the queue of women at the gates of Siemens on paydays to collect the pay bundles from Eckhardt and Herbert, with standing instructions to hurry to the markets and purchase food and necessities before prices went up. Many of the women of Germany had begun to burn banknotes in their stoves, because it was cheaper than buying firewood or briquettes. One man, who ordered a cup of coffee in Kranzlers, reported that the price had doubled by the time it was brought to his table.

In the affluent districts, such as Dahlem and Lichterfelde, Frederika Lenz, and others of her class, used family heirlooms, silver, and jewelry to barter with foreigners for their currency, which was in turn used to purchase commodities. What had been made scarce during the war years by the British blockade, was now increasingly out of reach for many, due to the declining buying power of the German mark.

On an evening in early December of that dreadful year, Herbert and Meira were again seated at his parents' dinner table, and the conversation centered on the woes of the country and the unfairness of the Treaty of Versailles. Frederika brought up the loss of the estate in Pomerania, and this was followed by a general discussion of the hyperinflation exacerbated by the demands for reparations. Hans Joachim listened to the heated comments until there was a lull in the conversation, then he cautiously began to present another point of view.

"The Allies are not the first to come up with the idea of reparations. I have an acquaintance, who told me in the strictest confidence, that his father, who was on the General Staff before the war, revealed that our government under the Emperor had formulated the same plan for Germany's enemies in 1914.

The hubris of our government leaders had allowed them to convince themselves, that the war would be very short, with Germany emerging as the victor. They had gone off the gold standard before the outbreak of hostilities, and felt it was safe to finance the war with credit. It was a foregone conclusion that Germany would be stronger after the war. So, you can see that the devaluation of our currency had actually begun during the war."

The others around the table stared at him wide-eyed. Frederika, whose own father had been on the General Staff, and whose brother had been an officer and a graduate of the War Academy, cried, "Hans

Joachim! That's outrageous. I never heard my father or my brother mention such a thing. That's traitorous talk, and you should advise your friend to shut his mouth!"

Herbert, as a veteran, was also agitated and added, "Yes, father, you would never convince my comrades that our government was capable of such despicable acts."

With a sigh, his father responded, "I said this came to me in the strictest confidence, because my source realizes, that this could cause great harm to come anyone putting forth such information and would of course be construed by many as Allied propaganda."

Meira, who up to this point had restrained herself, stated, "My mother says she has heard that people are blaming the Jews in the prewar government, and during the war for our present crisis. I can imagine, that anyone hearing what you have just revealed, Dr. Lenz, would probably accuse Jews of fabricating the story. There are families among my parents' circle of friends whose sons fought and died for Germany, and there are examples among my people such as Minister Rathenau, whose families have contributed to the culture and economy of this country going back generations. It doesn't seem to matter what effort Jews make for Germany, because when there is a crisis, the anti-Semites will immediately seize the opportunity to turn upon them."

The atmosphere in the candlelit dining room was depressed for the remainder of the evening.

Chapter Sixty-six

A Turning Point

After leaving his parents' home in a rage, Karlheinz Lenz walked the streets until he came to the S Bahn station of Lichterfelde-West. He boarded the train, which took him in the direction of the downtown area. After changing and transferring to buses and other trains, he crisscrossed the great city and nursed his anger and self-pity. Never having been able to easily meet other people like his brother could, he had spent much of his life alone and withdrawn. He had long since made his peace with being alone, but on this evening, the sense of loneliness engulfed him, and he felt a strong need to be with someone else.

Eventually his travels brought him to the Zoo station near Auguste-Viktoria-Platz and the Kaiser Wilhelm Memorial Church. As he stood in front of the great church, he was fascinated by the hustle and bustle of crowds going to and fro. He began to stroll toward the bright lights of nearby Kurfürstendamm. Standing near the juncture of Ku'damm and Tauentzienstraße trying to decide where to go next, he was approached by a young man who asked if he had a light for a cigarette. Replying that he did not smoke, the stranger seemed not to be disappointed, but instead asked what his plans were for the evening.

Karlheinz, who usually did not respond to strangers, felt suddenly grateful for contact with another human being. He answered he was not often in the city and wasn't familiar with the area. The young man suggested that perhaps they should go somewhere for a drink, to which Karlheinz agreed. They then introduced themselves, his new companion being named Egon Wolf. Egon suggested they walk to a nearby club which he knew. Not knowing anything to offer instead, Karlheinz agreed. They began to walk along Tauentzienstraße to Kleiststraße. As they walked, Egon showed an interest in Karlheinz that he had never felt from anyone before. He became relaxed and felt flattered by the new attention.

They came to a neon-lit establishment with the words *Kleist Kasino* displayed on the building. They were met at the door by a doorman who, upon recognizing Egon Wolf, admitted them. The interior presented itself in a manner which Karlheinz had never seen. He had been to a few neighborhood pubs, which were almost always smoky and frequented by people in nondescript dress, but he had never imagined anything like this.

Kleist Kasino had opened its doors in 1922 and quickly became one of Europe's most well-known gay bars. It attracted a large clientele of people from all walks of life, the homosexual crowd as well as ordinary citizens and tourists, all of whom were entertained by the ribald and bawdy transvestite shows and cabaret performances.

As Karlheinz took in the multicolored lighting and the carnival-like décor, he was fascinated by a large muscular man wearing a feather boa over his hairy chest and a large round lavender picture hat in a flower-bedecked swing swaying to and fro over the audience, singing in a falsetto voice a rendition of "*Komm' in meine Liebeslaube*" (Come into my bowery of love) to the accompaniment of a brassy orchestra, made up of burly men in short skirts, fishnet stockings and garters on the stage.

There seemed to be a large number of smartly dressed young men, who looked Egon and his new companion up and down, before returning to their drinks and conversations. Even with his lack of worldly experience, Karlheinz knew that he was in a new environment, which he had heretofore only heard of in whispers, but he didn't care. Egon steered them to a booth, in which were seated three young men, who seemed to recognize him immediately. He introduced Karlheinz to his friends, and they cordially made room, as they took in his tall, blond, Germanic good looks and began to enthusiastically inquire who he was and where he came from. Their easy manner made him feel comfortable and welcome. Soon he felt that he had found some new friends, which never had come easily to him before.

As the evening wore on, the effect of the environment, and several drinks, lulled Karlheinz into a drowsy and happy state. Sometime around two o'clock in the morning, Egon's friends made ready to leave, and Egon suggested that they too should go. As they walked outside, the chill suddenly reminded Karlheinz that he had no place to go. As if by inspiration, Egon suggested that he come home with him, to which Karlheinz and gratefully agreed. They retraced their steps along Kleistsraße to Wittenbergplatz, where there was an all-night taxi stand. They took a taxi to Egon's apartment on Windscheidstraße off Bismarckstraße in Charlottenburg. Karlheinz shared that night, and many nights to follow, with his new friend.

He was forever changed.

Chapter Sixty-seven

Posterity

Ursula was awakened again with violent nausea, as she had been for the past three days. But this morning, she was forced to hurry to the wash basin on the wash stand and empty her stomach with vomiting. Eckhardt, who was a sound sleeper, was awakened by her retching, and hurried to her side to hold her head and steady her on her feet. When the heaving subsided, he asked her, "What's the matter, darling? Have you caught something?"

She turned her wan face to him with a weak smile. "Don't worry, sweetheart. It'll soon pass. I must wash up for breakfast. Mama will have breakfast ready."

With a worried look, he watched her take the wash basin out the door and down the half flight to the toilet. When she returned, she already looked considerably better. She rinsed out the basin with water from the pitcher on the wash stand and took it down to the toilet. They hurried to dress in the frigid bedroom and went one flight down to Christina's flat for breakfast.

As the four of them, Ursula, Eckhardt, Christina and Rudi, began to eat, Eckhardt related the experiences Ursula had been having for the past several mornings with nausea and vomiting. Christina scrutinized Ursula closely, and then a smile played around her lips.

"You must see a doctor, but I think we are going to have a little stranger in our family."

Eckhardt and Rudi looked at her blankly, uncomprehending. Ursula, however, looked astonished at her mother and suddenly blurted, "You think I'm pregnant?"

"Well, I'm not a midwife or a doctor, but you show the early signs. I went through the same thing with each of my four kids."

Eckhardt and Rudi took in this revelation, and then broke into big smiles.

Turning to his brother-in-law, Rudi extended his hand and slapped him on the back. "What have you gone and done to my sister?"

Eckhardt, red-faced, retorted with a grin, "Get out of here, you punk!"

Turning to Rudi, Christina then stated, "You hurry up or you'll miss your bus."

Rudolf, now a young man of twenty, upon returning from Pomerania four years earlier, had undergone a course in auto mechanics but had become disillusioned after being laid off and not able to find steady employment after that. Seeing many of the best positions filled by veterans, who had gained much experience as mechanics during the war, he decided to apply to the city transit authority. He secured a job as a street car conductor. After building a good work record, he was offered an opening in the training program as a motorman, which he would become, as his father had before him.

As he went out the door, he laughed and flung over his shoulder, "Well, it's going to get crowded around here now."

Eckhardt finished his tea and roll and made ready to leave. He would have his second breakfast in the canteen at Siemens later in the morning. He bent over Ursula, and kissed her on the forehead as he bantered, "Well, we've gone and done it now, girl."

After the men had left, Christina queried Ursula, "When did you have your last period?"

"About six weeks ago, but I didn't think too much about it, because I've been late with my periods before."

"Well, we're second guessing. You need to go to the clinic and see a gynecologist right away."

Ursula agreed and promised to set up an appointment as soon as she got off work that afternoon. It was determined she had become pregnant in March 1924. It was a time of new hope for her and Eckhardt, but also for millions of other families across Germany.

§§§

The hyperinflation had been stopped at the end of 1923, by bold moves under the leadership of Gustav Stresemann, who had been appointed Chancellor on August 13, 1923. Without hesitation, he suspended seven articles of the Weimar constitution on September 26, 1923, in the midst of the financial chaos, and declared a State of

Emergency, thereby rendering Germany temporarily a military dictatorship.

Then on October 15, a new institution, the Rentenbank was established. This allowed a new currency to be issued under the Rentenmark Ordinance, equivalent in value to the prewar gold-based mark, or "gold mark." This was the brainchild of Hans Luther, of the Finance Ministry, and Hjalmar Schacht, managing director of the Darmstadt & National Bank. Schacht was appointed Commissioner for National Currency on November 13, 1923, and on November 15, printing of the devalued mark ceased.

The next day, on November 16, the new Rentenmark appeared. On November 20, the devalued mark was pegged to the Rentenmark at the exchange rate of a trillion to one. The hyperinflation was over, and Germany was back on the gold standard.

§§§

As the economy stabilized and prosperity began to slowly reappear across the country, the mood lifted, and people began to believe once again in the future. As the manufacture and export of goods picked up and jobs opened up, there was real money again in the pay envelopes.

Berlin began to regain its former luster, and the new prosperity revived the cultural life of the capital. Artists and writers were drawn to the city, and the renowned "Berliner Tempo" returned.

Chapter Sixty-eight

Celebration

As soon as it was confirmed that Ursula was indeed pregnant, she and Eckhardt decided that they would celebrate with their old friends, Herbert and Meira. Eckhardt left it up to Ursula to plan the evening, and she then telephoned Meira, who was ecstatic when she heard the good news. Ursula suggested they meet at Klärchen's Ballhaus for dinner and dancing, like old times. Meira hesitated for a moment when she heard this, and pointed out that Herbert, who had always been an excellent dancer, might be hesitant to try it because of his knee injury. She did go on to say, however, that his knee had responded surprisingly well to treatment and therapy when he returned home. He had even been able to walk, with a slight limp, without his cane. It was decided to move forward with their plans and leave it up to Herbert to decide whether or not he would like to try his luck on the dance floor.

This was Spring of 1924. The war was long over, the hyperinflation was behind them, life was becoming better and better. The latest dances were imported from America, and everything American was in high fashion. Some young men and women had begun to take on American names. Wilhelm became Billy, Friedrich now liked to be called Freddy and Johann was now Johnny. Their girlfriends were Betty, Mary, and Judy.

The friends met at their reserved table at Clärchen's. They looked around the room and marveled at the recent renovations which had been made to the place. When the giant menus were brought to them, they were astonished to see how the offerings had changed. The traditional German kitchen was still well represented with Wienerschnitzel and *Eisbein* (pork shank), but they now competed with heretofore unheard-of delicacies: Hungarian goulash, Russian Stroganoff, and American-style grilled steak.

The American Negro jazz orchestra was in full swing, with German and American hits intermixed. Couples on the dance floor were showing their expertise, and life was good.

As soon as they had placed their orders and were settled in with cocktails (another American import), the girls had their heads together discussing the choices of boys' names (of course it would be a boy). Herbert and Eckhardt smiled at each other in a spirit of contentment, with Eckhardt already taking on the look of a proud father.

"Well, old boy, you've beaten me to it," teased Herbert.

"Yeah, it caught me by surprise," responded his friend.

"Well, I have a little news of my own," added Herbert.

"I have decided to enter the university and follow in my father's footsteps. I'm gonna study medicine. Meira and I have talked it over, and she and my father have convinced me we can manage it."

"That's wonderful! Congratulations!" exclaimed Eckhardt.

Hearing the conversation, Ursula added, "Oh Herbert, I'm so proud of you. You'll make a wonderful doctor. You like people and people like you. You'd better watch out though, Meira. All the women will be making up ailments, in order to visit the handsome doctor."

Eckhardt burst out laughing, and Meira, pretending to be jealous, muttered, "Yes. I warned him about that. But as a nurse working in the profession, I'll be keeping an eye on him, and all my friends will too."

There was laughter all around, and Herbert turned beet red and grumbled, "Oh, sure. That sounds like a real problem," which brought more laughter.

The food was served and savored by the two couples, who were nourished by their mutual friendship as much as by what was eaten.

After enjoying dessert and coffee, the atmosphere of congeniality and contentment continued, until Ursula turned to her husband and said, "Come on. I want to dance. In a few months, I'm gonna have to bend over backward in order to keep from falling on my face. So, you come dance with your wife before she turns into a clumsy old cow."

Eckhardt chuckled and arose with the comment, "You're right. I'd better get out there before Herbert does and shows me up with his fancy steps."

Ursula and Eckhardt got into the swing of a fast fox trot, to the tune of the American hit, "You're Driving Me Crazy."

As he watched his friend, Herbert turned an idea over in his mind. *Do I dare try that? What if I take Meira out there and fall on my ass? But I know she loves to dance...*

Meira squeezed Herbert's hand with a smile of understanding. She was thrilled enough that he was simply able to walk without crutches.

Ursula led Eckhardt by the hand as they laughingly returned to the table. Their faces were flushed and shiny with perspiration, to which Herbert quipped, "You'd better come down here and do that every night, fella. You're really out of shape."

"Okay, wise guy."

At this, Herbert made his decision. *Yes, I can do this!*

As a slow fox trot began, Herbert stood up and mockingly bowed to his wife. "Madame, would you do me the honor?"

Smiling, Meira arose and curtsying, answered, "Of course, sir. But my mother has warned me about fellows like you, so you behave."

Laughing, Ursula and Eckhardt watched their friends as they blended into the couples moving around the dance floor. Herbert began to move Meira to the music with only a slightly discernible limp. But as the music progressed, this too disappeared. He gradually picked up the tempo, and they were soon moving gracefully to the music. Herbert looked smugly at his friends as he and Meira swung past the table.

Ursula turned to Eckhardt, "Look at him!"

"Yes, that's the old Herbert," he replied.

Meira, for her part, had a look of surprised bliss on her face. Life was indeed good.

Chapter Sixty-nine

Mein Kampf
(My Struggle)

An 18-year old young man born April 20, 1889, in Braunau am Inn, a small town near the German border in Austria, then part of the Austro-Hungarian Empire, was alone and dejected in Vienna on a day in 1903. He had seen himself as an artist and had even managed to sell sketches and postcards on the streets of the city, but his application for admission to the Vienna Academy of Arts and the School of Architecture was rejected. He had failed his school exams at age 15 and had not completed a formal education. So, he only managed to eke out a hand-to-mouth existence in the Austrian capital for the next several years. His name was Adolf Hitler.

It is believed that at this time he first became interested in politics and observed how the masses could be made to respond to certain themes. He was especially impressed by the anti-Semitic nationalist Christian-Socialist Party. He was Austrian, but had long been fascinated with Austria's vigorous, dynamic neighbor, Germany. In 1914, when World War I broke out, he volunteered to fight for the German Army, and gained respect as a corporal and a dispatch-runner. His several awards for bravery included the Iron Cross First Class. He was blinded by mustard gas in October of 1918 and was in the hospital when Germany surrendered. He was devastated by Germany's defeat, and fell into a state of deep depression, facing an uncertain future.

Small political groups had begun to form in the last years of the war. In March 1918, Anton Drexler formed one of these small groups. Drexler was a local locksmith and was bitterly opposed to the armistice of November 1918 and the revolutionary upheavals that followed. Drexler followed the views of militant nationalists, such as opposing the Treaty of Versailles. He held anti-Semitic, anti-monarchist and anti-Marxist views and also believed in the superiority of Germans, claiming to be part of an Aryan "master race." He accused international capitalism of being a Jewish-dominated movement and denounced capitalists for war profiteering. Drexler blamed the political violence and instability in Germany on the Weimar Republic for being out-of-touch with the masses, especially the lower classes. His small political party was called the *Deutsche Arbeiterpartei* (German Workers' Party), or DAP.

Following recovery from his war wounds, Hitler gained employment as a spy for the German Army and was ordered to attend a meeting of the DAP in September, 1919. Upon attending, he found he agreed with Drexler on his nationalistic, anti-Semitic views, but disagreed with how the party was organized. When the lectures concluded, Hitler got involved in a heated political argument with another visitor. In vehemently attacking the man's opinions, Hitler caught the attention of other party members in attendance. Impressed with his oratory skills, Drexler approached Hitler and encouraged him to join the DAP. On the orders of his army superiors, Hitler applied to join the party.

Once accepted, he quickly gained a reputation as a powerful orator, with his passion about the injustices forced on Germany by the Treaty of Versailles. Soon people were joining the party to see Hitler and hear his rousing speeches, which seemed to stir audiences to near hysteria and be willing to do whatever he suggested.

Ernst Röhm was a former military officer who had distinguished himself during the war. Seriously wounded in the Battle of Verdun in 1916, he had spent the remainder of the war as a staff officer. He became interested in politics and joined the DAP in 1919. It was soon thereafter that he met Hitler, and they became close friends.

One year later, the party changed its name to the *National Sozialistische Deutsche Arbeiter Partei,* or NSDAP. The name was abbreviated to Nazi. Hitler designed the party banner himself, placing a black swastika in a white circle on a red background. His bitter speeches against the Treaty of Versailles, other politicians, Communists and Jews, soon brought him widespread recognition, and in 1921, Hitler became the chairman of the NSDAP, replacing Anton Drexler.

Crowds were flocking to beer halls to hear Hitler's impassioned speeches. In order to protect gatherings of the Nazi Party from disruptions by Social Democrats (SPD) and Communists (KPD), and later to disrupt meetings of the other political parties, the small Nazi party began to organize and formalize groups of ex-soldiers and beer-hall brawlers. Many of the members were disgruntled war veterans like Hitler himself, and some even had prison records for being convicted of violent crimes. Röhm became the head of this newly-formed group. As the vanguard of Hitler's security forces, they quickly built a reputation as "thugs" who were given to violence with little provocation. By September 1921, the name *Sturmabteilung* (SA) (Stormtrooper) was being used informally for the group. The name was derived from the specialized assault troops during the war who used infiltration tactics and had been organized into small squads of a few soldiers each.

Brown was the original color of the uniforms for troops posted to Germany's former African colonies. After the war, with the loss of these colonies, the military surplus items became cheaply available and were distributed to the members of the SA. The SA then came to be known as *Braunhemden* (Brownshirts) and was dubbed *die braune Bewegung* (the brown movement). The SA became the guardians of Hitler and his meetings, but they were soon disrupting the meetings of opposing parties, fighting against their paramilitary units, and intimidating anyone they disagreed with, but especially Jews.

In 1922, the Nazi Party youth organization, called *Jugendbund der NSDAP* (Youth Organization of the NSDAP), was established. Its purpose was to recruit future members of the SA. Numerous youth movements existed across Germany prior to and especially after the war. The prominent ones were formed as political groups, which included the *Jugendbund.*

On November 8, 1923, Hitler made this his first attempt at seizing power. Gustav Kahr, the Prime Minister of the state of Bavaria, was to be the keynote speaker at one of Munich's largest beer halls, the *Bürgerbräukeller.* After the meeting had been in progress for some time, Röhm and 2,000 SA Brownshirts stormed into the hall allowing Hitler to take the stand and proclaim that the national revolution against the Weimar Republic had begun and to announce the formation of a new government. A riot ensued, the Brownshirts stormed the War Ministry and held it for sixteen hours. This led to several deaths, but the coup ultimately failed.

The failed attempt to overthrow the Weimar Government came to be known as the "Beer Hall Putsch." Hitler, Röhm, and eight others were arrested and tried for high treason and sentenced to fifteen years in prison in Landsberg, which was one of the most lenient institutions in the German prison system. Hitler only served nine months of his fifteen-year sentence, during which time he dictated most of his volume of *Mein Kampf* to his deputy, Rudolf Hess, and Emil Maurice. This propaganda work, comprised of falsehoods and anti-Semitic invective, clearly laid out his plan for transforming German society based on racial superiority.

Chapter Seventy

A New Beginning

Shortly after his wife announced her pregnancy, Eckhardt was promoted to Assistant Chief Electrician at Siemens with a substantial pay increase.

"You know darling, I've been thinking. With a new baby coming soon, do you think we should look for a new apartment?" Eckhardt suggested one morning soon after he had gotten his new promotion.

"I've watched your mother do a fantastic job of maintaining a home here for years. Considering the primitive conditions she has had to put up with, I've wondered how she did it. Briquette stoves for heating and cooking, hauling chamber pots up and down the stairs to the toilet, coping with rats in the hallway. Do we want to live that way?"

Ursula, somewhat taken aback at the harsh description of the home she had grown up in, replied defensively, "Just because we're now a little better off financially, are we too good for my family and the neighbors around here?"

"No, sweetheart. Not at all. It's just because now we can afford something a little better, I would like to make things easier for you and for our baby. What if we were able to take Christina and Rudi with us?" he continued.

Ursula brightened at that thought. "Maybe you're right. Let me talk to Mama about it.'

Later that afternoon, when she returned from work, Ursula approached her mother with the idea. Christina, however, did not respond enthusiastically.

"I've lived in Wedding all my life. I moved into this apartment with Detlev right after our wedding. We brought our children into the world and raised them here. I have lifelong friends and neighbors here. I think it's too late in life for me to make such big changes. You can't transplant old trees, you know."

When Ursula even suggested that Christina could help her with the new baby, that still did not sway her. "I managed to raise my children myself, and I had four close in age. With only one to look after, you'll do fine."

Discouraged, but not surprised at Christina's reaction, she reported the conversation back to Eckhardt.

Thoughtful for a moment, he replied, "Well, I can see where your mother is coming from. But I wonder what Rudi would think. Did you talk to him?"

"No, I think we'd better be careful with that. I could tell Mama was a bit hurt that we might be moving soon, and I wouldn't want to upset her further. If Rudi left, she might feel totally abandoned."

"I can see that, but Rudi is not a child, and he very likely will be striking out on his own one of these days, anyway" Eckhardt countered.

"That's true. Nevertheless, I think we should be careful. One thing at a time. When he hears about our move, he might bring up the subject himself. Rudi's like every other young person. He doesn't see a future for himself in Wedding" Ursula replied. "But I don't want to be the one blamed for taking him away from Mama.'

Eckhardt sighed with resignation. "Well then, I'll let you decide when, or if, the time might be right to at least make the offer to him to move with us."

The matter was left at that for the time being.

Chapter Seventy-one

The New House

It was decided they would begin looking for a home closer to Eckhardt's work, perhaps in Tegel, where he had lived with Herbert as a young bachelor before the war. Unexpectedly, he heard from a colleague at Siemens, whose father had passed away, that his mother would be selling her small house in the Gatow district of Spandau.

Eckhardt hurried home with this news, eager to tell Ursula about it. An appointment to view the house the following Saturday was made through Eckhardt's colleague.

It was a small two-storied thatched-roofed brick cottage one street away from the Havel river. Central heating with a coal-fired furnace in the basement and steam radiators on the first floor had been installed before the outbreak of the war. The kitchen had been recently upgraded with an electric range and a cold-water sink. A small cold pantry was located off the kitchen, but Eckhardt already had plans to purchase a modern refrigerator soon. There was a small lavatory with a flush toilet near the front door. A bedroom and a combination living and dining room completed the layout of the ground floor.

Upstairs, there were two small garret bedrooms tucked under the roof. In the back of the house was a small garden and storage shed. The property was bordered by a wall around the backyard and a wooden fence around the front. Along the north side of the house was a space large enough for a small car. This was important to Eckhardt, as he had become fascinated with automobiles, and had promised himself to have one in the not too distant future.

When she saw the house, Ursula was convinced right away they should have it. They paid the widow a deposit of 300 new Rentenmarks, with the understanding that the balance of the down payment of 1000 marks would be paid within 30 days or less. Since the recent issuance of the new currency, mortgages were not easily obtained, but with Eckhardt's good employment and work history with Siemens, he had been able to arrange a loan from the employees' credit system.

In a frenzy of excitement, they returned to Wedding and described what they had found to Christina. She was still opposed to moving, but Rudi, listening to the conversation, was instantly in support of his sister and brother-in-law. Ursula went on and on about the central heating, the electric range, and the convenient lavatory. Eckhardt spoke up and added he intended to extend steam heat to the upstairs rooms and would soon build a full bathroom on the back of the house with hot water.

Christina listened to the young people and their plans. *I wonder what it would have been like if I had been able to raise my babies with those modern conveniences. Maybe it would be fun to help Ursula with the baby in such comfort.*

As she looked around the old flat, she could understand why Ursula would want to start her family in a better environment. Perhaps it was time to move on, after all.

§§§

Herbert and Meira were delighted with the house. Meira proposed that she and Ursula begin the search for furniture together. Meira and Ursula were able to schedule their days off together the following week. They began to make the rounds of new and used furniture stores around the city. Because of the recent hard times and hyperinflation, many people had sold off their furniture in exchange for commodities and hard currency. As a result, extremely inexpensive but good quality furniture was everywhere. The two young women quickly determined, however, that much of the most attractive merchandise had come from large houses and was therefore oversized for the small house in Spandau.

Then Ursula hit on the idea, that perhaps the old lady selling the house, might be willing to sell some of her pieces already there. They made their way across the city and presented themselves at the woman's front door. Surprised at seeing them so soon, and without an appointment, she did not invite them in, until Ursula profusely apologized for the inconvenience and began to present her idea. At first, the old woman hesitated, then invited them in to further discuss it. When she had been there before, Ursula had not paid particular attention to the furnishings, as she was focused on the house itself, but now when she looked around, she was somewhat let down by what she saw.

The living room furniture were the best pieces in the house. They were representative of what had been in style during the last half of the previous century. Biedermeyer had been in fashion when the current owner had married and started her family. Her choices had been more modest versions of this, but some of the dark wood and not very comfortable design were what Ursula saw before her.

After further consideration, Ursula, together with Meira's agreement, decided to take the bedroom furnishings, and the small dining room table and chairs, and continue to look further for the living room.

As they walked to the bus stop, the two friends realized once again, they had much to be thankful for. Their husbands, although injured, had survived the war, and were engaged in building a good future.

Now Ursula was expecting Eckhardt's child and was looking forward to moving into her own new home. Meira was rising in a career in which she was valued and excelled. Herbert had found a new career goal in medicine. Yes, compared to many in these precarious times, they indeed had a great deal to be thankful for.

Chapter Seventy-two

Die Goldene Zwanziger Jahren
(The Golden Years of the '20s)

This phrase was coined to describe the short period after the hyperinflation which ended in November 1923, and the onset of the worldwide depression commencing with the stock market crash on Wall Street in October 1929.

Although Germany began to revive economically, with the injection of more than $25 billion of foreign money. More than half of this came from American loans, the rest being organized by American bankers as intermediaries. Financial and industrial expertise was also being provided by the American government and US corporations, but the white collar-middle class were not great beneficiaries of this so-called "golden age."

This group, comprised of managers, bureaucrats, bankers and clerks, did not receive the wage increases of the blue collar industrial sector. By the late 1920s, industrial sector wages began to surpass those of the middle class. Although unemployment decreased generally, it dragged on amongst white collar professionals, and almost half of these did not qualify for state unemployment relief.

The result was an increase of middle class resentment and a perception that the SPD (Socialist Party) dominated government and favored the blue-collar class at the expense of the once admired and respected part of German society – the middle class.

The rumor began to spread that this was an intentional and subtle form of class warfare intended to impose "socialism by stealth." The workers were represented by the SPD and KPD (Communist Party), but the middle class had no party which truly represented them. Therefore, by the late 1920s, Hitler's NSDAP was able to gain the attention of the disenchanted middle class.

German farmers were also adversely affected during the "Golden Age." By the mid-1920s, the importation of cheaper foreign food products forced them to improve productivity by investing in new technologies, such as tractors and farm machinery. This forced many farmers to borrow heavily to purchase this equipment. Unable to make payments, farmers then defaulted on their debts, and there was a marked increase of farm foreclosures.

The situation of German farmers became worse due to a global grain surplus in the mid-1920s, and in 1928, this led to small-scale riots – "the farmers' revenge" – protesting foreclosures and low market prices. Agricultural production fell by 1929 to less than three-quarters of its pre-war levels. Ultra-nationalist parties, such as the NSDAP, generated much propaganda using the slogan *Blut und Boden* (Blood and Soil) and its nationalistic connotations.

Many farmers struggling with debt and obstinate banks became very receptive to Nazi anti-Semitic propaganda, and to the rumors of conspiracies supposedly instigated by Jewish bankers and financiers.

In Berlin, however, much of the despair of the times was masked by the surge of culture and entertainment, represented by the glitz and glamour of the capital. After the tragedy of war, the scourge of the flu pandemic, the humiliation of defeat and terms of the Treaty of Versailles, the occupation of the industrial heartland of the Ruhr valley by the French, the hunger and despair caused by the period of hyperinflation, the German public was desperate for "normalcy" and relief.

The policies of Gustav Streseman – Germany's chancellor in 1922 and Foreign Minister from 1924 to 1929 – brought about the return of economic and political stability and fostered a new era of optimism and hope.

After the deprivations of the previous decade, the mood in Berlin was one of excess in many forms. Young people were not interested in saving money and conservative living, as their parents had been in Wilhelminian pre-war Berlin, but were more given over to spending and having a good time. As a result, places of entertainment sprang up everywhere. Cabarets and nightclubs were pervasive.

Berthold Kempinski, a wine merchant from Posen – at the time a German province, now in Poland – moved to Berlin in 1872 and established his wine-merchant's business on Friedrichstraße. In 1889, he opened the largest restaurant in Berlin on Leipzigerstraße, thereby launching his family business into the restaurant trade.

After his death in 1910, his heirs expanded into the hotel business with the construction in 1918 of the impressive Hotel Kempinski at

Kurfürstendamm 27, which today is the location of the Kempinski Hotel Bristol.

In 1928, the Kempinski company acquired the legendary Haus Vaterland on Potsdamer Platz. Such entrepreneurship was exemplified all over the city during the 1920s, with the establishment of new venues, and the upgrading and modernization of existing ones, such as Clärchen's Ballhaus.

Berlin became a magnet for artists, writers, musicians and architects. Many world-renowned names were established through their works in and around the 1920s, such as Berthold Brecht and Kurt Weil – *Dreigoschen Oper* (The Threepenny Opera), 1928 – Walter Gropius – *Bauhaus* (Design School), 1919-33, and Alexander Döblin – *Berlin Alexanderplatz* (the film), 1929.

The Romanisches Café was a café-bar established in 1916, on the eastern corner of Auguste-Viktoria-Platz – at the eastern end of Kurfürstendamm. It quickly developed into the most popular meeting place for artists in Berlin, especially after World War I. Writers, painters, actors, directors, journalists and critics gathered there. By the end of the twenties, however, growing unrest and violence in the city caused the Romanisches Café to decline. In 1927, Nazis instigated a riot on Kufürstendamm and targeted the café as a meeting place for left-wing intellectuals. With the Nazi takeover, and the resulting emigration of most of its clientele, the café ceased to be an artists' meeting place. (It was completely destroyed in an Allied air raid in 1943).

There were many who capitalized on the rowdy atmosphere of Berlin in the 1920s. The city became a center of the drug trade and the upsurge in crime which accompanied it. Prostitution, which had heretofore existed as a shadow "industry" came out in the open. Many members of both sexes turned to this "profession," as they discovered that more profit could be realized in a shorter amount of time than in a regular job.

There were streets in Berlin that were virtually turned into centers of the trade, which was "open for business" both day and night. The Kleist Kasino was one of hundreds of gay bars which sprang up all over the city and, indeed, Berlin became known as the gay capital of Europe in the 1920s.

In the background, behind all of the riotous living and debauchery, was a government desperately trying to establish the foundation of a democratic society, but the conflict of forces from both the extreme left and the extreme right, brought it all to an end in 1933.

Chapter Seventy-three

Roter Wedding
(Red Wedding)

In the election of 1925, the KPD (Communist Party) garnered over 52% of the vote in Berlin. The Nazis called it "the reddest city in Europe after Moscow." The district of Wedding had become the stronghold of the communist movement and came to be known as "*Roter Wedding.*"

Christina had been shocked and revolted by the murder of Rosa Luxembourg and Karl Liebknecht in 1919, as were many others. As a member of the working class living in the working-class district of Wedding, she had been surrounded by political discussions stating the aims of the Communist Party. Not a highly educated woman, she had not been particularly interested in politics earlier in life, but as the travails of the war, the death of her husband and two children in the Influenza pandemic of 1918, and the subsequent hardships during the postwar hyperinflation wore her down, she began to reflect on why she and her country had suffered so much.

As she heard more about Marxism and its stated goals for building a more equitable society, she began to wonder if perhaps it might not offer the deliverance from the grinding poverty and misery suffered by herself and those around her. She was drawn to the concept of socialism and the equal distribution of goods and services to all. One spring morning, shortly before Ursula and Eckhardt bought their house, while waiting for Mr. Schroeder to wrap her purchase of fresh rolls and bread, she was approached by a neighborly acquaintance she had known for several years. After the exchange of enquiries about their respective families, the woman asked Christina if she was going to the rally to be held in the evening in nearby Schiller Park.

The keynote speaker would be a young member of the KPD leadership, one Walther Ulbricht. (Ulbricht would play a leading role in the establishment of the DDR or *Deutsche Demokratische Republik* in East Germany after World War II).

After responding, she hadn't heard anything about it. Christina then listened to what the woman had to say about Ulbricht's inspiring speech she had heard at an earlier meeting.

"Why don't we go together," she suggested to Christina.

Glad to have an opportunity to interact with another woman near her own age, and to be able to get out of the flat for a while, she agreed to meet her neighbor in the corner pub after feeding her family. That evening at the table she informed them of her plans, to which Ursula raised a strong objection.

"You shouldn't be involved with those people, Mama. It's dangerous. Their meetings often turn into brawls when the Nazis arrive, and you could end up being hurt or thrown in jail by the police."

Eckhardt concurred. "If you want to know more about the Communist movement, you should read the writings of Marx and Lenin. Then if you are still interested, I would be glad to go with you to a meeting. But Ursula's right. Two unaccompanied women would become targets for rowdies that will be there."

Rudi, who had been listening to the conversation spoke up. "I'll go with you, Mama."

At this, Christina turned to her son with a grateful smile.

"Oh, would you? There, you two worriers. My big strong son will protect me," she shot at Eckhardt and Ursula.

Looking at his wife with resignation, Eckhardt shrugged his shoulders and sighed.

Ursula, still not comfortable with the idea of her mother being in such a situation, said, "Well, if you're determined. But Rudi, you get them out of there at the first sign of trouble, or if the Nazi Brownshirts even show up."

"I promise," he assured his sister, confident that he could certainly handle himself against any street thugs like the Nazis.

When they arrived at the park, a large crowd had already seated themselves on the benches provided, and many others having arrived later, stood under the trees or were milling about. Red banners were hung behind the speakers' podium, and everything seemed to project a festive mood. Others who were crossing the nearby Edinburgerstraße, held up traffic, and a harried traffic policeman was trying to maintain order. The meeting came to order with a record of the Communist anthem, *The Internationale*, played on a windup gramophone set before the microphone, followed by a short welcome speech made by a local party leader from Wedding.

Finally, the keynote speaker was introduced, and Walther Ulbricht began his speech. Having been born in Leipzig in Saxony, he spoke in a strong Saxon dialect, which was comical to Berliners. Low snickers ran through the audience, which were silenced by glares and mutterings from other listeners. Ulbricht seemed not to notice the disturbance, and continued with his remarks, commencing to expand upon the words of Marx and Lenin, extolling the vision of a new world of equality and socialist brotherhood.

The audience was settling in to take in the inspiring words of the speaker when a commotion was heard out on the street, with speeding trucks coming to a screeching halt. Young Brownshirts piled out and ran toward the crowd of listeners. The Communist counterpart of the Nazi Brownshirts, was a contingent of young men wearing red scarves around their necks and sworn to protect Ulbricht. The hapless audience, caught in the middle, scattered in all directions in panic.

Rudi, having been alerted by noise of the arriving trucks, had immediately taken the arms of the two women accompanying him and had pulled them away into the darkness behind the speakers' stand. He had purposely and wisely picked a spot on the outer edge of the crowd near the podium before the meeting had begun, in the event any danger should arise.

They made their way through the darkness. The clash between the two groups had developed into ghastly pandemonium. The shouts and curses were drowned out by screams of terror and pain. This was followed by the whistles and shouts of the arriving police, who had been standing at the ready on Barfußstraße bordering the southeast side of the park. Rudi and the terrified women made their way by a circuitous route back to their neighborhood, slinking through dark backstreets. Christina was shaking from shock and terror, and Rudi was quivering with rage. The thought that people could have their right to listen to a variety of ideas taken away by bullies filled him with a fury.

Chapter Seventy-four

A New Citizen

Eckhardt Detlev Meinert was born on Saturday, November 1, 1924, at 6:15 a.m. in the Siemens Company Medical Clinic with Dr. Horst Kirschner, a Siemens company doctor, attending. Little Eckhardt was a robust miniature of his father, weighing 3.5 kilograms (7.5 lb.) and was 50 centimeters (20 in.) long. Meira assisted with the delivery, which had gone smoothly. Ursula was in labor less than 45 minutes, and although exhausted, was radiant with a maternal glow.

When Eckhardt was called in after the delivery, he was ghostly pale with concern for his wife, but upon seeing her smiling and holding their handsome son, he burst into tears of relief. He insisted that Herbert be allowed into the delivery room, and when the two friends faced each other, Eckhardt now holding his son, Herbert too became misty-eyed. The two couples gathered around Ursula's bed and the bond of their friendship was deep and tangible

As was typical for the time, Ursula and the baby were kept in the clinic for four more days for observation. She would have preferred to have left the next day after the delivery. Eckhardt visited her and his son every afternoon after work and brought huge bouquets of flowers. Christina and Rudi, as proud grandmother and uncle, and Herbert and Meira contributed to the floral collection, until by the time Ursula was released, the room resembled a florist shop.

Having moved into their home in the early spring, Ursula had given up her job at KaDeWe where she had been assured by her supervisor a position would always be waiting for her. She spent the spring and summer months renovating the new home. She and Eckhardt had worked together painting and hanging wallpaper, and she made new curtains for every room in the house.

Eckhardt had kept his word and had built a bathroom addition on the back of the house, where plumbing was installed with hot water for the new bathtub and sink. For the present, it was decided to wait on the extension of steam heat for the upstairs bedrooms. The baby's crib was in the kitchen near the door leading into the master bedroom. All in all, they had managed to turn the little cottage into a cheerful, comfortable home for their family.

§§§

Christina had weighed the possibility of moving to Spandau with her daughter's family, but decided she preferred to stay in the old neighborhood in Wedding for the time being, especially now that she had made new acquaintances among the local KPD members. She had her widow's pension, and Rudi was by now a tram driver, so together they were financially secure.

She was not by nature a person who spent a great deal of time reading, but she attended the party meetings and read the pamphlets and articles made available to her. Although she and her husband had raised their family with a sense of pride in their self-sufficiency, she now began to believe the purpose of government was to oversee the distribution of goods and services to all members of the community – even if it meant surrender of some freedoms and life choices.

Ursula and Eckhardt, on the other hand, having made their way without much support from the government, felt that freedom to make life choices was worth the risk of being independent. Having succeeded by working for private enterprises – KaDeWe and Siemens – had proven that one could succeed in life without surrendering to the decisions of bureaucrats.

Rudi was undecided about his political beliefs, but was determined to accompany his mother to meetings, after the experience they had at the Spring rally in Schiller Park.

Chapter Seventy-five

Christmas 1924

With prosperity returning, the shops across the city were once again displaying a vast array of merchandise. KaDeWe on Wittenbergplatz was decked out in festive decoration, with beautiful displays in the show windows. The glass showcases on Kurfürstendamm were filled once again with luxury items as in prewar times. Crowds of shoppers once again thronged the major shopping districts on Unter den Linden, Kurfürstendamm and Tauentzienstraße. People had money once again and were eager to spend it.

Ursula was in high spirits as she prepared her new home for the holidays. The greatest and most recent gift this year was asleep in his crib in the warm kitchen, where his mother busied herself baking a variety of Christmas specialties – raisin-filled Stollen, Lebkuchen and Spekulatius cookies.

A large goose had been ordered to be served on Christmas Eve with Rotkohl and Knödeln. The ingredients for the Glühwein had been purchased and were ready for Eckhardt's expert hand in preparing the delicious drink, made from red wine, heated and spiced with cinnamon sticks, cloves, star aniseed, citrus, sugar, vanilla pods and rum.

Eckhardt would choose and purchase the Christmas tree, which would normally have been done by Ursula and himself together, but they had agreed they would not expose the new baby to the cold. There would be other Christmases when that would be a family affair.

Also, the trip to the Weihnachtsmarkt would have to wait for another year. It was agreed that Christina and Rudi would come and stay overnight on Christmas Eve. But again, because of the new baby, there would be no attendance at Christmas Eve services as in years past. This would also eliminate the need for any discussions about religion, about which Christina, influenced by her newly discovered Communist doctrine, was forming some new opinions. Herbert and Meira were expected to spend Christmas Eve with his parents in Dahlem but would come for supper the next evening.

Christmas Eve arrived, and the weather cooperated with cold but clear skies and Christina and Rudi made their way across the city by bus and subway. Most people made sure they reached their destinations early, as some transit lines ceased operation by 3 p.m. on Christmas Eve and Christmas day.

When they arrived at the cottage in Spandau they were greeted with embraces and laughter by their loved ones. The new member of the family seemed to sense the cheerful atmosphere in the house, and greeted his grandma with grins as she picked him up to hug him. Uncle Rudi impatiently waited his turn to hold his nephew, and the love was felt by everyone.

The house was filled with succulent odors, and the kitchen was so hot from days of cooking and baking it became necessary to open a window. Care was taken to place baby Eckhardt in his crib in the master bedroom to prevent him from getting a chill.

Ursula then resumed preparations for the evening feast while Christina prepared lunch. Eckhardt and Rudi withdrew to the parlor with two Schultheiss beers to discuss the upcoming *Fußball* match between the Berlin league, BFC Germania and SSV Ulm after the new year.

Ulm, being only 10 kilometers from Eckhardt's hometown of Blaubeuren, would of course have his support, while Rudi, a born Berliner would root for BFC. They shared a friendly rivalry, and there was much bantering, as each extolled the virtues of his team and made much of the supposed deficiencies of his team's opponent.

Then lunch was served, and after the table was cleared, the women began to prepare the goose for roasting and turned on the oven. Christina marveled at the convenience and cleanliness of Ursula's electric range and oven. Such luxury!

As the side dishes were prepared and set in the cold pantry, and with the goose in the oven, Ursula and her mother decided they would take a break with a nice cup of tea and sample the Spekulatius cookies. Eckhardt looked in the kitchen as the ladies sat at the small breakfast table with their treats and quipped, "Where are our goodies? We want a sample, too."

"Too bad," teased Ursula. "This is only for kitchen staff." She smiled and winked at Christina as she said this.

"Oh, come on," wailed Rudi. "That's not fair."

"We'd better give them some," responded Christina, "or we'll have three babies crying next."

Laughing, Ursula said, "Alright, little boys. Come get some, but one apiece."

As night fell, the big moment arrived, and the feast was spread on the dining room table. The four family members gathered around, and although Christina was somewhat indifferent to religion nowadays, she too bowed her head respectfully as Eckhardt offered a prayer of thanksgiving.

The goose was perfect, the Rotkohl added just the right accent with its sweet and sour goodness, the Knödeln were just soft enough, but not doughy, and the pickles and relishes that were homemade by Christina topped off the meal. Everyone ate until they couldn't eat another bite, and a satisfied lull fell over the table as the diners contemplated the remains of the dinner, illuminated by the candles on the table.

Finally, Eckhardt spoke up and suggested they have their dessert after lighting candles on the tree and opening their presents. This was agreed to all around. Then Eckhardt motioned to Rudi to follow him as he made his way to the back door.

Once outside, Eckhardt, in response to Rudi's questioning look, explained he needed help bringing Ursula's Christmas present into the house. Eckhardt showed the way to the garden shed with a small pocket flashlight. He opened the door and proudly shone the light on a gleaming white refrigerator. It had been placed on the small wagon used for gardening. Rudi was very impressed.

Together they pulled the wagon out of the shed and across the yard. When they reached the house, Eckhardt sent Rudi ahead to tell the women to go into the bedroom and close the door.

When he returned and assured Eckhardt all was in readiness, the two of them being very strong, struggled to lift the refrigerator over the back step and carry it into the kitchen. It was placed against the wall opposite the stove and plugged into the nearby outlet.

When all was ready, he instructed Rudi to open the bedroom door and tell the ladies to come out, but as soon as he looked into the bedroom, he hastily withdrew, embarrassed as his sister had decided to breast feed the baby while she waited.

All laughed, except Rudi. His mother chided him, "What's the matter with you? You've seen women feeding their babies before on the bus or on park benches in the summertime." Rudi mumbled something indistinct.

Eckhardt remarked, "Hurry up with that, before I change my mind and take this thing back."

Still holding her son to her breast, Ursula walked into the kitchen, followed by her mother. When they caught sight of the beautiful gleaming appliance, they both gasped.

"Eckhardt Meinert! What have you been up to?" said his astonished wife.

"Don't you like it?" he prodded.

"Like it! I can't find words to say how much I like it," she retorted. She carried the still nursing baby across the kitchen and kissed her husband, who embraced his wife and child.

Christina observed the little drama being played out before her, and in spite of herself breathed an unvoiced prayer of thanksgiving for her family, for her son-in-law and for his love for her daughter. Once again, she wished Detlev were here to see this.

Rudi, watching, thought to himself, *I want all of this someday, too.*

At last, the Christmas tree candles were lit, and as in years past, O, Tannenbaum was sung. Presents were exchanged with expressions of gratitude, and the evening began to wind down. The Christmas treats and Glühwein were served. As they savored the last of the wonderful day, they watched the tree candles slowly burn down as they contemplated how blessed they were.

Ursula spoke up, "I think about how much has happened since we had our Christmas ten years ago. I remember Papa playing his accordion, and Emil and Rudi playing with their toy wooden train. I remember Brigitta trying to be so grown up and become a woman. I remember Meira being there for her first Christmas and giving us the luxury chocolates from KaDeWe."

Turning to Eckhardt, she said, "Most of all, my darling, I remember you not being there and how afraid I was that we would never have another Christmas together."

He looked at her misty-eyed and replied, "I remember not being here, too, and how I missed you. I also remember that strange Christmas, when we and the British declared a Christmas truce and celebrated together between the trenches. I remember the young Englishman I met named William from Wiltshire.

We showed one another the pictures of our girlfriends. Both of you were so beautiful, you and his girl named Elizabeth. I wonder what ever happened to William. I hope he made it through the war and returned home to his Elizabeth."

All present contemplated what had just been discussed. The tree candles were extinguished, the dirty dishes and glassware put in the sink to be attended to the next morning, and everyone wished one another a happy Christmas as they embraced before going to their respective bedrooms.

The house was finally darkened, and peace settled over the little cottage and the great city.

Gute Nacht und frohe Weihnachten, Berlin.

Chapter Seventy-six

Raccoon Coats and the Laubfrosch
(Tree frog)

Herbert and Meira arrived at Eckhardt's and Ursula's house late in the afternoon of Christmas Day in a small bright green open automobile. Herbert was at the wheel with a big grin on his face, and Meira was seated beside him. They both were enshrouded in bulky raccoon coats, the latest fashion hit from America. Herbert was wearing a porkpie hat, and Meira a stylish cloche hat over her bobbed hair.

"Wow, man! Where did you get that?" blurted Eckhardt as he walked out to the car parked in front of his house.

"Papa surprised us with it as a Christmas present, and Meira surprised me with the news that she can already drive. She drove ambulances during the war and just needs to get her driver's license. She was the main reason Papa got it, because working the late shift at the hospital is getting more dangerous for women traveling alone at night on buses and streetcars."

By this time, Rudi came out, looked the shiny new vehicle over, and asked what it was. Herbert explained it was a 1924 Opel Laubfrosch and was the first car built on a moving assembly line in Germany. It got its nickname because of the green color.

Ursula and Christina then joined the admiring group standing around the car.

As Herbert and Meira stepped from the car with their coats reaching almost to the ground, Christina's eyes widened. "Oh, my god! Where did you get those coats? They look like fur tents."

This brought laughter all around.

"Mama, behave. Those are the latest fashion from America."

"From America!" Christina snorted. "I should have known."

The men grinned and the girls giggled. They were used to Christina's sardonic comments.

After congratulations had been extended to the proud owners, everyone made their way inside, where the cheerful house and lingering fragrances from holiday cooking put them into a relaxed and congenial mood.

Admiring the new raccoon coats, Eckhardt asked where they had been purchased and was astounded to receive the reply, "At Friedlanders."

Eyebrows went up at this. In surprise, Ursula blurted, "So, have you made things up with your father, Meira?"

Smiling, Meira explained, "Unfortunately, no. But I have good contact with Mama and my sister, Edna.

Herbert and I were strolling on Ku'damm one evening a couple of weeks ago, and we walked past Papa's store and saw the coats on display in the window. Herbert was fascinated and declared that he had to have one."

Herbert interrupted, "They're the latest thing with college students in America, and since I'm now a college student, myself, I want to be "collegiate," too."

This referred to a current American popular song entitled *Collegiate*. This brought a round of laughter.

Meira continued, "I slipped word to Mama, told her his size and asked her to get one for his Christmas present. She then had two delivered to her house, unbeknownst to Papa – one for Herbert and one for me. So, there you are. They're our Christmas presents from my Jewish parents, but Papa doesn't know about it."

Everyone had a good laugh at this, and Eckhardt volunteered, "I think we should get some, too. Don't you think so, dear? Definitely for you, Rudi. You too, Christina. You'd be a hit at your party meetings." More laughter.

"Don't be ridiculous, Eckhardt. Spare me your '*petit bourgeois*' indulgences," she sneered.

"Oh, come on now, Mama. You know he's teasing," said Ursula.

Christina mumbled to herself.

"Speaking of '*petit bourgeois'* indulgences, look what the *Weihnachtsmann* (Santa Claus) brought me," exclaimed Ursula proudly, pointing to her new refrigerator.

Meira was ecstatic. "Oh, Ursula! That's wonderful!"

After some discussion of how life was getting better, the group then seated themselves in the parlor.

"How was Christmas Eve in Dahlem?" Eckhardt asked.

Herbert and Meira exchanged glances. Then Herbert proceeded, "Where do I begin? With things getting better, Mama is back to some of her old ways as the daughter of the Prussian aristocracy.

Instead of all of the family decorating her house like normal people do, she had to have one of the most expensive florists in town come and do it – including putting up and decorating the Christmas tree! It looks like one of those overdone things in a department store.

Then for dinner last night, we had five complete courses, with a different wine for each course. I could tell Papa was a bit put out, but as usual he puts up with a lot to please Mama. All this for six people!"

"Six? I thought there were only four of you," exclaimed Eckhardt.

Herbert and Meira looked at each other again and paused for a moment.

"Yes, well now Karlheinz has a new friend that he stays with. His name is Egon Wolf, and is a pleasant enough fellow, but Karlheinz spends most of his time with him, to the exclusion of the rest of us.

Anyway, I told you about the row we had at my parents' house last summer after Rathenau was killed. Karlheinz stormed out of the house and hadn't spoken to my parents for months. Well, with Christmas coming on, my mother kept urging my father and me to talk to him and try to get him to come home for Christmas. As far as I was concerned, he could have stayed away and stewed in his own juice. And as things turned out yesterday, that probably would have been best," snorted Herbert.

"Nevertheless, I tracked him down by talking to some of his friends he's known for years and found out he hangs out with this Egon guy. They spend a lot of time at the Kleist Kasino."

"The Kleist Kasino?" interjected Rudi. "That *Schwuhllokal* (gay bar) in Schöneberg?"

"That's right," answered Herbert. "When I finally found Karlheinz and talked to him, at first he wasn't interested in seeing anyone in the family. Then I pointed out to him how much Mama has gone through with the war, worrying about me missing, the deaths of her parents, the loss of the estate, and now she can't see her youngest son. After he thought it over, he agreed to come for Christmas Eve on one condition: Egon comes too!

I asked why Egon wouldn't go home for Christmas, but Karlheinz explained that his father is a Lutheran pastor in Magdeburg, and his family has chucked him out because he's gay. I said I would check this out with Mama and Papa and get back to him.

When I told our parents about the situation, Mama's reaction was, 'Absolutely not!' My father reminded her that she'd been the one to insist that Karlheinz come home, so now there could be no backing out.

I was really surprised. I hadn't seen Papa stand up to her like that in a long time. Basically, he said, 'Your son has agreed to come home, and we'll all be together – including his friend'.

Mama started to argue, but when Papa puts on the doctor hat, he becomes the chief surgeon and is in charge."

This brought chuckles, to which Meira added, "Yes, I work with Doctor Lenz, and when he's on a case, everybody walks the chalk line."

"Well, anyway, to wind this long story up, we all sat around the table in our evening clothes – I had to loan Egon one of my tuxedos, because he's bigger than Karlheinz.

Egon turned out to be more pleasant than my brother and even managed to partly win Mama over. She commented afterward what a nice young man he was – and nice looking, too.

But Karlheinz sat there sulking like a bump and only gave short answers when asked a question. He spent most of his time glaring at my wife, which of course got under my skin. But I decided as long as he kept his mouth shut to her, I'd let it go."

Ursula turned to her friend and asked, "How did that make you feel, Meira?"

"Like Eckhardt said, as long as he didn't say anything insulting, I didn't let it bother me. Over a lifetime as a Jew, you learn to develop a thick skin early on, or you'll get your feelings hurt every day."

Everyone pondered this for a moment. Finally, Rudi spoke up, "You're an amazing girl, Meira. I know Karlheinz. He made me feel like crap most of the summer when I was on the estate. I'm surprised he has a friend at all. He's so full of himself, he doesn't know anybody else is around. He's got him and himself, and I guess the two of them are very happy together."

This brought another round of laughter.

"That's true," added Herbert. "Like I said, his friend Egon seems to be a nice, congenial fellow. I don't know how he puts up with my brother."

Then, a small cry came from the bedroom, and Ursula brought little Eckhardt out to greet everyone. Meira and Herbert immediately commented on how good he looked and how he was growing.

When it was time for dinner, which was really a supper of cold cuts, cheese and potato salad, the conversation moved on from Karlheinz, and old memories were brought up. People who were gone were remembered, as in the conversation the evening before. Eckhardt again related the story about the Christmas truce of 1914, and this led to a discussion of how people from different backgrounds can find a common ground at times like Christmas. Herbert referred to the holidays he had spent with Madam Fournier and her daughter during the war, and how he often thought of them and wondered how things turned out for them.

Meira then referred to her first Christmas with the family ten years prior and stated she could never express how much the love and friendship they had shared over the years meant to her. And most especially how grateful she was for her husband.

"He's my Christmas present every day of the year." He looked lovingly at his wife, which reflected the same sentiment.

Eckhardt and Ursula exchanged glances, which expressed more love than words could say.

Chapter Seventy-seven

Hanukkah 5684
(1924)

The Jewish festival of Hanukkah dates back to the second century BC, when the Holy Land was ruled by Syrian Greeks known as the Seleucids, who were determined to replace Hebrew culture with Greek culture and eliminate the belief in one God. A small group of faithful Jews under the leadership of Judah of Maccabee revolted against the Greeks, drove them from the Holy Land, reclaimed and rededicated the Temple in Jerusalem to the service of the God of Israel.

However, when they attempted to light the seven-branched candelabra, or menorah, they found only one cruse of consecrated oil which had not been contaminated by the Greeks. They lit the menorah with the one-day supply of oil, but it miraculously lasted eight days before new oil could be prepared according to the ordinances of ritual purity. Hanukkah, also known as "The festival of lights," commemorates these miracles.

The Hanukkah festival for the year 1924, or on the Jewish calendar 5684, commenced with Hanukkah I on Thursday, December 25, and ended with Hanukkah VI on Tuesday, December 30. As was the practice for Jews everywhere, the first candle was lit on the menorah in the Friedlander home on the first festival day by Benjamin Friedlander. As the Hanukkah miracle involved oil, foods were fried in oil. Latkes, or potato pancakes were prepared by Golda and her daughter Edna, and served with applesauce and sour cream, along with sufganya, or jelly-filled doughnuts, after the lighting of the first Hanukkah candle.

Golda and Edna were mindful of the empty chair which had formerly been occupied by Meira. As she gazed at it, Golda's eyes filled with tears, and her husband observing this, warned, "I know what you're thinking, Golda. Don't even say it. I will say it again: that girl is dead to us and I don't even want to hear her name mentioned in this house." At this, his wife bowed her head and tried to stifle the sobs that caused tears to flow freely. Edna also began to cry.

"Come on, ladies. We've been all through this before. Are you going to spoil the holiday? Let's eat and then play dreidel," came from the obdurate father.

Dreidel is a game played with a four-sided spinning top embossed with the Hebrew letters, *nun, gimmel, hei* and *shin,* which, when placed together, is an acronym for *nes gadol hayah sham (*a great miracle happened there). The prizes for the winners would be a pot of coins, nuts, or other treats, which is won as determined by which letter the dreidel lands on when spun.

Both women looked at him blankly. Finally, Golda said defiantly, "I want my daughter back."

Benjamin, feeling his anger rise, said, "What are you whining about, woman? You have your daughter. She's sitting across from you now. You have no other."

Chapter Seventy-eight

A New Proselyte

On a warm July afternoon in 1925, Karlheinz was strolling along Kantstraße, when he came to Savignyplatz and noticed a bookstore he hadn't seen before. He stepped inside and was refreshed by the cool interior and the comforting odor of books. As he looked at new publications being offered on the front counter, a picture of Adolf Hitler on the jacket of a book entitled *Mein Kampf* caught his eye. He had heard of this man as the one who had initiated an unsuccessful rebellion in Munich two years earlier and had been sentenced to prison for treason. He had also heard that he had organized a new political party known as the NSDAP, commonly known as Nazis. Hitler had also been known as an opponent of the Jews, who he believed had been largely responsible for causing the instability, which led to World War I, and for the humiliation of Germany's defeat, a position with which Karlheinz was in agreement.

As he leafed through the text, he found many quotes explaining why the Jew is to be regarded as the enemy of western civilization. Deciding that he had to learn more about this fascinating author, he purchased the book, and finding a bench under a shady tree, began to find many ideas which resonated with his own thoughts and feelings.

Later, when he was seated across from Egon Wolf in the apartment they now shared, reading aloud from his new purchase, he was surprised his friend did not pick up on everything from the book. As a matter of fact, Egon reacted to some passages quite differently, cautioning, "That sounds dangerous to me. I'd be careful about spouting some of those ideas aloud." They bickered a bit, but finally Karlheinz sulked and withdrew to the bedroom, where he could delve into the volume in peace.

Several days later, on a Sunday, at his mother's urging, he and Egon joined his family in Dahlem for dinner. This time Meira was not present, as she had to cover for another nurse.

When it came time for coffee and dessert, Karlheinz began to extol the virtues of Adolf Hitler and his wonderful new book. After listening for a few minutes, his father spoke up saying, "That's rubbish! I have several distinguished Jewish colleagues, whom I have known and worked with for many years, and who are outstanding doctors and fine men."

At this point, Frederika inquired, "Who is this Hitler? I've heard he's a radical troublemaker and should have been hanged for inciting that trouble in Munich, which caused several people to be killed. Besides, I believe he was only a corporal in the war, wasn't he? If my father were alive, he would have something to say about soldiers from the lower ranks who forget their place and cause trouble."

Herbert, observing the exchange going on before him, had several thoughts running through his mind. He was glad Meira was not there to hear the venomous denunciation of her people, and he was proud of his father for his rational rebuttal, but not surprised. Hans Joachim Lenz had always represented himself as a compassionate, fair-minded individual, who was respected by all who knew him.

As for his mother, she had responded in typical fashion for her: class conscious. This came automatically to her, and although she was trying to be more open-minded, due largely to the influence of her husband and himself, she still reflected the influence of her class and upbringing. He also noticed that his brother's friend seemed ill-at ease and did not have anything to say in support of Karlheinz.

After more debating, with which Karlheinz became more agitated verging on outright anger, Hans Joachim ended the discussion.

"In any case, I don't put too much stock in the words of a man who is known to associate with thugs, viciously attacks a whole group of people with unsubstantiated rhetoric and seeks to instigate a race war. I also believe that Germany needs to join the rest of the western world in developing a society based on democratic process. We have seen what restricting the rights of expression and justice in Russia has led to. Therefore, Karlheinz, I must ask you not to bring up these ideas in my house again. I'm just so thankful that Meira was not here to hear this."

To this, Herbert added, "Thanks, Father. I'm glad she wasn't here for this, too, and I would also like to point out that I knew Jewish soldiers in the trenches who fought for this country as hard as any man. And you, brother, you'd better be careful choosing your friends in these times, and I don't mean you Egon. I mean those Nazis. They're troublemakers who are going to get a lot of people hurt, so you just watch out."

Egon interrupted, "As one who isn't a member of this family, I hope that I'm not out of place by adding to this conversation. But thank you, Herbert. I agree with you. I've told Karlheinz the same thing you've just said. I wish he'd never found this book. And I hope he'll avoid these people, too."

As Karlheinz stood up, his father said, "I need to speak to you, Karlheinz."

The two of them then stepped out into the back garden, and Hans Joachim led the way to the rose arbor. Turning to his son, he said, "I know your mother has been giving you money for quite a while, and I haven't said anything to her about it, but if you insist on pursuing this Nazi business, I'll see to it that she stops. If you'll abandon it, I'll reinstate your allowance and support you, if you'll enter the university and prepare a career for yourself.

As for your friend Egon, I would encourage you to either return home, or find a small place for yourself. I don't insist on it, but I can only advise you that openly associating with homosexuals can't help your reputation. What you do privately and discreetly is your own business, but a reputation is something no one should squander."

Karlheinz digested what his father said without a retort, and controlling his emotions, replied, "I'll think about it, Father."

They returned to the house where Herbert and Egon were discussing the changes taking place in Berlin and the opportunities which would increase in the future. Karlheinz thanked his mother for dinner, and he and his friend left, relieved to be away from the fastidious atmosphere.

Chapter Seventy-nine

The Air Age

Rudi was driving tram 5256 on the Lichterfelde line late one afternoon in September when two young men boarded and sat in the seat directly behind him. He overheard their excited chatter about what a great day it had been for flying. He was suddenly all ears, and in spite of the rule not to chat with passengers, he asked where they had been flying.

"We belong to the Akaflieg Berlin flying club" responded one young man. "That's the acronym for *Akademische Fliegergruppe* (Academic Flyers Group). We are aeronautical engineering students at the Technical University, and we fly gliders at Kammermark Airfield near Pritzwalk. Are you interested in aviation?"

Rudi turned and blurted, "Absolutely! I'm not supposed to talk on the job, but could I meet you sometime and learn more about what you do?"

"Of course," was the reply. "Let me give you the telephone number of our club. You can call, and they'll answer your questions, or you can leave a message for me and I'll contact you."

A car horn blared, bringing his attention back to his driving. He was startled to see that he had accelerated dramatically.

Rudi was handed a card with the logo of the flying club.

"Thanks so much. I'll definitely be calling you."

"Hope to hear from you" was the answer. "By the way, my name is Klaus Dieterle, and this is Erik Vorbauer."

"I'm Rudi Bellon. Thanks again. I'll be in touch."

The two aviators got off at the next stop, giving Rudi a hearty wave and a smile as they walked away.

Rudi thought about what he had encountered. His curiosity was whetted, and he looked forward to his next meeting with the pair.

The next day on his lunch break, he called the number on the card, and the young woman who answered the phone was friendly and helpful. When Rudi explained that he wanted to get in touch with either one of the two men whose names he repeated. She stated that she'd been told he might call and told him the club would be meeting that evening in the *Mensa* (cafeteria) on the university campus. He was welcome to attend.

He could hardly contain his excitement as he continued his shift, and upon turning his tram over to his relief for the evening shift, hurried to the tram stop for the line that ran up Hardenbergstraße to the Technical University.

When he entered the large cafeteria, he looked for his new acquaintances in the crowd of students, but Klaus Dieterle spotted him first and stood up while waving him over to the group sitting at a long table in the center of the room. When he reached the table, Rudi saw about twenty robust-looking young men laughing and carrying on several conversations at once. Klaus and Erik Vorbauer greeted him and shook his hand. Then Klaus proceeded to introduce him to the others. He was warmly received, and he took a seat across from Klaus and Erik. Erik volunteered to fetch him a beer from the canteen, but Rudi declined, not wanting to put anyone to any trouble. Klaus spoke up and stated, "Come on, man. I want him to get one for me, too."

Erik growled, "Since when am I your new barmaid?"

"Since I got the last two for you, so you owe me," rebutted his friend.

"Okay, you got me there," said Erik moving off to the canteen.

"Get me one," shouted one of the others.

"Me too," added another.

"Poor Erik," commented Klaus. "You'd be surprised how many he can manage with those big hands of his, like a barmaid at Oktoberfest." This brought laughter all around.

One of the others spoke up, to Rudi, "So, Rudi, why are you interested in airplanes?"

"Actually, I don't know anything about airplanes, but a couple of years ago I went out to Tempelhof Field to watch one of the Zeppelin airships land. I found it fascinating and have spent some of my days-off there watching the planes take off."

"You don't want to waste your time watching Zeppelins. Those old gasbags are like whales rolling around in the sky. Pay attention to airplanes. That's real flying," interjected Klaus.

That brought forth nods and comments of agreement around the table.

Meanwhile, Erik returned with six one-litre mugs of beer—three in each hand.

"See, Erika, I knew you could do it," chided Klaus.

"Keep it up, and you'll get yours over your head," growled Erik.

The light-hearted laughter and joking continued for a while, until a tall thin blond young man stood up and tapped a spoon on the side of his beer mug for attention.

"We have some items of business to take care of, gentlemen. Let's get it over with and then go see what the girls are up to."

More laughter.

There were several issues that were discussed: a group needed to take responsibility for finding new storage facilities for the gliders with winter coming on, as they were losing their current storage place, which was being sold for agricultural use; with some people getting automobiles, would there be enough vehicles to transport people next summer by car? The train took too long to travel the 108 kilometers (67 miles) to Pritzwalk (northwest of Berlin) with all the stops.

"Besides, if everyone shared gasoline it would be cheaper, and we can come and go when we please," the speaker added.

These, and several other matters were discussed, until finally someone turned to Rudi and asked, "When did you enroll in the aeronautical engineering program? I've never seen you on campus."

An awkward silence followed until Klaus spoke up and said, "Rudi isn't a student here. We met downtown and I invited him to come and listen to us to see if he's interested in pursuing aviation."

Everyone considered this information for a few moments, and then one of the students said, "I recently heard that a new flight school has started up out at the end of Heerstraße in Staaken."

"That's right," added another. "*Deutsche Verkehrfliegerschule* (German Transport Flying School). You should check it out."

"Thanks. I really appreciate that," responded Rudi.

"I know what," Klaus exclaimed. "Why don't we go with you? I'm curious to see what they're doing out there."

"Good idea," added Erik. "Let's meet here next Saturday for lunch, and then we'll head out."

Glad to have some new friends and excited about his new venture, Rudi and some of the others then left to check out some new clubs in town and perhaps meet some of the newly independent saucy Berlin girls.

Chapter Eighty

Generations Clash

When Rudi told his mother about his new craze for aviation, she looked at him in dismay for a moment before answering.

"Where did you ever get such ideas? In the first place, that costs money, and we are comfortable living as we are. But there's nothing extra for things like flying clubs. Also, I'm surprised those fellows gave you the time of day. They're all probably from well-to-do families who have nothing to do with people like us. Did you tell them you live in Wedding? Of course not! Because you knew they'd have tossed you out on your ear if you had."

"You know what, Mama? You're a snob, only in the other direction. You need to look around. The world is changing. All that class crap you grew up with is over. The Kaiser and people like him are gone. Nobody pays any attention to titles and all that stuff anymore. Klaus and Erik are super guys, and their friends I met are just like them. You go to all those Communist meetings and take in all that propaganda about class struggles and doing away with the '*petit bourgeoisie*', which might have been valid before the war. But now, people respect someone who can better himself by his own efforts without some Kommissar to tell him how to live his life."

At this, his mother laughed and said, "Are you sure those fellows aren't Americans? You sound just like what we are warned about at our meetings. Be careful around capitalists. They'll have you believe they're your friend, until they decide you have something they want or figure out how they can use you. Then, after they have you under their thumb, it's all over with 'friendship'."

At this, Rudi put on his coat and cap and said, "I'm going out. I can't listen to any more of your negative Bolshevik crap. I wish you'd never started hanging out with those people. You used to be such an open, friendly person. But you've become bitter and suspicious and measure everyone by their political convictions. Those that don't measure up to your judgements are automatically seen as an enemy.

Tell me, do you have any friends anymore except Communists? I bet you even think Eckhardt and Ursula are '*petit bourgeois*'. I'm surprised you can even be in the same room with Herbert and Meira. I hate to think what your new Communist friends would like to do to Herbert's parents."

Tears welled up in Christina's eyes. Never had one of her children spoken up to her or Detlev in such a manner. As Rudi went out the door, she felt her world collapsing. Perhaps she had been too rash in criticizing his new friends and belittling his new interest. She began to wonder if she really had changed so much. She would ask Ursula.

§§§

True to their word, Klaus and Erik were waiting for him when he entered the cafeteria. They had the only lunch item on the menu for the day – *Eintopf* (one pot) – a stew of vegetables and sausages cooked in one pot. After finishing off their lunch with a beer, they stepped outside and started in the opposite direction from the bus stop, which startled Rudi.

"The bus is that way," exclaimed Rudi.

"No bus today," said Klaus with a grin.

As they neared a Ford Model T roadster parked at the curb, Klaus explained, "I persuaded my brother to let me use his car while he's on holiday in Italy."

He reached into the car and set the emergency brake, pushed the spark control up to retard the spark, pulled the hand throttle half way down, turned the gas valve on, and walked around to the front of the car. He gave the crank a half turn. The car immediately sprang to life, and the three of them climbed in from the passenger's side, as there was no door on the driver's side.

They headed northwest on Hardenbergstraße to Das Knie ("the knee" – today Erik Reuterplatz), turned left onto Bismarckstraße to Kaiserdamm and onto Heerstraße. They drove the 13 kilometers (8 miles) to Staaken airfield, laughing and joking all the way. When they saw attractive girls on the sidewalks, they honked the "oogah" horn and waved. Sometimes the girls waved back. It was a bright early autumn day and some of the leaves were just starting to turn. It was good to be young.

When they reached the airfield, they could see groups of gliders parked on the grass next to one of the runways and many young men standing around in groups. A car was parked on the edge of the runway with one rear wheel raised up on a jack and a cable drum bolted on in place of the wheel. The cable stretched out about 100 feet on the grass and would be hooked to the nose of a glider, waiting some distance down the grass strip. As the car engine was revved up, the drum rotated, the cable was quickly wound up, and the glider swiftly became airborne.

Klaus parked the car. He, Erik and Rudi got out and walked toward the nearest group of young men. As they drew nearer, heads began to turn in their direction. Klaus stepped forward and introduced them, and the response from the group was friendly. One tall fellow extended his hand to Klaus stating, "I'm Helmut Stock. I'm an instructor here. What can I do for you?"

With a motion toward Erik, Klaus explained, "Erik and I are members of Akaflieg Berlin at the TU, and our friend Rudi here isn't a student and can't qualify for our club, but he's intensely interested in flying. We wondered if you might be able to help him out."

Unsmiling, the instructor looked Rudi up and down. Finally, after a moment, he asked Rudi, "What do you do for a living?"

Rudi blushed and stammering, replied, "I am a tram driver for the Berlin transit authority."

Grinning, the instructor chided him, "So you want to drive something that will leave the ground."

This brought laughter all around as Rudi blushed even more and mumbled "I never thought of it that way, but perhaps you're right."

Helmut Stock smiled at this and said, "Let's walk over to the office and I can explain what we do here."

Turning to the group of students who had been listening to the conversation, Stock said, "As soon as that glider comes down, Mueller, you take ours up next."

"Yes, Sir," responded the young man.

Klaus and Erik then assured Rudi they would be glad to accompany him and the instructor, if he wished, but Rudi said that would not be necessary. The two then became engaged in conversation with the young students as Rudi and the instructor walked away.

Just as they reached the office shack near a hanger, a two-seat trainer biplane landed on the end of the runway.

"What's that?" Rudi asked, pointing to the taxiing aircraft.

"That's an Albatros L 68, one of our mainstay trainers. A rugged little beast. It's takes a lot of abuse from people like you," the instructor teased.

Rudi grinned in response, pleased to be included already among fliers.

After they were seated at the instructor's desk, he began to explain the program. The school was subsidized by the German government, and the newly formed Luft Hansa airline would join in supporting the school in the near future. The stated mission of the school was to train commercial pilots for the growing air transport industry.

With historical hindsight, it is now known that glider and aircraft training was promoted covertly to lay the foundation for a new German Airforce, which was forbidden by the Versailles Treaty.

The requirements for entry were the successful completion of a battery of tests. The applicant must have completed secondary school and be in good health. A medical examination was required to confirm this. The student would be expected to pay for registration fees and tuition, but when this was a financial hardship, financial assistance was available if the candidate met all the other requirements. The instructor then handed Rudi a brochure and asked if he had any questions.

"Only one. When can I start?"

Helmut Stock grinned at this eager response and was glad to see that the young man was really enthusiastic.

Chapter Eighty-one

The Invoice

There was a soft knock on Benjamin Friedlander's office door one morning in the Fall of 1925.

"Come in," he responded.

Klara Morgenstern, his bookkeeper, opened the door and asked, "May I speak to you for a moment, Mr. Friedlander?"

"Of course. Have a seat."

"I was filing some invoices for storage, and I came across an invoice that aroused my curiosity. I found an invoice from December ordering two of our raccoon coats to be delivered to your home. I don't recall you placing that order, which you always do when something is taken out of inventory. Do you remember doing that?"

"Two raccoon coats? What would I do with two raccoon coats?"

The bookkeeper smirked and said, "I wondered about that myself. I thought maybe your wife decided to get them for you both, so you could stroll Ku'damm with all the stylish young people."

Frowning, Benjamin growled, "Not funny, Miss Morgenstern. It's not your place to comment on my wife's and my age."

"I'm sorry, Mr. Friedlander. I didn't mean to imply that you and Mrs. Friedlander are old."

"Well, we are, and you need to show more respect for your elders."

The poor girl blushed, thinking to herself Mr. Friedlander had really become sour during the past year or so.

"Anyway, thank you for bringing this to my attention. Let me have that invoice. Ah ha! I see my wife signed for it. Thank you again, Miss Morgenstern. I'll look into it. That will be all."

"Yes, Sir, Mr. Friedlander. Thank you, Mr. Friedlander," the girl said hastily, glad to back out of the situation. She softly closed the door.

After she left, Benjamin sat holding the invoice in his hand and turning the matter over in his mind.

Two raccoon coats! Delivered to my house shortly before Hanukkah! What has Golda been up to?

Then it hit him like a flash! He remembered seeing Herbert and Meira standing before his show window, looking at the raccoon coat displayed there a few days before the date on the invoice. He remembered being torn, wanting to go and greet his daughter, who was often in his thoughts, but deciding *No*! He had declared his position to her, to his wife and to his other daughter, and decided that he was committed to his course of action but had thought no more about it.

That evening as he arrived home for dinner, he found his wife in the kitchen, which was filled with the savory odor of roast chicken. He could see that she had set aside a pan of *kugel*, (noodle pudding) one of his favorites. He kissed his wife on the cheek and was about to launch forth with his investigation of the invoice, when his elder daughter, Edna, came into the kitchen, and smiling, kissed him on the cheek, greeting him with, "Hello, Papa."

He decided to postpone his enquiry until after dinner, and perhaps even until he and his wife retired. He was learning not to start confrontations on an empty stomach.

After enjoying his wife's excellent cooking, he retired to the parlor to read his paper, while his wife and daughter cleared the table and washed and put away the dishes. Although his questions kept eating at him, he held his peace and told himself to start calmly questioning his wife.

After she brought coffee to him, and his daughter had retired to her room, he handed the invoice to her and asked, "What do you know about this, Golda?"

His wife blanched when she saw the document in his hand. After a moment of silence, her mouth set in determination, she said, "Yes, I ordered them!"

"What for? Did you intend to wear one and give the other one to Edna? I think you both are a little mature for that. Do you think that will help Edna to catch a man?"

"There you go again. Belittling Edna and making her out to be a hopeless old maid!"

"Well, what would you call her? She's 33 and hasn't got a beau in sight. Or maybe you're reserving her for some Goy, like her sister married!"

"Don't go there with me, Benjamin! I ordered them because Meira informed me that they had seen them in our store window and wanted them for her and Herbert. Our son-in-law. *Not some Goy*!"

Feeling his temper rising, he flung back, "And you did all that without talking to me about it?"

"What good would it have done? Would you have allowed it? Of course not! That might be mistaken as a peace offering from you – and you certainly wouldn't want to send that signal, would you?"

After a moment of trying to calm himself before responding, he said, "You are so different from a Jewish wife like my mother. You've become headstrong and stubborn, just like that other daughter of yours."

"Yes, SHE *IS* MY DAUGHTER!" shouted Golda.

Benjamin opened his mouth to respond, but Golda cut him off.

"No! *You* listen, Benjamin," she said emphatically. "Yes, she's my daughter, and I'm proud of her. She's a fine woman, who has a fine husband, who loves her, respects her, and treats her well.

As far as comparing me to your mother, you're right! I'm the daughter of one of the most successful bankers in this city. No, let's change that – in this country! Not some farm girl from Poland! If that's what you wanted, maybe you should have gone back to Poland and had some village matchmaker find you a wife!"

Furious and shaken by his wife's defiance, he roared, "I thought I told you and Edna to stay away from that girl."

"You did. But I chose to do otherwise. And I intend to do more of what I choose from now on! You might as well get used to it. I'm glad this came out in the open, because I WILL see my daughter, and you can decide what you're going to do about it. Good night!"

With that, Golda Friedlander stalked out of the room and called over her shoulder, "I will be sleeping in Meira's old room until further notice!"

Benjamin stared at the empty doorway aghast.

Chapter Eighty-two

Athen an der Spree
(Athens on the Spree)

The year 1926 brought exciting changes to the bustling capital. Because of the amalgamation of the twenty-plus districts into the metropolis of Berlin, the result of the Greater Berlin Law of 1920, it now became the largest industrial city in Europe and the third largest municipality in the world.

Domestic and foreign companies relocated to the German capital or established headquarters there. Ford Motor Company established their European sales headquarters in Berlin in 1925. The automobile had taken over the wide boulevards, with the exception being only a few old horse-drawn cabs used by sightseers and tourists.

The urban rail system, the Stadtbahn (commonly called the S-Bahn), which had originally been powered by steam locomotives, had begun to be converted to electricity in 1914. The work, delayed by World War I, was completely electrified between 1926 and 1929.

Tempelhof, which had been a military parade ground, was opened as an inner-city airport on October 8, 1923, and the new airline, Deutsche Luft Hansa, founded on January 6, 1926, in Berlin, inaugurated its first flight from Tempelhof on April 6, 1926, with a Fokker F.11 bound for Zurich via Halle, Erfurt and Stuttgart.

The Funkturm, the newly constructed radio tower, which opened on September 3, 1926, adjacent to the fair pavilion in Charlottenburg-Wilmersdorf, was constructed of a steel framework similar to the Eiffel Tower. It is 150 meters (490 feet) high and includes at the height of 52 meters, a restaurant reached by an elevator. It is no longer used for broadcasting and was taken out of service in 1973.

Babelsberg in Potsdam is the home of Universum Film AG (abbreviated in its logo as UFA). This studio was established on December 18, 1917, and by the 1920s, became the largest film studio in Europe, indeed one could say the "Hollywood" of Europe. Many famous movie stars had their start with UFA, including Marlene Dietrich, Emil Jannigs, Josef von Sternberg, Pola Negri, and Lillian

Harvey. In addition to UFA, film studios also existed in Weißensee and Woltersdorf. In connection with the film industry, great movie palaces were constructed, particularly along Kurfürstendamm, in which full symphony orchestras performed to accompany silent films.

Berlin became a magnet for artists, musicians and writers, making the Romanisches Café across from the Kaiser Wilhelm Memorial Church their chief meeting place. Some of the famous names from the literary world who spent some of their most creative years there during the twenties include Franz Kafka, Bertolt Brecht, Viktor Nabokov and Christopher Isherwood.

Isherwood is interesting to note, because he wrote his *Berlin Stories* there, which became the background for the play/film *Cabaret.*

Another side of 1920s Berlin that developed with the freedom of the Weimar Republic was the upsurge of entertainments catering to every taste. In addition to the previously highlighted Kleist Kasino, it has been estimated that by the mid-twenties over 500 homosexual and lesbian bars and clubs existed in the city, some of which were patronized by customers other than gay people. The transvestite shows, like those presented in the notorious Cabaret Eldorado, and cabaret performances, such as can be seen in the film *Cabaret,* were popular with visitors to Berlin, including many foreign tourists.

Prostitution was widespread, with the range of gender and "specialties" being unlimited. The Blue Stocking in Linienstraße featured prostitutes who had suffered amputations or loss of limbs, which was especially popular with disabled war veterans. It has been suggested that perhaps this was because they felt less inhibited with partners who suffered the same disabilities as themselves.

It is understandable that many Germans who lived through the next two decades of police-state terror and war nostalgically regard the mid- to late twenties as a golden age in Berlin. It was a time of booming development, new technologies, entrepreneurship, creative energy, scientific advances, and yes, unrestricted entertainment and pleasure, in an atmosphere of freedom that had never before been experienced in a city stifled by Prussian repression and conservatism.

But it was soon to come to an end.

Part VI

Gathering Darkness

Chapter Eighty-three

Political Confrontation

Behind all the bright lights and fun, there was a darkness developing, which all the good times couldn't prevent. Despite the successes of the Weimar Republic, it nevertheless was not popular with many people. Partly because of the attitude of cooperation with the Allies, and effort made to accommodate the demands of the Versailles Treaty, the Weimar government was seen as feckless by some, especially among leaders in the military. They felt the government allowed Germany to be humiliated before the world. But on a practical level, the Weimar leaders were trying to walk a fine line and use moderation within the limited latitude they had.

Berlin was seen as leftist and was dubbed by the rising Nazis as the "reddest city in Europe after Moscow," the Communists having won 52.2 percent of the vote in the 1925 municipal elections. The Nazi party had very little support until the Great Depression.

Joseph Goebbels, a journalist and holder of a PhD from Heidelberg University, came to Hitler's attention during what he called his "quiet years" between 1926 and 1929. Goebbels enjoyed a quick rise in the developing Nazi hierarchy, due to his huge talent for speech making and developing propaganda. As a highly educated man, he was a rarity among the early Nazis. But as a little man who walked with a limp resulting from infantile paralysis, and who wore a built-up shoe on his right foot.

The implementation of Goebbels' new campaign was not initially well received in Berlin. In fact, the Nazis had an uphill battle, especially among the working class, who were generally more in support of the Communists. In addition, Goebbels labored under a handicap due to his appearance. Berliners, who are known for their harsh humor, immediately seized the opportunity to disparage his handicap with cruel jokes.

One afternoon while shopping at an open-air market, Christina Bellon overheard two women discussing Goebbels.

The first woman, with a sardonic smile, asked the question:

"What does Goebbels carry in that box of a foot?"

"I don't know. What?"

"Batteries for his loudspeaker of a mouth."

Bystanders burst forth with gales of laughter.

Hitler named Goebbels his "Gauleiter in Berlin," and in October 1926, he was sent to the capital. At once, Goebbels undertook the formidable task of reorganizing and creating publicity for the previously ignored Nazi Party.

This proved to be a good training ground, preparing him for his future role as Propaganda Minister. He gained recognition for the Party through his organization of meetings and speeches. He later published a newspaper in 1927, *Der Angriff* (The Attack), plastered posters all over the city and instigated confrontations with the Communists.

He had been in Berlin barely a week when he organized a march through a Communist stronghold, Neukölln, which developed into a street riot. His efforts began to bear fruit, as the Party membership grew. His Stormtroopers, however, once went too far when they beat up an elderly pastor, who had heckled Goebbels during a Party rally.

Police then declared the Nazi party illegal and forbade any Nazi speech making in Berlin and the entire state of Prussia. The restriction was soon lifted in the spring of 1927, when Hitler came to Berlin and gave a speech to a crowd of approximately 5,000 supporters in the Sportpalast, the popular venue for sports and cultural events (built in 1910 and demolished in 1973).

Soon, the SA Brownshirts began to appear all over the city. Their role, in Goebbels' view, was the "conquest of the street." This was meant to reconcile the two conflicting worldviews: nationalism and "true socialism" – free of Marxism.

Chapter Eighty-four

Benjamin Friedlander vs. *Die braune Bewegung* (the Brown Movement)

"You, Nazi scum, pack up and get away from my store!" shouted Benjamin Friedlander at the young SA Brownshirts passing out leaflets in front of his store one morning in January 1927. One of them clenched his fists and took a step toward the angry store owner.

"Come on, Heinz. Let's go," said his comrade to him, catching hold of his sleeve. "We can take care of him some other time."

Hesitating a moment, the angry Brownshirt shouted at Benjamin, "Okay, Jew. We'll leave now, but I'll remember you. We have a score to settle."

Folding up their stand and packing up their leaflets, they glared at Benjamin, who was trembling with anger and fear as they moved down the block.

Shaking and pale, he entered his store where his employees and a few customers stood frozen from shock as they watched the drama unfolding through the large windows.

His manager hurried up to him. "Are you alright, Mr. Friedlander?"

"Yes, thank you," was the response as Benjamin moved up the three steps to his office.

He was anything but "alright." Trembling, he removed his topcoat and went to his liquor cabinet to pour himself a stiff shot of schnapps. He fell into his chair and took deep breaths as he felt the liquor warm him and begin to steady his nerves. As he looked through his office window at his employees going about their work, he noticed the number of customers slowly diminish as they concluded their purchases and depart or leave without buying anything.

He felt a new apprehension: could this be a sign of things to come? He could well imagine that incidents such as had taken place today could keep customers away, either because they were afraid of being involved in such violence, or even perhaps because they harbored some anti-Semitic sentiments of their own, which they had not previously confronted in themselves.

He tried to compose himself and return to the sales floor as soon as possible, but inwardly he was plagued by a new anxiety.

Could such things really happen in a highly civilized country like his beloved Germany, the land of poets and thinkers?

At this time, things were still uncertain for the Nazis, but Goebbels was working overtime to persuade anyone who would listen, even Communists, to become Nazis. In his attacks on Marxism, he claimed Jews were behind the movement. This theme was repeated whenever Goebbels made speeches at Nazi Party meetings, such as was planned for February 11, 1927.

Chapter Eighty-five

Big Confrontation and Bloody Brawl

"I must insist you stay away from that rally, Mama," Rudi said to Christina.

"I know I promised you I would avoid situations which could turn ugly, Son, but this is an important opportunity to show the Nazis we will not be intimidated. Our block leaders have asked everyone to show solidarity by marching through the city to show them we are united and to confront them at their own meeting."

"That's crazy! You're telling me you want to walk into the hornet's nest? Those people are killers, and you being an old woman will not stop them from beating you right into the ground, along with anyone else they can catch. No, Mama. I won't allow it."

"Allow? Who do you think you are? I'm still an independent adult, even if I am an 'old woman,' as you put it. I'm going, whether you come or not!"

Turning on his heel, Rudi stormed out of the flat shouting over his shoulder, "I'm gonna get Eckhardt. Maybe he can talk some sense into your head."

This was the second time Christina and her son had had a flare up over her politics. This time she would stand her ground.

Under the circumstances, Rudi felt the expense of a taxi was justified. He went to the taxi stand two blocks away, and stepping into the smoky interior of the cab, gave the driver Eckhardt's and Ursula's address. How he wished his sister and her husband had gotten their telephone for which they had recently applied. The waiting period could be up to six months – or longer in outlying districts.

Arriving at the cottage in Spandau, he asked the driver to wait while he hurried to the front door and knocked. Ursula, surprised to see her brother on the door step, smiled and asked what he was doing there after the dinner hour.

"I'm sorry, Ursula, but I need to speak to Eckhardt right away."

"Well, come in and tell me what's on your mind."

Eckhardt, hearing voices at the front door, stepped up behind his wife and seeing Rudi exclaimed, "Well, this is a welcome surprise. What brings you here at this time of night?"

Rudi stepped inside and quickly explained that his mother was determined to attend a big Communist Party rally the next day, which would conclude with a march to the Nazi meeting, where there was sure to be bloodshed. He needed Eckhardt's help to dissuade her.

"Oh, you must go, sweetheart. You boys have got to stop her," cried Ursula. "I don't know what's gotten into her since she started going to those Communist meetings."

"I have a taxi waiting outside," interjected Rudi. "I wish Ursula could come, too, but I realize she has the baby, and it's bitter cold outside."

"Let's go," said Eckhardt, as he turned to put on his coat and cap.

When they reached the flat in Wedding, they were surprised to find two middle-aged men in the kitchen talking to Christina. She introduced them as the block leader and his secretary from the local Communist headquarters, whom she had summoned for support.

The block leader, a burly worker with the city maintenance department, began immediately in a strident voice to point out the importance of tomorrow's meeting and that it was imperative that Mrs. Bellon attend. There would be other women there, and even some with children. But the men would protect them if things got rough.

Eckhardt, not one to be easily intimidated, interrupted the man and declared, "I'm sorry, but that's out of the question. Rudi has always accompanied her to your meetings, but he's as opposed to this one as I and my wife, who also happens to be Mrs. Bellon's daughter.

I've heard from acquaintances that the Nazis are expecting you people to start something, and they have brought in reinforcements from as far away as Leipzig and Magdeburg. Why, in heaven's name, would you have women and children there?"

"If the Nazis see children, then we are sure they won't start any violence and will listen to us. Goebbels has been trying to recruit our members to join the Nazi Party, and if they see how united our members are, they'll know that's a futile effort."

"So, you're using children as shields? That's the most irresponsible and despicable thing I have ever heard!" retorted Eckhardt, to which Rudi nodded his head in agreement and added, "In any case, my mother will not be there!"

At this, the block leader, used to being in charge and now red-faced, blurted, "It's vital that she be there!"

"Wait a minute," interjected Christina. "I have something to say about this."

Eckhardt turned his steady gaze upon her and said in a low voice, "We need to talk, Christina."

She had always admired and respected her son-in-law. His unwavering gaze and calm determined voice subdued her.

Turning to the block leader, Eckhardt stated flatly, "The matter is not up for debate and is closed. You need to leave!"

The burly man, trembling with rage, turned to his companion, "Let's go! You can't talk to this kind of people!" As they made their way to the door, he threatened, "But mark my word. The day will come when you *will* listen to us, whether you like it or not!"

"Out! Get out right now!" shouted Rudi.

§§§

As Rudi and Eckhardt, and many others, had feared, the confrontation turned into a bloody brawl between the Nazis and Communists. Beer glasses, chairs and tables flew through the air and severely injured people were left lying on the floor covered with blood. It was seen as a triumph by the Nazis, who beat up about 200 Communists, and chased them from the hall.

When national elections were held on May 29, 1927, the Nazis had poor results, but Goebbels won a seat in the Reichstag. However, the majority of Germans were not interested in the Nazis because times were good, and things seemed to be going very well without them. The economy was improving, inflation was under control, and more and more people were working.

But an ominous turning point had been reached: Berlin's Jews now became the lightning rod for Goebbels's "conquest of the street."

Chapter Eighty-six

Haus Vaterland
(House Fatherland)

The throb of the great metropolis continued. As spring and summer of 1928 approached, more and more automobiles continued to throng the boulevards, and Ku'damm was filled with crowds of people seeking excitement and pleasure. The great movie palaces were filled to capacity, and the dance halls and casinos were open until the early hours. American dances were the rage with young people. Josephine Baker, an American black entertainer, had electrified Berlin by introducing the Charleston two years before and the dance was to be seen in every dance hall.

As warm weather approached, the beaches in and around the city were inundated with old and young enjoying the warmth of the short northern summer, the most popular being the wide beach at *Wannsee*, a large bay on the Havel river. This is Europe's largest inland beach and can accommodate up to 30,000 visitors. Approximately ten percent of the total area of 355,000 square meters, or 87 acres, is given over to nude bathing.

The most talked-about entertainment venue was the new Haus Vaterland, which opened on September 1st on the southwest side of Potsdamer Platz and was dubbed 'a department store of pleasure'. The six-story sandstone-faced building had been built in 1912 as an office building but was leased by the Kempinski family of restaurant and hotel fame. In it were constructed 12 themed restaurants, a large cinema, a variety theatre, the 'Palm Court' ballroom, and the largest coffee house in Berlin.

Some examples of the themed restaurants included the Löwenbräu on the third floor, which was a Bavarian beer garden with barmaids dressed in *Dirndlkleider* (traditional dresses). The *Terrasse Rheinland* (Rhineland Terrace), also on the third floor, featured an artificial river which flowed past a recreation of the Rhine valley countryside, and which was visited hourly by a simulated thunderstorm, with rain and lightning, followed by a fake sunburst.

On the fourth floor was the Wild West Bar, a complete recreation of an American saloon with swinging doors at the entrance and waiters in cowboy outfits and ten-gallon hats serving American cocktails. Entertainment included a jazz band and showgirls and black-face minstrel shows.

Soon after this amazing establishment opened, Eckhardt, Ursula, Herbert and Meira planned to make an evening of it there. Christina, now resigned to staying away from the big party rallies because of the danger. She agreed to come to Spandau to take care of little Eckhardt in order to free up Ursula for the evening, although she secretly preferred they use his middle name of Detlev.

Ursula and Meira had purchased new outfits of dropped-waist knee-high dresses, Ursula's a deep rose georgette trimmed with beads, with matching colored high-heeled 'touch ups' shoes, and a white feather boa around her shoulders. Meira's was a jade silk, with a strand of pearls, white high heeled mary jane pumps and a cream-colored feather boa. They both had bobbed hair and were in high fashion for the period and wore head bands of material and color to match their dresses, topped off with corresponding colored ostrich plumes. They were as fashionable as could be imagined for the period in which they lived.

Herbert wore a navy-blue blazer, a pale blue shirt with a yellow silk tie with blue polka dots and white pleated front trousers, with black and white wing tip shoes. Eckhardt, being by nature more conservative than his friend, opted for a black pin striped suit and vest, plain white shirt and red bow tie with black alligator shoes and a black fedora hat.

When Herbert and Meira came to pick up their friends, it was not in the little green 'Laubfrosch,' but in Dr. Lenz's sleek new midnight blue Mercedes 460 sedan, which he had insisted on loaning to his son.

As the happy group started down the Ruhlebener Straße leading to Spandauer Damm, Eckhardt commented on the whispered smoothness of the big eight-cylinder car as it rolled effortlessly along the boulevard. Eventually, they came to Das Knie and onto the Charlottenburger Chaussee. There they joined dense traffic gliding through the Tiergarten in the direction of the Brandenburg Gate. Upon passing through the gate and entering Pariser Platz, they turned right toward the brightly-lit Haus Vaterland on the southwest side of Potsdamer Platz. They glided up to the curb and were greeted by a valet who assisted the ladies out of the car, and after all had stepped onto the curb, he drove the car away to reserved parking along the Stresemannstraße.

After the entry fee of one mark was paid, the four friends found themselves in the impressive marble entrance hall. After taking in the lavish décor, they decided to eat at the Grinzing café. The tables were covered with dazzling white damask tablecloths, the starched corners hanging stiffly at attention. As they took their seats, they marveled at the beautiful diorama of old Vienna and the Danube. They watched in amusement as a model electric train ran through the room, crossing bridges spanning canals on which model ships sailed.

They looked over the giant menus and discussed the many examples of Viennese cuisine. The ladies both decided on the traditional *Wienerschnitzel* (succulent veal cutlets breaded and fried) and served with noodles and vegetables. Eckhardt chose *Tafelspitz* (beef boiled in broth) and served with vegetables, and Herbert decided on goulash served with dumplings and *Rotkohl* (red cabbage cooked with apples).

Upon the waiter's recommendation, they ordered a good fruity Austrian wine, *Zweigelt*, with their dinner. They savored their meal and the good wine as they listened to the small orchestra play musical favorites from Johann Strauss, both the father and the son, Waldteufel, Lanner, and other Viennese waltz composers. They all agreed that one could not end a Viennese supper without *Sachertorte* (chocolate cake made famous by the Café Sacher in nineteenth century Vienna), and served with any one of many varieties of freshly ground coffee topped with a dollop of unsweetened whipped cream.

But they had more to see. They looked in several of the other themed restaurants and decided one of their favorites was the Wild West Saloon, with its strange American cocktails. Herbert, though, couldn't wait any longer to try out the Charleston, so they entered the huge Palm Court ballroom and managed to secure a table. Ursula and

Meira ordered champagne, but Eckhardt and Herbert had their old standby, cold Schultheiss beer.

They were awed by the grandeur of the room and the large dance orchestra playing a mix of German fox trots, the American Charleston, and the seductive tango from Argentina. Eckhardt stayed for the most part with the foxtrots, but Herbert danced with both girls to show off how quickly he could adapt to any dance. At first, Ursula hesitated to try the Charleston, but finally, with Herbert's coaching, picked up on the energetic rhythm, and threw herself into it. She became so delighted with the dance, that she insisted her shy husband try it. To please her, Eckhardt reluctantly let her drag him onto the floor as the band struck up the American hit, 'Five Foot Two.' He was miserable, but he stuck it out to the end.

"I'm sorry, Honey, but that's just not me," he lamented.

"Okay, baby," Ursula teased. "You gave it a good try. I'll leave you alone if you'll dance the next slow one with me."

"Deal," he responded, as he escaped to the table.

Soon the band struck the sultry tune, 'Tango Amor'. Meira, although proficient at the Charleston, preferred the dark, mysterious tango. As soon as the music started, the lights were dimmed and Meira took her husband by the hand and said smiling, "This one is for you and me."

The mysterious music seemed to set off Meira's exotic beauty. Her husband appeared to be taken in completely by his wife's sensuous movements, as they soon were the most elegant couple on the floor, and other couples stepped back to watch as they captivated all onlookers. They took on a beauty that seemed to transport them to another world. At the conclusion of the dance, the orchestra leader applauded, and everyone took up the applause. Eckhardt and Ursula stood up, and soon others joined them as the applause continued.

Then Meira became embarrassed, and ducking her head, returned red-faced to the table. "I feel like a fool," she confided to Ursula. "I don't know what came over me. I don't like to be a show-off. It must have been too much champagne."

“Unlike me,” said Herbert, laughing, as he came up behind her. This brought laughter from Eckhardt and Ursula, and from others within earshot at other tables.

“Darling, you were magnificent!” he said to Meira. “I didn’t know you had that kind of rhythm in you. Let’s do the next tango.”

“No, that’s enough for tonight,” she answered. “As a matter of fact, we need to get home. Does anyone realize how late it is?”

Eckhardt looked at his watch, “Oh, my gosh! It’s after two o’clock. It’s a good thing tomorrow is Saturday.”

Haus Vaterland
GASTSTÄTTEN G·M·B·H
BETRIEB KEMPINSKI · BERLIN

Just A Little Tip How To See "Haus Vaterland"

From the Vestibule broad staircases and lifts lead to the lofty MAIN HALL, in itself certainly worth seeing. Extending several floors upward it tends to give the visitor the first impression of the magnitude of this world-famed Amusement-Palace, which indeed may be considered the centre of Metropolitan life and its events.

Only a few steps to the right of this MAIN HALL is the JAPANESE TEAROOM, a tastefully decorated place full of that Eastern atmosphere and of lovely comfort, and Japanese in attendance.

Not far from there Vienna air breezes in the GRINZING. Here they serve you the famous "Heurige" in true Vienna style, here you hear the old Viennese songs played by a ladies' band, and cabaret numbers offer gay pastime. The Panorama shows in the valley the old Donau-Metropolis with the characteristic steeples of the Stephansdom.

Going a floor higher and we come into the "LÖWENBRÄU", a typical old-fashioned Bavarian beer-house. A native band plays "Schuhplattler" (clogdances) and many other old peasant dances of the German South. There Bavarian variety performances, going well with Munich beer, and making the best entertainment for him who desires to transplant himself into the realm of the Bavarian Alps. The view offered of the Zugspitze and the Eibsee nurses such illusion.

From the gallery of the "LÖWENBRÄU" you walk straight into the "WILD WEST BAR". This odd room in the style of a blockhouse, makes you feel like being way-out in the real prairie. You will find whisky bottles standing on the tables and of course there is music, and the American songs and melodies sung just like across the big pond.

Next to the "WILD WEST BAR" you will find the "CSARDA", newly decorated. Here is Hungarian wine, music and that dancing so full of passion and temperament. Not a quiet minute in here, and a feeling of that romance of the wide Hungarian Steppe overcomes you.

On the same floor there is the PALMENSAAL, with its fantastic interior decorations, and when illuminated at night, a picture of fairyland, such as imagination cannot better paint it. There is a large dancing-floor, an excellent music band, cabaret and good humour and fun everywhere.

Below the PALMENSAAL the Orient has gotten alive in way of a TURKISH CAFÉ, from where you can see the Golden Horn stretched out before you.

And going a few steps further you run into the BREMER KOMBÜSE where grog, punch, claret and beer are served just as they did in olden times in the Bremen-Drinking-Rooms. This place will especially attract the merry sea-farers.

The heart of this big establishments is the "RHEINTERRASSE" with its wonderful Panorama of the old Rhine, delighting everybody, as the view appears so real, especially when from time to time, wind, clouds and a thunderstorm enliven the landscape. Here you will find daily variety shows with the best class of artists. You sit comfortably at small tables and enjoy, besides these performances, all that the well-known Kempinski cuisine and the famous Kempinski wine-caves have to offer you.

On the right of the RHEINTERRASSE you will find the SPANISH BODEGA, where red Portwine and sweet Malaga are on tap and original wine barrels all around. Really, in there Spain does not seem to you so very far away!

Before leaving the House our way leads through the KAFFEE VATERLAND. This is a most imposing establishment with a gallery running all round in an oval. There is a large orchestra consisting of high class musicians, giving concerts from the afternoon until late at night.

5000. 537.

Flyer given to tourists at Haus Vaterland, 1930's

Chapter Eighty-seven

Deutsche Verkehrsfliegerschule
(German Flight Traffic School)

Rudi was in his element. From his first moment of flight in a glider with his instructor, he knew he had found his calling. What he, and most of the other students at the Deutsche Verkehrsfliegerschule didn't realize, was that they were part of a core of future pilots to be trained for the restoration of the Luftwaffe. Under the terms of the Versailles Treaty, Germany was prohibited from rebuilding a military air force. Therefore, flight schools were established in the 1920s all over Germany, auspiciously for training pilots for the budding commercial air industry and for sport aviation. Staaken itself would, within the next decade, become an important military airfield of strategic importance.

Rudi, of course, was unaware of all of this, and he took what he was told on face value. He had passed all of his entrance exams with flying colors and had quickly proven himself to be a natural pilot. He soon soloed in gliders and was ready, after less than two months, to begin flight training in a powered aircraft. Helmut Stock very soon recognized Rudi as a young man with great potential as an aviator and took him under his wing.

Rudi flew his first solo on a cool November day, after only eight hours of instruction in the Albatross.

Initially, he was limited to practicing landings and takeoffs around the field, but he was eager to make his first cross-country flight. He and Helmut completed a flight to Magdeburg within two weeks after his first solo. A week later, he flew to Magdeburg solo, a distance of 129 kilometers, followed the next day with a flight to Leipzig – 149 kilometers.

Rudi continued to build up hours and experience, which prepared him to take his written exam in March, and his flight check immediately thereafter. He became a licensed pilot shortly before Christmas of 1928.

He continued working as a tram driver and attending flight school, as time allowed, in preparation for his commercial pilot exam. After successfully passing his written exam, and the rigorous flight test, Rudi Bellon became a commercial transport pilot in June 1929.

He applied for a position with the new Luft Hansa airline and was hired as a copilot on the Berlin-Munich-Stuttgart-Berlin route. He was launched on his new career in less than a year after he had met Klaus and Erik on the Lichterfelde tram.

§§§

Christina Bellon was, of course, understandably proud of her son. *If only Detlev could have been here to share the joy.* When she shared her elation with her neighbors, they were awestruck that one from their midst had accomplished so much, and for the most part they extended hearty congratulations to her and to Rudi.

However, when she related the news to some colleagues at a Communist party meeting, she met a few instances of hostility. The burly block leader, in fact, made it a point to warn her that she could expect her son to take on dangerous '*petit bourgeois*' attitudes by associating with the well-to do, who could afford expensive air travel. Somewhat stung by this negativity, she decided in the future to keep comments regarding her family strictly to herself.

Ursula and Eckhardt were very supportive of her brother and promised to be among his passengers as soon as they could save enough for airfare. In fact, Eckhardt was excited to go to Württemberg again and take his wife and baby, whom his mother had never met. He was also eager to show his wife the beautiful village and surrounding countryside where he had grown up. He longed to take her for a walk beside the Blau River and see the swans on the clear, blue water of the Blautopf. Indeed, as he thought about it, he felt a strong pang of homesickness he hadn't experienced for many years.

Herbert and Meira joined his parents and brother for dinner one evening in August, a few weeks after Rudi had resigned from the transit authority and begun his flying career. It gave Herbert great pleasure to announce Rudi's new position at the dinner table, knowing that Karlheinz and Rudi had never reconciled their differences after the summer at Schloß Hohenberg, and also how Karlheinz had displayed his arrogance in regarding Rudi as someone of less importance than himself. Dr. Meinert and his wife, Frederika, were delighted at the news, and insisted that Herbert extend their best wishes and congratulations to Rudi.

Karlheinz, on the other hand, frowned and glowered in silence until his brother prodded him, "Isn't that great, brother? See what the little 'urchin,' as you called him, has accomplished?"

Herbert couldn't resist challenging Karlheinz further, "If someone from his background can do it, think what a person with your advantages could be doing."

At this, Karlheinz retorted, "I don't know what this country is coming to, when people like him can rise so far above their place. It's a disgrace!"

Hans Joachim then spoke up, "How can you talk like that? On the contrary, it shows great hope for any country that can move away from class mentality and allow anyone to rise to any heights through their own effort and ability. Don't you agree, my dear?"

Frederika, after pausing for a moment, replied, "Yes, of course. But I can also understand how Karlheinz feels. Losing the estate affected him more than any of us, even as much as we all loved the place.

You have to see that those of us who were raised in a society where station was important were taught that everyone has his or her place. It's hard for some of us to see people from lower levels of society coming up and even posing a threat to those of us who believed our place in society was secure.

Believe me, I wish the young man well, and I am trying hard to understand that the world I grew up with is no longer there." After a pause, she added, "And perhaps in the long run that's better and more just."

Turning to her younger son, she continued, "Your father is right, dear. The estate and that way of life is gone. You must let go of the past and find your place in this changing world. This young man, Rudi, and people like him, are the future."

Meira listened to all of this and thought of her own grandparents, how they had come from nothing and what they had accomplished. She thought to herself, *Yes, Madam. But my people have been making something out of nothing over and over for thousands of years. My grandparents and my father could say a great deal about sacrifice, diligence, determination and hard work.*

But knowing that Karlheinz, with his attitudes, was no friend of Jews, she decided to keep her thoughts to herself and discuss them later with her husband.

Chapter Eighty-eight

Auf Wiedersehen, Wedding
(Goodbye, Wedding)

Christina was aroused from a deep sleep, as she felt the brush of fur against her cheek. As she slowly became conscious, she realized a warm animal was attempting to burrow under her *Eiderdecke* (down comforter). In doing so, a long hairless tail trailed across her neck. Now fully awake, she realized that a large rat had somehow managed to climb onto her bed. She jumped up and threw the Eiderdecke on the floor, causing the rodent to fall with a loud squeak. Before she could find her shoe to throw at it, the bold animal ran across the floor through the open door of her bedroom, across the room where Rudi was asleep and out the door leading into the hall, which had somehow been left ajar.

She shouted at her son, who in alarm ran to his mother, who, ashen-faced, was trembling in the doorway. When she related the disgusting incident to her son, he shouted, "That's it! We're finding a better place to live. Since this place has changed ownership, it has really gone downhill, and it wasn't much to start with."

Since he began his new airline career, he had been considering a move and tried to convince his mother it would be a good idea. She was reluctant to leave the old neighborhood, where she had lived all her life and knew everyone in her building, and many up and down the street. But with this most recent experience, she agreed she was ready to consider something better. Especially now that Rudi's income was considerably more than before.

Berlin has come to be known as the capital of Classical Modernism, the architectural movement that developed after World War I under the influence of Walter Gropius, the founder of the world-famous school of design, Bauhaus, in Weimar in 1919. He, Ludwig Mies van der Rohe, Le Corbusier and Frank Lloyd Wright in America are considered to be among the foremost pioneers of modernist design and architecture. Many of the modern apartment buildings from that era survive today, and many are included on the UNESCO World Heritage list. They typify the modern concept of apartment design, featuring light airy spaces with large windows leading onto balconies, and with the modern conveniences of central heating and bathrooms. This, in stark contrast to the dank, dark, dreary apartments built around sunless inner courtyards constructed in the last decades of the nineteenth century.

After talking with some colleagues at Luft Hansa, a young woman who had recently started with the airline as a stewardess and who lived in the Treptow district, advised him that some new apartment blocks on Kiefholzstraße near the intersection of Dammweg in Treptow were almost ready to receive new tenants. After informing his mother of this, they traveled together to view the new projects.

They were modern flats with centrally heated steam radiators and indoor bathrooms with flush toilets. The kitchen was wired for electricity and could accommodate modern electric stoves and refrigerators. The location was much more convenient, as it was closer to Tempelhof airport, which would shorten Rudi's commute to and from work. The rent was considerably more than the cold water flat in Wedding, but Rudi and his mother decided they could do no better, and the added comfort and convenience made it well worth it.

"Look, Mama," enthused Rudi. "No more handling briquettes and stoking fires on winter mornings, and you won't get up and see ice on the inside of the windows."

"Yes, and I was just thinking how much more pleasant it would have been to raise children here. When you children were babies, your father or I would have to get up in the middle of the night and stoke the fire to keep the room warm.

Now we can keep ourselves clean in this beautiful bathroom, and I won't have to go downstairs in the morning and empty those nasty chamber pots.

We must get a refrigerator and range right away for the kitchen. Imagine how much better we'll be able to eat, with fresh fruit and vegetables on hand every day. And the elevator! No more walking up three flights of stairs.

Oh, Rudi! Aren't we lucky to be able to live here?"

They paid a deposit on a new apartment. Rudi smiled at his mother's excitement and could relate to everything she said.

Then came the matter of new furniture. She wanted new things, except for a few old pieces, such as her bed and dresser, which had been in her family since her mother's parents' time, more than a century earlier.

She gave notice to the building manager in Wedding, explaining that she would be moving as soon as the new apartment was ready for occupancy, which she expected to be within the month.

When she next shopped at Schroeder's bread shop, and was telling Mr. Schroeder about her moving plans, she was overheard by one of her neighbors of long-time acquaintance, who was very inquisitive about the new apartment.

"So, you'll have all indoor plumbing and central heat?"

"Yes, Mrs. Kraemer. It's wonderful. You should look into it for yourself. You're getting up there in years, like me, and it's not getting easier to build fires and get up and down the stairs."

"Yes, that's true, but I don't know if I could afford it. You have your son's help, and all I have is my widow's pension. I'll think about it."

"I've heard there's financial aid available for war widows like you" Christina informed her neighbor. "I don't know much about it, as I haven't needed to look into it because of my son's help. After I'm moved in, you must come and visit me and see if it's something you might like."

"Well, thank you Mrs. Bellon. I'd really like to see one of those new apartments. I see them being built, and I've wondered what they look like inside. You've given me something to think about. Best wishes to you in your new home."

As she walked away, Christina thought about her old neighbor, and realized how much she would miss her, and people like her in the old neighborhood.

Chapter Eighty-nine

Rudi's Infatuation

"Rudi, are you going to lunch now?"

Rudi turned at the sound of the feminine voice behind him.

"Hello, Erika. Yes, I'm gonna eat in the restaurant across from the terminal building. You wanna join me?"

Erika Brandt was a petite brunette of 20, who had been taken on by Luft Hansa as a stewardess shortly after Rudi had been hired as a copilot. She had brought the construction of the new apartment buildings in Treptow to his attention, which prompted the move of his mother and himself from Wedding in the summer of 1929.

Waiting for her to catch up to him, Rudi looked at her pretty heart-shaped face and stylishly bobbed dark brown hair and wondered what she found interesting in him. The captain of the new Junkers G24 airliner, and Rudi's superior, had flirted with Erika ceaselessly from day one. Although she was courteous to the man, she had deflected his attempts to get closer to her. The large, well-built blond pilot, and a veteran flier of the war, was perplexed and jealous when he saw how her face lit up when Rudi appeared.

No, Max Bayer was not used to being rebuffed by women. As a matter of fact, most women flocked around him, smiled and simpered to gain his attention. But Erika Brandt only turned on her charm with Rudi.

Together they crossed Tempelhofer Damm and made their way to the small family-owned restaurant on the corner of Manfred von Richthofen Straße. Upon entering, the stout middle-aged wife of the owner greeted them with a broad smile. Rudi, being a regular patron, had his favorite table in a nook near the window overlooking the small courtyard behind the building, which was shaded by a large sycamore tree. As the proprietress showed them to their table, she looked approvingly at the young girl in her dark blue well-fitting uniform, a feminine counterpart to the uniformed young pilot.

After pondering the selections on the hand-written menus, Rudi suggested the Eintopf, a house specialty of steak, peas and carrots over a layer of French fries served in a small clay pot. Erika followed his suggestion. The cheerful proprietress took the order to her husband, the talented cook out of sight in the back kitchen.

"How are you and your mother settling into to your new home?" she queried.

"It's wonderful! I'm so glad to have Mama out of that dump in Wedding. Did I tell you about the rat that got in her bed?"

"A rat! How horrible! Did it bite her?"

"No. Fortunately, it was more terrified of Mama than she was of it. She was just furious. Anyway, your tip about the new apartments came along just at the right time."

"I'm glad it worked out so well for you both," she responded with a smile.

"Are you and your family thinking about moving into one of those new places?"

"Oh, no. We live in a house on Baumschulenweg that my grandfather Brandt built in 1885. My mother would never give up her garden, and my father has his woodworking shop in the backyard."

"Sounds very nice. I'd like to have a house someday. My sister and her husband bought a small house out in Spandau almost two years ago. They really love it, especially since they have a new baby."

"I love Spandau. It would be nice to live out there along the Havel river," Erika replied.

After a few more minutes of conversation, which was helping them to get to know one another better, their food arrived. Erika asked for a glass of red wine and Rudi had a beer. After taking a bite, Erika enthused, "This is delicious! I'll be eating here more often. And it's so convenient to Tempelhof. Thanks for bringing me here."

Rudi, pleased with himself, was feeling very content in the presence of this lovely girl. He had no experience with women and was surprised at himself for being so at ease in her company. As they ate, Rudi felt her eyes on him, and he inadvertently began to blush.

With a light laugh, she commented, "You're blushing!"

"It's hot in here," he blustered. "Don't you find it warm in here?"

"No, I'm fine. Why don't you take your jacket off?"

"Good idea," he muttered, annoyed at himself. He thought he had everything perfectly under control.

As they walked to the bus stop after dinner, they passed a taxi stand, and Rudi got the impulse to take a taxi. Taking Erika by the arm, he steered her to the lead car idling at the front of the line.

"What are you doing," she asked, somewhat startled.

"I want to see where you live, if you don't mind."

With a look of complete astonishment, she allowed herself to be escorted to the car.

"Do you travel like this all the time," she teased.

"Only on special occasions. Today is one of those," he answered confidently.

They were both very quiet on the ride to Baumschulenweg, which took them around the south side of Templehof through Neukölln. When the taxi stopped in front of the tidy stucco house, Erika turned to Rudi and asked, "Would you like to come in and meet my parents?"

Somewhat startled at the suddenness of the offer, he hesitated before answering. "That would be great, but are you sure I might not be interrupting something, or perhaps make it uncomfortable for your parents, coming so unexpectedly?"

"Oh, they'll be glad to meet you. I've told them about you."

Surprised at this information, Rudi suddenly felt shy and countered, "Well, I hope they won't be disappointed."

"Oh, don't worry. They're not expecting much," she teased, with a laugh as she walked away from the taxi.

Rudi looked after her, wondering what she meant by her last remark. As he paid the driver, he noticed the man watching him with an amused smile. Frowning, he turned to walk to the front door where she stood waiting with a mischievous smile.

As they entered the front hall, Erika called out, "I'm home, Mama. I brought someone to meet you."

At this, a small, delicate-featured woman who strongly resembled her daughter came out of the kitchen wiping her hands on her apron.

Extending a hand to Rudi, she said, "Hello. You must be Rudi Bellon. I'm happy to meet you. We've heard so much about you."

Realizing she had said too much, she looked apologetically at her daughter, who was frowning at her mother.

"Hello, Mrs. Brandt," said Rudi extending his hand and taking her small hand in a warm handshake.

"Come," interjected Erika. "You must meet my father. Where is he, Mama?"

"He's gone to buy some materials for his woodworking project, but he should be back soon. Would you like to have a seat in the parlor? I can make tea, if you like," offered Mrs. Brandt.

"Oh, thank you, Mrs. Brandt. We just had lunch, and I must get home, but thank you again."

"You must come for dinner soon. I'll send word to you with Erika. You can meet my husband, then. He'll be sorry he missed you."

"I would look forward to that. I'm happy to have met you, Mrs. Brandt."

Turning to Erika, he said, "Thanks for inviting me in. I'll see you tomorrow morning."

"I'll walk you out," Erika replied.

As they walked to the front gate, he said to her, "Your mother is very kind. I was thinking she looks a lot like you."

"I take that as a compliment. People have always said that, and my mother was a very beautiful woman when she was young."

"She still is. And so is her daughter."

At this, she beamed a radiant smile and shook his hand, holding it a little longer.

Feeling very confident, he turned and walked toward the bus stop on Köpenickerlandstraße.

Chapter Ninety

The Crash

"I don't like the sound of that," muttered Hans Joachim Lenz, as he listened to the news broadcast on the evening of Wednesday, October 23, 1929.

Looking up from her book, *Im Westen Nichts Neues* (All Quiet on the Western Front), the anti-war novel by the German author and war veteran Erich Remarque, Frederika asked, "What's that, dear?"

"The American Stock Market is declining."

"What does that mean?" she inquired further.

"It means that the values of stocks have declined so rapidly that people are watching their investments evaporate before their eyes.

It reminds me of our currency devaluation which started back in '21, which led to the hyperinflation. You remember, we lost all of our savings. Now I could lose again, with my stock portfolio becoming worthless."

"Well, why don't you sell your stocks right away?"

"That's what people are doing, which is causing the market to collapse even faster."

"So, what are you going to do?" asked Frederika – a sense of dread overcoming her.

"I'm going to keep an eye on it. I'll call my broker tomorrow and discuss it with him."

The next day, Thursday, October 24, 1929, the Great Crash took place on Wall Street. The date came to be known in history books as "Black Thursday."

By the time Hans Joachim, and millions of others across the world decided to sell their stocks and try to salvage something from the economic wreckage, it was too late. Hans Joachim had left word with his broker to sell if the market reached the point they had agreed upon.

On Friday morning, the broker called him at the clinic to tell him his stocks had declined so fast overnight, there was nothing left. Shaking and numb with shock, Hans Joachim looked at the receiver in his hand as if he didn't know what to do with it, until he finally realized he had to hang it up.

With shaking hands, he lit a cigarette, and took a few puffs on it until he began to feel nauseous. He crushed it out and knew he had to call his wife.

"Hello, Frederika. We are wiped out!"

He heard her begin to sob. "Hello. Did you hear me, darling?"

After a prolonged pause, she responded in a quavering voice, "Wiped out? How can we be wiped out?"

"There's nothing left in the stock portfolio. It's all gone!"

Fortunately, Hans Joachim had the resources before the War to pay off his home mortgage, so that now in the face of the economic crisis, his family was not faced with homelessness. But the experiences of the war years with the blockade, and the postwar years leading up to the period of hyperinflation, had taught him well. He knew how to adjust to hard times.

"We will have to let all of the staff go with a month's notice," he announced at breakfast a week after the crash.

"Oh, no," cried Frederika. "I can't go through all that again!"

"I'm sorry my dear, and I'm sorry for our loyal servants, but the signs are very clear that this is going to be a very severe blow to our country. We've been enjoying a false prosperity for the last few years, supported by foreign loans, primarily from the United States. Now their economy is collapsing as well.

The banks there simply do not have the funds to continue to support our banks. Also, we have enjoyed the benefit of exporting goods to them in vast quantities, which they are no longer in a position to import, as their own industries are also losing their markets.

In addition, I hear that their Congress is under great pressure to raise tariffs on all imports to protect their industries. So, you see, Frederika, without their loans and their markets, we can expect nothing in the foreseeable future from the United States, or anyone else."

Later that evening at dinner, Hans Joachim reiterated what he had said earlier that morning. Numb with the shock of hearing this again from her husband, and only half understanding what he was saying,

Frederika looked at him in a daze. Wordlessly she got up from the table and left the room. Left alone at the table staring at his half-empty plate, he finally arose with a sigh and prepared to leave for the clinic.

The effects of that black October overwhelmed German society at all levels. As in New York, when many jumped out of skyscraper windows, suicide rates across the world rose rapidly and extremely so in Germany.

Industries began layoffs and cutbacks immediately in anticipation of hard times to come. Christmas 1929 was already far less festive and brilliant than the year before.

Chapter Ninety-one

Frederika's Decline

Frederika seemed not to recover. During the War, except for the period when Herbert was missing, and in the hard times following, she had shown resilience and determination to overcome – even at the time of the loss of Schloß Hohenberg.

Now, however, she wandered aimlessly around the house and only responded to attempts to engage her in conversation with listless indifference. She was in the depths of despair and brooded on her disappointments with her children—Herbert's rebellious refusal to go the university before the War and subsequent marriage outside of his class to a Jewish girl, the wrenching sorrow from the death of a little girl in the early years of her marriage, Karlheinz's disinterest in women, and his relationship with his friend, and finally his growing fascination with the rowdy young men in the Nazi movement.

When it came time to give notice to her household staff, she performed the duty with seeming detachment. Their longtime cook was retained half-time. With no one to maintain them, the immaculate rooms and garden slipped into neglect, as dust accumulated, and weeds overtook the lawns and flowerbeds.

After the Christmas holidays of 1930, the dark bleakness of the northern winter descended upon the city, and long lines again began to appear at soup kitchens and shelters for the homeless. Whole families with small children turned to begging. Camps for the homeless began to appear in the parks of the city and woodlands in the suburban areas.

Hans Joachim saw all this on a daily basis as he traveled to and from the clinic by public transportation, having stored his car for the duration. But he no longer discussed any of this with his wife, who spent more and more time alone in another bedroom, often not arising until midday or late afternoon.

Their bridge of communication became more and more obscure, and he lay awake through many sleepless nights alone in what had been their shared room. She had moved into a guest room down the hall.

As the months dragged on and warm weather and longer days returned, he hoped his wife would begin to take an interest in her garden, which had always been for her a great source of pride. But it was not to be. Herbert and Meira came to dinners less and less frequently, as these were prepared with diminishing commodities by their long-suffering cook. Karlheinz appeared rarely at these times, and it was due to real effort from the rest of the family that any response from Frederika occurred.

Summer passed and the cool days of autumn returned and the employment picture grew dire. Herbert was able to continue at the university, but Meira was able to support them only with help from Hans Joachim, as she and many others in the medical field, including doctors, were forced to practice often without pay from patients who were penniless. Health insurance connected to employment diminished as unemployment grew, and even some doctors found themselves among the homeless. Often, patients paid doctors with scarce commodities brought in from the countryside.

§§§

Frederika continued to decline as autumn moved into winter. She lost all interest in food, and her normally fresh complexion became sallow, with dark circles forming under her eyes. At the beginning of December, she took to her bed, and Hans Joachim, who had pulled many patients back from the brink of death, had no success with his wife. He began consulting with other doctors, and they, like himself, were not able to come up with a conclusive diagnosis.

Then came the hallucinations. The few friends who came to visit from time to time stopped coming after they experienced Frederika's sudden off-topic replies. Someone would be talking to her and suddenly she would interrupt, looking past the person speaking, as if seeing someone else standing behind him or her. She would begin something like, "Hello, Mama. Did you see Papa today? I asked you to tell him I wanted to go to Berlin this weekend." Then came the non-recognition of a family member or friend.

"Who are you?"

"It's me, Mama. Herbert."

"No, you're not Herbert. You're a nice man who brings me flowers, but you're not my little Herbert."

One night shortly before Christmas, long after Hans Joachim had retired, the house was enveloped in still darkness. Frederika lay in her bed humming to herself, when she saw a little girl standing beside her bed. At first, she was startled, until she realized that she was seeing her little Gerlinda.

"Hello, darling. Where have you been?"

"I've been playing with Herbert in the nursery. He let me ride his rocking horse."

"That's nice, sweetheart. Come give Mommy a kiss."

"I can't, Mama. I have to go now."

"No, please don't go!"

Turning to leave the room, the little figure said, "Come with me, Mama."

Frederika arose from her bed and followed the child out into the hall, which ran along the gallery overlooking the entry hall below. As the little figure reached the railing, she turned and smiled at her mother just as Frederika drew near her. As she started to reach for the child, who seemed to be beyond the railing floating in the air, Frederika, bending over the railing to do so, lost her balance and suddenly felt as if she were moving through space. She felt no fear but instead felt a sense of ecstasy as she embraced her daughter.

Hearing a muffled thud from the front entry hall, Hans Joachim sat straight up in his bed. As his head cleared, he wondered if perhaps someone had broken into the house. He cautiously arose and opened his bedroom door. Hearing nothing, but seeing light coming from Frederika's partially open door, he called, "Frederika? Are you alright, dear?"

Getting no response, he went to her door and peered into the room. Seeing the bed empty, he turned and walked along the gallery railing. Then out of the corner of his eye, he saw something on the floor of the entrance hall below. In the semi-darkness, he could make out the form of his wife lying on the floor. A sudden panic overtook him as he ran down the curved stairway. She was face up, and in the half-light coming through the elliptical transom over the front door, he could see a relaxed smile on her face.

§§§

The recently installed telephone rang shrilly in the hall of Herbert and Meira's apartment. Meira arose and made her way through the darkness. She answered with her voice lowered so as not to awaken Herbert.

"Lenz residence."

"Meira, I need to speak to Herbert."

"What is it? Can I take a message? He's asleep and has an exam tomorrow."

"Meira, Frederika is dead."

She stared blankly into the darkness, unable to take in what she had just heard.

"What happened?"

Hans Joachim, usually a man with great self-control, began to sob and answer almost incoherently.

"She fell over the railing of the gallery onto the floor of the entry hall. Please let me speak to my son."

"Of course. One moment."

Returning to the bedroom, she shook her husband by the shoulder.

"Darling, wake up. Your father is on the phone."

Groggily he muttered, "My father? What time is it?"

"Never mind. Speak to him."

Taking the phone, Herbert mumbled, "Yes, Papa. What's the matter?"

Meira had switched on the hall light and watched her husband's face. As he was given the terrible news, she saw his face blanch.

"Yes, Papa. We'll be right there."

Shaking, he replaced the receiver and turned to Meira as she embraced him. His shoulders shook as he buried his face in her shoulder, and she could feel his tears through the sheer material of her nightgown. After a few moments, he declared, “We must go to Dahlem right away. Papa is alone there and needs us.”

After dressing in a hurry, they went downstairs and out into the cold darkness to their car. On the drive to Dahlem, Herbert explained as best he could what had happened and wondered aloud why his mother had fallen over the bannister.

Hans Joachim was on his knees beside his wife holding her head in his lap and moaning, “Oh, Frederika, why did you do it?”

Herbert and Meira gently helped him to his feet and into the large parlor. After all three were seated on a long sofa, Herbert on one side and Meira on the other, arms around Hans Joachim’s shoulders, they let him sob and repeatedly ask, “Why did she fall? Why would she do such a thing?”

After several minutes, when Hans Joachim became calmer, he asked, “Where is Karlheinz?” Karlheinz still lived with his friend, Egon Wolf, whose apartment had no telephone.

Herbert replied, “I will go and find him. You stay with Papa, Meira, and in the meantime, call Grieneisen mortuary to come for Mama.”

Hearing this, Hans Joachim first protested that he didn’t want anyone touching her. Then his medical training took over and he agreed that it should be done.

Chapter Ninety-two

Search for Karlheinz

Herbert drove across the city to bring the tragic news to his brother. Upon arrival at the apartment building, he found the nameplate with the names Wolf/Lenz and rang the bell. Receiving no response, he tried again. A voice inquired over the speaker, "Yes, who is it?"

"Egon, this is Herbert, Karlheinz's brother. I need to speak to him."

"Sorry, Herbert. He's not here, but you can come up."

When the buzzer sounded, Herbert opened the door and entered the building. He went up two flights. Down the dimly-lit hallway, he saw light coming from an open door. He knocked softly, and Egon said, "Come in."

Egon, dressed in his bathrobe, stood in the doorway of the small kitchen.

"So, where is Karlheinz," Herbert inquired.

Egon said bitterly, "I don't know. I haven't seen him for several days. Since he started hanging out with those Nazi Brownshirts, he doesn't have time for his old friends anymore."

Annoyed at this bit of news, but not having time to go into the matter more deeply, Herbert stated, "I don't like to hear that. I'd like to talk to you more about it, but right now I need to get word to Karlheinz that our mother is dead."

Egon, startled, look at him wide-eyed. "Oh, Herbert. I'm really sorry to hear that. What happened?"

Herbert then recounted the tragedy, to which Egon responded, "Karlheinz will be devastated. He has said more than once he felt closer to his mother than anyone else in the family. Please don't take offense."

"No offense taken. We've all known that for years. Do you have any idea where he might be now?"

"I'm sorry, but as I said, I don't see him for days at a time. It seems he's always going to some party meeting or rally, but he doesn't tell me anything specific. You might try enquiring at the Nazi party headquarters on Lützowstraße."

"Oh, I know where that is. Yes, I'll see what I can find out there. In the meantime, if you hear from him, please tell him about our mother and tell him to contact me or our father."

"I will. I'm sorry for your loss, Herbert. I appreciated the courtesy your family showed me at your home. If there's anything at all I can do for you, be sure and let me know."

Herbert thanked Egon for his offer and left.

As he descended the stairs, he thought to himself, I wish my brother hadn't chosen that lifestyle, but at least he's lucky to have a friend like Egon – if he only had enough sense to see it.

When he arrived there, the building housing the Nazi Party Headquarters was still locked. He had to wait in his parked car a short while, when a black Mercedes sedan parked in front of him. Two stout SA men in their brown uniforms got out and proceeded to unlock the door and enter. He followed them into the building. As he entered, he saw the two walking down a long hallway lined on both sides with offices. They entered one, and Herbert hastened his step, reaching the door just as one of the men was closing it.

"Excuse me," he began. "Could you please help me?"

Being that it was first thing in the morning, and not being in the best of spirits, one of the two answered in a surly tone, "What do you want?"

"I'm looking for my brother. It's urgent." He then explained the circumstances of his mother's death.

"What's his name and what unit is he attached to?"

"Karlheinz Lenz. I didn't know he was member of your organization, and I don't know anything about his unit."

The second SA man standing inside the office and hearing the exchange stepped forward and interjected, "Karlheinz Lenz, did you say? He's not a member of the SA, but he always hangs around with those other homos from Münich. Is that faggot your brother? I wouldn't spread that around, if I were you. Unless maybe you're one, too," the man added, with a challenging glare.

Herbert's face was enflamed by embarrassment and anger. Knowing that losing his temper would only bring trouble, he bit his lip.

After a moment, the antagonist sobered and replied, "They all follow Ernst Röhm – the Führer's old buddy. Find him, and they won't be far away."

At this point, his comrade frowned and cautioned, "Careful, Horst. Just answer the man's question. Do you know where they might be?"

Refusing to be intimidated, the accuser responded, "Probably all in bed together!"

The other SA man quickly took Herbert by the arm and ushered him into the hallway, closing the door behind him. "Don't pay any attention to my friend. He hates homos and shoots his mouth off too much. Sorry we couldn't help you."

Sensing that he was causing a disturbance, and not wanting to bring any more attention to himself or his family, he thanked the man and made his way to the street and to his car.

Upon returning to Dahlem and to his parents' home, he found Meira alone in the house. "Where's Papa?"

"After the men from Grieneisen's removed your mother's body, your father was in such an agitated state that he didn't want to stay here and decided to go into the clinic. I assured him that we'd be in contact with him as soon as you got back with Karlheinz. Where's Karlheinz?"

"I went to their apartment, but he wasn't there. Egon says he hasn't seen him in days. Apparently, he has taken up with a new crowd – a bunch of Brownshirts from Münich, who are friends of Ernst Röhm. Egon's not happy about it, but what can you do?

I went by the Nazi party headquarters, and that didn't go well. One fellow there really hasn't anything good to say about Karlheinz's new friends. Anyway, that was a total waste of time. I'm glad Mother wasn't here to hear about this.

I'm exhausted, so I'm gonna lie down for a while, and then I'll try to think of some other way to find my idiot brother."

“Don’t say that, especially not in front of your father,” admonished Meira. “He’s been through enough in the last 24 hours. He doesn’t need you or anyone else to run down his other son!”

“I’m sorry. You’re right, of course. It’s just I wish that kid would grow up. He’d better. He doesn’t have his Mama now to make excuses for him and clean up his messes.”

“You just go lie down. I called the clinic and explained the circumstance, so I’ll be here to take any calls that might come.

Later, we need to pick up your father and go to Grieneisen’s and make the funeral and burial arrangements.” With that, she gave her husband a kiss and held him in her arms for a moment before he trudged wearily up the stairs to his old bedroom.

Chapter Ninety-three

Karlheinz is Told

The phone on the hall stand rang, startling Meira from her nap in a large upholstered chair in the front parlor.

"Lenz residence. Meira Lenz speaking," she spoke into the elegant ivory colored receiver.

"Egon Wolf here. May I speak to Herbert, please?"

"I'm sorry, Mr. Wolf, but he's asleep. May I take a message?"

"I was downtown for lunch at Aschinger's and I ran into two fellows who are part of the crowd Karlheinz runs around with. I explained that Herbert was looking for him and why. They said they were returning from an all-night party in Potsdam, where they and others, including Karlheinz had been. They all plan to go to the El Dorado Club this evening. If Herbert can go there this evening after eleven o'clock or so, he can probably find Karlheinz."

"Thank you, Mr. Wolf. Thank you so much. I'll tell him."

Later in the afternoon, Herbert came downstairs and Meira related the news from the phone call. Upon hearing the name of the location where he would likely find his brother, he snorted derisively and said, "The Eldorado Club! Why am I not surprised!"

"What's the Eldorado Club?" asked Meira with a puzzled look.

"It's a queer bar on Lutherstraße that's famous for transvestite shows. It's not only popular with queers and lesbians, but it's also considered one of the night spots in Berlin that attracts politicians, artists and tourists. One of the fellows that I served with in France told me about it, and thought it was a spectacle not to be missed. As far as I know, though, he wasn't queer. He had been here before the war with friends, who went there out of curiosity."

"So, do you want me to go with you tonight?" asked Meira.

"No, I don't think that's something you would want to see."

At this Meira laughed. "Don't forget. I saw and heard plenty when I was a nurse in that field hospital. I'm not easily shocked."

Herbert grumbled, "Well, you're not in a field hospital now, and I wouldn't be comfortable with you there."

"Well, I just hope one of those boys doesn't try to pick up my handsome husband," she teased.

At this Herbert turned red in the face and retorted, "That's not funny, Meira!"

"I'm sorry. I know you're taking all this very hard, and I don't mean to make it worse for you. You do what you think is best, and I support you."

§§§

Hans Joachim returned home late after dinner and collapsed into a deep leather chair and was asleep at once. Herbert had decided to withhold all of the news concerning his brother, and his father only briefly asked about him during dinner. Herbert stated that he was going to find Karlheinz later in the evening. When his father didn't inquire further, Herbert didn't elaborate.

Leaving his wife to look after his father, Herbert drove across the city, arriving at the El Dorado Club shortly before eleven p.m. He entered the establishment and was assailed by the noisy hubbub and laughter. The room was decorated with colored lights and mirrored balls which revolved and threw reflections on the walls and on the patrons. As he made his way through the crowds, he looked over the heads and tried to see into the dark corners where groups of men and women were seated at the tables. Some of the patrons looked him up and down, making him uneasy.

Then, after much pushing against people, he came to the dance floor where all varieties of couples jostled one another, men with men, men with women, and women with women. He spotted his brother locked in the embrace of a husky SA man. As he watched, the music stopped, and the dancers made their way back to their seats. The SA man had his arm around Karlheinz's waist, and leaned over and kissed his brother's face.

As the two of them reached a booth where other young Brownshirts were seated close together, Herbert stepped forward, and in a loud voice called, "Karlheinz!"

As his brother turned, he, seeing Herbert standing there, turned pale and asked, "What are you doing here?"

One of the other SA men interrupted. "You know him, Karlheinz? Have him come over here and have a drink. He's a bit on the old side, but that's okay with me."

The ensuing laughter was cut short by Karlheinz shouting, "Shut up, you idiots!"

"Come here" Herbert responded. "I need to talk to you."

As he pulled Karlheinz aside, he bent his head close to Karlheinz's ear, and said softly, "Mother is dead!"

At this, Karlheinz staggered and said, "What did you say?"

"You heard me. Come with me, and I'll tell you all about it."

In a daze, Karlheinz turned to his companions and said, "I have to go."

His erstwhile partner said, "But sweetie, you promised me another dance."

Not answering, he followed his older brother out to the street and got in the car.

Chapter Ninety-four

Terror

The damp chill hit Benjamin Friedlander in the face as he locked the door of his store late on an early January evening in 1932. He had worked later than usual after closing time. His staff had long since gone home, leaving him alone in his office as he pored over catalogues of merchandise, which, for the most part, he could no longer afford. The bitter effects of the Depression had forced him to discontinue carrying many of the high-quality goods people had come to expect from Friedlander's.

Then, of course – also due to the extreme hard times – his client base had shrunk considerably in the past two years. As a result, he had had to revert to practices he utilized in the beginning years of his career, namely, custom tailoring. As in former times, he had found skilled tailors in the eastern European community of the city – Jewish and Gentile.

As he hurried to the streetcar stop, he was one of few pedestrians. The late evening crowds in the downtown area of former times were no longer to be seen. The few people now on the street, were mostly people like himself, who had practical reasons to be out and about. Those out seeking pleasure were scarce, as the financial crisis had cut across all classes.

Consequently, some business establishments, restaurants and cafes, stores selling luxury merchandise, and even some theaters, had shortened their business hours. Some had been driven out of business. The great boulevards now had less glitter, and one felt an atmosphere of despair.

After a long wait, the southwest bound streetcar traveling toward his home in Charlottenburg arrived. Benjamin boarded and found a seat in the front section of the car. Being lost in thought, he hardly noticed other passengers moving up and down the aisle as they seated themselves. As the car rolled along, the swaying motion soon lulled Benjamin into an exhausted doze.

After a while, at a stop near Luna Park, four rowdy young SA men boarded, and with boisterous laughter and loud voices, found seats a few rows behind Benjamin. He, being aroused and slightly annoyed, looked back at them with a frown. They, seeing him looking in their direction, arrogantly looked back with challenging expressions.

Then, one of them with a startled look of recognition, glared at him fixedly with hostility, and leaned over and murmured to his seat partner. Benjamin, realizing that he was the object of this threatening attention, focused on the hostile face of the young Nazi. With a shock, he realized he was staring into the face of the young *Stormtrooper*, whom he had chased away from in front of his store on that January morning five years earlier. He recalled the threat the man had made: "*We have a score to settle.*"

The words cut through his brain like a hot knife.

He averted his gaze and felt numb, as a cold sweat of terror washed over him. He could hear the rumble of their voices, punctuated with menacing laughter. Panicked, he considered his options.

His tram stop was one station past Luna Park, and he was grateful it was a station which was normally crowded, so as to offer some protection. Then it occurred to him that due to the late hour and the amusement park being closed for the winter months, this hope was not realistic. Nevertheless, he decided to take the chance, and made ready to bolt out of the tram and attempt to lose himself among other passengers doing the same.

As the car stopped, he remained seated until the doors opened, and then jumped up and made a dash for the exit, pushing his way through others waiting to disembark. The young *Stormtroopers* seeing his move, sprang up and ran to the rear door, just as Benjamin jumped off the last step of the front door.

As he hastened through people milling about, he ducked into a small side street leading to the nearby Church of the Nazarene, hoping to find sanctuary there. The SA men jumped off the bottom step of the tram and looked around for their prey.

Just as Benjamin rounded the corner leading into the narrow dark street, one of his pursuers shouted, "There he is!" and gave chase.

"Stop, Jew, or you'll be sorry!"

Benjamin summoned up all his reserve energy and broke into a run. He could hear the shouting, cursing men closing in behind him. It was no use. The younger, more fit Brownshirts quickly overtook him, and one grabbed his coat collar and threw him to the ground. They then dragged him into a nearby underground public toilet. As they entered, two men relieving themselves looked up in startled alarm.

"You bastards clear out!" shouted one of the Nazis. Without argument, the two raced up the stairs, not wanting to be involved in what they saw to be a dangerous situation.

The Stormtroopers then threw Benjamin down on the wet, filthy floor and began to go to work on him. He curled himself into the fetal position, as fists and booted kicks rained down upon him.

"*Dreckjude*!"

"We're gonna get rid of you vermin!"

"Kike bastard!"

Curses and invective and blows continued for what seemed an eternity. Blood flooded his nose and mouth. After the initial pain, his body went into shock, and soon he slid into unconsciousness.

As the bullies finished their attack, they relieved themselves on their victim, laughing and congratulating themselves, and gave him one last kick before leaving.

After a while, a man entered the facility to answer nature's call and saw the body on the floor. As he drew near, he determined that the unconscious man had been badly beaten but was breathing.

He ran back up the stairs and at a nearby phone box called the police. Returning downstairs to the toilet, he tried to communicate with Benjamin, but to no avail. He went to the sink and moistened his handkerchief, which he then used to clean some of the blood and filth away from the victim's bloody nose and mouth. He had no sooner completed this task as well as he could, when the police arrived and soon thereafter the ambulance attendants.

Benjamin was taken to the emergency room of nearby Martin Luther Hospital. It was soon determined he had suffered two broken ribs and a fractured skull. His ribs were bound, and after being washed and dressed in a gown, he was given pain medication and put to bed, to be kept under close observation for the next twenty-four hours.

This experience was to be the beginning of an ordeal that would involve his whole family.

Chapter Ninety-five

A Family Reunites

"Friedel-Crafts reactions are a set of reactions developed by Charles Friedel and James Crafts in 1877 to attach substituents to an aromatic ring. The two main types of these reactions are: alkylation reactions and acylation reactions, both of which proceed by electrophilic aromatic substitution."

Herbert knew that a question asking for this definition would appear somewhere on the test coming up in two days. He frowned in impatience, not being a lover of organic chemistry. He had had several discussions with other pre-medical students, and with his father, about the necessity of pre-med students having to study organic chemistry at all. Hans Joachim had laughed and conceded that the same question had been debated when he was a medical student as well. His concentration was interrupted by the shrill ringing of the telephone.

"Now what?" he grumbled to himself, as he shuffled across the room in his pajamas and slippers.

"Lenz residence," he muttered into the device.

"Hello, Herbert? This is Edna Friedlander. May I speak to Meira, please?"

"Hello, Edna. She's on duty at the clinic. What can I do for you?"

"Papa is in the hospital. He was attacked coming home this evening and is badly hurt," Edna stammered, fighting to control herself.

"Attacked? What do you mean attacked?"

"Some rowdies caught him near Luna Park and beat him up and left him in a public toilet. A man found him and called the police and the ambulance. He's in Martin Luther hospital with some broken ribs and a fractured skull.

The police interviewed a witness who saw four Nazi Brownshirts leaving the toilet shortly before Papa was found. They probably did it. Please, can you get hold of Meira and tell her. Mama and I are at the hospital, and I'm calling you from there."

"I'll go get Meira right away. We'll be there as soon as we can. Tell your mother we're on our way."

Herbert immediately called the nurses station at Charité Hospital and told the head nurse about the situation. He asked if someone could relieve Meira, and the woman assured him it would be taken care of. Thanking her, he asked that Meira be notified he was on his way to pick her up.

He quickly dressed and rushed down to his car. He raced across town to the Charité and was relieved to see Meira waiting outside in front of the main entrance as he drove up on the circular driveway.

As she got into the car, she peppered him with questions, to which he replied, "I'm gonna find out who those bastards are."

When they arrived at the Martin Luther Hospital and walked into the lobby, they found Edna waiting for them. As they walked toward the elevator, she explained that Benjamin had been taken to the radiology department for X-rays and evaluation. They left the elevator and walked to the waiting area, where they found Golda sitting white-faced and almost in shock. As Meira embraced her mother, the woman broke down.

"Oh, Meira! I'm so glad you came. You too, Herbert. Who could have done such a thing to Benjamin? What did he ever do to deserve this?"

"I'm sorry to say it, Mrs. Friedlander, but if Nazis did it, they don't need a reason," Herbert replied. "They're thugs. They're filled with so much propaganda, they look for opportunities to bully someone. Anyone!"

"And we know they hate Jews," Meira added.

Meira and Edna sat on both sides of their mother with their arms around her. Gradually, she became calmer, taking comfort from both her children.

Chapter Ninety-six

Political Upheaval

On the night when Herbert picked him up at the El Dorado Club, Karlheinz, after his initial grief, stared out the car window on the way home. He was contentious and surly throughout the time of grief and the funeral. He had only short answers for anyone who asked about his welfare or expressed sympathy.

Only after his mother's burial did he approach his brother in the library with the question, "Are you gonna tell Papa where you found me?"

"He hasn't asked, and I have no intention of telling him. You've already been enough of a disappointment to him, and far be it from me to add to his grief."

Smarting under the rebuke, Karlheinz retorted, "I've been a disappointment! You have room to talk! You with your Hebe wife!"

At this, Herbert flared, "Don't start with me, Karlheinz! And don't use that tone when you mention my wife! Look at the kind of people you run around with!"

"My friends don't judge me, and they respect me!"

"Respect you! Don't be an idiot! They like to be seen with you, because you're the son of an eminent surgeon in this city. Being with you gives them a kind of respectability. They're using you! And are you using your allowance to impress them? The minute you no longer buy them drinks, you become an embarrassment to them and they'll drop you like a hot rock! Grow up, man!"

At this, Karlheinz charged out of the library red-faced with fury, and walked out the front door, slamming it behind him.

Hearing the uproar, Meira appeared and asked, "What's happening?"

Hanging his head, Herbert answered, "I lost my temper with my brother again. I so wanted to avoid a confrontation at this time."

Putting her arm around her husband's shoulder, Meira said in a soothing tone, "Don't blame yourself. He's been rude and obnoxious since you brought him home."

"What are we gonna tell Papa?" lamented Herbert.

"We'll tell him Karlheinz wants to be alone with his grief."

"My father's not stupid, and he knows Karlheinz. But you're right. We'll try to make it as easy for him as we can."

§§§

"Damn!" burst forth from Hans Joachim Lenz as he threw down his copy of *Berliner Morgenpost* on the morning of March 14, 1932.

"What's the matter?" inquired Herbert as he helped Meira set the family dining room table for breakfast.

"Hitler and the Nazis got 30.1 percent of the popular vote in the election yesterday! Where is this country headed?"

"Yes, but Hindenburg almost got an absolute majority with 49.6 percent," replied Herbert.

"Well, almost there is not good enough," grumbled his father.

Just then Meira came out of the kitchen with a freshly brewed pot of coffee and stated, "Breakfast is on the table, gentlemen. Come and eat. Later with politics."

As they sat down and began to pass around the fresh rolls, the phone rang in the hall.

"I'll answer it," volunteered Meira.

"Dr. Lenz residence," she announced.

For a moment, Meira thought they had been disconnected. Then the insolent tone of Karlheinz's voice snarled abruptly, "Who's this?"

"This is Meira Lenz."

"What're you doing there?" came the challenging voice.

"Herbert and I have been helping your father clear out some of your mother's things and taking care of him."

"By 'taking care of him,' do you mean taking advantage of his grief and helping yourself to my mother's jewelry and valuable things?"

Not wanting to get into a dispute with Karlheinz, Meira asked frigidly, "To whom did you want to speak, Karlheinz?"

"Both of them, but put Herbert on the phone first."

She returned to the dining room and said, "Your brother wants to speak to you, Herbert."

"I wonder what he wants?" As he arose from the table and picked up the receiver, Herbert answered, "Yes, Karlheinz. What is it?"

"Well, what do you think of the election results? Our man, Hitler, is really coming up in the world, don't you think," he exulted.

"Yes, you could say that. But don't get carried away. Since no one won with a clear majority, there's bound to be a second election. Then we'll see.

By the way, do you know anything about what happened to Meira's father?"

"Meira's father? What happened to the old Kike?"

Ignoring the insult, Herbert replied, "He was beaten up and left in a public toilet near Luna Park a couple of months ago. He suffered some broken ribs and a skull fracture. Meira has been nursing him at home since he got out of the hospital. Hopefully, he'll be able to go back to the store half days pretty soon."

"Why would you ask me if I know anything about it?" came the belligerent response.

"Because he's told us that four Brownshirts did it."

"So? There are a lot of them here now. Besides, if he got beaten up by any of them, he had it coming! He probably antagonized them somehow. You know how Jews are. They're insolent bastards who don't know when to keep their mouths shut. Anyway, I don't know anything about it. Let me speak to Papa."

"Alright, Karlheinz. But don't provoke him. You might apologize for leaving in a rage without telling him goodbye."

"Don't tell me what to do! Put him on!"

Reluctantly, he called his father to the phone. "It's Karlheinz."

"I can imagine what he wants. He probably wants to crow about the election outcome," sighed Hans Joachim.

As Herbert returned to the dining room, he shook his head as he spoke to Meira. "I really wonder where he thinks this is gonna lead us."

"Well, most importantly, he's making contact with your father. Any kind of contact is better than none," inserted Meira. "Look at my *own* father. He was belligerent when he finally remembered why we had fallen out, but with my mother's and sister's coaxing, and my showing him I wanted to give him the best care possible, he has softened to the point that he'll speak to me. We just don't discuss my marriage to you. Not yet."

Chapter Ninety-seven

Healing Begins

After Hans Joachim had left to go to Charité and Herbert to the university, Meira mused about what she had said to her husband earlier. She thought back on the terrible evening in February and the fear she shared with her mother and sister. They had soon settled into a routine of taking turns sitting by his bedside as he struggled to regain consciousness.

She sat observing her father, head and chest swathed in bandages. He was attached to intravenous feeding and medication tubes, motionless and still except for the rise and fall of his chest, the only sign of life in his battered body. Meira imagined how she would feel now if he had been killed. She resolved to make every effort to reconcile the differences that separated them, as far as it was in her power to do so.

As close as they had been, she had always looked forward to his coming home during her growing-up years. She remembered the joyful excursions she and her sister had enjoyed when he had taken them to the Zoo or Luna Park. She recalled the sun-filled days when they had taken the ferry to *Pfaueninsel* (Peacock Island) and seen the peacocks. They were delighted when he helped them build sand castles on the beach at Wannsee. The trips to Potsdam to visit *Der Alte Fritz* (Old Fritz) – Friedrich the Great's – palace of Sans Soucci, walks through the Tiergarten, and picnics in the Grünewald were memories she cherished.

Yes, he had always been a devoted father, and she was confident that under his hurt and disappointment with her choice of a husband, he still loved her. And she loved him and would not give up until she had his acceptance of her now.

In the days that followed, Benjamin's condition remained virtually unchanged, until one morning about one month after the attack, he opened his eyes and struggled to focus on his surroundings.

His wife's face bent near his and he heard her softly say, "Hello, my love."

"Golda?" he managed in a raspy voice. "Where am I?"

"You're in the hospital, and you're in good hands."

As he internalized this information, he asked, "Where is Edna?"

"She'll be here soon, and Meira, too."

At this, he struggled to remember why the mention of her name disturbed him.

His brow was furrowed in concentration, as he fought to reestablish his memory. He studied his wife's face, then asked, "Why does hearing her name bother me?"

"Never mind that" Golda answered. "She is your daughter and has been here helping to take care of you and loves you as much as Edna and I do."

Frowning, and still disturbed that the mention of his youngest daughter's name made him uncomfortable, but not remembering why, he was suddenly very drowsy and too tired to sort it out now. He murmured groggily, "I need to rest now."

§§§

As soon as their mother called them with the good news that their father had awakened, Edna and Meira met in the main lobby of the hospital and hurried upstairs to his bedside. Benjamin, by now sitting up and taking some liquid nourishment, was startled to see the two girls enter his room together.

"Hello, Papa," they chorused, then hurried across the room to embrace him.

Still not able to recall the issue he had with Meira, he asked her, "Where have you been?"

Not knowing how to answer, Meira looked at her mother for help. Golda picked up the cue and interjected, "She's been here with us helping take care of you. We're all here together now, and that's what's important."

Frowning and still not satisfied, but deciding he would think more about it later, Benjamin then smiled and said, "I'm so happy my beautiful girls are here."

Chapter Ninety-eight

Weimar's Last Days

Since no candidate for president won an absolute majority of votes in the first round of the election on March 13, it became necessary to hold a second round on April 10. Hindenburg, running as an independent, competed with Hitler, representing the Nazis, and Erik Thälmann, the candidate for the Communist Party. Hindenburg came in first with 53.0%, Hitler was second with 36.8%, and Thälmann placed third with 10.2%. Although the Nazis failed to win the presidency, their gain in the second round represented garnering over more than two million additional votes between March 13 and April 10, 1932.

Herbert and Meira had joined their friends in Spandau, Eckhardt and Ursula, on the second election night for dinner. They were gathered around the radio as the results came in, and Ursula commented, "Well, I'm sure Mama and her Communist friends are disappointed that they did so badly."

"Yes. And thank God for that!" stated Eckhardt flatly. "But I'm uneasy about the gains the Nazis made, even though they didn't win. I guess we shouldn't be surprised. The country is bitter and frustrated over the events since the war. Except for the relatively good times of five years during the last half of the twenties, we have gone from one catastrophe to the next. And people are sick and tired of hearing we were the only ones responsible for the war.

Except for the Americans helping us with their loans until the crash of '29, the rest of the world, particularly the British and the French, have pushed all the war blame off on us."

"That's true," agreed Herbert, "but I don't think people are right in giving up on democracy. Our government has not made the most of the opportunities they've had since the war, it's true, but let's face it: we don't have a long history of individual rights and self-determination like the British, or even the French.

Our society has been under the control of authoritarian leadership for centuries. The last time our people tried to stand up for their rights was in 1848, and we know how that turned out. As a result, millions emigrated to America and other countries, where they have been able to enjoy greater freedom."

"Yes," responded Eckhardt. "It takes time for a society to break the mentality of unquestioning obedience, and we have been trying it in one of the most difficult periods in our history. But I don't like the things we hear about the Nazis. They have become more and more aggressive and intolerant. I shudder to think what they would be like if they were in power."

"And Hindenburg. He's over eighty and in poor health. I hear he didn't even want to be in politics, but his sense of patriotism gave him no choice."

The air of relief that the elected president did not represent either of the two radical ideologies, was mixed with apprehension and concern that the power vacuum, which would develop if something happened to him, might be filled by one of them. These were desperate times, and the people of Germany were ready to undertake desperate measures to prevent the return of starvation and sickness of the recent past.

The Great Depression hit America hard, and the effects on American society during those years has been well documented, but the impact on Germany was even worse. The "prosperous" last five years of the Weimar economy in the late 1920s had been propped up mainly by American loans, more so than by industrial production and exports. Several German and Austrian banks failed due to loss of consumer confidence in addition to the decrease of demand for German products. The United States, which had been the largest purchaser of German exports, raised tariff barriers to protect its own manufacturers.

The result was that by 1932, German industrial production dropped to 58 percent of the 1928 levels, which in turn brought about massive unemployment. By late 1929, 1.5 million Germans were unemployed. One year later, there were more than 3 million, and by the end of 1932, 6 million, or 26 per cent, were without work.

Reports from that time state that packing-crate encampments of the homeless had sprung up in suburbs and parks. Young men could be seen all over the city trying to eke out an existence any way they could, begging, trying to sell shoe-laces, shining shoes, opening car doors, lining up at the Labor Exchange seeking casual day employment, hanging around public toilets and bars offering to prostitute themselves, stealing, picking up cigarettes butts off the street, etc.

The Weimar government responded dismally to the situation. Rather than trying to stimulate the economy with the creation of job programs, such as were developed during the Roosevelt administration in the United States (WPA, CCC, etc.), the administration under the leadership of Chancellor Heinrich Brüning increased taxes, ostensibly to reduce the budget deficit, and then went on to implement wage cuts and spending reductions to lower prices.

Even though these policies were rejected by the legislative body, the Reichstag, President Hindenburg supported Brüning as he declared them to be "emergency decrees" in 1930. Understandably, these measures failed, and instead increased unemployment and public misery rather than alleviating it. They also brought about more government instability and division among the political parties.

The great beneficiary of all this was Adolf Hitler, who later declared the period had brought him unprecedented contentment. As public confidence in the Weimar government decreased, Nazi Party membership increased to record levels.

Chapter Ninety-nine

Nostalgia

Christina absentmindedly watered the geraniums on the balcony of her apartment on Kiefholzstraße in Treptow. She was bored! She and Rudi had been living in the new apartment over two years, and the convenience and comfort of a modern domicile was very exciting in the beginning. But now, she missed the old neighborhood in Wedding. She had made her way back several times since leaving in the summer of 1929 and was welcomed by some of her old friends and neighbors. However, over time she felt the closeness she'd enjoyed with them had dwindled.

Her old long-time acquaintance, Mrs. Krämer, had visited her a few times in Treptow, but this ceased during the past year due to Mrs. Krämer's failing health. On her last visit, she brought Christina the sad news that Mr. Schröder, the baker, had passed away.

"Yes, Mrs. Bellon. It was a real shock for poor Mrs. Schröder. She awoke one morning last month and found her husband dead beside her. Just imagine! He was already cold and stiff when she discovered him."

"I wish I had known. Was the service well attended?"

"Well, you know how it is. The old neighborhood has changed, and quite a few of our old friends and neighbors have moved away, like you. So, except for the two children and their families, there were only a few neighbors there.

One can't blame them, though. Look at your beautiful apartment. And your bathroom! You know how people say, 'Happiness is not a flush toilet.' But when I have to make my way down to that dark, cold hole of a toilet on the mezzanine, I'd like to try a little of that unhappiness."

They both laughed at this.

"Oh, yes. I remember, but how much time can you spend on the toilet? Sometimes, I get a little lonely here. I don't know anyone in the building. Most of the tenants are younger people, and with the hard times, in some families, husband and wife are both working. I get out and go to the shops, but I hardly ever see anyone I know."

"But tell me, what is Mrs. Schröder going to do now? She can't run the bakery by herself."

"That's true, and neither of her children are interested in taking it over. Besides, they too had moved away from Wedding as soon as they could. The daughter doesn't even live in Berlin anymore. She married a fellow from Hamburg and has lived there almost ten years. So, I don't know what she can do. In times like these, it would be hard to find anyone who would want to take over a bakery in a neighborhood like ours."

They finished their coffee and cake, and Mrs. Krämer stated she must leave in order to get home before dark.

As she finished watering her plants, Christina turned all this over in her mind. In spite of the changes, she sometimes entertained the thought that she perhaps should never have left her old home. What if she were to move back?

§§§

"You think you'd like to do what?" Ursula looked at her mother, incredulous.

"Oh, come on, Christina," Eckhardt teased. "You know you're not serious. Remember the rat?"

"And don't forget the ice on the inside of your window in the wintertime," added Ursula.

"I know, I know, but I am so bored and lonesome. Rudi's gone so much of the time flying. And I do appreciate the modern apartment, but I find myself cleaning it two or three times a week, just for something to do.

I've gone out in the countryside a few times foraging like I used to do during the war, but I'm not so young anymore, and Rudi gets after me because he has enough income, and I don't really need to do that. I made the trip out to Zossen last summer, but I didn't have the energy to walk out to the farm, so I just got back on the train and came home."

She had come out to Spandau to see her grandchild, have dinner and stay overnight with her daughter and husband, and was glad to have someone to talk to. She told them she was thinking about moving back to Wedding, mostly to see how Ursula and Eckhardt would react. She wasn't surprised at their response, and deep inside she knew she didn't want to do that. But she was so lonesome.

"Well, I think I'd like to go to bed," she stated.

"Of course, Mama. By the way, Eckhardt installed electric heaters in the rooms upstairs, so feel free to make yourself comfortable. And put that idea about moving back to Wedding out of your mind. You can come here anytime you feel bored and lonely."

"Thank you, dear. Goodnight." With that, she gave her daughter a kiss on the cheek and turned to Eckhart before starting up the stairs, and said affectionately, "Goodnight to you, too, son."

"Goodnight, Mama. Sleep well."

Ursula and Eckhardt looked at one another as Christina trudged up the stairs. After a moment, Eckhardt shook his head as he picked up his copy of *Berliner Tageblatt,* and Ursula went to check on "little" Eckhardt, now a robust youngster of eight, having had his birthday on November 1.

Later, as she and her husband were lying in bed, she turned to him and asked softly, "What are we going to do about Mama?"

"What do you have in mind, Ursula?"

"Well, I know Mama. If she makes up her mind to move back to Wedding, she'll do it, no matter what we think or say about it. I can't imagine her going back to that lifestyle, now that she's had something better. She thinks she would take up with old friends and acquaintances there, but as she said herself, many of them have moved away, or have died. Many of those that are still there are getting up in years—like herself—and are dealing with health issues like Mrs. Krämer, or have passed on like Mr. Schröder. I can predict that she would very shortly learn life there would not be like she remembers it."

Eckhardt listened to this without comment and turned it all over in his mind.

"What are you thinking," probed his wife.

"Why don't we have her come and live here with us," he responded.

"Really? Would you consider such a thing?"

"Don't act so surprised. I could tell you were working up to this," he teased, giving his wife a gentle nudge.

"Oh Sweetheart! You remind me over and over how lucky I am to have you. Mama loves you, you know. I bet she'd accept gladly, if she knew you had suggested it."

Smiling to himself in the darkness, he then turned to his wife, and with an embrace, whispered, "I think I fell in love with your family about the same time I fell in love with you."

She snuggled against her husband and kissed him passionately. The warm intimacy of the night enveloped them as peace settled over the little cottage in Spandau.

Chapter One-hundred

Convalescence and Intimidation

Benjamin continued to mend over the spring and summer months of 1932. He gratefully allowed his daughter Edna to work with his manager in running the store during the time he was confined to his bed. Gradually, he regained his strength and moved slowly about the house.

By the end of May, he returned to the store for an hour at a time, allowing Edna to drive him there in his car. Little by little, he was able to extend his time, until by July he could work half days. As he traveled back and forth, he was shocked by the sight of more and more vagrants and derelicts on the streets. The long queues in front of the soup kitchens, which had been established in vacant shops and businesses that had been forced to close, had increased in the time since his attack in February.

As he stepped from his car in front of his store, he was embarrassed by the resentful stares of shabbily clad panhandlers in front of the buildings. Sometimes women with young children approached him holding their hands outstretched. He began to carry small denominations of currency and coins for the purpose of providing them with temporary relief. Intermingled with the crowds were the Brownshirts, with their stands displaying propaganda posters and pamphlets.

One September morning as Edna drew the car up to the curb in front of the store, he spotted a pair of them established near the entrance, as they had been five years earlier, and he started to walk past them with his face averted without comment. As he drew nearer to the entrance, he heard a raucous shout from one of them, "Hey, Jew! Remember me?"

As he looked up, he found himself staring into the face of the ringleader of the Nazis who had beaten him up!

Blood drained from his face as the shock of seeing his tormentor again in broad daylight hit him. He quickly opened the door as the laughter followed him, accompanied by the taunts, "That's it, Jew! Run away! We're not through with you yet."

As he entered the store, he was oblivious to the greetings offered him by the staff, and he stumbled on trembling legs to his office. Edna soon followed after parking the car behind the building.

"I couldn't hear what those Nazis were saying to you, Papa. What was it?"

Looking at her trembling father seated at his desk, shaking as he poured himself a brandy, she instinctively knew.

"Are those the men that beat you up last winter?"

"One of them, yes. He's the one I chased away from here over five years ago, and he has never forgotten it."

"I'm going to call the police," stated Edna as she reached for the phone on his desk.

"Oh no, don't do that. It will only make things worse," he pleaded.

"How much worse can it get, Papa? You need to identify them as the ones who attacked you. They won't stop unless you put an end to it."

With that, she took the receiver off its hook and told the operator to connect with the police. After a moment, a male voice came on the phone and Edna outlined the situation. When the man on the other end heard the name "Friedlander," he responded, "Is that the clothing store on Ku'damm?"

"Yes. Could you please send someone right away?"

There was a long silence until Edna asked, "Hello? Are you still there? Can you send someone here, please?"

"Yes, I understand."

The man immediately hung up.

Edna stared at the receiver in her hand before replacing it on its cradle.

"Please take me home Edna," her father said.

"You have to wait until the police come, Papa. You'll have to make a statement."

This was answered by an anguished groan.

"Look out front, Edna. See if those men are still there."

Edna peered out the office window, which allowed a view through the front store windows. The two Brownshirts were nowhere to be seen.

"They've packed up and left, Papa."

"Oh, that's good," replied Benjamin with relief.

"No, that's bad, Papa. Now you can no longer identify them for the police."

This got no response from her father.

After more than a half-hour, two policemen entered the store and were directed to the office. Edna met them at the door and explained what had happened, to which the older of the two turned to Benjamin, "Well, Mr. Friedlander, did you provoke them or say anything to them?"

"No, of course not, but the one who called after me was one of those that attacked me last February near Luna Park. He was also the one I told to get away from my store over five years ago."

"Well, then you did provoke them," responded the officer with a smirk.

"But that was a long time ago, and I didn't want Nazis bothering my customers as they came and went from my store."

With a sardonic grin to his colleague, the officer replied, "You'd better learn to know who you pick your battles with, don't you think?"

At this Edna interjected, "Are you saying my father is to blame for this whole thing?"

At this, the man turned to her, and with raised voice said, "I'm not talking to you! I'm questioning your father! If I want to hear from you, I'll let you know."

Caught off guard, Edna began to protest, "I think I have a right…"

The policeman cut her off, "I'll explain your rights – if I choose – but since you can't keep your mouth shut, you can leave. You step outside! Now!"

With a helpless glance at her shaking, white-faced father, she reluctantly stepped outside the office. Through the window she watched in anguish as she saw the two officers harassing her father.

She could not make out what was being said, but she could hear the raised voices and see her father begin to break down in tears. She was outraged and embarrassed, as the scene was being taken in by staff and customers, many of whom hurried out the door after paying for their purchases or put their selections back on a shelf or table and left.

Finally, the two officers came out and stated, “There is nothing to report here, as your father can’t tell us any more about the alleged attackers. Of course, there aren’t any Brownshirts outside your store now.”

As the two men walked through the store, the people watching stepped aside.

§§§

“It was terrible, Meira. Papa was devastated. I’m afraid he’s going to have a nervous breakdown.”

“Oh, Edna. I’m sorry all this has fallen on you. How’s Mama holding up?”

“Well, as you can imagine, she’s very distraught as well. You know, Papa is more down now than I have ever seen him. You know how he’s always been so confidant and used to being in charge, but he’s really in need of support now. Would you consider coming over and bringing Herbert?”

“Do you think that would be a good thing?”

“Yes, I do. Papa was grateful for your help when he was convalescing last winter. I think it’s time for him to get past some of his prejudices and get to know your husband. Herbert is strong, and Papa needs the support of another man.”

Meira paused before answering.

“Well, I’ll talk it over with Herbert when he gets home from class this evening, and you perhaps should have Mama talk to Papa. If he’s not opposed to the idea, we can come over tomorrow afternoon.”

Meira told her husband about all that had happened at the store that afternoon and the conversation she’d had with her sister.

Herbert listened without comment and after a pause replied, “I’m so sorry to hear that your father had to go through such an ordeal. Do you think he’d want to have me involved? I mean, if I can be of any help, then of course I’m glad to do what I can. But remember he has had mistreatment today from Gentile Germans – first the Brownshirts and then the rude policemen. Don't you think having to deal with another Gentile German might upset him?"

"You're my husband, and as such, we're all involved with each other as family. He needs to understand that, and I'll suggest that to Edna. I know she'll certainly emphasize it to Mama."

"Alright. Call Edna and tell her we will be out tomorrow afternoon about 4 o'clock."

§§§

The next day at the appointed time, Herbert and Meira drove out to Charlottenburg and were greeted cordially at the door by Golda Friedlander. They found Benjamin seated in the front parlor in his large leather chair. Upon seeing Herbert in his house for the first time, he looked uneasy, but was cautiously courteous to his son-in-law. After enquiring how he was feeling, the group listened and let the distraught man relate the incidents of the day before in his own words.

"Imagine how I felt. I was humiliated in my own store in front of my staff and customers. Worse than the insults of the Nazis, was the disrespectful treatment I received from the policemen. I can't get over it!"

"Well Papa, you must try to do just that. Dwelling on it will do you no good. More importantly, we must decide what to do next," admonished Meira.

At this point Herbert spoke up. "I've told my father about the attack you suffered last winter, Mr. Friedlander, and he discussed it with some of his friends and colleagues at the clinic, some of whom are Jewish as well. These Nazis have grown bolder during the past months, especially after the gains they made in the last two elections.

One of my father's friends, Dr. Eisenberg, went out to his car one morning and found the windows smashed and a dead rat tied to the steering wheel. My father – and some of the other non-Jewish doctors – protested to the Police President, who promised to follow up on the matter."

"What's the matter with people?" lamented Edna.

Herbert explained, "It's the Nazis' propaganda, combined with people's frustration and anxiety about the economic crisis we're going through. Goebbels is making the most out of the situation and whipping up everyone's anger and growing resentment. That hasn't really gone away since the war. Many people listen to the Nazis and let themselves be persuaded that someone else is to blame for all their misery – the Allies, the wealthy, the Jews, etc."

"I would never have believed that such barbarians as the Brownshirts could get away with what they have done to me in my country," lamented Benjamin. "All my life I've been proud to live in the most cultured country on earth. I've always been proud to consider myself German. I've always believed that with our great educational tradition and talent for hard work and organization, we would again take our place among the great nations."

Muted by empathy for the suffering man, the group waited.

Finally, Herbert spoke up. "I'll discuss this whole matter with my father. He was outraged when I told him what happened to you last winter, and I am sure he'll not let this disgrace from yesterday rest."

Benjamin gazed at his son-in-law with new respect.

"You're a good man, Mr. Lenz. I'm sorry I've been so stubborn and wasted so much time getting to know you. I should have known my daughter would not attach herself to a man unless he were of the highest character. Please forgive me."

"Don't berate yourself, sir. I understand how hard it is for someone to break with strong traditions. My own mother had to suffer much because of the class distinctions that she grew up with, and I think it may have had something to do with her death."

Meira looked at him. She had never heard him refer to his mother's death this way before.

Soon, it became apparent that Benjamin was exhausted and needed his bed. Meira arose and embraced her father and then her mother. Herbert shook Benjamin's hand and promised to get in touch with his father and report back to the Friedlanders as soon as possible. Edna walked them to the door and hugged her sister tightly, expressing her gratitude again for their support.

As they drove away, Herbert said grimly, "We have work to do."

Chapter One-hundred-one

Gentile Support

"Friedlander is right!" exclaimed Hans Joachim Lenz. "No man should have to suffer the outrages he has had to endure in a highly civilized country like Germany!"

"I agree with you, Papa. Many people would agree with you. Nevertheless, that's where we're at in this country at the present time. The question still remains, 'What are we going to do about it?'"

Nodding his head at Herbert's challenge, Hans Joachim muttered, "Yes, what are we going to do about it?" Then he declared, "I'll make an appointment with the Police President and speak to him myself. I'm not closely acquainted with the man, but I know Albert Grzesinski is an honorable man and is no friend of the Nazis. Last year he tried to muzzle Hitler and have him deported as an undesirable alien, but Chancellor Brüning wouldn't sign the deportation order."

"If you would do that, Papa, I'm sure Meira's family would be most grateful. Please let me know right away how it comes out."

§§§

"Papa, how are you?" Meira asked her father on the phone a few days later.

"I'm feeling better. I really appreciate you and Herbert coming the other evening. Your husband is a fine man. I should never have doubted your wisdom in marrying him."

"We're happy to help you in any way we can. I'm glad you finally got to meet my husband. Yes, you're right. Herbert is a wonderful man and husband, and I love him. I'm sure you'll come to love him, too.

Doctor Lenz has spoken with the Police President, and Mr. Grzesinski apologized for the behavior of the officers at your store. He pointed out that, unfortunately, the Nazis have been successful in unofficially 'recruiting' some of the police. When it comes to his attention, he sees that they are disciplined, or even dismissed from the police department. He further suggested that you might consider having a bodyguard until the political situation can be stabilized. He's confident that Hitler cannot last.

In fact, in addition to trying to have him deported, Mr. Grzesinski has referred to Hitler as 'the foreigner' and found it 'lamentable' that he should be negotiating with the government 'instead of being chased away with a dog whip'.

He suggested that you might consider taking on a long-time acquaintance of his and former colleague, now retired, who also finds Hitler and the Nazis to be an odious disgrace to our country. He was a police captain with over forty years' service with the department. Mr. Grzesinski is confidant he would prove to be a capable and trustworthy guardian for you and would welcome some extra income. If you're interested, you may contact Mr. Grzesinski at his office and discuss it with him. His secretary will put you right through."

Gratified that such a prominent person would take an interest in his dilemma, Benjamin was relieved to learn that such protection might be available to him.

"Please convey my deepest gratitude to Dr. Lenz for his time and trouble. I'm sorry to inconvenience him with my concerns, but I am most grateful. I'll follow up on his suggestion first thing in the morning."

"Good, Papa. You can see that Herbert comes from good stock. He's just like his father – always concerned for the unfortunate and willing to help where he can."

"Yes, apparently that apple didn't fall very far from the tree," quipped Benjamin.

Laughing, Meira replied, "Very well put, Papa."

§§§

"Good morning, Mr. Wollner. I'm Benjamin Friedlander, and I have just spoken to the Police President, Albert Grzesinski. He suggested that I might contact you, which I hope is not an imposition."

"Yes, Mr. Friedlander. I've been expecting your call. I know about the disgraceful attack you suffered at the hands of those Nazi hoodlums last winter and the harassment you have suffered since. I add my apologies to those of Mr. Grzesinski for the ill-treatment and humiliation imposed upon you by officers of our police department. Please permit me to assure you that such behavior is not typical for the Berlin police."

"Yes, I understand, Mr. Wollner. Not unexpectedly, I was informed that some officers have been influenced by Nazi propaganda, like many others nowadays I fear. So, since you have been apprised of my dilemma and my need for some protection, would you consider taking on the responsibility for my safety? I assure you I will make every effort to make it worth your while, but unfortunately, my financial resources have been considerably reduced due to the present economic crisis in our country. Could I suggest that we have a meeting at your convenience to discuss the matter?"

"Of course, Mr. Friedlander. If I can, I'll be happy to be of service to you. I would be happy to meet with you as soon as possible."

"Excellent! May I suggest that we meet here at my home tomorrow at 10 o'clock? I apologize for inconveniencing you, but I would rather not venture out on my own."

"Tomorrow will be perfect, and don't consider it an inconvenience."

"Thank you, Mr. Wollner. I look forward to seeing you here tomorrow at ten."

Kurt Wollner was a large, muscular man in excellent health, who was a widower in his late sixties. He had established a reputation during his forty years with the Berlin Police Department as a fearless defender of the peace and safety of the citizens of the city. He was respected by other members of the department as a man of character and unshakable honesty. He never wavered in his dedication to upholding the law in a fair and unbiased manner, never being swayed by enticements to let expediency cloud his judgement.

It was agreed that he would henceforth serve as chauffeur and bodyguard for Benjamin and members of his family, and he assured his new employer that he would not only personally dedicate himself to the task of securing his safety but would also not hesitate to call for backup from officers whose integrity he knew could be relied upon.

He was acquainted with many policemen whom he knew would not be taken in by propaganda—not from Nazis, or Communists, or any other group that employed radical means in their quest for power.

It was also suggested by Golda that, as Mr. Wollner was a single man living alone in a large apartment in Wilmersdorf, he might consider taking two unoccupied rooms on the third floor of their house – rent free, of course.

Kurt Wollner was surprised and grateful when this offer was made but replied that he would like to consider the matter before deciding. He had a grown son and daughter, who were accustomed to bringing their children to visit their grandfather, and dinners were frequently held in his flat, which had been the family home where he and his wife had raised their children. Then, Golda insisted that in lieu of taking up residence in the Friedlander home, Kurt Wollner would take breakfast with them every weekday morning at 7:30. After that, he would drive Benjamin to the store and assist as needed for the balance of the day. Finally, he'd drive Benjamin home and join them for dinner before returning to his own home for the night. The new routine soon proved to be successful, and Kurt Wollner and Benjamin Friedlander formed a bond which would develop into a lifelong friendship.

Chapter One-hundred-two

Friendship Lost

Egon Wolf turned the key in his front door and entered his apartment early on a Friday morning in November. The odor of cigarette smoke, beer, whiskey and unwashed bodies hit him as he stepped into the vestibule. Young men in various stages of undress and nudity lay sprawled on the living room floor. Expecting the worst, he went into his bedroom and found Karlheinz and two other men in his bed.

"Karlheinz, get up, you bastard!" he shouted as he yanked the bed covers off his friend and the other two unknown young men, all three passed out drunk, as were the occupants on the living room floor. Returning from a three-day trip to Leipzig, where he had visited his ailing mother, Egon had never expected his friend to take such advantage of his generosity and hospitality.

"What do you want? Leave me alone," Karlheinz grumbled groggily.

"Get up and get this scum out of here now!" commanded the outraged Egon.

"What are you getting so worked up about?" retorted Karlheinz. "Go out in the living room and pick yourself out a snuggle buddy and leave us alone."

Shaking with anger, Egon marched back into the living room and began shoving the bodies lying on the floor with his foot. As they began to regain consciousness, the "guests" responded to their tormentor with growls and profanity.

Staggering down the hall, Karlheinz shouted obscenities at Egon, and upon reaching him, shoved him violently against the wall. "Stop, or I'll knock you on your ass!"

Egon shoved back, and the tussle degenerated quickly into a fight. As the combatants exchanged blows and careened around the room, they stepped upon bodies and smashed into furniture, knocking over tables and lamps. By this time, Karlheinz's two bedmates joined the fray, pulling the two erstwhile friends apart.

Karlheinz and Egon, breathing hard with blood pouring from their noses and mouths, glared at one another with newly-developed hatred.

"How could you do this to me," gasped Egon.

"I thought you were coming back on Saturday, so I invited some of my friends to sleep over. Anyway, what are you being such an ass for, you faggot?"

The color drained from Egon's battered face as he tried to regain his composure. "I thought you were my friend."

"I'm sick of you!" Karlheinz responded. "Look around. These are real men, and you're gonna be lucky if they don't finish what I started and beat the shit out of you."

Tears began to form in Egon's eyes as he took the abuse. The others began to gather up their uniforms, muttering threats and sneering insults at the hapless Egon.

§§§

Unshaven and disheveled, Karheinz appeared at his father's house after gathering up his few personal belongings and flinging a final threat at Egon. "You watch yourself, faggot. I haven't decided how to deal with you, but I'll think of something."

Meeting his father's housekeeper in the hallway as he started up the stairs, he declared, "I'm moving back home. Where's my father?"

"He's at the clinic where he usually is at this time of day," replied the astonished woman.

"Well, I'm tired and I'm going to take a nap. Is my bedroom made up?"

"I'm sorry, sir, but your father has kept some of the unused bedrooms closed up since your mother died. I can make up the bed right away."

"Yes. Do that now," he commanded. "Is there any coffee left from breakfast?"

"Yes, sir. There should still be some on the stove. I can heat it up for you."

"No, I can do that," as he started toward the kitchen. "You make the bed."

“Yes, sir,” responded the flustered woman.

Learning that his youngest son had returned home to stay surprised Hans Joachim when he returned to his house that afternoon. He asked the housekeeper, “Where is he?”

“He came home about midmorning and went to bed,” she reported.

“And still in bed? How did he look?”

“He was unshaven and not looking good,” responded the woman reluctantly, not eager to get involved in family matters of her employer.

At this Dr. Lenz frowned, and muttered, “If he thinks he’s going to just move in here when it suits him, after not even giving me a call for weeks on end, he’ll find out differently.”

With that he started up the stairs and walking resolutely to his son’s door, knocked firmly.

§§§

Still smarting from his father’s reprimand and ultimatum, Karlheinz sat brooding on the subway to Kurfürstendamm reflecting on the worst confrontation he had ever had with his father.

He had been in deep sleep when he slowly registered the pounding on his door. “Let me alone,” he shouted at his tormentor in an alcoholic stupor.

“I’ll let you alone after I have straightened you out on a few things. Open this door! ” his father had shouted.

Finally, on unsteady feet, Karlheinz had staggered to the door and opened it to face a furious, red-faced father.

“What do you mean showing up here after not even calling for weeks at a time?” challenged Hans Joachim. “Why are you even here?”

Sulking before answering, Karlheinz looked at him, “Egon kicked me out.”

His father frowned at this news. “Now what happened?”

“I invited a few friends over while he was in Leipzig visiting his mother, and he came home a day earlier than I expected. He doesn’t like 'em, and so he came in and started yelling at us. We had a fight and he told us to get out."

Hans Joachim then stated, "Your mother and I would have been happier if you had taken up with a nice girl, but since you didn't, we at least were glad you were involved with a decent fellow. Egon showed himself to be a courteous, respectful young man when he was here. Now you've probably lost your friendship with him. You've become more difficult to understand since you've been hanging around those ruffian Brownshirts. Mark my words, you're going to live to regret your association with them. They're bad news! But if you think you're going to loaf around here very long living off your allowance, you'd better think again! And know this, I'll be glad to help you enter the university. But if you're not willing to do that, you get a job or move out!"

"Where am I going to get a job in times like these?" countered Karlheinz.

"I agree, it won't be easy. But if I help you, I'm sure we can find something. At any rate, I expect you to do something besides hanging out with thugs, getting drunk, and making a nuisance of yourself."

At this, Karlheinz scowled darkly and muttered something to himself.

"What did you say?"

"Nothing."

"Well, I'm going to leave you to think it over, but know this: I mean what I say."

With that, Hans Joachim walked through the door, closing it firmly behind him.

Karlheinz lay on the bed a long time before finally rousing himself with the determination to go downtown and find the "friends" that his father had so scathingly denounced.

Chapter One-hundred-three

Relocation

"It's a boy!" shouted an exultant Eckhardt into the phone to Herbert. He and Ursula had almost given up hope of having any more children. Little Eckhardt, now eight years old, was of course the center of attention in their lives, but they had thought about having more and finally decided not to wait any longer.

§§§

"Now, Mama, you must not put off moving to Spandau any longer," admonished Ursula to her mother as she proudly held the new little family member to her breast. "I will really need your help, and I want you to be an important person in my children's lives," she continued.

Christina sat near her daughter and new grandson and was touched that Ursula would want her in their home.

"Where will you put me? You only have two rooms upstairs, and one is little Eckhardt's."

"In the beginning, the baby will sleep downstairs in the kitchen near our room as Little Eckhardt did when he was born. Later, Detlev will share the room with his brother. That leaves the other room for you. Come on, Mama, it will be good for them. Besides, remember how six of us managed to live together in that little apartment in Wedding. We would have thought we were royalty having a room for just two of us."

Christina laughed at this.

"Yes, we were so poor. But we didn't know it, because everyone else we knew was living the same way, or some even worse. Well, I'll talk it over with Rudi. He would be here today, but he's flying."

"I'm sure he'll agree with me that this would be the best thing for all of us," Eckhardt interjected, as the beaming proud father standing at the foot of Ursula's bed holding little Eckhardt's hand.

As for little Eckhardt, he was silently considering what to make of the new little stranger who was now the focus of everyone in the room's attention, instead of himself.

Just at that moment, Herbert and Meira entered the room, having driven to the clinic immediately after Eckhardt's phone call.

"You did it again! Congratulations, you two!" exclaimed Herbert.

"Now, see, Ursula, aren't you glad you took my father's advice to have your delivery in a hospital instead of in your little house in Spandau?" he added.

"I only wish I had had such an option when my babies were born," chimed in Christina. "They all had their first glimpse of light in our little kitchen, where they were delivered. A neighbor woman had to boil water on that old charcoal stove, and I had to lie on the kitchen table. Detlev and the children were exiled to the other two rooms. You, young people don't know how well off you are, but I'm so happy you have it better than we did."

The listeners contemplated what she had said. The mood was lightened as the two couples chattered away about the newcomer. The proud parents beamed and basked in all the warmth of the moment.

Little Eckhardt watched and listened to what was being said with growing apprehension.

§§§

Meira brooded on the drive home from the hospital.

"What's wrong, darling?" Herbert finally asked.

"I was just thinking how happy Ursula is."

Herbert drove on without comment for a moment. "You're thinking of their children, aren't you?"

"Yes. We've been married about as long as they have, and I've never missed a period. Doesn't it bother you that we've never conceived?" she asked wistfully.

"Of course, it does, and I don't understand it either."

They both were lost in their thoughts for the rest of the drive.

After arriving home, Meira noticed that Herbert seemed immersed in thought with a slight frown on his face, which was truly out of character for him. Herbert, the one who was always ready with a smile and who cheered others up, seemed to be deeply disturbed.

Later, as they lay in bed, Meira ventured forth with a suggestion, "What if I get a fertility test? Would you be alright with that?"

"What makes you think there's anything wrong with you? You told me your periods have always been regular."

"Well, that doesn't mean everything is normal. Let's talk to your father about it."

"If that will make you feel better, I'll call him tomorrow."

"Or I can speak to him. I see him at the clinic almost every day," she offered.

"Let me speak to him first, alright?" he countered.

"If that's what you want, but let's find out soon."

§§§

"I spoke to Papa today on my lunch break. He would like to see both of us this evening and suggested we go out to his house for supper," Herbert told his wife upon arriving home.

"Good. We can do that, but we mustn't stay long. I have to be in for an early surgery in the morning with another doctor."

When they arrived at the Lenz home, they were met by Hans Joachim at the door.

"Please come in. I'm here alone most evenings unless I have guests. I can arrange for Cook to stay then. Otherwise I've had to cut her back to part time. She and the housekeeper are the only staff I've got these days. These are hard times, and I can barely afford to keep them at all, but I can't just let them go. They've been so loyal and dependable over the years."

They sat down at the kitchen table to their simple meal of cold cuts, bread and cheese. Meira reported that they had seen Ursula and Eckhardt's new baby. And he was beautiful. This led into the discussion of why they were there.

"Now I don't mean to embarrass you two, but as you have asked for my advice I need to know a few details."

With a smile, Herbert replied, "Don't worry about that, Papa. Remember Meira is a nurse and we are all adults here. Feel free to ask us anything you like."

"Before I say anything, do you have any idea why Meira hasn't gotten pregnant?" Hans Joachim asked.

"If you mean do we have a good relationship, I can only say it's wonderful," Meira countered. "My periods have always been good and regular, and I am in good health."

"We've never used contraceptives, if you're wondering about that," added Herbert.

"Well, then I don't know what else there is to say," replied his father.

They lapsed into silence as they continued their meal. Finally, Hans Joachim spoke up,

"I'm going to recommend that Meira see a colleague of mine. I've known him for years and he's one of the most eminent gynecologists in the country. As a young man, he was in the service of the royal family. I will call him tomorrow and set up an appointment, if you like."

Meira nodded in agreement.

After sitting with Hans Joachim in the library for a short while, they left to return home. Enroute, Meira turned to her husband, and taking him by the arm asked, "Don't you think this is the right thing to do?"

"Yes. We should have done this years ago," responded Herbert.

§§§

"Ursula is right, Mama. You need to put that idea of moving back to Wedding right out of you head. I've heard you say, 'Happiness is not a flush toilet,' and I understand what you mean, but going back to that cold-water flat is not a good alternative, either.

I'm sorry you're not happy here, and I hate to leave you alone for days at a time, but at least we have income when others are starving. I think Ursula and Eckhardt's offer for you to move in with them is a great idea. You won't be alone, and you will be with your grandchildren. And Eckhardt loves you like a son."

Christina looked at Rudi thoughtfully. Then she had another idea. "How are you and Erika Brandt getting along?"

At this, Rudi turned to her blushing.

"Right now, she's a little put out with me. A few weeks ago, I had to sit in for another pilot on the run from Berlin to Vienna, and there's this stunning little stewardess from Bavaria on that flight. Her name is Gudrun Stegmeier, and she's full of fun and a flirt. She has a reputation of being a little racy with some of the other pilots. Anyway, during our layover in Vienna, she, the other pilot, Axel Breymeyer, and I were staying in the same hotel. They have a good restaurant there, and we had dinner together.

Afterward, we went out to Grinzing to one of the Heuriger (wineries) and enjoyed some of the late-season wines. Gudrun had too much and got silly. She flirted with Axel and me until we decided it was time to go back to town.

After we got back to the hotel, she continued to lean up against me and even tried to kiss me going up the stairs. Axel was taking it all in and was a little jealous that she paid more attention to me than to him. I thought we would all go to our separate rooms, but Gudrun still wanted us to go to one room together. Axel was agreeable to that, even though he's married with two kids. But by this time, I was tired and went to my own room. I left the two of them arguing in the hall about what they were going to do next, and I went to bed."

"Is that all, Rudi?" she asked.

Rudi blushed and dropped his gaze. *I should know better than to try to get past Mama*, he thought ruefully to himself.

After a long pause, he muttered in a low voice, "I was asleep and woke up when I realized Gudrun was in bed with me and kissing my neck. I didn't mean for anything to happen after that."

Christina didn't respond but waited patiently.

Finally, she asked, "Did you tell Erika about this?"

"I wanted to, but I waited too long. Gudrun got to her first."

Again, Christina waited.

Rudi then continued, "She told Erika we had a 'good time' in Vienna. I tried to start up a conversation with Axel about the return flight, but he just gave me short answers, while Gudrun sulked in the corner. I don't know what he knew.

The next time I saw Erika, she was very cool and withdrawn. I asked her to go to the movies, but she said she didn't feel well. I let it go until the following weekend after we returned from our regular flight from Munich and Stuttgart.

That Saturday morning, I went to Erika's house and knocked on the door. Her mother answered and invited me in. Erika was in the kitchen and was still cool towards me. After a while, I suggested we take a walk. At first, she said she had to help her mother with some baking – until Mrs. Brandt said she could take care of it – and persuaded Erika to go with me.

As we walked along, I asked why she was acting that way. She told me that she had heard from Gudrun about our 'good time in Vienna'.

That made me angry, and I took her home and left."

"Do you love her?" asked Christina.

Rudi hesitated a moment before answering.

"Yes, I do. But I don't see a future for us."

Christina twisted her wedding band that Detlev had given her so many years ago, then said, "If she is the mature woman you've said she is, she'll appreciate you telling her the truth. Explain what happened and emphasize you didn't try to start anything with the other girl. If she cares about you and if she knows this Gudrun, she no doubt sees how she acts toward other men.

She'll be hurt, and she might not forgive you right away, but I'm sure she sees people every day in her work and knows none of us are perfect. We all make mistakes, and often it's harder to forgive ourselves than it is to forgive another person.

One thing for sure, you can't try to continue with Erika if you don't resolve this issue first. It will haunt you, and it will sour any relationship you might have with her. She'll come around. But if she doesn't, she's not the girl for you."

He was relieved that he had confided in his mother, but he dreaded to face Erika. *Mama is right! I have to get this resolved as soon as possible.*

After her conversation with Rudi, Christina decided she would take Ursula and Eckhardt up on their offer. Leaving Rudi alone and unhindered in his apartment helped him decide how he wanted to live his own life.

§§§

"That's wonderful, Mama," said Ursula when Christina was over for supper the next evening. "Eckhardt will get Herbert to come and get you in his car on Saturday. Will that work for you?"

"That will be fine. I don't have much, just my clothes. The furniture will be there for Rudi."

"How does he feel about your moving out?"

"He thinks it'll be a good thing for me. Hopefully, it'll be a good thing for you and your family, too."

"Why would it not be a good thing?" retorted Ursula, as she continued to feed little Detlev. "Just think, you can be moved in here for Christmas."

Chapter One-hundred-four

Rudi Searches his Soul

The dark silence of the apartment met Rudi as he opened the door. Returning from his flight to southern Germany, cold, hungry and tired, he realized again how much he was going to miss his mother.

At least the rooms were warm. A central heating plant served apartment buildings for several blocks around. The heating season usually ran from October 1st to April 30th, unless an extreme change in the weather dictated otherwise. He thought about how it would have been if he were coming home to the old flat in Wedding when no one was there. Dark. Musty. Icy cold.

After changing from his uniform into his flannel pajamas, he rummaged around in the small refrigerator and settled on cheese and ham and made a sandwich, which he prepared with slices of rye bread.

He opened a bottle of Bären Kindl beer and settled himself on the living room sofa and turned on the small radio. The news was on, and it was disturbing, as usual. The Nazis had staged another "counterdemonstration" against the Communists, who had held a large convention in their meeting hall in Kreuzberg. As usual, it had turned violent.

He thought about his mother and her past narrow escapes from such confrontations. Another good reason she had gotten out of Wedding. Since she was now living in Spandau, it would be less convenient for her to attend these rallies, and hopefully, over time, she would become less involved with the Communists.

Like many Germans, Rudi had by now become so discouraged with politics in the country, that he avoided political discussions and more or less followed the now popular maxim *Politik ohne mich* (politics without me). After listening a few more minutes to the news, he switched to another station playing popular music, including some of the latest American hits. His meager knowledge of English did not permit him to understand the lyrics, but he liked the sound of the big orchestras.

Erika had become a fan of the big American musical productions and American orchestra music. They'd seen the musical *One Hour With You* starring Jeanette MacDonald at the Gloria Palast on Ku'damm, and Erika, when she thought she was unobserved, could often be heard humming the title song.

He was relieved and grateful that she had finally softened toward him, after he explained the circumstances. At first, she was skeptical as to how much Rudi had had to do with encouraging Gudrun that night in Vienna. But then, thinking it over, she knew Rudi well enough to realize that his openness was typical of his character. He didn't come across as a person capable of much deception.

Gudrun, on the other hand, was a shameless little flirt. Erika had seen enough and heard enough about her to believe Rudi when he described how she had come onto him. After a few days, she let Rudi know the incident was past and she didn't want to think about it again.

As he looked around the room, he began to imagine that Erika was there with him. The more he thought about the idea, the better he felt about it. He knew Erika was very fond of him and maybe even loved him. *I love her. And I want her.*

On a layover in Munich a year or so before, they had almost been intimate. They had been in a small café in Munich, when she unexpectedly leaned over and kissed him. He was surprised at how quickly his pulse quickened and he felt heat flash through his body.

They left shortly thereafter to return to their hotel and decided to take a stroll through the English Garden. It was a warm summer evening, and the stars shone down on the old town. As they walked among the trees, he grasped her hand and held it tightly.

After some moments, they stopped, and he pulled her into an arbor and passionately kissed her. Their embrace became more intense, and after a few moments she pulled back and whispered, "I care for you very much Rudi, but I don't want to become one of those girls who help reinforce the reputation of being a popular bedmate with sexy pilots."

Somewhat disappointed, but chastened, he turned what she said over in his mind, as they walked to the hotel.

§§§

"I wish Rudi would ask that girl to marry him. I know he loves her," Christina confided to Ursula as they worked together in Ursula's small kitchen baking the traditional Christmas cookies and breads.

"Let's have the two of them over for dinner," Ursula responded. "We should get to know her better and help Rudi feel she is already part of the family."

So, the following Saturday, Christina spent most of the day preparing one of her specialties, *Sauerbraten* (German pot roast) served with glazed carrots and *Spätzle* (homemade noodles pressed through a special sieve over boiling water).

When a knock came on the door, little Eckhardt shouted, "I'll get it," and rushed to open the door before anyone else could.

Upon opening the door and seeing Rudi standing there with Erika, little Eckhardt blurted, "You're pretty!"

This produced laughter all around, as the astonished young woman blushed to the roots of her hair.

"Well, now that we have introductions taken care of, please come in and join us," said Ursula warmly.

They were soon seated in the small living room, where Christina sat holding little Detlev on her lap. After some minutes of Erika answering questions with help from Rudi about how they met and some background on Erika's family, Ursula announced dinner and they all gathered at the table. Little Eckhardt insisted he wanted to sit next to Erika, and Erika responded she would be happy to have such a handsome young man sit next to her. At this the smitten boy blushed.

"Now we're even for you making me blush earlier," quipped Erika.

The congeniality that developed around the table put everyone at ease. Rudi sat proudly across from his sweetheart, and now knew he wanted her in his life forever.

On the way home, as they sat close together on the subway, he moved restlessly in his seat until Erika turned to him and asked, "What's the matter?"

Their eyes met. Red-faced, Rudi stammered hoarsely, "I love you."

Staring at him, she whispered after a pause, "I love you, too."

Holding her gaze, he then decided to purchase a ring the following week and propose to her on Christmas Eve, which he did. She joyfully accepted, and they set a wedding date for the following May.

Chapter One-hundred-five

Nightfall

While waiting for Kurt Wollner to bring his car around to the front entrance of his home, Benjamin Friedlander sat in his large leather chair in his library browsing through several copies of *Berliner Morgenpost*. He had been watching events in the Reichstag for several months with growing concern. Since the July election, the government had become so fragmented that forming a majority government of pro-republican parties (of which there were over 20) was impossible. The election of July 31, 1932, produced no majority.

The Nazis became for the first time the largest party in the Reichstag, with the Communists trailing in second place. The two strong anti-democratic parties now comprised a majority (called a "negative majority," as the two would never have formed an alliance).

In the year 1932, there were three successive chancellors. Heinrich Brüning resigned in May due to a conflict with President Hindenburg, who then appointed Franz von Papen as chancellor. Franz von Papen became involved in secret meetings with Hitler, which led to his dismissal by Hindenburg, who then replaced him with Kurt von Schleicher on December 2, 1932. He became the last chancellor of the Weimar Republic.

December of 1932 was a tumultuous month in the Reichstag. Four days after the appointment of von Schleicher on December 6th, the Communists tried to introduce a motion of no-confidence, but the Nazis succeeded in having the motion postponed. The next day, 50 Nazi and Communist deputies brawled in the lobby of the Reichstag, smashing a large chandelier and injuring six people.

Later, riding in his car seated next to Kurt Wollner, who was driving, Benjamin asked him, "What do you make of all this uproar in the Reichstag?"

Thoughtful for a moment before answering, the former policeman said, "I see dark days ahead for this country."

"Although I wish it were otherwise, I do, too," responded Benjamin. "If things continue like this, I am especially concerned for the Jews."

They drove on for a time along Bismarckstraße to the traffic rotary of Das Knie and turned into Hardenbergstraße, where they encountered a large contingent of students from the Technical University carrying pro-Nazi posters and swastika flags and accompanied by brown-shirted SA men marching toward Ku'damm. All traffic was blocked in both directions. Seeing this, Benjamin blanched and began to tremble.

"Come, Kurt. Let's go back home. I can't deal with this today."

"I completely agree, Mr. Friedlander. This is what I meant when I said I see dark days ahead."

§§§

"Well, Mrs.Lenz, I am happy to report that the fertility tests came back perfectly normal," the congenial gynecologist stated. "There is absolutely no reason you shouldn't conceive. Have you considered having your husband tested as well?"

With mixed feelings, Meira smiled and replied, "Thank you, doctor. I'm very relieved I have that behind me. As for my husband, I can't speak for him, but I'll tell him what you've suggested."

"I know men can be very sensitive when questions are raised concerning their virility, but I've seen several young men who, for one reason or another, are sterile. I think going through the war has a lot to do with it. Was your husband injured in the war?"

"Yes, he had a knee shattered by machine gun fire and was taken care of by a French farm-woman. He was under her care for many months before he was seen by an army surgeon."

At this, the doctor frowned slightly. "I don't know how a knee injury could have affected his testicles, but stranger things have happened. Please encourage him to come and see me."

On the way home, Meira thought about her conversation with the doctor and wondered how Herbert would react to his suggestion.

§§§

"Guess what! I've been promoted to captain on the new Junkers trimotor." Rudi was elated by his upgraded status with Luft Hansa. After having completed training on the Junkers JU-52 airliner several months earlier and having been assigned to the Berlin-Munich-Salzburg route as copilot, he had been hoping to have this new opportunity.

Congratulations were extended all around by his family as they sat together for Christmas Eve dinner at Eckhardt's and Ursula's house. Erika, seated beside him, smiled with pride at her soon-to-be husband. She had persuaded the Luft Hansa Flight Director to assign her as stewardess on the same flight.

"I'll take over my new responsibility on Monday after Christmas," he announced proudly.

"And I'm going to be with him to keep all those brazen girls away. He was always so handsome in his uniform, but now with four stripes, he'll be irresistible," teased Erika.

This brought laughs around the table, and little Eckhardt looked round-eyed at his heroic uncle. He had already decided he wanted to be a pilot just like his uncle when he grew up. Rudi had promised him a ride in the new plane in the coming weeks after the holidays, when he would be taken on an overnight jaunt with his uncle and soon-to-be aunt. He turned and looked adoringly at her – still smitten.

Although the general holiday mood across the country was considerably dampened by the political instability for Christmas of 1932, the Meinert and Lenz families took strength from one another. They pushed aside all gloominess, so that the atmosphere was warm and jovial as they began to savor the delectable Christmas meal prepared by Christina and Ursula.

The gifts and the tree lighting awaited them, to the delight and anticipation of little Eckhardt. Baby Detlev in his crib reminded all present of the infant of long ago whose name they celebrated.

§§§

Dr. Lenz looked wistfully at Herbert and Meira as they seated themselves at the large dining table. The succulent dinner had been prepared by his faithful cook, and they knew from experience of years past, she would have done herself proud. How she managed to acquire the ingredients with the shortages in many of the shops was a miracle.

As he looked around the table, Hans Joachim paused for a long moment looking at his son and his wife, whose mood was somewhat subdued by the news they had received from his fertility tests days before. Herbert would never be able to father children. His sperm count was zero. Meira, seated next to her husband, held his hand. Herbert was very quiet, but knowing his son's strength, Hans Joachim was confident that with Meira's support, the two of them would see this trial through successfully together.

Contemplating the chairs which were occupied by his own wife and his younger son in years past, Hans Joachim silently prayed, "Oh, Frederika, how I miss you, darling. Where is our boy? Please watch over him. Merry Christmas, sweetheart."

§§§

Benjamin, Golda and Edna Friedlander prepared to begin the festival of Hanukkah, which commenced on December 23 and would continue to December 31. They were grateful to be together and shared the realization that they would need to bond tightly in the coming days. Intimidated by the catastrophic events which had befallen Benjamin, they felt for the first time in their lives surrounded and cut off by dark forces, which began to be more and more evident in the beleaguered country. Golda with her head covered by a shawl, began the blessing of the Hanukkah meal.

Epilogue

The gleaming Junkers trimotor rumbled down the northern east-west runway at Tempelhof airport on Sunday, January 29, 1933, and became airborne. Heading west, Rudi then turned the plane gently southward toward the Bavarian capital.

Typical for Berlin at that time of year, the day was clear and cold. The sun shone brightly, and the sky was a brilliant blue. As they gained altitude, Erika began to make meal preparations in the tiny galley for the 15 passengers on board.

Today, the menu was Wienerschnitzel with Rotkohl and Spätzle served with beer or wine.

Rudi was in his element. Feeling the soft rumble of the three BMW 132 (770 hp) radial engines through his seat, he felt a great level of satisfaction. He reflected how he, a poor tenement boy from Wedding, had managed to make his way to his present situation: a captain for Germany's flagship airline.

His thoughts turned to Erika, serving the noonday meal to the passengers, a combination of international and domestic leaders of business and government. He then thought of their upcoming marriage and the subsequent establishment of a home in their beautiful apartment. Yes, life was good, in spite of the current uncertainties in the country and around the world.

As she sat in her jump seat behind the flight deck, Erika was content and relaxed after having cleared away the remains of lunch. She gazed out the window at the landscape sliding away beneath the plane. Germany was indeed a beautiful country, and the rolling hills and green fields bespoke a peace that was not disturbed by the struggles and conflicts of people. The sun was soon low in the West, and as they flew southward, the clear skies gave way to an overcast, which slowly turned into a cloud cover.

She then stood up and peered over her fiancé's shoulder at the distant Alps. Noting lightning over the mountains in the direction of Salzburg, she spoke to Rudi in his ear, "It looks like a storm is brewing."

“Yes,” he replied. “Lightning in the wintertime is very unusual. That must be a big storm. It looks like our landing could be really rough.”

§§§

As political upheaval continued to increase and remaining confidence in the government evaporated, President Hindenburg reluctantly appointed Adolf Hitler Chancellor of Germany on January 30, 1933.

SIGILLVM · BVRGENSIVM · DE · BERLINSUM

PRESENTING

Brandenburg II
The Ninth Circle of Hell

by
James Cloud

Available Now

Turn the page for a preview of

THE NINTH CIRCLE OF HELL

Excerpt from Prologue

Since 1914, the senseless killing fields of Ypres, Passchendaele, the Somme and the Spanish Influenza pandemic had combined to destroy an entire generation. The allied naval blockade brought starvation and deprivation upon the women and children left behind to fend for themselves. Following their bitter defeat in World War I, Germany was held totally responsible. The subsequent humiliation imposed by the Versailles Treaty required Germany to make reparation payments in gold, resulting in the incredible hyperinflation of the early 1920's and the complete collapse of the nation's currency. Following a brief recovery, the worldwide Depression in 1929 caused massive unemployment, and by the end of 1932, 6 million, or 26% of Germans were without work.

This unleashed chaos, with a rise in street fighting and terror brought about by the conflicting ideologies of the National Socialists and Communists. The nation was on the brink of civil war, and the German people were desperate for a leader to take control of the calamitous situation and restore order and stability. Adolf Hitler promised to be that leader.

Chapter One

In Flammen
Up in Flames

Monday, February 27, 1933 - 9:00 p.m.

"The Reichstag is burning!"

Deutsche Luft Hansa Flight Captain Rudi Bellon was approaching Berlin on his flight from Munich and watching the glow of a huge fire in the center of the city. Not yet having access to two-way radio communication to enquire what was burning, Rudi banked the Junker trimotor in a wide arc over the city center as he prepared his landing approach at Tempelhof Airport in southwest Berlin.

"It's the Reichstag!" he exclaimed to his crew and passengers whose noses were pressed to their windows.

"I can't believe it!"

"Look at that!"

Easing the three throttles back, Rudi descended for a low altitude steep turn over the glowing fire.

In the hospital below, nurse Meira Lenz, had been continuously assisting in emergency surgery since the beginning of her morning shift. She had just removed her shoes to ease her burning feet and aching back and was relaxing with a cup of tea in the canteen of the Surgical Clinic at Charité Hospital. She heard the roar of an airplane flying low overhead, followed by a young doctor shouting in the hallway that the Reichstag was ablaze. The building served as the seat of parliament of the German Empire. She thrust her shoes onto her sore feet and joined the throng of doctors and nurses hurrying to the third-floor windows, which faced south toward the burning Reichstag across the Spree River. The flames lit up the night sky and were reflected in the water. The frozen faces stared aghast at the spectacle.

"Da geht unsere Demokratie in Flammen auf!" (There goes our democracy up in flames), murmured a voice in Meira's ear. She turned and looked into the face of her father-in-law, Dr. Hans Joachim Lenz, chief surgeon at Charité Hospital. His face was marred by a saddened expression as he placed a hand upon her shoulder. Looking at those around her, Meira saw several faces wet with tears.

"Enough about democracy!" blurted young surgeon Helmut Köhler, understudy to Dr. Lenz.

"That's how I feel," added Gerhard Ziegler, assistant anesthesiologist. "What has democracy gotten us? Those democratic weaklings in the government have been nothing better than ass-kissers for the Allies, especially Britain and France."

"Exactly!" responded Dr. Köhler. "Hitler shows strength as a leader. We've been pushed around long enough. I'm optimistic that the new Chancellor will get this country back on its feet. I think he'll clean house." He did not elaborate on just how Hitler would accomplish that, but listeners agreed with nodding heads.

Sensing that any further comments were unadvisable, Dr. Lenz put his arm around Meira's shoulders as they moved away from the window and walked down the hall to the elevators. He shook his head and in a low voice confided, "I am seriously worried about the future of this country. I can understand the frustration of people like those young hotheads back there, but I can't believe that empowering a man like Hitler will do anything but make the situation worse – much worse."

Listening to her father-in-law, whom she loved and respected, Meira turned his words over in her mind. "I agree with you," she replied. "Hitler and his followers are rowdies and bullies. They have given evidence they have it in for anyone who opposes them or doesn't measure up to their standards of what it takes to be a 'good German'. Look at what happened to my father. He loves this country and always considered himself to be a patriotic German. His parents walked here from Russia with nothing. They were able to raise themselves up because of the opportunities available in a civilized dynamic country. The beating he got from those Nazis last year shattered him." She stifled a sob. "I don't think he'll ever recover."

Hans Joachim Lenz listened with bowed head and after a moment responded, "I am as ashamed of my people as I have ever been. This is not typical of Germans. But when we look around at the things that have taken place here in the last few years, I'm beginning to have doubts. And now the parliament building is being destroyed as we speak – a symbolic end of the first real democratic experiment that has ever taken place in our country's history."

Placing her hand on his arm, she gave it a gentle squeeze. "Oh, Papa, if only everyone was as compassionate and good as you and my husband. I am so proud to be a part of your family."

In the western suburb of Spandau, Eckhardt Meinert, his wife Ursula and her mother Christina Bellon were listening to the *"Zwei Augen"* (Two Eyes) tango with the Paul Godwin Tanz Orchester on the radio at home. The broadcast was interrupted by the emergency announcement the Reichstag was on fire. Hurrying out to their backyard, they could see the glow over the central part of the city.

"How awful!" exclaimed Ursula.

"How could that happen?" cried Christina.

Wide-eyed, Eckhardt gazed at the spectacle with a blank stare. "Eckhardt, what's wrong?" asked Ursula, shaking his arm. Receiving no answer, she shook him again. As his eyes began to focus, he turned to her and said, "I have an ominous feeling. It reminds me of the flames I saw from the trenches."

The bitter February air blasted their faces as Karlheinz Lenz and his new lover, SA Lieutenant Lutz Steinhauer, raced northwest on the Avus speedway through the Grunewald forest. Lutz was driving his open black Mercedes SSK roadster. The *Sicherheits Abteilung* (SA) were Hitler's security division, known as "storm troopers" or "Brownshirts." Dressed in their black leather coats and leather racing helmets, they were enroute to a party in the diplomatic quarter of Tiergarten. The radio blared. Karlheinz mimicked the dusky voice of Zarah Leander, a recently arrived singer from Sweden, doing a rendition of *"Das gibt's nur einmal"* (That Happens Only Once). An announcer interrupted the music with the newsflash that the Reichstag was burning.

"Good riddance!" blurted Lutz.

Looking at his friend with surprise, Karlheinz retorted, "What?"

Lutz continued, "It's just a rat's nest for diddling old men who didn't get anything done for Germany! Thank God for Hitler!"

Karlheinz, being a passive individual, did not respond and looked at his friend, startled at the vehement outburst. They raced toward the city center on Charlottenburger Chausee through the Tiergarten to Brandenburg Gate to see the inferno.

It had been just four weeks since the new chancellor had been sworn in.

ABOUT THE AUTHOR

James Cloud is a retired educator with more than 30 years of experience teaching History, Government, U.S. Citizenship Preparation, German and English as a Second Language. Among his awards are The Adult Educator of the Year in Utah.

Cloud was born and brought up in Las Vegas, New Mexico shortly before the outbreak of World War II. In 1942, he entered Miss Kohn's first grade class. Mr. Lingnau, his mother's grocer, was German. He was a very nice man who used to give the children candy. When it was pointed out that Miss Kohn was Jewish, it was the first time he had ever heard that word. As the children began to hear more about the war and the treatment of the Jewish people in Europe, it created a great curiosity about the conflict between the Germans in Europe, who were viewed as the "bad guys" and the Jews. *Why would such nice people hate each other?* In Las Vegas, New Mexico they didn't. This created a dilemma for Cloud, leading to a life-long interest in these two cultures.

As a young adult, the author traveled to Germany, learned the language and was accepted into the Institute of Arts in West Berlin, completing a degree in Industrial Design and an apprenticeship at Siemens. While living in Germany, he worked as an interpreter for the British Military Mission during the Cold War years and developed an intimate knowledge of both East and West Berlin.

Returning to the States, Cloud married and completed a Master's Degree in German Linguistics and Literature at California State University at Fullerton.

He began writing his first novel, *Brandenburg: A Story of Berlin*, at the age of Eighty, bringing together his impressions gained over a lifetime of teaching and interacting with many nationalities and cultures – most especially with German and Jewish people.

He has attempted to provide an account of life in Germany as told from the German perspective, as compared to the many books about that era told from an Allied point of view so we can have a better understanding of the events that ultimately led up to the tragedy of the Holocaust and a ruinous war.

Made in the USA
Las Vegas, NV
30 April 2024